My
Father's
Daughter

ALSO EDITED BY IRENE ZAHAVA

Anthologies
Finding Courage
Hear The Silence
Lesbian Love Stories
Love, Struggle, and Change
Speaking For Ourselves
Through Other Eyes
Word of Mouth

The WomanSleuth Mystery Series
The WomanSleuth Anthology
The Second WomanSleuth Anthology
The Third WomanSleuth Anthology

Journals
Earth Songs
Moonflower
Water Spirit

My Father's Daughter

Stories by Women

EDITED BY IRENE ZAHAVA

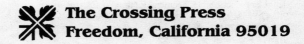 The Crossing Press
Freedom, California 95019

Grateful acknowledgment is made for permission to use the following previously published material:

"Auto Repair," by Rosalind Warren. Originally appeared in *Seventeen*, November 1988. Copyright © 1988 by Rosalind Warren. Reprinted by permission of the author.

"Automatic Timer," by Lynda Barry. Copyright © 1990 by Lynda Barry. Originally appeared in *Mother Jones*, January 1990. Reprinted by permission of the author.

"The Day My Father Kicked Me Out," from *The Notebooks of Leni Clare and Other Short Stories* by Sandy Boucher. Copyright © 1982 by Sandy Boucher. Reprinted by permission of the author.

"Dropping Anchor," from *Trespassing and Other Stories* by Valerie Miner. Copyright © 1989 by Valerie Miner. Reprinted by permission of the author and The Crossing Press.

"Extremes of High and Low Regard," by Lou Robinson. Originally appeared, in an earlier version, in *Top Stories*, copyright © 1988 by Lou Robinson. Reprinted by permission of the author.

"Lumps," by Harriet Malinowitz. Originally appeared in *The Massachusetts Review*, Winter 1979. Copyright © 1979 by Harriet Malinowitz. Reprinted by permission of the author.

"My Father's Darling," from *Useful Gifts* by Carole L. Glickfeld. Copyright © 1989 by Carole L. Glickfeld. Reprinted by permission of the author and The University of Georgia Press. Originally appeared in *Crossroads*.

"My Father's Daughter" is reprinted from *God's Snake* by Irini Spanidou, by permission of W.W. Norton & Co., Inc. Copyright © 1986 by Irini Spanidou.

"My Room at Night," by Judy Freespirit from *Across The Generations IV*, edited by Marcy Alancraig and Paula Ross. Copyright © 1985 by Judy Freespirit. Reprinted by permission of the author.

"My Sister's Marriage," by Cynthia Rich. Originally appeared in *Mademoiselle*. Copyright © 1955 by Cynthia Rich. Reprinted by permission of the author.

"People Should Not Die in June in South Texas," by Gloria E. Anzaldúa. From a work-in-progress, *Entreguerras entremundos*, forthcoming from Spinsters/Aunt Lute. An earlier version appeared in *My Story's On: Ordinary Women, Extraordinary Lives*, edited by Paula Ross. Copyright © 1989 by Gloria E. Anzaldúa and printed by permission of the author.

"Strike It Rich," from *The Question She Put to Herself* by Maureen Brady. Copyright © 1987 by Maureen Brady. Reprinted by permission of the author and The Crossing Press.

"Stroke" copyright © 1988 by The Ontario Review, Inc. From *The Assignation*, by Joyce Carol Oates, first published by The Ecco Press in 1988. Reprinted by permission.

"A Sudden Trip Home in the Spring" from *You Can't Keep a Good Woman Down* by Alice Walker. Copyright © 1971 by Alice Walker. Reprinted by permission of Harcourt Brace Jovanovich, Inc.

"The Thorn," from *Temporary Shelter* by Mary Gordon. Copyright © 1975, 1978, 1981, 1982, 1983, 1984, 1985, 1986, 1987 by Mary Gordon. Reprinted by permission of Random House, Inc.

"What a Sky," from *Lantern Slides* by Edna O'Brien. Copyright © 1990 by Edna O'Brien. Reprinted by permission of Farrar, Straus and Giroux, Inc.

"Zami: A New Spelling of My Name" (an excerpt), from *Zami: A New Spelling of My Name*, biomythography by Audre Lorde. Copyright © 1982 by Audre Lorde. Reprinted by permission of The Crossing Press.

Library of Congress Cataloging-in-Publication Data

My father's daughter : stories by women / edited by Irene Zahava.
    p. cm.
    Includes bibliographical references.
    ISBN 0-89594-424-3 -- ISBN 0-89594-423-5 (pbk.)
    1. Short stories, American--Women authors. 2. Fathers and
daughters--Fiction. 3. Women--Fiction. I. Zahava, Irene.
PS647.W6M9 1990
813'.01083520431--dc20
                                                90-40977
                                                  CIP

Dedicated to my father,
Morton Levinson

Contents

Preface

I am my father's daughter. This fact would be obvious to anyone who looked at the two of us together. But beyond the similarities of our physical features there are the similarities of personality.

We both tend to be sentimental and, more often than either of us want to admit, we lean toward self pity. We go out of our way to be kind to strangers but we can be very hard on the people we are close to. We are impatient and quickly lose our tempers, especially in restaurants, where we expect the service and the food to be impeccable. We each expect to get our own way and are convinced that our opinions are the right ones. Neither of us can sit through a television program without talking incessantly, and we've been known to flip channels and watch five programs at the same time.

When I was four years old, my father bought me a Daniel Boone cap and took me to my first movie. He taught me how to swim, and he ran behind me and my bicycle just minutes after the training wheels were removed. When we danced together at family parties, people said how graceful and light on our feet we were. He taught me about faith, tolerance, and rebellion.

I know that I love him. I also know that he infuriates me more than anyone else. I have thought about him constantly for the fourteen months I've been working on this anthology and dreaded the day I'd have to write about him in a preface. All this time I've been telling myself "I can't do it, I can't do it, I can't do it." Today I finally did it. My father would say, "So what's the big deal?"

Irene Zahava
May 10, 1990

My Father's Daughter

IRINI SPANIDOU

I have a picture of my father and myself published in a newspaper. The caption reads, "Man Carrying Child Crosses The Narrows of Euripus." My father is swimming on his side. He holds a rope in his teeth. The other end of the rope is tied around the inner tube from a tire. I'm hanging inside the tube, my face small, barely visible. I must be about two. I stare over the tube's rim thoughtfully, my eyes hurtful, earnest. They show no fear but fatalism, profound sadness and sagacity — yet the mouth smiles at the camera with pleading, helpless innocence.

My father was a student at the Chalkida Military School at the time. He had trained to cross the channel all summer. The water in the narrows runs for six hours North and for six hours South, with the inflow and outflow of the tide. As the current changes direction, the undertow becomes treacherous. The small boats that cross the channel back and forth stay anchored at the shore and the sea is empty. Every evening at this time, he swam against the current, taking me with him — a man testing his endurance, a small child in a tire bobbing in his wake like flotsam.

I do not remember this from experience. My father often repeated the story to friends in later years, roaring with laughter as he added, "Old Mavros was on the drawbridge once and saw me. He's a brigadier general now — he was colonel then. 'You'll drown the child, Karystine!' he hollered. 'You'll drown the child.'"

When I was nine, the summer I went back home after living with my grandparents, he was stationed in Chalkida again, a teacher at the military school this time. The first day, he took me to these same waters to teach me how to swim.

Raising my body with his hands under my stomach, he said, "Relax and you'll float. Move your arms about."

I was told to float and I floated.

He took his arms away and said, "Now, swim!"

I swam.

He taught me the different strokes and how to flip on my back when I was tired. "You don't need to touch bottom to rest," he said. "You can go as far out in the sea as you like. You must know your own strength. Think beforehand, 'If I go that far out, will I be able to swim back?'"

There was no life-saver now, no rope. Connecting me to him, ever stronger, was the power of his will. His presence clamped around my heart like an iron brace. It did not displace Grandma's love, but it blackened it, snuffing out the last glimmer of happiness I had felt living with her.

I read all day in my room, door and shutters closed because the glare of the sun hurt my eyes. I read in darkness, kneeling on the floor, a book propped on the edge of my bed, slowly sliding my finger beneath each word.

People in books were unhappy, as I was, but their unhappiness was beautiful, I thought. The more a book made me cry, the more I loved it. Books did not have an autonomous existence, I realized. Behind each book I could feel a live presence, the writer, his voice vibrant in my mind's ear. Even when a character died at the end, the voice was still alive. It was like magic.

I want to write, too, I thought. If I write my suffering down in a book, it will become beautiful. I tried to write but my hand moved slowly and it tired me. My mind was too fast for my hand. I'll have to wait till I grow up and can write faster, I thought.

I wrote poems, however. Poems were short. They were not about suffering, my poems. They were like songs. They came to my mind as a tune. I wrote down the words and all by themselves they rhymed. I wrote a poem about the lemon tree in the yard and one about a centipede and one about the Greek flag.

I recited them for Mama.

"Aha!" said my godfather. "A budding artist."

My godfather, Leandre, was a painter. He had rented the house next to ours, Chalkida being a resort, and with my father's fortuitous stationing there, he thought it a good opportunity for them all to be together.

He was chunky and bald, a garrulous, free-spirited man, with a roguish incivility that endeared him to women and amused the men. He had been my father's best friend since childhood.

My father used to say to him, "Who would have thought you would turn out an artist? Had I only known, Leandre! Now here I am, stuck — my best friend an artist!"

Both men laughed.

He painted pictures with muddled outlines, broad, coarse strokes of jarring colors and called them, "Ostrich Saluting Danger," "Stone, Patient" and "Uranium." He was working on another called "Euripus' Suicide," a blur of blues and yellows. I knew from school Euripus had killed himself, drowning in the waters now bearing his name, because he could not explain why the current in the channel, every six hours, changed. I thought I could not understand the picture because it was not finished yet. When one day he said it was done, my

3

father and I went to see it.

It looked no different.

My godfather tried to explain his picture. "It's what you see," he said.

"Where is Euripus?"

"It's his spirit I've painted."

"His spirit is blue and yellow?"

My godfather laughed. "We Greeks were the first people to puzzle over and try to explain the mystery of the world — to make science out of primitive wonder," he said. "First of all peoples, we posited reason. We tried to explain the workings of the world through logic. Do you know what logic is?"

"Yes, but I don't know how to say it."

"Look at my shoes. They are muddy. Why are they muddy?"

"Because there's mud on them."

"Why is there mud on them?"

"Because there's mud outside and you stepped on it."

"Why is there mud outside?"

"Because it rained."

"Now, this is logical thinking: The mind asks, 'Why are Godfather's shoes muddy?' Logic answers, 'Godfather came in from outside. If there is mud on his shoes, there must be mud outside. If there's mud outside, it must have rained. Therefore, Godfather's shoes are muddy because it rained.'"

I had known that without thinking! Nevertheless, I pursued with the same method: Why did it rain? Because there were rain clouds in the sky. Why were there rain clouds in the sky? Because we had bad weather. Why did we have bad weather? Because God was angry. Godfather's shoes were muddy because God was angry!

"There you have it," Godfather said. "Euripus. He could not explain the tide logically. He knew the moon caused it. But *why?* It defied reason.

"Men have killed themselves despairing over love, men have killed themselves despairing over life, and a Greek kills

himself over the limits of reason! That's pride, Annio. Hear
me? That's *pride!*"

He pointed at the painting. "That's what I've tried to say
here," he said. "With colors."

"I see. Blue is for the sea and yellow for pride."

"You get ten in Logic and zero in Art, Anna," my father
said, laughing. Then addressing my godfather, "For a while
there I was scared you might have passed artistic sensibility on
to her — along with the baptismal oil."

"She may surprise you yet. 'Mars's child is Apollo's step-
child.'"

"Eat your tongue, Leandre!"

A few days later, coming unexpectedly in my room, my
father found me reading *Lassie, Come Home* and crying. He
grabbed the book away from my hands and slapped me.

"That should give you cause for crying," he said. "Blub-
bering like a moonstruck idiot! Reading sentimental trash!
And I who praised your mind! Get out of my sight!"

For days after this incident, he did not speak to me. When
I was in the same room with him, he ignored me, not deigning
to even show me his contempt. This vengeful silence, spiteful
and calculated, much meaner punishment than a whipping, he
prolonged at will. He did not love me any more, I thought.
Never again would he love me. I was a weakling, unworthy of
him. I did not deserve his esteem. Who, what, was I, if my
father treated me as though I did not exist?

One day, in late afternoon, as he and my godfather were
getting ready to go to the beach, he turned to me and said, "Put
on your swimsuit!"

I ran to my room and changed. When I came out, they had
left.

"Mama, do you think Daddy meant I should go along?"

"Yes," she said. "Run! Go."

Her anxious voice flowed through me like a chill. She's
frightened for me, I thought. Why? Why is she frightened?

She came with me to the door, opened it and, stepping

aside from the cascade of sunlight suddenly flooding the room, stood in the shadow, her beautiful face desolate, her silence the muteness of a life smothered by futile longing, her inexpressible love, her shackled joy.

She watched from the house as I ran to meet my father, her worried eyes boring into my back, pushing me toward panic. I ran faster.

When I got to the beach, my father and Godfather Leandros were already in the water. I sat on their towel and waited. I was afraid my father might not want me in the water with him. When he came out, he said, "Well, go in! Don't you want to swim?"

He gave me a push to make me stand up and smiled. He has forgiven me, I thought. Just like that!

I ran in the sea and, overjoyed, swam, far out to the deep, then turned around and treaded water, looking back at the beach. My father and my godfather sat on the sand, smoking and talking, their wet hair tousled in the breeze. The blue, gleaming water surrounded me, still and serene, enclosing me in its beauty, wistful as in a dream. My father looked up and waved, then lay down on his back. Suddenly, the keen absolving joy I had felt when I first dove in the water drained from me. I felt empty inside, a heavy emptiness, weighing me down. The sea began to ripple — gently, caressingly on the surface, churning with treachery underneath. The current is changing, I thought. I started to swim back, frantic. For every stroke I went forward, I was drawn two back, or so it seemed.

"The tide's coming on!" I screamed.

My godfather jumped up and ran toward the sea. My father ran after him. He fell on him, holding him back. They fought, then moved apart, my father standing at the edge of the water, my godfather a little behind him. My godfather's face was slack with anxiety, my father's rigid, stern.

I must not show fear, I thought. I beat on the water with my arms as I swam, beating my fear to death. My fear made me want to live. I had to live to kill my fear. I swam harder, with all my might. I no longer thought or felt anything. When my feet touched bottom and I could wade, my body started to shake. It continued to shake, even after I was out of the water.

"You are inhuman, Stephane," my godfather said to my father.

"If every time a toddler stumbles you catch him, he'll never walk. She's a good swimmer."

"'It's the good swimmer who drowns.'"

"Yes. And: 'The mother of the brave shall mourn.' I know all the proverbs. You know what I say? What I learned in the war: You are a man or you are cannon fodder."

"She's a girl, Stephane."

"A girl! She's my daughter! She's my pride."

"'Pride comes before a fall.'"

"It seems to me I've heard from your very lips an oration about the Greek spirit — about our reason and pride."

"It's been our undoing."

"Our glory," my father said, bending to pick up his cigarettes lying on the beach. Seeing the pack was empty, he walked over to the kiosk on the sidewalk to buy another one, then came back. He put his arm around me.

My father thinks I'm brave — I swam ashore, I thought. I must always be brave, so my father stays proud.

"It's time we head home," he said.

My godfather followed, a few steps behind.

Every day from then on, I swam farther and farther out — farther than anyone else swam — out to the deep where the water held Euripus' haunted soul. I was exhilarated. I was swimming in Euripus' proud spirit. I was swimming out where the waters, reaching back beyond memory, drenched in history, were immortal.

Waiting for the Beep

LAURA DAVIS

I'm trying to make a seven letter word out of "X E P R S I T." Ex-strip? Stripex? Prestix? Expirts? Janice and I sitting at the kitchen table, hot into our late night Scrabble game. The phone rings in my study. I can't make out the voice, exactly, but I wait for the beep that will tell me the message is over. Whoever it is is droning on and on. I continue staring at the letters in front of me. "Sorry I'm taking so long," I say, rearranging the tiles around on the rack once again. Sexpits? Sex Tips?

"Abby?" Roommate number two, Ellie, is sitting next to the phone machine, working at the computer. "I think you should come listen to this," she says. "It's pretty weird."

Another crank call, I think. But it isn't a crank. It's my father. He's speaking in a strange monotone. "This is a special telephone made just for me. If I push one, I get Carlotta. If I push two, I get daughter. If anything should ever happen to me, all I have to remember is one for lover, two for daughter . . ."

Sam is singing the glories of his telephone on my answering machine. I know he loves modern technology, but really?

A knot of panic wrenches my stomach. Something is very wrong. His voice is flat and dry, like the life has been squeezed from it. This is getting to be familiar. Crises with Sam. In the past year, three heart attacks. Two months before that, Carlotta and I nursed him through a series of mini-strokes.

Sam is making a little song out of our initials. "One for 'C,' two for 'A.' One for 'C,' two for 'A.' If anything ever happens to me, my angels will arrive. . . ."

Ellie puts her hand on my shoulder. I remind myself to breathe. Janice suppresses a giggle. "Do you think he's drunk?"

"No, the doctors told him to quit after the first heart attack. As far as I know, he did."

"Something he ate?"

"Are you kidding? He wants to write a healthy heart cook-book for kitchen novices! Just yesterday he made cookies out of vegetarian burger mix! Cardiac cookies: no salt, no sugar, no flavor."

Sam is picking out a tune with the buttons on his telephone. He's singing Carlotta's and my name in terrible two-part harmony. "Something is really wrong." My voice falters. "Sam's a better musician than that."

I take a big gulp of air and reach for the phone. Janice and Ellie flank me. "Hello, Dad? It's Abby. Are you okay?"

"Oh, I'm just fine. Just fine. But the most amazing thing just happened. I was just talking about you and there you are on the phone. Isn't it incredible? When you really want some-thing it just appears. . . ."

Stroke symptoms, I think . . . tingling, numbness, slurred speech . . . "Dad, listen to me. You sound funny. Are you dizzy or anything?"

"No, I feel just fine."

"How about your vision? Do things look normal?"

"Everything looks just great. In fact, everything looks

terrific."

"Do you feel sick or anything?"

"Nope. I feel great."

I'm not sure what to say next. "Well, you just sound a little strange."

"No, no," he insists. "I feel great. I couldn't feel better."

My concern suddenly clouds with old anger. "Have you been drinking?" Ellie tightens her grip on my arm.

"Nope, haven't drank a thing. I told you I wasn't going to do that anymore. One for Carlotta. Two for Abby."

"Have you taken your medicine today? How much blood pressure medicine did you take?"

"Just the regular, but you know I was cleaning my apartment today and I did find a couple of hits of LSD. They were just these dots on a piece of paper. I hadn't seen them in five years, and I just wanted to see if they were still any good."

"You're tripping?" I cover the receiver with my hand. "He took two hits of acid." Janice tries not to giggle. I glare at her.

"Yes, I took them about an hour ago. I was feeling good and I wanted to call my only daughter. All I had to do is press two and there you were, like magic . . ."

"Look Dad, I have to get off the phone now. How about if I call you back in a few minutes . . ." Janice pantomimes driving a car. "Or maybe I'll just come over. Yeah, I'll come over in a little while. Is that okay?"

"I pressed two and my angel is coming over. I can't think of anyone I'd rather see. I just press two and . . ."

"Dad, I'm going to hang up now. I'll see you in a few minutes. Look, would you mind staying put till I get there?"

"I'll be right here when my angel arrives . . ."

The second I hang up, the phone rings again. That damned auto-dialer. But it's not him. It's Carlotta. "Do you know what he did? He took acid. He's so stupid. How could he do that? He has a heart condition and now he takes LSD. He could have a heart attack. I don't know what to do. I'm so mad at him . . ."

Carlotta is fifteen years younger than Sam. She met him through the Singletarians, a social offshoot of the Unitarian church. He'd been more exciting and unusual and energetic than men her age, but in the last year she'd found herself nursing a man whose health was failing. She'd hung in there. I had to hand it to her. Sam wasn't easy. They'd been going out, steadily, for seven years, and he stubbornly refused to live with her or get married. She was traditional and wanted to be his wife. He wanted his independence. He got his way, and she stuck by him.

"He's just trying to kill himself." Carlotta's voice started to rise in pitch. "He's going to die tonight."

"Listen, Carlotta. I just talked to him. Sam's going to be okay. He'll come down. Look, do you think you can drive? Why don't you meet me over at Project Artaud in half an hour? I'm going to hang up and call the Haight-Ashbury drug hotline. I'll call you right back."

Janice's head is in her hands over the aborted Scrabble game. Half-laughing, half-crying, little snorting noises erupt from her open mouth. "We'll come with you," she says.

Ellie, our resident student nurse, walks in carrying the Physicians' Desk Reference. She leafs through the index, looking up lysergic acid. "Well, it's a long shot, but maybe I can find something in here."

"Yeah," I say. "What to do when a seventy year old white male with a heart condition takes two five-year-old hits of Windowpane."

I pick up the phone and dial 411. "Can I have the number of the Haight-Ashbury Drug Hotline?" I wait for the number, scribble it down. Then to Janice: "This is the nineteen-*nineties,* not the nineteen-*sixties!*"

I dial. Let it ring ten, fifteen, twenty times. "I can't believe it! It's a drug hotline and they don't answer!"

Finally, a mellow male voice: "Haight-Ashbury Drug Hotline."

11

"Hi. My seventy year old father just took two hits of acid. He's had three heart attacks and a stroke in the last year, and I want to know what to do."

"Wow," the FM voice replies. "You have a really hip dad."

"Listen, are you a drug hotline or not? My father has a heart condition. He just took two hits of acid and I want to know what to do."

"Just go over and talk to him. You know, just talk him down."

"Listen, is he in danger? Can't you give me some information? You're a *drug hotline!*"

"Well, I don't really know anything about taking acid and heart attacks."

"Well, I suggest you call someone to find out," I spit back angrily. "Isn't there a doctor you can call? This is not a joke. This is my father."

"Okay, okay! Give me your number. I'll call you right back."

I'm waiting for the man to call back. I lace up my battered white Reeboks and pull my black leather jacket off the coat rack. "Did he have to do it at eleven on a Tuesday night? I'm going to be up all night."

"Well, I hope he's having a good time, at least," Janice says gently. "What a way for an old hippie to go."

Creating a banner headline between my hands, I add, "Yeah, can you see it now? Seventy-year-old music teacher turned lawyer drops dead after taking acid. He is survived by his thirty-four year old lesbian daughter, his fifty-three year old Chicana lover, a social worker for the city of San Francisco . . ." My laughter grows hysterical, then stops abruptly. "Why do I feel like a parent with a teenage child? What am I going to say to him?"

"It's Sam, Abby. He's your buddy. He loves you. You're just going to have to go over there and figure it out."

The phone rings. I leap for it. The FM voice is urgent this

time. "Get your father to the emergency room right away."

I start crying. I mouth "emergency room" to Janice and Ellie.

"Ask him if you need an ambulance," Ellie says, flipping through the phone book for emergency numbers.

"Do I need an ambulance?"

"No, just drive him over. The doctor's worried about his blood pressure. He could have another heart attack."

I hang up the phone. Look at my friends, my eyes searching for something to hold on to.

"Do you want us to come?" Ellie asks.

"No, Carlotta's gonna meet me over there." Closing the velcro on the top of my dirty white sneakers, I breathe in more air, trying to make myself bigger.

"We'll keep the phone by the bed," Ellie adds. "Call any time you need us."

I run out of the house, grunt a hello at the gang of guys who hang out in front of our house, getting loaded and protecting the neighborhood, run a block and a half to 28th Street where my car is wedged between two others on a steep hill.

It's a five-maneuver parking space. Turn the wheel all the way to the left. Let up on the clutch slightly. Kiss the bumper in back. And stop. Turn the wheel all the way to the right. Kiss the bumper in front. And stop. Turn all the way to the left . . .

I get out in four maneuvers, my front bumper scraping the corner of the bumper ahead of me. I run the stop and head south toward the Mission District: La Cumbre — the best steak burritos with cheese. Old Wives' Tales — the women's bookstore. Nicaraguan and El Salvadoran restaurants. Osento women's bathhouse, my home away from home. The stores on lower 24th Street that sell three kinds of plantanos, ten kinds of fresh chilis and two sizes of handmade corn tortillas. The low riders double parked and blocking traffic. The sounds and smells of the Latin district that separates my house from his.

I love it. A real city neighborhood: dangerous and alive.

The streets are a blur, an obstacle course of blinking lights and jaywalkers and double-parked cars. I run a red light and don't look back for cops. Make it to 16th and Alabama in five minutes — record time. Take the cement stairs at Project Artaud two at a time. My eyes gloss over the brightly colored acrylic murals that wind up the stairwells. This place has come a long way from its former life as an American Can Company factory.

I reach Sam's door and pause. A big metal fire door decorated with little orange stick-on circles arched around in a free flung spiral. Cracked open less than a foot, it's held at bay by a dirty roll of carpet remnants. Pausing to listen, I hear him talking in a loud, excited monotone about the wonders of his auto-dialer.

Sam is alone, sitting on his bed, talking into the speaker phone, a beatific smile on his face. I smile, despite myself. Yep, this is Sam all right. Tripping his brains out, oblivious to danger. He looks funny around the eyes—pupilless—but he's definitely still alive.

I breathe again, a ragged breath that snags on the way out: a sigh.

I look past him into his room. Against the wall is the shopping cart he liberated from the Safeway parking lot. Two years ago he covered it with crepe paper and helium balloons for our annual jaunt in the San Francisco Gay and Lesbian parade. He attached a brightly colored magic marker masthead with two poles: San Francisco Parents and Friends of Lesbians and Gays. Inside the cart was a conga drum and a variety of percussion instruments. We made a lot of noise pushing it down Market Street to the cheers of thousands, Carlotta on one side of me, Sam on the other.

This year the cart stayed neglected in the corner, piled with dirty clothes, and I cried through the whole parade, Janice and Ellie on either side of me. Sam was recuperating in the hospital after his third heart attack. He told me the worst part of getting sick was not being in the parade.

I turn to watch Sam talk into his speaker phone. ". . . and now, Crystal, I get to talk to you." He speaks robustly, with great pleasure. "This telephone is really just the most incredible thing . . ."

Oh, it's Crystal, his next door neighbor. I'd met her a couple of times at those giant Artaud parties. She's humoring him, I think to myself. All the artists and old hippies who live here probably think it's great. "What a character," they'll say to each other. "Sam was tripping last night. Did you talk to him?" My rage spews up suddenly. Don't they care about him? He's had three heart attacks. Don't they realize he could again?

Sam looks up and notices me. Maybe it's my negative energy. "Abby!" He says my name with awe. What a miracle that I've suddenly appeared, his angel before him. "Why, it's Abby," he tells Crystal. "My daughter, Abby." He extends his arm. I crawl into it, loving and reluctant. He looks at me, beaming with spiritual love and openness. I can't but smile. So far, he's having a good trip. I take his hand and feel for his pulse. It's racing.

"Hi, Abby," Crystal says brightly. "How are you?" I hate speaker phones.

"Uh, Dad, do you think you could get off the phone?"

"Get off the phone?"

"Yeah," I flounder. "I'd like to spend some time with you. It's hard when you're talking to someone else."

"My lovely daughter wants to spend time with me," he tells Crystal. "I must go. But I will call again . . ." He clicks off the phone with a flourish and turns to face me.

I hesitate. "So how is it going?"

"Abby, it's so good to see you. You know, you look really beautiful tonight. It's your cheekbones. They're just shining..." I take his hand, one finger on the vein, pulsing, pulsing, out of control.

"So, Dad," I begin again. "I'm glad I came over. I really wanted to see you . . ."

"You've always been beautiful, but tonight, well, you're just so much more radiant. It's like there's light just streaming from your face . . ." He traces my cheeks with his forefinger, lost in wonder.

These may be your last moments with your father. As he sings the glories of your face. I examine his face, the wrinkles, the scar above his nose where a beam had fallen on him, the soft blue eyes without pupils. Janice is right, I think to myself. What a way to go. At least he's going to die happy.

"Dad," I say gently, "thank you. I'm glad you're enjoying my face. But you know I was kind of worried about you."

"Worried about me? Why? I feel wonderful. I'm perfectly fine. I'm visiting with my only daughter who I love, who has the most marvelous face I've ever seen . . ."

Carlotta walks in. She holds herself stiffly, trying not to cry. I disentangle myself and put my arm around her. I say softly, "I'm working on it. We have to take him to the hospital. Do you know where his Medicare card is?"

Sam stands up and flows over to her. She stiffens under his hug.

"Dad," I say, "now that Carlotta is here, we have to go to the hospital. All three of us." I say it slowly, calmly, matter-of-fact. Like a mother telling her toddler it's time for bed. Firm, unyielding. You will eat your vegetables. You will put your toys away.

He looks from one of us to the other, surprised. I watch it hit him, the awareness of danger. Playtime is over. "Oh, so this is what this is about. Oh, oh, oh." Some of the light leaves his face. His trip is changing. I don't sense any panic, not yet anyway. He's taking it better than I thought.

"You both think I need to go?" he asks, hoping for a reprieve. Carlotta, wordless, nods at him. I pick up his hand, stroke it again. His pulse races off the map. He looks like a scared little boy. Under the wrinkles and set of his face, he is scared, an expression of soft innocent shock. He no longer looks like my father, the one who's there, for better or worse.

16

He looks lost and I am his anchor. I keep the pressure on his hand steady. "The doctors are worried about your blood pressure."

"Okay," he says, resigned.

I feel guilty for spoiling his fun.

Carlotta gathers up Sam's belongings. He joins in, searching for his medicine. "It's after eleven," he says, his voice somber now. "I forgot to take my eleven o'clock pill."

"Dad, you just took acid. I don't think it really matters. Let's just go to the hospital. If they want you to have it, they can give it to you there." But he's into puttering. He's been to the hospital before. He knows the routine. He searches for his jacket and his glasses. He gets to keep some dignity this way. He goes through all eight pockets of his dirty Banana Republic vest, looking for his Medicare card. I hope there aren't too many fascinating things in there to distract him. Like his nitroglycerin. Or dirty tissues. I decide to give him five minutes.

In the car, the seat belt chafes. I grip the wheel too tightly. Someone cuts me off and I scream, "You goddamn motherfucking asshole!" I don't say a word to Sam. I feel like those parents whose missing kid is found after forty-eight hours and the first thing they do is slap the kid across the face.

We head for San Francisco General. The big charity hospital. The emergency room, full of gunshot wounds, abused kids, smack overdoses, crack cocaine babies, the homeless people I try not to look at on the streets. I feel ashamed. This is where my uninsured, stubborn, proud father gets his medical care. This is where I lived in the hospital for a week just a couple of months ago, cardiac intensive care, sleeping on the floor, a stiff pretzel, wondering if we'd both be alive in the morning. My father a number on a Medicare card, a faceless aging hippie statistic.

The hospital parking lot is full. The cars are circling like sharks. There are five ahead of us already. I head back to the street. Pull into a bus zone. I'll get towed, but so what.

The white lights glare down dispassionately. They see everything; they smell the odors of death and hopelessness. I tuck my hand in Sam's arm. Carlotta's on the other side. I breathe through my mouth so I don't have to smell the smell of ten thousand sweats, ten thousand fears. People die here.

We follow the yellow duct tape line on the floor to the reception desk. The glass separating us from the staff is thick. I wonder if it's bulletproof. The nurses sit there, talking to each other, disinterested. We're walking; it can't be too critical. We wait for the punchline to someone's story before we get their attention. I look at the clock, impatiently. It's 12:35. "What seems to be the problem?" a male nurse finally asks. His voice is tired, but has an unmistakable lilt.

No one speaks. I refuse to answer for Sam, so he says it deadpan: "I've been getting treated here by Doctor Bartlett for a heart condition. I was in cardiac ICU two months ago, in June. I took some acid a couple of hours ago." He says it as if they were two aspirin. "And they," he motions at us, "were worried about my blood pressure."

"You took LSD?"

"Yeah, that's right."

"How much?"

"Two hits."

"How old are you?"

"Seventy."

The man doesn't flinch. If this is a new one to him, he doesn't show it. He cuffs Sam immediately to check his blood pressure. With his other hand, he sticks a thermometer in his mouth. He tosses a clipboard at me. "Here, fill this out." He looks me over, wondering if I'm tripping too. Or maybe I'm the one who gave it to him.

I write down the Medicare numbers. Carlotta pulls out the little black book that lists Sam's medications. "He didn't take his eleven o'clock pill," I say lamely, wanting to make it clear I'm not a co-conspirator.

18

His blood pressure is dangerously high, 220 over 160. "Good thing you came in," the nurse says. "Go over there anu sit down. We'll call you."

"But is he in danger?" I ask. "What are you going to do?"

"We'll call you."

The waiting room reeks. A lot of people here haven't showered in a long time. Everyone's eyes are downcast, except the few people who never stop talking to themselves. We sit down in three plastic chairs, Sam in the middle. He's wired and can't stop talking. The headline of the *Chronicle*, lying on the floor, gives him an idea. It's something about third world debt. He starts lecturing to me, loudly, in his worst condescending voice, on the evils of multinational corporations in the third world.

"ALL THESE COMPANIES GO DOWN TO THESE COUNTRIES AND EXPLOIT THE PEOPLE THERE. EVERYTHING IN THIS WORLD COMES DOWN TO GREED. ALL THESE PEOPLE CARE ABOUT IS PROFIT AND MAKING MONEY."

His voice pounds my face. I back up in my chair. He isn't giving me any room. The man across from us, whose arm is covered with soiled bandages, gets up and walks to the other side of the room. Several other people glare in our direction.

"THE U.S. HAS SYSTEMATICALLY GONE THROUGH ALL THE COUNTRIES OF CENTRAL AND SOUTH AMERICA AND EXPLOITED THE PEOPLE TO MAKE MONEY. DO YOU KNOW THAT THE U.S. USES MOST OF THE WORLD'S RESOURCES AND ONLY PRODUCES A SMALL PERCENTAGE?"

The guards ignore Sam's tirade, probably assuming he's just another crazy person. I want to yell at them, "He's not really this way. I don't really have a father like this."

Sam's voice grows louder and nastier: "THAT'S WHY THE WHOLE WORLD IS FALLING APART. IT'S BECAUSE OF OUR GREED. THE U.S. AND THEIR MONROE DOCTRINE THAT HAVE RUINED AND EXPLOITED SO MANY NATIONS . . ."

I try not to look at him. I imagine a big plastic bubble

around myself. I wish I had a pair of socks to shove in his mouth.

"ABBY, THIS IS VERY IMPORTANT. I REALLY THINK YOU SHOULD LISTEN TO THIS. IT'S BECAUSE OF OUR POLICIES THAT WARS ARE HAPPENING THROUGHOUT CENTRAL AMERICA. WE INSTIGATE AND FEED THOSE WARS. IT'S ALL BECAUSE OF OUR FINANCIAL INTERESTS. IT'S ALWAYS BEEN THIS WAY. IT'S OUR MULTINATIONAL CORPORATIONS THAT ARE DOING ALL THE DAMAGE."

His voice is staccato, fortissimo, each word accentuated with a touch of violence. He spits as he talks. Everyone is watching us now. Even the guys who talk to themselves are silent. Maybe they're boning up for their next monologue. I press back into the plastic incline of my chair.

"DO YOU KNOW THAT PEOPLE ALL OVER THE WORLD HATE AMERICANS? THAT PEOPLE SPIT ON AMERICANS BECAUSE WE ARE THE ONE COUNTRY THAT DOESN'T KNOW HOW TO COEXIST WITH OTHER COUNTRIES?"

As if seeing me for the first time, he turns his venom on me. "And you! You sit there with your leather jacket and your fancy yuppie sneakers. You're part of the problem. You're a consumer. You buy things manufactured on the slave labor of third world countries."

I sit frozen. A puddle forms on the floor in front of him, where his wet words land. I hate him. He is no longer my father. This is not the man I call twice a week to chat about nothing in particular, the one who still pays for me at the movies, who sends me the latest clippings from the daily legal rag about lesbian custody cases. This is not the man with whom I double-date. He isn't the one on a first name basis with all my lesbian friends, who comes for brunch regularly, who still draws me funny cartoons and pictures, even though I'm thirty-four. This is not the man who's supported every decision I've made as an adult. This isn't my father. I stare straight ahead of me. I crack my knuckles over and over, even though it hurts. I refuse to look at him.

"ABBY, AS YOUR FATHER I THINK IT'S VERY IMPORTANT THAT YOU UNDERSTAND THE WAY THE WORLD WORKS. PEOPLE ARE GREEDY. THEY KILL INNOCENT PEOPLE JUST SO THEY DON'T LOSE MONEY. AND YOU'RE PART OF IT!"

What does he think I am, a Republican? I decide to find the nurse.

"I DON'T KNOW WHY YOU'RE GETTING UP, ABBY. WHAT I'M TELLING YOU IS VERY IMPORTANT . . ." His voice echoes off my back as I walk away.

"We've been sitting here for over an hour," I tell the nurse who checked us in. "I want to know what's going on." He's absorbed in the Daily Crossword. Reluctantly, he sets it aside and lazily looks through the clipboard sheets, trying to remember who I am.

"I'm the one whose father, the one with the heart condition, took acid."

"Oh yeah," he says. "I remember you." He's cranky. "Look, I told you we'd call as soon as we're ready."

"But what about his blood pressure? It was dangerously high when he came in an hour ago."

"That's why we want him to be here. If anything happens, we can whisk him right upstairs."

"You're going to wait until he has a heart attack to do anything? Another heart attack could kill him." I should have taken him to another hospital. But where?

"We're watching him."

"You're not watching him. We're sitting out there in that pit you call a waiting room. He could keel over and die."

"Is he dizzy?"

"No."

"Is he experiencing heart pain?"

"No."

"Is he sweating?"

"No."

"Is he short of breath?"

"No."

"Well?" he says impatiently, leaving out the, "what do you expect me to do about it?"

"Can't you do something? Give him an antidote or something?"

He looks at me like I'm crazy. "He's just going to have to come down. That's all."

This is getting nowhere. I decide to try humor. "Look, we've been here for an hour already. He's out there spouting off about multinational corporations. I'm getting a lecture on the history of the United Fruit Company." I emphasize the words, "Fruit Company," hoping to strike a familiar chord. It's clear this nurse is a faggot, albeit a grumpy one. "I mean, my father's tripping on acid, lecturing me about a Fruit Company!" I stroke my leather jacket and give him the dykiest look I can muster.

He emits a small smile, despite himself. "I'll see what I can do."

I walk back to my seat, bracing myself for a concise political history of the *contras*. Miraculously, Sam is quiet. Carlotta is holding his hand. He has that lost look on his face again. I pick up his other hand and stroke it. His hands are soft and wrinkled and gnarled. They aren't my father's hands anymore. They're the hands of an old man.

A doctor with a white lab coat comes into the room. "Mr. Berger?"

Sam stands up. We get up too. The doctor stops us: "Family members aren't allowed in emergency." There is no room for bargaining.

"What are you going to do with him?" I ask, stalling for time.

"Hook him up to a blood pressure monitor and watch him." He turns and leads Sam away. I want to follow, to sit by his side, but I obey dully. My usually spunky self drips out the bottom of my feet, creating a soft puddle on the floor. There's some way I'm failing here. Letting death take him. I keep thinking someone else would make a scene, would fight back, would take him to a different hospital. But maybe that person would have a different father.

Defeated, Carlotta and I return to our seats. I know we are sharing the same thoughts: Have we just seen Sam alive for the last time? Here? Like this? We look at each other briefly, and then away. I see the shame and fear in her eyes too. "Want a magazine?" I ask.

"Sure," she says, grateful.

I look at the clock: a quarter to two.

I toss Carlotta a copy of *McCalls*. I leaf through the magazines and choose a mail order catalogue for Day Timers, wonderful desktop organizers for the busy executive. The basic day timer has five functions on every page, and you get them all, in a personalized leather-bound case for only $49.95. I like reading about them. It reminds me that I have a life outside of this, a professional life with order, schedules, deadlines.

I read the catalog cover to cover, every page, carefully studying the variations of Day Timer for every executive lifestyle. I decide the one for me is on page 37 and costs $69.99. I look around to see that no one is watching me. Then I tear out the order blank and shove it in my pocket. I have a plan. I know what I'm going to do tomorrow.

The TV has switched over to a test pattern. Carlotta says she's exhausted. "Why don't you go out and take a nap in the car?" I suggest. "If anything happens I'll come out and find you." I give her the keys, try to imagine her sleeping in a bus zone in the middle of the Mission District at three in the morning. "Try to get some sleep," I tell her. "He'll still be awake tomorrow."

I check in with the nurse. "Nothing new." I return to a different seat, hoping it might improve my perspective. It doesn't. I read an article in *McCalls* about "throwaway"

23

teenagers. I'm reading the third paragraph for the fourth time without absorbing a word, when the janitor comes in to roust out the homeless. Probably this is the daily 3:00 a.m. ritual. He makes us stand up while he slowly, methodically washes the floor. It takes half an hour. One toothless man gives him a hard time and the guards throw him out. I stand against the wall, behind the white line, where he tells us to wait. I watch the second hand make its jagged way around the face of the big institutional clock. I wonder how Carlotta is doing in the car. How Sam is, strapped down, flat on his back with tubes and monitors down the hall. Talk about a bum trip. Maybe we shouldn't have bothered him. Just left him alone at Artaud, oblivious and happy.

I press myself back up against the wall to avoid the head of the mop, and think back twenty years to Sam's first acid trip. We'd been camping in Rocky Mountain National Park with my best friend Vicky and my big brother David, who went to the University of Colorado. I was a new teenager, and this was my first real visit with Sam since he left our home in New Jersey and moved to California to "find himself." I was dazzled to have a hippie dad. In our month together we smoked pot, visited communes, drove to Colorado, and went camping together in the mountains.

We were grilling hot dogs over an open campfire one night, and Sam kept going on and on about the colors of the flames and the magic of the fire. He was loud then too, enunciating every word carefully about the incredible way the hot dogs cooked and sizzled. He kept talking about the color orange. Something was wrong, but I didn't know what it was. He kept saying the same dumb things over and over, as if they were the most important things in the world. My measly little hot dog charred and shriveled on my stick. It didn't taste good, like things cooked on a campfire usually do. The next day David told me he'd turned Sam on to acid.

The janitor motions to us brusquely. There are five of us left. We sit down again. I look vainly around the room for something to do.

Sam and I had dropped acid together once, when I was twenty-one. I'd just moved to California and I was finally angry at him for abandoning us. He'd come off his pedestal in a big way. We were both visiting my cousin in the Santa Cruz mountains. Someone offered us some Orange Sunshine and we took it. We ended up peaking together under the apex in a small pyramid house, sitting cross-legged, knee to knee. I said, "You know your leaving really changed my whole life. It's hard for me to trust people, to believe that things can last."

"I never thought about how it would affect you," he said. "I just needed to get away. I had to find myself. I just couldn't live that way anymore. It had nothing to do with you."

"It changed my life, Dad. It was really hard."

"I'm sorry," he said, meaning it. He took my hands and his eyes teared up. "I never wanted to hurt you."

That was my last acid trip. This is Sam's. If he makes it through till morning, I think, I'll go over to his house with a police dog and sniff around for drugs. "Okay, Dad, hand them over," I imagine myself saying. "You're busted."

At five o'clock, Carlotta stumbles back in. She says she was looking forward to going back to her job with the homeless. "It'll be a piece of cake after this." We discuss a dozen ways to kill Sam in the morning. Carlotta comes up with my favorite: throw the telephone answering machine into the bathtub with him.

We talk about what the trip may have meant for him, why he might have done it. Maybe it's his way of expressing his fears of death, his frustration at physical limits. "Maybe now he'll be able to talk about these things," she says. I hope so too. What's that thing they talk about in psychology books? The window of opportunity?

At 6:30, they lead him out. He still hasn't come down, though his blood pressure has. He talks to us as if nothing unusual had happened. "You stupid kid," I want to yell at him, but I wrap my arm around him instead. We walk together out to the car, Sam in the middle. It's still waiting for us in the bus zone. There is no ticket on the windshield.

I drop Sam and Carlotta off at Artaud, go home, leave a note on the table that says, "Sam's okay. I'm sleeping," and fall into bed. I wake up with a raging headache, take three Advil and walk into the kitchen. Ellie's home, cooking cauliflower curry. I look up at our dinosaur clock. It's five o'clock. I've lost the whole day. My mind ranges over the work I haven't done. "That asshole," I think to myself.

"So?" Ellie queries.

"So? So, it's five o'clock. I just woke up. I'm going to be up all night. Again." I sit on a kitchen chair, pick at the salad she's made, and fill her in.

Midway through dinner, the phone rings. After the beep, I hear his voice. I get up and answer.

"Hi," I say, icy.

"I just called to see how you are."

"I just woke up from sleeping all day. I missed a deadline today. Now I'm going to be up all night. My schedule's totally thrown off." I'm not giving him an inch. "And how are you?" I ask, venom dripping off each word.

"I'm feeling better," he says.

"And?"

"And?"

"And is that all?"

"I just wanted to hear your voice."

"Just wanted to hear my voice?" Are we on the same planet, or what? "Why don't you try, 'Abby, I'm really sorry about last night. I realize you and Carlotta were up all night. I guess I was just feeling scared about being sick, tired of so many limitations. I wanted to be young again.'"

"Why do you always have to read so much into everything? I am sorry you were up all night and I'm grateful for what you did. But I wasn't trying to prove anything. I came across a little acid and I just happened to take it."

"You've had three heart attacks and a stroke." I yell. "You don't just happen to take acid!" Janice and Ellie creep into the doorway. They didn't want to miss any of this.

"Well, I did. I just wanted to see if the acid was good anymore."

"Dad, as far as I'm concerned, what you did last night was a suicide attempt."

"It was no such thing," he snaps, indignant. "It was there and I took it. That's all there is to it."

"That's bullshit, Dad. You're a seventy-year-old man who's had three heart attacks and a stroke. You're not a fucking teenager! That was a cry for help. You mean to tell me you don't have any feelings about your body suddenly falling apart? You've been hospitalized four times in the last year! You never talk about your heart attacks. You've got to be scared."

"I don't know what you're talking about. I'm not scared. I'm not harboring any secret feelings. Everybody dies. That's reality. I've had a good life. I've done everything I wanted to."

"And it's coming to an end. Over. Finito. You don't believe in God. You don't believe in reincarnation. You don't even believe your essence returns to the soil so plants can grow. You're of 'the worms crawl in, the worms crawl out' school of death. Doesn't that bother you? That you're just going to stop existing?"

"I've made my peace with death."

"Well, I haven't! I don't want you to die." Janice and Ellie inch closer. Janice takes my free hand. I look out the dirty sliding-glass window onto the street below. The guys downstairs are getting rowdy, mouthing off to each other. Maybe there'll be a fight. "Aren't you going to miss anything?" I ask Sam after a moment. "Aren't you going to miss Carlotta?" My voice rises crazily. "Aren't you going to miss me?"

"How could I miss you? I'll be dead."

"Oh, you're impossible!"

"No, *you're* impossible. You're always trying to presume what I feel. Don't you think people can live and die without always having hidden motivations, without thinking about everything? Dying is a natural part of life. People have been doing it for centuries."

"I hate this. Not only did I stay up all night, but it didn't even do any good. I thought maybe going through all this would at least enable us to talk about what's really happening."

"What's really happening is my daughter keeps trying to put words into my mouth, keeps trying to find meaning where there isn't any. That's what's really going on."

"Dad, I hate it when you're like this. I can't talk to you anymore. I'm hanging up."

I refuse to talk to Sam for three weeks. I rage with Janice and Ellie at home, commiserate with Carlotta on the changes Sam is going through, talk in therapy about losing the father I've known. I have long conversations with friends who've cared for aging, ailing parents. Sara, whose father is having a heart valve replaced, suggests starting a chapter of the "Daughters Against Daddy Death" club. Sally sends me a list of books on grief and death and dying, which I dutifully purchase and never read. I keep them perched precariously by the side of my bed, a wandering pile. As the days go by, I stop hoping for a Marcus Welby ending, yet I refuse to return Sam's phone calls. I'm punishing him, practicing for his death.

I write to my friend Meg, whose father has been dead for many years, and tell her I'm grieving for Sam. She shoots back a note, short and to the point: "What are you doing, grieving now? Wait till he dies first. You'll have the rest of your life to grieve. Why do you need a headstart? Make the most of each moment you have now."

The next day, Janice and I are deep into Scrabble. She's just played REQUIRE on the triple word score, with the Q on the double letter. One hundred twenty-eight points. There's no way I can recover.

The phone rings. The machine clicks on. It's Sam. He's singing again, in his normal "Sam is always musical" voice, picking out the tune as he goes along.

"I haven't seen my daughter Abby in too long. She has not called and life is passing by. I wonder if she will pick up the phone . . ."

"Go ahead, answer it," Janice urges. "The game can wait."

I look at her, smile, then go over to the phone. "Hi, Dad, it's me."

Zami:
A New Spelling
of My Name
(excerpt)

AUDRE LORDE

Except for political matters, my father was a man of few words. But he carried on extensive conversations with himself in the bathroom every morning.

During the last years of the war, my father could be found more often away from home than not, or at best, sleeping a few hours before going back out to his night job at the war plant.

My mother would rush home from the office, market, fuss with us a little, and fix supper. Phyllis, Helen, or I would have put on the rice or potatoes already, and maybe my mother had seasoned some meat earlier in the day and left it on the stove with a note for one of us to turn on the fire low under the pot when we came home. Or perhaps there would be something left on purpose from last night's supper ("Leave some of that for your father's dinner tomorrow!"). On those afternoons, I didn't wait for my mother to come home. Instead, I packed the food up myself and took off downtown on the bus, headed for my father's office.

I heated each separate portion until it was piping hot. Carefully, I packed the hot rice and savory bits of meat stew or spicy chicken and gravy into scoured milk bottles which we saved for that purpose. I packed the vegetables separately in their own bottle, with a little pat of butter if we could get it, or margarine, on top. I wrapped each bottle in layers of newspapers, and then in an old towel, to keep the food warm. Placing them in a shopping bag together with the shirt and sweater that my mother had left for me to take to my father, I set off by bus down to the office, heavy with a sense of mission and accomplishment.

The bus from Washington Heights ran downtown and across 125th Street. I got off at Lenox Avenue, and walked the three blocks up to the office, past bars and grocery stores and small groups of people in lively conversation on the street.

Sometimes when I arrived, my father was downstairs in the office already, poring over receipt books or taxes or bills. Sometimes he was still asleep in a room upstairs, and the janitor had to go up and knock on the room door to waken him. I was never allowed to go upstairs, nor to enter the room where my father slept. I always wondered what mysteries occurred "upstairs," and what it was up there my parents never wanted me to see. I think it was that same vulnerability that had so shocked and embarrassed me the day I peered into their bedroom at home. His ordinary humanity.

When my father came downstairs, I kissed him hello, and he went into the back of the office to wash his face and hands preparatory to eating. I spread out the meal carefully, on a special desk in the back room. If anyone came in to see my father while he was eating, I wrote out a receipt, proudly, or relayed the message to him in the back room. For my father, eating was too human a pastime to allow just anyone to see him at it.

If no one came in, I sat quietly in the back room and watched him eat. He was meticulously neat, placing his bones in even rows on the paper towel beside his plate. Sometimes my father looked up and saw me watching him, and he reached out and gave me a morsel of meat or a taste of rice and gravy from his plate.

Other times I sat with my book, quietly reading, but secretly waiting and hoping for this special treat. Even if I had already just eaten the same food, or even if it was some dish I did not particularly like, these tastes of my father's food from his plate in the back room of his office had an enchantment to them that was delicious and magical, and precious. They form the fondest and closest memories I have of warm moments shared with my father. There were not many.

When my father was finished with his meal, I rinsed out the bottles, and washed his dish and silverware. I placed them back upon the shelf especially cleared for them, and covered them with the cloth napkin that was kept there for that purpose, to protect them from the dust of the back room. I carefully repacked the bottles into the shopping bag, and took the nickel carfare that my father gave me for the bus trip back. I kissed him goodbye and headed for home.

Sometimes no more than two or three sentences passed between us during the whole time we were together in the office. But I remember those evenings, particularly in the springtime, as very special and satisfying times.

The Dangerous Beauty of the Open Road

ELLEN SHEA

I usually cruise at about 70 — over the speed limit, but not enough to be conspicuous. Troopers are really after the ones that break 90, the guy who weaves through traffic like a shuttlecock through a loom. Most truckers are happy to hover at 70, an even clip. If you keep up with the flow of the rigs and don't pass too many, you'll do all right.

For safety's sake I have a CB, everybody does, but I don't like all that chatter when I'm driving and I don't like people calling me whenever they feel like it. So I always keep it turned down. Instead I watch for signals that show there's a speed trap up ahead — the sudden choke in traffic like a clogged sink, truckers on the other side coming toward you and flashing their lights in warning. When I pass the trap doing a sedate 55, around the bend I flash my lights in return for the trucks on the other side. Just doing my part.

Driving a car is one of my earliest memories. I held onto

33

the steering wheel and he worked the pedals. I was standing on my father's thighs and he was really steering, else we would have gone right off the road, but still I'll never forget the incredible power I felt. I turned the wheel to the right, and the car (obeying me) swung gently to the right. I was making it *go*. I didn't think these words; I was too young. But I knew it anyway: I liked controlling this car, forcing it to do my bidding. That was driving. "Fast," I said to my father, which is of course his version of the story, and the speedometer needle jumped from 5 to 10. "Whoosh," my father told me "'Atta girl. You already drive better than your mama." I don't remember my mother being in the car any of the times I was allowed to drive.

My business is legitimate, no secret packages taped underneath the truck or anything, but I don't want to get stopped. Too many speeding tickets will put me right out of commission. And I can't stand having to be polite to those troopers who are, universally, pricks. With their mirror sunglasses and tough guy hats, their jaws working with Wrigley's Spearmint, they live to catch a drug-runner or an escaped convict. Instead they get moving violations and road accidents from here to kingdom come, and lost assholes from Ohio. They want to see your fear when they pull you over and step up to your window, and if you don't trot it out nice for them, they get nasty until you knuckle.

One of them stopped me in Pennsylvania somewhere for doing "19 miles over the speed limit, Ma'am." He saw a girl driving a truck, short hair, muscles on her tan, ropy arms. He wanted to quiz me about who I was and where I was going and why. I got bored with this and told him that last I heard, it was still a free country and did he just want to give me a ticket, or not. His sunglasses hid his eyes, but I could feel their chill.

"What's a dyke like you doing around here?" he said, low and mean, a big grin on his face. "All our girls around here like men, sweetheart, so you're wasting your time." He said this,

I swear. Also, he was all of 22 years old.

I kept my mouth shut and took the ticket, then pulled off the shoulder nice and slow. That's what you have to do when you're a stranger, you have to eat this shit right on up, with a pleasant smile on your face. Swallow it down like a good girl. Or you'll be force fed something worse.

I've been a stranger for a while now, and I've learned some valuable things that way.

I inherited the truck from my father. Believe me, there're better legacies you can have. Still and all, somehow I always knew I'd end up taking over his business and motoring that truck down every interstate in the country. She's a small rig and I can handle her fine. She responds to my touch with an amazing eagerness; I can usually get her to do things my father never could. For instance, start up on days when the temperature drops to 20 below. My father called all his trucks Red, like a horse or a dog. Here comes the believable part: of course he showed his Reds more care and attention, maybe even affection, than he ever showed me or my mother.

Driving was my father's life. That and drinking. If you put the two together you can understand a whole lot without my even saying it. How he lived, how he died, what kind of man he was. Even so, my father respected me a lot, or that's what I think. Maybe because I could control the truck, because I'm an ace driver. Because I am as tough and sour as he ever wanted to be.

I tell people I was born in a truck. This isn't true, but it might as well be. It makes for a good story.

It seems that when my mother's time came, my father was out back working on a truck, one of the early Reds. As my mother tells it, she waddled into the yard clutching at her belly and my father asked if couldn't she hang on for five more minutes so's he could finish with the shocks. My mother threw a socket wrench at his head, and missed. Then my father loaded her up in the truck and took her to the hospital where I was born 20 minutes later. My mother likes to tell this story, especially the part about the throwing of the wrench.

"Of course she missed," my father confided in me once, "she could never throw worth a damn. I only took her to the hospital so I wouldn't have to look for my tools all the hell over the place."

"I only missed," my mother would say, "because I was having contractions every two minutes. You almost got born in that truck, and then what would he've done? Run screaming from the place, most likely. Down to the bar to steady his nerves."

So I often tell people that I was born on the road and will probably die on the road, which may well turn out to be true.

Most people do not belong behind the wheel of a car. They don't give IQ tests before they hand out drivers' licenses, and it shows. People who left off school in the third grade, people who can't operate a toaster, people who think New Mexico is in South America — all these people get in their cars every day and drive around for a while. I happen to think that driving requires concentration and skill, deft hand-eye coordination, the ability to think fast on your feet, and instantaneous reaction time. So you see what we're up against.

Truckers must cultivate some rare patience if they're to survive on the job. It's a matter of just going along with it, I tell myself, instead of reacting every time some dim-witted feeble brain cuts you off to do 25 in the left lane of the thruway. The Zen of driving is essential to remember. Certainly, I wish death upon these people, but only in the most benign sort of way, and I will not do anything to facilitate it.

Only, most drivers take such fearsome stupid chances, riding around in their little instruments of death. A two-ton trailer rig can crush a car like it was a cheap beer can, so all that's left is some scrap metal and round pellets of shatter-proof glass scattered across the road. And the bodies. I've seen some accidents, more than I care to remember. You cannot believe what a person looks like when he's been pulled from the wreckage of yet another fiberglass sports car. He will be half-chewed and partially digested and spit out of some demented creature's mouth. State troopers, the young ones, will retch, but the truckers will only turn white because they've usually seen it before, and when they stop to help they know it's almost always too late.

"This is no life for a girl," my mother tells me every time I visit, which isn't too frequently anymore.

"If I was a boy, what would you say?" I asked her once.

My mother laughed. "That it wasn't much of a life for a boy, either." She looked at me hard. "But I guess that's what your father always wanted you to be. A boy. So I shouldn't be too surprised on how you turned out."

That wasn't exactly true, but my mother would naturally see it that way. "I turned out fine," I told her.

"Well," said my mother. She sidestepped this point. "Some day you're gonna want children. Then what?"

Strange that she didn't mention a man. Maybe she knew that wasn't a problem, that I could always have a man, if and when I wanted one.

"No children," I said. "I couldn't take care of a child. I can barely take care of me."

My mother snorted and looked away, out the window and over the hills. "That's what they all say," she told me. "That's what I said. And now look."

Now look, I thought. You only had the one. But before I could say anything more my mother went on.

"You don't want to regret it," she said. "You don't want to wake up one day, old and alone. No children, no family, no real home. I'm not gonna be around forever," she added, though of course she would. My mother was built to last. "Just a truck," she said now. "Is that what you want? Truck's not gonna take care of you when you get sick. Truck's not gonna sleep with you when you're lonesome. Truck's not gonna bury you when you die." Her voice was hard and I knew she was thinking of my father.

There were no guarantees, I told her. "You can't expect happiness," I said. "Just because you do all the right things, what you're supposed to. It doesn't work like that. You can't count on anything, you know that."

"You're wrong," my mother said. She walked to the kitchen sink and leaned on it, gazing into the drain. "You can always count on some things. You can count on ending up with less than you started out with."

I left her standing there, her face to the window hiding tears, or maybe hiding that there were no tears at all. I backed Red down the driveway and tried not to gun the motor as I drove away.

I like to drive fast, yes. Fast and steady. I train myself, but still I have not much patience with the dawdlers, the meek of heart, the older ones who peer over the steering wheel convinced they can still do it, our flaming youth whose greatest thrill is to challenge truckers and play chicken to pass the night away. I never play; they end up buzzing around me like so many harmless gnats. I will sooner pull over than engage them in battle, though many truckers do. Maybe out of boredom, ego, a sense of impending doom.

These are things I hate: break-down, construction, alternate routes, detours, drawbridges, inexplicable slow-ups, heavy beach traffic, rush hour, Friday night exodus during ski and sun seasons, Sunday night returns to the city. I hate driving in the middle of the day, with the general populace. I like those sweet empty hours before dawn. Between three and five in the morning I drive my best, just me and the other truckers. We are terribly courteous to one another, for the most part, as we hurtle through that dead zone finally free of the rest of the driving world.

I used to have a quote written on a piece of paper bag and Scotch-taped to my dashboard. This is what it said:

> The truck devoured the road with high-singing tires, and I rode throned in the lofty, rocking cab, listening to the driver telling me stories about all the people who lived in the places we passed, and what went on in the houses we saw.

It's from a book by Thomas Merton, called *The Seven-Storey Mountain*. I tried to find it in a bookstore once in El Paso, but they'd never even heard of it. I'm sure a better bookstore in a bigger city would have it, except I don't even bother to look for it anymore.

One day I was giving a lift to a trucker I knew slightly, whose rig broke down 20 miles outside of town.

"What's this?" he said, and peeled the quote off the dashboard.

"Nothing," I told him. "Something from a book that I like."

"Something from a book," he said dubiously, and read it. "Sounds like *poetry* or something." He made a gagging noise. When I didn't answer, he said, "You dress kind of funny, too, come to think of it." And laughing, he crumpled up the old brown paper and let the wind snatch it from his hand.

By this time I knew the sentence by heart, so I decided it would be safer to keep it in my head and not on the dashboard. A truck is not a place to fill up with clutter; you can get attached to objects even quicker than to people. That was a good lesson to learn.

Now my truck has very little, but it's complete unto itself. I've got a sleeping bag stashed in the back in case I'm fed up with trucker motels or I want to catch a quick nap somewhere. I have a battery-powered hot plate and three thermoses, a bottle of Jim Beam and one of vodka, a tape deck, plenty of magazines, and a whole medicine cabinet full of stuff, including all the pills that get traded around in truck stops like they were baseball cards for flipping. I have everything I need.

But when I need something more, I stop at a motel or some roadie bar on the outskirts of any town. A place usually with live shit-kicker music and beer for 30 cents a glass.

The sex is almost always very good. Sometimes exceptional. I only take people passing through, like me. I rely on my gift, which I like to think I was given at birth, the way some people have a knack for mathematics or foreign languages. I have a gift for picking the right ones, who will never surprise me, because I don't like surprises. I look for humor and tenderness and passion, and something of grief, since that's what gives people strength and sympathy. As good a combination as you'll ever find.

And then, on those cool motel sheets with the TV turned down low and its blue-white light baptizing our bodies, we go to town, go to town all night sometimes, and my instinct never fails me and I never get hurt. Unless I want to be.

Besides my father's love of driving, his attachment to liquor, and his affection for Red, I've also inherited his intense absorption in food. This is a trait that most truckers share, maybe because a meal breaks up the tedium of a long day and gives you something to look forward to.

I remember my father eating dinner at home, plowing steadily and silently through his London broil and mashed potatoes with an unwavering focus that fascinated me. My mother and I could talk around him and through him, without expecting a response until he'd wiped his mouth and pushed his plate back, and woke up.

Most of the waitresses at truck stops are named Fran or Adele or Missy and they always seem to wear the same beige and orange polyester uniforms. They'll give pie on the house to the truckers they know, and keep the coffee coming without ever having to be asked for a re-fill. Invariably the older ones feel sorry for me — a lamb lost in wolf territory — and take very good care of me. They bring me choice pieces of pot roast, an extra slab of meat loaf, always the white meat fried chicken, the last slice of chocolate layer cake that's over-sized. They can be friendly at times, and so can the men, but the women truckers are a different story.

The other women truckers are a breed apart; they're not like me. Or I'm not like them. They travel with elaborate hair dryers and curling irons and nail polishing kits. They favor matching outfits, pastel sets usually, and tight designer jeans.

I think of them sometimes as I finger-dry my hair in some tiny motel bathroom. I look at my favorite, comfortable clothes in the mirror, grimed and wrinkled, and try to imagine myself working them over with a portable travel iron. I conjure up a picture of filing my plastic press-on nails at night by the glow of the TV. This game never fails to cheer me up, so when I stroll into the coffee shop I almost laugh at the sight of these wondrous creations at their tables, fixing their lipstick in a compact mirror. Their eyes slide right over me. I'm not a man, I'm not a girl, they can't see what I am so they don't see me at all.

Every once in a while, though, one of them will give me careful information on some truckers: who's safe, who I'm to watch out for, who's supposed to be a killer in bed. Or outside bed.

They shouldn't worry. I carry a gun and I know how to use it. I've shot two men because they neither of them believed that I would or could.

Sometimes I think I am a cowboy, sitting high in the saddle as I ride out alone on Red at sunset; my gun not slung low on my hips but strapped to an ankle holster. It chafes and leaves an imprint on my skin, but I no longer feel it except as a comforting presence nestled against my leg.

My gun is illegal. I would carry a knife, except I don't ever want to be that close to danger in order to protect myself.

Driving at night you need your wits about you. The headlights can trick you into a glaze and you're dreaming awake. You don't want to be on cruise control in a truck at night, hugging the wild corners of a two-lane blacktop. You want to be all there, driving, and let the truck know who's boss.

What would happen if I lost my concentration and let Red take over? Then what? Would she turn on the trail for home? Wander off into the underbrush exploring? I keep her on too tight a rein to find out. If I'm done with my delivery quota for the day, I usually stop most nights pretty early. Then I can be on my way before dawn and cover a fair distance before the sun even breaks.

One night or early morning I came home from catting around town to find my father passed out on the stairs, presumably on his way up to bed. As I was used to finding my father in various states of consciousness, this was not too unusual. I only clucked to myself, an angry cluck, and because this time I refused to rouse him and spirit him off to his bed, I kicked him in the side as I went upstairs.

I know how that sounds, but regardless, I did it, and didn't feel too bad for doing it. Maybe it was meant to get him up, or maybe not. When you live with a drunk for a while you learn to exact your revenge in small ways that only you can know about, in ways the drunk cannot possibly retaliate for. It wasn't a kick that would've broken a rib — it would've probably left a bruise, a soreness the next day to add to the general soreness. I was just doing my part, heaping on the guilt, so he'd be forced to wonder the next day: where did that one come from? Did someone sucker punch me in the bar? What door did I go careening off of?

So I kicked him, and as I did, he moaned a little, a small groan that didn't manage to bring him up from whatever depths he was in, and I hesitated, thinking he would wake and then I'd have to help him up. But he didn't wake, and was silent. So I switched off the light and went on up to bed.

Later that morning I was awakened myself by the sound of my mother screaming, over and over. I'd heard my mother scream before, certainly, but not like this. I rolled out of bed

and hit the floor running. She was on the stairs next to my
father, who hadn't moved a limb since I'd seen him six hours
earlier. My mother's eyes were wide and shiny with terror and
she was pulling the skin of her cheeks down with both hands,
like a parody of some woman in shock. She couldn't form any
words, but she didn't have to. I called an ambulance and then
I led my mother away from him, into the kitchen, while we
waited for it to come. Then I made sure there wasn't anything
I could do, and there wasn't.

Like in murder mysteries, I asked the attending doctor to
pinpoint the time of death. Unlike murder mysteries, he
couldn't really tell me. Some time between three and five in
the a.m. is what he'd said. I'd come home about 3:30 that
morning.

Once I read an article that mentioned how when a person
dies he usually has a little air left in his lungs. If you move the
body, the sound of the air escaping creates a small sound, like
a moan or a groan. Sometimes this can fool you, the article
said, into actually believing the person was still alive when he
wasn't.

The fact of the matter remains, there is no way out of this
one. I kicked a dead man on the stairs in my house. Or I kicked
a man who was engaged in dying. The doctor allowed to me,
privately, that my father was not only drunk as the old skunk
when he died of a massive coronary, but that his liver was
greatly enlarged. "The drink killed him," the doctor told me,
shaking his head with a show of sadness. "I'm not telling your
mother. But that's what killed him, sure as I'm sitting here."

I didn't care much what killed him, but I cared when.
There was another possibility, the one I favor the least.
Suppose it hadn't happened yet. Suppose my father was just
taking his customary breather after spending seven hours in
the bar, and I could've roused him. Gotten him to his feet,
maybe even gotten him to yell at me, to maybe take a swing
at my head. Then he would've had his heart attack and I

43

could've saved him. In this fantasy, he stayed in the hospital two months, quit drinking and smoking, came home, and was a nice man who liked to shoot pool with his daughter and tinker with his truck and take his wife out to Clam Night at the Holiday Inn.

But this is what I believe in my heart: I kicked my father who was barely cold, half an hour dead, and kicking him, dislodged the last breath he'd ever hold in his lungs.

Because we live in modern times, only hitchhikers I will occasionally pick up are the young girls. Sometimes they just want to get into town, but more often than not they're running away. Running from fathers who beat them or have sex with them, husbands who beat them and rape them when they've had too much to drink. We may live in modern times, but in small towns everywhere girls are still getting married at fifteen.

They are usually surprised and not always pleased to see that I am a woman. They buy into the stereotypes very early and are suspicious of why I have stopped for them. They cannot seem to realize that it is the men they must watch out for. I've heard stories about truckers who'll pick up young girls and boys to see what they can get, take them where they want to go in return for a quick blowjob or a roll around the back of the truck. I don't know if I believe this; most truckers get paid by the load and even a 15 minute break can mean missing a warehouse deadline. Nevertheless, I've met some slimy characters on the road and I wouldn't want to be fresh-faced and fourteen, sitting in the passenger seat.

I stopped for one girl outside Yellow Springs; she claimed to be eighteen but I didn't think she'd see that age for another three years yet.

"I never seen a lady trucker before," she confided to me.

I allowed as how we weren't all that common.

"What made you want to be a trucker when you grew up?" she said.

That made me think. Not having too much ambition herself other than to have babies, she just assumed that's the way it was done. You decided to drive a truck at age three, and then there you were.

It was curious, but no one had ever asked me why. My mother knew why, or thought she knew. My friends shook their heads and secretly enjoyed it — I was someone they were comfortably sorry for, and then they felt better about their own lives. My father's friends, who were all truckers, nodded their heads and told me I'd be sorry. This girl suddenly asked me why and I didn't have an answer.

The pause went on too long for her. "Guess you get to see a lot of places," she decided. "You don't gotta answer to no one, right? Your own boss and all that." She settled my life neatly and moved on to hers, which was much more messy. I left her off in a city that was slightly out of my way. I didn't ask for anything in return.

I've been through all 48 mainland states. While it's true I've seen an awful lot of the country, I haven't seen that many cities. It's not that I don't like people or crowds or noise. Sometimes I do. But those places, they're none of them my home. And I don't belong; I'm not even visiting. It's not like travelling to a place to see friends you know, or to soak up some exotic atmosphere. I'm only passing through. While I'm passing through, I imagine the lives that I never quite see, each one complicated and thorough, with its own history and its own address book filled with other people's names and lives. Sometimes I see a brief flash of people I will never know — I'll pass a lawn party or a wedding letting out of a church, an old man and woman sitting on a porch swing, two children beating each other up with plastic pails and shovels. They never see me. I'm a truck going by. I leave no trace or memory, but I carry them all with me wherever I go.

Mostly I measure how far I've come and how far I'm going by road signs. I chart my progress across the country by hours (how long will it take me to get to Shreveport). Sometimes I picture my truck as a little blip on a huge road map. That's me, traversing all those red and blue lines, skimming past insignificant dots that are towns easy to forget. Forging through the larger congested dots that mean big cities. And there's me and Red, making short work of all those endless lines . . . where do they all go? A grid that stops when you get to the edge of the map. And where do we go from there?

One day my father and I were out in the back working on Red. There was something clearly wrong with her transmission. Though neither of us knew squat about fixing transmissions we were banging away regardless. We were both decked out in our oldest clothes and grimed up; now and then we'd chug from warmish cans of Budweiser. Just like a beer commercial, me and my father. I was working hard, not thinking of anything and not talking much either when suddenly I got that unmistakable feeling when someone's looking at you. I glanced up and it was my father.

He was staring at me as if it were the first time he'd ever laid eyes on me. It came over in such a flash I knew it had to be true — he was looking at me not like a daughter, or even a woman, but as a stranger. Someone who puzzled the hell out of him, someone who didn't belong in his backyard. He stood there, examining me, not a hint of smile on his face. It wasn't a mean look, though, not like he'd decided to hate me. No, because in that instant he didn't know me well enough to hate me. But there was something unpleasant there all the same.

"What," I said, to break the spell.

He shook his head. "Nothing," he said. "Just . . . you're an odd fish, you know? Some kind of odd fish." He dropped his eyes.

"Yeah, and you're a queer duck," I told him, and we both sort of laughed so that the moment was over and we went back to work.

He couldn't understand how this odd fish came to be. He

46

never made the connection that it was him who spawned me.

I've driven in some weather. In wretched Texas heat, where it hit 114 and cars and trucks were littered on the side of the road, steaming, like some freshly killed animals. In rain and snow storms that could make you believe in Jesus, when the back end of Red would go fishtailing down the highway. That sickening skid feeling when the wheels have no grip and no gravity, the weightless suspension of your heart as you steer into the skid, always into the skid, where you don't want to go, teaching your foot not to slam on the brake and send you slithering down an embankment end over end over end.

I've seen tornado weather. I played chicken with a twister, trying to beat it to the next truck stop. There's no more unnatural weather on this earth, though some truckers will claim the Santa Ana winds can make them believe in hell.

The tornado was supposed to be heading away from the direction I was going in, but in its perversity, its fickle black soul, buttonhooked back toward me. I was in South Dakota, next service area 34 miles, when I saw the dark blot on the horizon. It loomed up fast, bouncing on its merry pogo stick way, that eerie howling making my hackles rise like a dog.

The sky was a color that no sky ever had the right to be, a sickly yellow-gray like the end of the world. I pulled Red off onto the shoulder and got out, leaving both windows open. The radio had been bleating warnings every three minutes about what to do if you were unlucky enough to get caught. I was apparently the only one in sight who had. Even though I knew that staying in the truck would only give me the illusion of safety since the twister could toss it like a Matchbox truck, it was still the hardest thing I'd ever done, to climb down out of Red and throw myself into a drainage ditch. When the tornado passed over, screaming, I screamed too.

There was a moment of absolute stillness when all the air seemed to have been sucked up by a huge, invisible pair of lungs. Then dirt and rocks and branches and sod were churning around me, and the twister was gone on its weird, whistling way. I sat up and watched it dance down the highway, touching down lightly here and there, kicking up all manner of things in its wake. I was left behind in my drainage ditch, holding clumps of weeds in my tight fists as if I might fall off the face of the earth.

A while later some people drove by, hailed me as a survivor, and plied me with warm whiskey until I could emerge from my lair shaky but alive, alive-o.

My mother didn't fall apart until after it was all over. Up until then she'd held herself together well enough, for the sake of all the people who'd come to show their respects. She considered it vulgar to break down in front of them. So she was quite the gracious hostess even after the burial, inviting everyone back to the house for a ham and a turkey that she'd cooked herself, the night before. Neighbors had brought in casseroles, candied and glazed and microwaveable, and all manner of pies, including rhubarb, which I hated.

My mother's face was flushed. She darted from one cluster of people to the next, emptying ash trays, re-filling their highballs, urging food. She was giddy with the company, the first successful party she'd ever thrown. She didn't want anyone to leave and when she waved goodbye to each person at the door ("Thanks for coming — safe home now") I expected her to invite them all back to do it again the next weekend. When the last drunk and gorged guest had gone, my mother wandered restless and empty through the house, ending up in the kitchen where I sat with my watery rye.

"What a mess," she said, and sunk into a chair.

"You spent a lot of money," I said.

"And if I did," she said. "Your father deserved a fine send-off. What's money to me now, anyway?"

"Nothing," I said. "Nothing. Only the truck is going to need a few things, if I'm to carry on the business."

"Don't you dare," my mother told me. "Don't you dare

mention that truck to me. Tonight." Tears rolled slowly down her face and dripped off her jaw. She seemed too tired or too hopeless to wipe them away. I wanted to get her a tissue but my mother would have interpreted that as pity, something you did for a child or an old person.

"He loved you the best, you know," she said.

"He called me an odd fish," I told her.

"And so you are," she said. "But he loved you the best. Out of the both of us, he loved you the best."

I said, "He had a funny way of showing it."

My mother slapped me full across the face with a ferocious suddenness and my neck cracked. Then she went to bed.

Once I needed some time off so I flew to England for two months and traveled around. I could've rented a car, but I thought that's what I was trying to get away from. Instead I got myself a Britrail pass and spent my time as a passenger. But in my dreams there, I was always driving. Sometimes I was even driving a train, careening down the tracks, hugging a hairpin turn around the edge of a cliff. Always I could feel the pull of the train underneath me, responding to my touch.

In a pub out in the west country, a small trainman's place called The Goat's Head, I sipped the local ale and became the object of some curiosity being as I was American, female, and alone. The natives had a collective accent so thick and fanciful that I could hardly believe we were speaking the same language at times. By the third or fourth round — the local brew being more potent than any beer I'd ever had before — I was floating on the rhythms of their speech. I absorbed most of what they were saying more from the pattern and lilt of their phrasing rather than understand the words themselves.

The fellow next to me, a train engineer, finally found out that I drove a truck back home in the States.

"Cor!" he said. "Lorries. Driving a lorry cross that swaping big country of yours." Never mind that I was a girl, I became his hero. I'd never made anyone's face light up before.

It seemed that I'd hit upon his dream — of driving for days and never seeing the ocean, but only the flat and unbreakable expanse of land stretching in front, the sky meeting the earth in a faraway horizon and knowing that you could drive to that point and still keep going. It was the hunger of someone who lives on an island. It was the ancient yearning for the New World, and I discovered with some surprise that I was away from my own land and I was homesick.

We drank and talked of lorries all evening until the bar-keep called time. The train engineer offered me a walk to clear our heads and the walk ended in his flat for a nightcap. Contrary to what I'd heard about the British, he was a good and fervent lover. And if he was off exploring some unknown landscape, driving in search of who knows where, I could excuse him for that. Because I found I was off there, too, driving to the edges of some precipice that I couldn't quite see.

My mother has an owl collection. She collects all types of owls without discrimination for quality or craftsmanship: ceramic, glass, wood, plastic, and those hideous ones made out of shells glued together. "Why don't you collect something?" my mother tells me. "It's a good hobby."

I don't have any room for clutter, for collections, for anything that needs preserving and dusting. But one day I realized I'd taken my mother's advice after all. I collect the names of places — towns I've seen and driven by, even towns that were just a sign on the road.

I liked the ones best that had some history to them, history someone in a bar would tell me. Like Baby Head, Texas, which apparently was named when a raiding Comanche captured and killed a white baby and put its head on a pole on the mountain. Or 88, Kentucky, because the postmaster couldn't read or write. I also liked Bill, Wyoming, so called after the first name of most of its citizens.

Then there's the ones I just like the sound of: Cat Mash, Alabama; Slaughter Beach, Delaware; Rough and Ready,

California; Experiment, Georgia. West Virginia has towns called War and Mud and Odd. Kentucky has Dwarf and Viper. Texas is the hands-down winner, though. Texas has a love for one-word towns that may or may not be descriptive, like Small and Scurry and Fry, Lawn and Pancake; Necessity, Fairy, Pep, and Goodnight.

I keep the list in my back pocket, not taped to the dash-board. Sometimes at night I take it out and read the names to myself. The names all make a kind of poetry, a lullaby that puts me to sleep.

When I was still pretty small, my father and mother took me to an amusement park. This was fairly unusual, as they weren't that big on family-type outings. Seems like once they had me, they expected me to entertain myself. But we ended up at this amusement park where there was a ride I was wild to try. It involved cars and trucks that you could really drive. The brakes worked, and the steering. They rode gently around a track powered by electricity, like a trolley.

I remember you had to be a certain height to qualify for this ride and I had to strain to reach the line they'd painted for where your head should be. Finally, my turn was up and I climbed into a milk truck. This was much better than bumper cars, where all I wanted to do was drive in peace and all the other kids kept ramming me. The track wound in and out of trees, alongside a small pond, and through a tunnel. I properly observed traffic signals and the flashing railroad crossing sign. I was supremely, thoroughly pleased with myself. I could drive. This was all there was to it — I had always been certain it would be easy and there was no reason to wait until I was grown up to do it.

When I passed my parents waiting at the fence, I tooted the horn and waved like an old pro.

"That's my girl," said my father. His face was split wide with a grin. My mother was looking the other way and didn't see me go by.

51

•

It's not just my mother. Other people tell me that it's not much of a life for a girl. Sometimes men will shake their heads in wonderment at me — a woman whose code they cannot crack. Or so they think. A woman who forsakes hearth and home, who does not campaign for bedroom furniture and bassinets. A woman who can change a car tire in twelve minutes flat (if the bolts aren't rusted on), and sleeps many nights in many strange and empty beds, and is not afraid of the dark. A woman who can be alone and not talk to herself.

They watch me pull out of the parking lot after sharing a meal or more than a meal; their eyes follow me as I merge Red smoothly into the flow of traffic. They admire me and yet there is still something underneath that respect, something I once saw in my father's eyes: a puzzlement which can only be resolved in contempt. The women they all know do not do this, do not behave this way. Therefore, what does that make me?

But I've seen some things. I drove through a meteor shower one night and finally stopped along with everyone else who could not keep their eyes on the road. Our faces turned up to the heavens, we watched hundreds of shooting stars trace tails across the sky until we could no longer absorb such a vision and so abandoned it.

I've seen a palace in South Dakota decorated entirely with corn, and a house built with candy, like in Hansel and Gretel. I've driven toward a town that rose up from the desert floor like a citadel, shimmering with heat, that never grew any larger as I approached.

I once saw a trucker hit a deer, a large buck, probably eight points, and we both stopped and helped each other haul him bleeding and unconscious into the back of his truck by way of the electronic ramp. We drove to the city and found the closest veterinarian, who couldn't save the buck's life. Neither the other trucker nor I took the antlers, and the vet charged us fifty dollars for the privilege of making money off the carcass.

I once saw a trucker deliberately swerve to hit a dog who'd run out in the road.

I once saw a topless dancer sit down on her runway and sob after a trucker had thrown a wad of crumpled bills at her feet and yelled to buy herself a good support bra.

I met a man who confessed over too many beers that he was in love with his own mother. "She'll let me take her to the movies, but that's it," he said, "what can I do?"

I've never been visited by aliens from another planet but once saw a UFO. It hovered over a nearby mountain, shimmering with lights, exactly the way it's supposed to do.

I once saw a man killed in a bar, knifed by his best friend over a woman, of course. From that I learned that we have so much blood in us, it is not to be believed. And I learned that no one, no matter how brave, will move to restrain a man driven mad by love.

I once saw a whole field of bats rise up around me from where I scared them from their feasting. I felt the rush of air from the silent flutter of their wings but not a one touched me.

I once saw true love in the face beside me in bed one morning, and I left that same day. I was young and only wanted to jump in my truck, to drive, and it was only several years later that I remembered and understood that look, what it meant.

Some days when I'm tooling down the road, not thinking much of anything, I feel like one of those creatures in Pac-Man. A round head and a big mouth, gobbling up the road, swallowing that white line as fast as I can. It's fun for a while but it can get too hypnotic. Then I get mesmerized by the road and forget where I'm going. You can miss an exit like that. You can lose yourself.

I read an article in a magazine once about the hazards of scuba diving, how a diver can get nitrogen narcosis if he swims down too far. Then he can't tell down from up, and he's so deliriously happy he doesn't care, just keeps swimming further and further toward the bottom of the ocean. Who knows if he ever reaches it. But he never comes back.

Rapture of the deep, it's called.

I've felt it, too, driving late at night. You can follow the pull of your own headlights right off the highway, as you're going round a bend. Lured like a bug to its own senseless, dreamy ecstatic death. That's the dangerous beauty of the open road.

When I'm not on the road, I have a place to stay. I don't always sleep in my truck or in motels. People might expect I live in a small efficiency apartment fully furnished, but no. I live in a large old ramshackle house, hardly furnished at all. I have a phone only because my mother insisted, though no television, no washer and dryer, no microwave, no matching dishes.

"Why don't you buy yourself a comfortable couch?" my mother often says. "Why can't you get yourself a decent set of china, at least?" This is what my mother means by having a home. I don't know, maybe if I had all that I'd be a different person, settle down amongst all the things I'd collected, and never venture forth from such a cozy place.

In back of the house where I live for about 87 days out of the year is a meadow stretching toward the hills and a small copse of trees. When I'm there, I stand at twilight with a drink in my hand and survey all I see. The bats swoop out to search for food, stars begin to spangle the sky, the trees rustle. It's all very pretty. Then I walk around to the front of the house and sit on the steps so I can see the traffic. I watch the cars and trucks go past, their headlights holding them fast to the track.

My heart lifts and I yearn to be one of them driving by. I will only catch a glimpse of that girl sitting on the steps watching the traffic, and wonder who she is, what her life is like, before I turn my eyes away from her and back to the open road.

Stroke

JOYCE CAROL OATES

Her father was not an old man but he'd had a sudden stroke and it was serious they said so she terminated her lecture — she had "done" West Germany and Belgium and had only Holland, that is, Amsterdam, ahead — and flew home on the earliest available flight, arriving at John F. Kennedy Airport at what was presumably the late afternoon while simultaneously the late morning of the very day she'd started in, thinking God don't let him die, don't let him die God though not in the nuances of prayer, you cannot after all have an angry prayer nor had she believed in God for a very long time. She rented a car and drove for another day or what seemed like another day until she began to hallucinate and heard her own voice raised in grief and wonder in the car so she stopped at a motel just off the interstate highway where she couldn't sleep moving about the room in the semidark — she had kept the bathroom light on, and the door just slightly ajar— and lying on top of the corduroy bedspread that smelled like stale smoke and hair oil and then something, some presence, in the room woke her at dawn (though dawn was still dark), teeth chattering with cold, Is that you Daddy? Daddy is that you? — and her shaking fingers switched on the light and of course she was alone.

At the hospital the next morning at 10:15 she went directly to the fifth floor where her father had a private room and there was the woman who was her stepmother waiting for her, waiting to hug her in an embrace that hurt, beginning to choke and cry, It's bad, this woman was saying, and Try not to excite him, please, this woman was saying, and her nostrils contracted from the woman's perfumy smell, Oh no you don't, she was thinking, smiling where the woman couldn't see, you don't seduce this baby, oh no. These were not her words precisely nor was their cadence hers but she had no time to consider the strangeness of it, and at her father's bedside too she was in control speaking calmly and lucidly not about to break down like her stepmother seeing Daddy's right eye blurred and milky like a marble egg fixed on some distance beyond her head but the left eye was Daddy's old good eye shining, wasn't it, with love fierce as hurt.

They squeezed each other's fingers hard, these two, in code. Oh they knew each other! — they knew! They whispered so others (in the corridor outside the room) could not hear. At first she laughed entertaining Daddy with quick-capsule accounts of traveling in Europe, hotel nights and hotel breakfasts and embassy dinners and limousines and interviewers and it seemed he listened intently as always smiling and smirking his old good eye shining with humor and their old complicity in offhandedness in skepticism regarding all that was not, you might say, them; the two of them; the one that the two of them became, at such times; when they were together, that is; and others, though close (in the corridor outside the room, for instance), excluded. She was gay and witty and entertaining taking no notice of the plasterish color of Daddy's skin, or the tubes and transparent things, what snaked into his right forearm at the elbow where it was bruised and his skinny blue-veined ankle exposed so strangely, you might almost say luridly, at the corner of the bed, and there was the catheter in the groin which she could not see and of which she did not think, nor did she hear the strange labored breathing in the room nor did she smell the smell in the room that transfixed her nostrils. Daddy seemed to be asking about Amsterdam wasn't it? or the flight over the ocean wasn't it? or *her* health — wasn't it? and then he was trying to explain with the one still-living side of his mouth a way of getting out of, it seemed to be the city, maybe this city or maybe another city, how some people, the word was maybe "citizens" or maybe "civilians," were trapped, but others, the smart ones, had already left taking back-routes and avoiding thoroughfares where they would be picked off from the sky, the sky was the danger Daddy said, or seemed to be saying, plucking at her hand, or trying to pluck at her hand, and she listened and nodded, quickly, avidly. Oh yes. They had to leave at once Daddy said, he'd been a man of power and eloquence and enormous manly charm and just the smallest vein of cruelty in his old life but now his great need his only remaining human need was to make his daughter comprehend the simplest of human truths and she was at his bedside for that purpose. Don't worry she said I know where the border is, we won't be turned back. I don't want to be late he said his good eye spilling tears. She said, We *won't* be late, and so it went there at his bedside where no one else could hear and the words were strange spitty syllables, harsh consonants some would have thought merely sounds, merely sounds and not human sounds at that, and she began to feel the entire right side of her face freeze in its awful grimace and the left side, the still-living side, quiver and ripple like water churning alive with feeding fish with the need to explain, the need to make known all it is you know because this is all that remains of you now, the fiercest most terrible need of all existence and it was there in the room with her like a living thing, a presence, not her father and not herself but born

57

of the conjunction of the two of them for which she'd flown home and driven so many hours and afterward when she was crying angrily and the woman who was her stepmother tried to quiet her, tried to trap her again in that embrace and quiet her she said, He knows what you are planning, she said throwing off the arms, the trap, — he knows, and so do I.

Auto
Repair

ROSALIND WARREN

There's no place to go in Detroit
that's half as fun as getting there. Especially in my daddy's
Olds. The closest thing to heaven on earth is being on the freeway when Aretha comes on. Her soaring voice is telling me to
floor it. I turn the volume up until the music is coming from
inside me and go as fast as I can.

I don't want you to think that I don't drive responsibly. I
am a responsible driver. Responsible, but accelerated. I go to
the community college, though I'm just seventeen, because
I'm accelerated. I still live at home, though. So I can drive my
daddy's Olds.

My father taught me to drive when I was fourteen. He took
me to the parking lot at the Tel-Twelve Mall, told me to get behind the wheel, sat back in the passenger seat, and lit a cigar.
"Do your worst, babe," he said.

He put on the country-western station and Earl Scruggs
and Ricky Scaggs sang love songs as we lurched around the

lot. Dad slouched back in the reclining seat and gave me advice. "Don't squash that poodle, honey." "Watch out for the Winnebago." One morning he gave me a key ring with the keys to seventeen cars. "They're all yours, Mercy," he said. I gave him a bear hug and he smiled. "Sure wish your mom could see you now," he said.

Mom died when I was only two. She died in her car, a red Trans Am. Coming home from the supermarket one night, she was broadsided by a drunk car-door salesman in a Lincoln Continental. The car was totaled. She was killed instantly. The groceries in the trunk survived.

Dad didn't junk the car. He had it towed home. He rebuilt it. He wanted to salvage something, he says. Repairing the car made him feel better. He started collecting them. He buys wrecks and puts them back together again. It's like a hobby. He tells me it's therapy. "Auto repair — the poor man's analysis," he says. He must have over twenty cars now, plus junkers he keeps for parts.

Some of Dad's cars are stashed in friends' garages; some are out in our driveway or sitting in the backyard. We've got a peach-colored Studebaker down in the basement, because he took it apart in the driveway one summer and reassembled it down there, just to see if he could.

Everything in Detroit comes down to cars. If you don't work on the line like my dad, you work for a company that makes car-door handles or cruise controls. Or plastic saints for the dashboard. Or you're that company's lawyer, or the shrink the auto execs go to, or the funeral director that puts them all in the ground. Remember that guy who was buried sitting behind the wheel of his Caddy? He wasn't a Detroit man, but he had the right idea. Detroit is all auto showrooms, muffler shops, and intersections with a gas station on each corner. Motown babies are born groping for the steering wheel, and by the time a local kid is five she can call out the model and year of every car that drives by.

My dad never remarried. He's got girlfriends. He's got

me. He's got reconstituted Chevys, Fords, Pontiacs, a Studebaker in the basement, and job security. He's got pals on the line to go drinking with.

When he gets too drunk to drive, he phones me from a bar and I drive out to get him. His friends help him into the backseat. He sits with his feet up and lights a cigar.

"Where to?" I ask.

"East of the sun, west of the moon," he'll say if he's really sloshed.

"Dad?"

"Anywhere you want, babe," he says. "It's all the same to me."

The streets around Detroit — long, wide roads under a big midwestern sky — are made for cruising. I'll drive down Woodward Avenue. We'll put the radio on or just sit quiet and watch the world go by. Woodward is the main drag — miles of glittering neon signs and fast-food stands. Everybody in this city learned to drive on this street. Sometimes we'll cruise all the way out to Dearborn to see Ford Motor Company World Headquarters, a complex of gleaming skyscrapers sitting all by itself in the middle of nowhere. Or downtown to the Detroit River to see the Renaissance Center, which was supposed to revitalize the inner city but didn't. Or to Canada, crossing through the tunnel under the river, driving through sleepy downtown Windsor, and returning across the Ambassador Bridge. I drive by my mom's cemetery. Over the entrance is a sign in lovely pink neon script — Roseview Cemetery — that I remember from way before I had any idea what it meant.

Eventually Dad falls asleep and I drive home.

I fell in love with Todd in his daddy's Eldorado.

My daddy didn't take to Todd at first. "He's too short for you," he said. "He looks like a hoodlum." Dad was wrong about that. Todd was a rich kid from Bloomfield Hills. He wore faded jeans and a beat-up leather jacket because it looked cool, not because he couldn't afford better. He had long dark hair, beautiful gray eyes, and loads of nervous energy, and he

61

played lead guitar in the Clone Brothers, a local band. He was at our place watching television with a crowd of my friends. A girl I didn't like had brought him, so I started flirting with him.

I could sense Dad lurking by the front door later on as I walked Todd to his car. The girl he'd been with was long gone. Todd got into the Eldorado, and I leaned in the window of that gorgeous black car and kissed him. That's when I fell in love. Todd didn't seem too surprised — as if strange girls leaned in his car window and kissed him all the time.

"Call me," I said, dizzy.

We gazed into each other's eyes. Then he turned the key in the ignition and the engine blew up.

The next thing I know I'm sitting on our front lawn, with Todd and my father running around the car yelling instructions to each other, trying to get our old fire extinguisher to work and swatting at the burning Eldorado with blankets. A crowd of neighbors came out to cheer them on, but the Eldorado burned to a crisp.

Dad decided to like Todd then, either because he felt sorry for him or because he wanted his car for parts.

But Todd didn't phone. Maybe because our kiss had set his car on fire. I didn't see him again till months later. His band was playing at a bar out in Ypsilanti, and Dad went to see them without telling me. I guess he was getting sick of my moping around the house telling him how the love of my life had passed me by. Dad ended up having a pretty good time. After the last set, Todd drove my father home.

Todd rang the doorbell. It was late, and I came to the door in my pajamas. He was the last person I'd expected to see.

"Guess what?" Todd said.

I didn't have to guess — I could hear my daddy snoring away in the backseat of Todd's new Chevy.

"Let him rest," said Todd. He got out his guitar and I put on a bathrobe, and we sat on the warm hood of Todd's car, where he recycled all the love songs he'd written for his last girlfriend. Between the songs we kissed.

Hours later the car door opened and Dad stepped out. "What a night!" he said.

He squinted at us sitting there on the hood. I could tell he didn't really remember Todd's driving him home.

"Nice car," he said. "Is it ours?"

He circled the Chevy, patting the hood, stooping to admire the whitewalls, tracing the chrome with a fingertip. Finishing, he bowed to us and shuffled toward the house, still wrapped in the blanket I'd thrown over him. He looked like the drawing in my grade school civics textbook of Pontiac, the Indian chief for whom the city of Pontiac and later the car were named.

He paused on the front steps. "Call me if you need help putting any fires out," he said.

Todd phoned the next night.

"Want to come over?" he asked. He gave me directions to his house. It wasn't till I got there that I recognized the neighborhood, a posh subdivision that had gone up a few years back. When it was new, my friends and I used to cruise through and laugh at how grand and silly the houses were. They were all monsters, each flashier than the last. And Todd lived in the grandest one. It was a little castle, complete with three turrets, a (waterless) moat, and a fake drawbridge.

Todd met me at the door with a skinny girl with wild red curls and thick glasses. She looked about twelve.

"I'm baby-sitting," he said. "My parents are out of town. This is my sister, Gladys. She's a computer nerd."

"Computer hacker," Gladys corrected. "Want me to access your school records and change all your grades to A's?"

"They already are."

"Cool." She grinned. "If you're so smart what are you doing with my brother?"

Todd gave her a friendly shove. "Come on," he said to me. He led me through the place, which looked like something out of a magazine, to his room, which was ten times the size of my room at home. Guitars and stereo equipment lined one wall, and his record collection took up half of another. I'd never seen anything like it. We sat down on his bed.

"Where are your parents?" I asked.

"Geneva." He sounded almost apologetic.

Silence.

"I missed you," he said finally. Then we started kissing, and I felt at home again, even in that outlandish place.

We got to the point where if we'd been in a car, we'd have dusted ourselves off and gone to get coffee someplace on Woodward and talk. I'd never known anyone whose parents vanished to Geneva and left them a castle to hang out in. I wasn't entirely comfortable about it. I began wondering how I was going to get out of this. Did I really want to?

Then Todd stopped kissing me and looked into my eyes. I waited.

"Want to climb a tree?" he asked.

Climb? A tree?

"We have to take Gladys, though. I'm responsible for her."

"A tree?" I asked.

"You'll see," he said. "It'll be fun."

It was. The three of us drove to Ferndale, a small residential neighborhood. "We used to live here," said Todd as we cruised through the quiet streets. "Then Grandpa died and Mom inherited." We got out of the car at a sleepy little park. There was an old beech with thick, sprawling branches — perfect for climbing.

"This is my favorite place," Todd said when the three of us had climbed up to the top. We sat in the branches, looking out over the park and talking. When we ran out of things to say, Todd and Gladys sang me Elvis songs. I'd never been happier.

"And what have you been up to?" asked Dad when I got home.

•

Todd and I started going out. We usually took his car. I'd sit beside him, my head against his shoulder and the radio playing. He'd chain-smoke and we'd cruise and talk for hours. Or I'd just sit, quiet, feeling so happy I wanted to freeze the whole thing and stash it in a time capsule somewhere.

All this bliss made Dad a little nervous. "Don't get in over your head," he warned one night while he and I watched the Tigers pulverize the Red Sox on television.

"Too late," I said.

"He's a real nice kid," said Dad. "But he's got a few problems." I got a kick out of that. Dad spoke as if Todd were a faulty engine that needed a few days in the shop.

"What kind of problems?"

"You think that boy spends a tenth the time thinking about you that you spend thinking about him?"

"This is a relationship, Dad, not a see-saw."

"Do you two ever talk about anything besides his music and his band and his plans? Ever talk about *your* plans?"

"I don't need to talk about my plans."

"That's not the point," he said, "and you know it."

Of course I knew it, though I wasn't going to tell him so. I wasn't stupid. I knew deep down that I was in love with Todd and that Todd was in love with me being in love with Todd. As neat and talented as he was, he was too insecure and unsure of himself to be able to focus on me. But that would change. I'd make it change.

It was as if Dad could read my mind.

"That boy's a do-it-yourself model," he said. "You deserve a finished product."

I blew up at him. "I'm not one of your cars!" I said. "Don't try to take me apart and put me back the way you want."

He smiled. "Okay, honey," he said. "I'll back off. But maybe you'll listen to an expert." He took a folded-up piece of yellowed newspaper from his wallet and pushed it across the table to me. It was an old Ann Landers column about how to tell love from infatuation. I asked how long he'd been carrying it around.

"Five, six years," he said. "You never know when something like this could come in handy."

"I was only eleven when you clipped it?"

"Just thinking ahead," he said, rummaging around in his wallet. "The concerned single parent."

"The overprotective single parent," I said. "The nosy, interfering single parent." I told him I didn't give a hoot about what some old lady had to say five years ago about love. I was happier than I'd been ever with Todd. Dad would just have to trust me.

He kept poking around in his wallet. Finally he took out my mom's high school graduation photo and sighed. "You're the spitting image," he said. "On the outside. But on the inside you're just as pigheaded as your old man."

"I could do a lot worse," I said.

A few weeks later Todd and I were sitting in his car parked in our driveway, and Todd told me that he wanted to break it off. "It's getting too serious," he said.

I had the feeling that wasn't it at all. He'd found someone new to listen to his love songs. He just didn't have the nerve to tell me. I tried to joke.

"You want it to be more shallow?" I asked.

He stared at me, looking as if he were about to cry. I could tell he wasn't enjoying this, and my heart went out to him. Then I realized that if I didn't stop myself, I'd end up comforting *him* for leaving me.

"Ann Landers tried to warn me about you," I said. I got out of the car, slammed the door, and went to my daddy's Olds, parked right behind Todd's Chevy. I started her up and began searching for a good radio station.

Todd came over and leaned in my window.

"Where're you going?" he asked. "You live here."

"East of the sun, west of the moon," I said.

"Can't we be friends?" he asked.

I was so angry I wanted to back up my daddy's Olds, floor her, and smash right into Todd's beautiful new car. You break my heart, I'll wreck your Chevy. But I'm my father's daughter —I couldn't do that to an innocent auto. Instead I found Stevie Wonder on the dial and took off with a squeal of tires. Todd ran after me, but I floored it until he was just a tiny dot in the rearview mirror.

The music was good. It carried me through our subdivision and the quiet side streets over to Telegraph Avenue. I decided to drive down Telegraph, past all the Mile Roads. Ten Mile Road, by the all-night kosher Dunkin' Donuts. Eleven Mile Road, by my old high school. Twelve Mile Road. All the lights were with me and I was cruising. I love this car, I was thinking. Nothing can get me in here. It's when you get out of your car that the trouble starts.

There was a groan from the backseat, and my daddy's face appeared in the rearview. "Apparently a man can't take a little nap in his own Oldsmobile without getting hijacked?" he said.

"What on earth are you doing back there?" I asked.

"I was sleeping," he said. "It's usually real peaceful back here."

I glared at him. I didn't need this. Not now.

We rode a few minutes, silent. I could see it was funny. And I knew he loved me. Still, I had planned to drive for hours —a heartbroken blond racing down the freeway at night with tears in her eyes. A real American cliché.

Having Dad pop up in the backseat like that kind of ruined the picture.

"Are we headed anywhere in particular?" he asked a few miles later.

"Nope."

"Care to talk about it?"

I didn't really. I wanted to drive. Alone. I wanted to drive for miles and miles and dwell on my sorrow. But it was too late for that.

"There's a twenty-four-hour car wash out on Lone Pine Road," Dad said. "Your mom and I used to go there to talk. If we couldn't get things straightened out, we figured at least the car would get clean." He smiled. "We don't have to talk if you don't want to. But the car could use washing."

The most miserable night of my life and we're talking about whether the car needs washing.

Of course, on the other hand, the car did need washing. It couldn't *hurt* to wash the car. At the next intersection I turned toward Lone Pine Road, switched over to the country station, and gave the full weight of my foot to the accelerator. Dad leaned forward to squeeze my shoulder, then settled back in his seat, smiling. "No rush," he said. "We've got all night."

It wasn't that I stopped feeling sad. There was a heaviness in my chest that I knew would stay with me awhile. But as we cruised along, the idea of driving in the middle of the night to take a beat-up Oldsmobile through a car wash for a heart-to-heart talk with my old man didn't seem so bad.

What
A Sky

EDNA O'BRIEN

The clouds — dark, massed and purposeful — raced across the sky. At one moment a gap appeared, a vault of blue so deep it looked like a cavity into which one could vanish, but soon the clouds swept across it like trailing curtains, removing it from sight. There were showers on and off — heavy showers — and in some fields the water had lodged in shallow pools where the cows stood impassively, gaping. The crows were incorrigible. Being inside the car, she could not actually hear their cawing, but she knew it very well and remembered how long ago she used to listen and try to decipher whether it denoted death or something less catastrophic.

As she mounted the granite steps of the nursing home, her face, of its own accord, folded into a false, obedient smile. A few old people sat in the hall, one woman praying on her big black horn rosary beads and a man staring listlessly through the long rain-splashed window, muttering, as if by his mutters he could will a visitor, or maybe the priest to give him the last rites. One of the women tells her that her father has been looking forward to her visit and that he has come to the front door several times. This makes her quake, and she digs her fingernails into her palms for fortitude. As she crosses the threshold of his little bedroom, the first question he fires at her is "What kept you?," and very politely she explains that the car ordered to fetch her from her hotel was a little late in arriving.

"I was expecting you two hours ago," he says. His mood is foul and his hair is standing on end, tufts of gray hair sprouting like Lucifer's.

"How are you?" she says.

He tells her that he is terrible and complains of a pain in the back from the shoulder down, a pain like the stab of a knife. She asks if it is rheumatism. He says how would he know, but, whatever it is, it is shocking, and to emphasize his discomfort he opens his mouth and lets out a groan. The first few minutes are taken up with showing him the presents that she has brought, but he is too disgruntled to appreciate them. She coaxes him to try on the pullover, but he won't. Suddenly he gets out of bed and goes to the lavatory. The lavatory adjoins the bedroom; it is merely a cupboard with fittings and fixtures. She sits in the overheated bedroom listening, while trying not to listen. She stares out of the opened window; the view is of a swamp, while above, in a pale untrammelled bit of whey-colored sky, the crows are flying at different altitudes and cawing mercilessly. They are so jet they look silken, and listening to them, while trying not to listen to her father, she thinks that if he closes the lavatory door perhaps all will not be so awful; but he will not close the lavatory door and he will not apologize. He comes out with his pajamas streeling around his legs, his walk impaired as he goes toward the bed, across which his lunchtray has been slung. His legs like candles, white and spindly, foreshadow her own old age, and she wonders with a shudder if she will end up in a place like this.

"Wash your hands Dad," she says as he strips the bedcovers back. There is a second's balk as he looks at her, and the look has the dehumanized rage of a trapped animal, but for some reason he concedes and crosses to the little basin and gives his hands or rather his right hand, a cursory splash. He dries it by laying the hand on the towel that hangs at the side of the basin. It is a towel that she recognizes from home — dark blue with orange splashes. Even this simple recollection pierces; she can smell the towel, she can remember it drying on top of the range, she can feel it without touching it. The towel, like every other item in that embattled house, has got inside her brain and remained there like furniture inside a room. The white cyclamen that she has brought is staring at her, the flowers like butterflies and the tiny buds like pencil tips, and it is this she obliges herself to see in order to generate a little cheerfulness.

"I spent Christmas Day all by myself."

"No, Dad, you didn't," she says, and reminds him that a relative came and took him out to lunch.

"I tell you, I spent Christmas Day all by myself," he says, and now it is her turn to bristle.

"You were with Agatha. Remember?" she says.

"What do you know about it?" he says, staring at her, and she looks away, blaming herself for having lost control. He follows her with those eyes, then raises his hands up like a suppliant. One hand is raw and red. "Eczema," he says almost proudly. The other hand is knobbly, the fingers bunched together like forked twigs. He says he got that affliction from foddering cattle winter after winter. Then he tells her to go to the wardrobe. There are three dark suits, some tweed jackets, and a hideous light-blue gabardine that a young nun made him buy before he went on holiday to a convent in New Mexico. He praises this young nun, Sister Declan, praises her good humor, her buoyant spirit, her generosity, and her innate sense of sacrifice. As a young girl, it seems, this young nun preferred to sit in the kitchen with her father, devising possible hurley games, or discussing hurley games that had been, instead of galivanting with boys. He mentions how the nun's father died suddenly, choked to death while having his tea, but he shows no sign of pity or shock, and she thinks that in some crevice of his scalding mind he believes the nun has adopted him, which perhaps she has. The young nun has recently been sent away to the same convent in New Mexico, and the daughter thinks that perhaps it was punishment, perhaps she was getting too fond of this lonely, irascible man. No knowing.

"A great girl, the best friend I ever had," he says. Wedged among the suits in the cupboard is the dark frieze coat that belongs to the bygone days, to his youth. Were she to put her hand in a pocket, she might find an old penny or a stone that he had picked up on his walks, the long walks he took to stamp out his ire. He says to look in the beige suitcase, which she does. It is already packed with belongings, summer things, and gallantly he announces that he intends to visit the young nun again, to make the journey across the sea, telling how he will probably arrive in the middle of the night, as he did before, and Sister Declan and a few of the others will be waiting inside the convent gate to give him a regal welcome.

"I may not even come back," he says boastfully. On the top shelf of the wardrobe are various pairs of socks, and handkerchiefs — new handkerchiefs and torn ones — empty whiskey bottles, and two large framed photographs. He tells her to hand down one of those photographs, and for the millionth time she looks at the likeness of his mother and father. His mother seems formidable, with a topknot of curls, and a white laced bodice that even in the faded photograph looks like armor. His father, who is seated, looks meeker and more compliant.

"Seven years of age when I lost my mother and father, within a month of each other," he says, and his voice is now like gravel. He grits his teeth.

What would they have made of him, his daughter wonders. Would their love have tamed him? Would he be different? Would she herself be different? "Was it very hard?" she asks, but without real tenderness.

"Hard? What are you talking about?" he says. "To be brought out into a yard and put in a pony and trap and dumped on relations?"

She knows that were she to really feel for him she would inquire about the trap, the cushion he sat on, if there was a rug for his knees, what kind of coat he wore, and the color of his hair then; but she does not ask these things. "Did they beat you?" she asks, as a form of conciliation.

"You were beaten if you deserved it," he says, and goes on to talk about their rancor and how he survived it, how he developed his independence, how he found excitement and sport in horses and was a legend even as a young lad for being able to break any horse. He remembers his boarding school and how he hated it, then his gadding days, then when still young — too young, he adds — meeting his future wife, and his daughter knows that soon he will cry, and talk of his dead wife and the marble tombstone that he erected to her memory, and that he will tell how much it cost and how much the hospital bill was, and how he never left her, or any one of the family, short of money for furniture or food. His voice is passing through me, the daughter thinks, as is his stare and his need and the upright sprouts of steel-colored hair and the over-pink plates of false teeth in a glass beer tumbler. She feels glued to the spot, feels as if she has lost her will and the use of her limbs, and thinks, This is how it has always been. Looking away to avoid his gaze, her eyes light on his slippers. They are made of felt, green and red felt; there are holes in them and she wishes that she had bought him a new pair. He says to hand him the brown envelope that is above the washbasin. The envelope contains photographs of himself taken in New Mexico. In them, he has the air of a suitor, and the pose and look that he has assumed take at least thirty years off his age.

At that moment, one of the senior nuns comes in, welcomes her, offers her a cup of tea, and remarks on how well she looks. He says that no one looks as well as he does and proffers

73

the photos. He recounts his visit to the States again — how the stewardesses were amazed at his age and his vitality, and how everyone danced attendance on him. The nun and the daughter exchange a look. They have a strategy. They have corresponded about it, the nun's last letter enclosing a greeting card from him, in which he begged his daughter to come. From its tone she deduced that he had changed, that he had become mollified; but he has not, he is the same, she thinks.

"Now talk to your father," the nun says, then stands there, hands folded into her wide black sleeves, while the daughter says to her father, "Why don't you eat in the dining room, Dad?"

"I don't want to eat in the dining room," he says, like a corrected child. The nun reminds him that he is alone too much, that he cries too much, that if he mingled it would do him some good.

"They're ignorant, they're ignorant people," he says of the other inmates.

"They can't all be ignorant," both the nun and the daughter say at the same moment.

"I tell you they're all ignorant!" he says, his eyes glaring.

"But you wouldn't be so lonely, Dad," his daughter says, feeling a wave of pity for him.

"Who says I'm lonely?" he says roughly, sabotaging that pity, and he lists the number of friends he has, the motorcars he has access to, the bookmakers he knows, the horse trainers that he is on first names with, and the countless houses where he is welcome at any hour of day or night throughout the year.

To cheer him up, the nun rushes out and shouts to a little girl in the pantry across the way to bring the pot of tea now and the plate of biscuits. Watching the tea being poured, he insists the cup be so full that when the milk is added it slops over onto the saucer, but he does not notice, does not care.

"Thank you, thank you, Sister," he says. He used not to say thank you and she wonders if perhaps Sister Declan had told him that courtesy was one way to win back the love of recalcitrant ones. He mashes the biscuits on his gums and then suddenly brightens as he remembers the night in the house of some neighbors when their dog attacked him. He had gone there to convalesce from shingles. He launches into a description of the dog, a German shepherd, and his own poor self coming down in the night to make a cup of tea, and this dog flying at him and his arm going up in self-defense, the dog mauling him, and the miracle that he was not eaten to death. He charts the three days of agony before he was brought to the hospital, the arm being set, being in a sling for two months, and the little electric saw that the county surgeon used to remove the plaster.

"My God, what I had to suffer!" he says. The nun has already left, whispering some excuse.

"Poor Dad," his daughter says. She is determined to be nice, admitting how wretched his life is, always has been.

"You have no idea," he says, as he contrasts his present abode, a dungeon, with his own lovely limestone house that is going to ruin. He recalls his fifty-odd years in that house — the comforts, the blazing fire, the mutton dinners followed by rice pudding that his wife served. She reminds him that the house belongs to his son now and then she flinches, remembering that between them, also, there is a breach.

"He's no bloody good," he says and prefers instead to linger on his incarceration here.

"No mutton here; it's all beef," he says.

"Don't they have any sheep?" she says, stupidly.

"It's no life for a father," he says, and she realizes that he is about to ask for the guarantee that she cannot give.

She takes the tea tray and lays it on the hallway floor, then praises the kindness of nuns and of nurses and asks the name of the matron, so that she can give her a gift of money. He does not answer. In that terrible pause, as if on cue, one crow alights on a dip of barbed wire outside the window and lets out a series of hoarse exclamations. She is about to say it, about to spring the pleasant surprise. She has come to take him out for the day.

That is her plan. The delay in her arrival at the nursing home was due to her calling at a splendid hotel to ask if they did lunches late. When she got here from London, late the previous night, she had stayed in a more commercial hotel in the town, where she was kept awake most of the night by the noise of cattle. It was near an abattoir, and in the very early hours of the morning she could hear the cattle arriving, their bawling, their pitiful bawling, and then their various slippings and slobberings, and the shouts of the men who got them out of the trailers or the lorries and into the pens, and then other shouts, indeterminable shouts of men. She had lain in the very warm hotel room and allowed her mind to wander back to the time when her father bought and sold cattle, driving them on foot to the town, sometimes with the help of a simpleton, often failing to sell the beasts and having to drive them home again, with the subsequent wrangling and sparring over debts. She thinks that indeed he was not cut out for a life with cattle and foddering but that he was made for grander things, and it is with a rush of pleasure that she contemplates the surprise for him. She has already vetted the hotel, admitting, it is true, a minor disappointment that the service did not seem as august as the gardens or the imposing hallway with its massive portraits and beautiful staircase. When she visited to inquire about lunch, a rather vacant young boy said that no, they did not do lunches, but that possibly they could manage sandwiches, cheese or ham. Yet the atmosphere would exhilarate him, and, sitting there in the nursing home with him now, she luxuriates in her own bit of private cheer. Has she not met someone, a man whose very voice, whose crisp manner fill her with verve and happiness? She barely knows him, but when he telephoned and imagined her surrounded by motley admirers, she did not disabuse him of his fantasy. She recalls, not without mischief, how that very morning in the market town she bought embroidered pillowcases and linen sheets, in anticipation of the day or the night when he would cross her bedroom doorway. The thought of this future tryst softens her toward the old man, her father, and for a moment the two men revolve in her thoughts like two halves of a slow-moving apparition. As for the new one, she knows why she bought pillow slips and costly sheets: because she wants her surroundings not only to be beautiful for him but to carry the vestiges of her past, such sacred things as flowers and linen, and all of a sudden, with unnerving clarity, she fears that she wants this new man to partake of her whole past — to know it in all its pain and permutations.

The moment has come to announce the treat, to encourage her father to get up and dress, to lead him down the hallway, holding his arm protectively so that the others will see that he is cherished, then to humor him in the car, to ply him with cigarettes, and to find in the hotel the snuggest little sitting room — in short, to give him a sense of well-being, to while away a few hours. It will be a talking point with him for weeks to come, instead of the eczema or the broken arm. Something is impeding her. She wants to do it, indeed she will do it, but she keeps delaying. She tries to examine what it is that is making her stall. Is it the physical act of helping him to dress, because he will, of course, insist on being helped? No, a nun will do that. Is it the thought of his being happy that bothers her? No, it is not that; she wants with all her heart to see him happy. Is it the fear of the service in the hotel being a disappointment, sandwiches being a letdown when he would have preferred soup and a meat course? No, it is not that, since, after all, the service is not her responsibility. What she dreads is the intimacy, being with him at all. She foresees that something awful will occur. He will break down and beg her to show him the love that he knows she is withholding; then, seeing that she cannot, will not, yield, he will grow furious, they will both grow furious, there will be the most terrible showdown, a slinging match of words, curses, buried grievances, maybe even blows. Yes, she will do it in a few minutes; she will clap her hands, jump up off the chair, and in a singsong

voice say, "We're late, we're late, for a very important date."
She is rehearsing it, even envisaging the awkward smile that
will come over his face, the melting, and his saying, "Are you
sure you can afford it, darling?," while at the same moment
ordering her to open the wardrobe and choose his suit.

Each time she moves in her chair to do it, something awful
gets between her and the nice gesture. It is like a phobia, like
someone too terrified to enter the water but standing at its
edge. Yet she knows that if she were to succumb, it would not
only be an afternoon's respite for him, it would be for her some
enormous leap. Her heart has been hardening now for some
time, and when moved to pity by something she can no longer
show her feelings — all her feelings are for the privacy of her
bedroom. Her heart is becoming a stone, but this gesture, this
reach will soften her again and make her, if not the doting
child, at least the eager young girl who brought home school
reports or trophies that she had won, craving to be praised by
him, this young girl who only recited the verses of "Fontenoy"
in place of singing a song. He had repeatedly told her that she
could not sing, that she was tone-deaf.

Outside, the clouds have begun to mass for another downpour, and she realizes that there are tears in her eyes. She bends
down, pretending to tie her shoe, because she does not want
him to see these tears. She saw that it was perverse not to let
him partake of this crumb of emotion, but also saw that
nothing would be helped by it. He did not know her; he
couldn't — his own life tore at him like a mad dog. Why isn't
she stirring herself? Soon she will. He is talking non-stop,
animated now by the saga of his passport and how he had to
get it in such a hurry for his trip to America. He tells her to fetch
it from the drawer, and she does. It is very new, with only one
official entry, and that in itself conveys to her more than his
words ever could: the paucity and barrenness of his life. He
tells how the day he got that passport was the jolliest day he
ever spent, how he had to go to Dublin to get it, how the nuns
tut-tutted, said nobody could get a passport in that length of

time because of all the red tape, but how he guaranteed that he would. He describes the wet day, one of the wettest days ever, how Biddy the hackney driver didn't even want to set out, said they would be marooned, and how he told her to stop flapping and get her coat on. He relives the drive, the very early morning, the floods, the fallen boughs, and Biddy and himself on the rocky road to Dublin, smoking fags and singing, Biddy all the while teasing him, saying that it is not a passport that he is going for but a mistress, a rendezvous.

"So you got the passport immediately," the daughter says, to ingratiate herself.

"Straightaway. I had the influence — I told the nuns here to ring the Dáil, to ring my T.D., and, by God, they did."

She asks the name of the T.D., but he has no interest in telling that, goes on to say how in the passport office a cheeky young girl asked why he was going to the States, and how he told her he was going there to dig for gold. He is now warming to his tale, and she hears again about the air journey, the nice stewardesses, the two meals that came on a little plastic tray, and about how when he stepped out he saw his name on a big placard, and later, inside the convent gate, nuns waiting to receive him.

Suddenly she knows that she cannot take him out; perhaps she will do it on the morrow, but she cannot do it now; and so she makes to rise in her chair.

He senses it, his eyes now hard like granite. "You're not leaving?" he says.

"I have to; the driver could only wait the hour," she says feebly.

He gets out of bed, says he will at least see her to the front door, but she persuades him not to. He stares at her as if he is reading her mind, as if he knows the generous impulse that she has defected on. In that moment she dislikes herself even more than she has ever disliked him. Tomorrow she will indeed visit, before leaving, and they will patch it up, but she knows that she has missed something, something incalculable, a moment of grace. The downpour has stopped and the sky, drained of cloud, is like an immense gray sieve, sieving a greater grayness. As she rises to leave, she feels that her heart is in shreds, all over the room. She has left it in his keeping, but he is wildly, helplessly looking for his own.

A Sudden Trip Home in the Spring

for the Wellesley Class

ALICE WALKER

Sarah walked slowly off the tennis court, fingering the back of her head, feeling the sturdy dark hair that grew there. She was popular. As she walked along the path toward Talfinger Hall her friends fell into place around her. They formed a warm jostling group of six. Sarah, because she was taller than the rest, saw the messenger first.

"Miss Davis," he said, standing still until the group came abreast of him, "I've got a telegram for ye." Brian was Irish and always quite respectful. He stood with his cap in his hand until Sarah took the telegram. Then he gave a nod that included all the young ladies before he turned away. He was young and good-looking, though annoyingly servile, and Sarah's friends twittered.

"Well, open it!" someone cried, for Sarah stood staring at the yellow envelope, turning it over and over in her hand.

"Look at her," said one of the girls, "isn't she beautiful! Such eyes, and hair, and *skin!*"

Sarah's tall, caplike hair framed a face of soft brown angles, high cheekbones and large dark eyes. Her eyes enchanted her friends because they always seemed to know more, and to find more of life amusing, or sad, than Sarah cared to tell.

Her friends often teased Sarah about her beauty; they loved dragging her out of her room so that their boyfriends, naive and worldly young men from Princeton and Yale, could see her. They never guessed she found this distasteful. She was gentle with her friends, and her outrage at their tactlessness did not show. She was most often inclined to pity them, though embarrassment sometimes drove her to fraudulent expressions. Now she smiled and raised eyes and arms to heaven. She acknowledged their unearned curiosity as a mother endures the prying impatience of a child. Her friends beamed love and envy upon her as she tore open the telegram.

"He's dead," she said.

Her friends reached out for the telegram, their eyes on Sarah.

"It's her father," one of them said softly. "He died yesterday. Oh, Sarah," the girl whimpered, "I'm so sorry!"

"Me too." "So am I." "Is there anything we can do?"

But Sarah had walked away, head high and neck stiff.

"So graceful!" one of her friends said.

"Like a proud gazelle," said another. Then they all trooped to their dormitories to change for supper.

Talfinger Hall was a pleasant dorm. The common room just off the entrance had been made into a small modern art gallery with some very good original paintings, lithographs and collages. Pieces were constantly being stolen. Some of the girls could not resist an honest-to-God Chagall, signed (in the plate) by his own hand, though they could have afforded to purchase one from the gallery in town. Sarah Davis's room was next door to the gallery, but her walls were covered with inexpensive Gauguin reproductions, a Rubens ("The Head of a Negro"), a Modigliani and a Picasso. There was a full wall of her own drawings, all of black women. She found black men impossible to draw or to paint; she could not bear to trace defeat onto blank pages. Her women figures were matronly, massive of arm, with a weary victory showing in their eyes. Surrounded by Sarah's drawings was a red SNCC poster of a man holding a small girl whose face nestled in his shoulder. Sarah often felt she was the little girl whose face no one could see.

To leave Talfinger even for a few days filled Sarah with fear. Talfinger was her home now; it suited her better than any home she'd ever known. Perhaps she loved it because in winter there was a fragrant fireplace and snow outside her window. When hadn't she dreamed of fireplaces that really warmed, snow that almost pleasantly froze? Georgia seemed far away as she packed; she did not want to leave New York, where, her grandfather had liked to say, "the devil hung out and caught young gals by the front of their dresses." He had always believed the South the best place to live on earth (never mind that certain people invariably marred the landscape), and swore he expected to die no more than a few miles from where he had been born. There was tenacity even in the gray frame house he lived in, and in scrawny animals on his farm who regularly reproduced. He was the first person Sarah wanted to see when she got home.

There was a knock on the door of the adjoining bathroom, and Sarah's suite mate entered, a loud Bach concerto just finishing behind her. At first she stuck just her head into the room, but seeing Sarah fully dressed she trudged in and plopped down on the bed. She was a heavy blonde girl with large milk-white legs. Her eyes were small and her neck usually gray with grime.

"My, don't you look gorgeous," she said.

"Ah, Pam," said Sarah, waving her hand in disgust. In Georgia she knew that even to Pam she would be just another ordinarily attractive colored girl. In Georgia there were a million girls better looking. Pam wouldn't know that, of

course; she'd never been to Georgia; she'd never even seen a
black person to speak to, that is, before she met Sarah. One of
her first poetic observations about Sarah was that she was "a
poppy in a field of winter roses." She had found it weird that
Sarah did not own more than one coat.

"Say listen, Sarah," said Pam, "I heard about your father.
I'm sorry. I really am."

"Thanks," said Sarah.

"Is there anything we can do? I thought, well, maybe
you'd want my father to get somebody to fly you down. He'd
go himself but he's taking Mother to Madeira this week. You
wouldn't have to worry about trains and things."

Pamela's father was one of the richest men in the world,
though no one ever mentioned it. Pam only alluded to it at
times of crisis, when a friend might benefit from the use of a
private plane, train, or ship; or, if someone wanted to study the
characteristics of a totally secluded village, island or mountain, she might offer one of theirs. Sarah could not comprehend such wealth, and was always annoyed because Pam
didn't look more like a billionaire's daughter. A billionaire's
daughter, Sarah thought, should really be less horsey and
brush her teeth more often.

"Gonna tell me what you're brooding about?" asked Pam.

Sarah stood in front of the radiator, her fingers resting on
the window seat. Down below girls were coming up the hill
from supper.

"I'm thinking," she said, "of the child's duty to his parents
after they are dead."

"Is that all?"

"Do you know," asked Sarah, "about Richard Wright and
his father?"

Pamela frowned. Sarah looked down at her.

"Oh, I forgot," she said with a sigh, "they don't teach
Wright here. The poshest school in the U.S., and the girls come
out ignorant." She looked at her watch, saw she had twenty
minutes before her train. "Really," she said almost inaudibly,

"why Tears Eliot, Ezratic Pound, and even Sara Teacake, and no Wright?" She and Pamela thought e.e. cummings very clever with his perceptive spelling of great literary names.

"Is he a poet then?" asked Pam. She adored poetry, all poetry. Half of America's poetry she had, of course, not read, for the simple reason that she had never heard of it.

"No," said Sarah, "he wasn't a poet." She felt weary. "He was a man who wrote, a man who had trouble with his father." She began to walk about the room, and came to stand below the picture of the old man and the little girl.

"When he was a child," she continued, "his father ran off with another woman, and one day when Richard and his mother went to ask him for money to buy food he laughingly rejected them. Richard, being very young, thought his father Godlike. Big, omnipotent, unpredictable, undependable and cruel. Entirely in control of his universe. Just like a god. But, many years later, after Wright had become a famous writer, he went down to Mississippi to visit his father. He found, instead of God, just an old watery-eyed field hand, bent from plowing, his teeth gone, smelling of manure. Richard realized that the most daring thing his 'God' had done was run off with that other woman."

"So?" asked Pam. "What 'duty' did he feel he owed the old man?"

"So," said Sarah, "that's what Wright wondered as he peered into that old shifty-eyed Mississippi Negro face. What was the duty of the son of a destroyed man? The son of a man whose vision had stopped at the edge of fields that weren't even his. Who was Wright without his father? Was he Wright the great writer? Wright the Communist? Wright the French farmer? Wright whose white wife could never accompany him to Mississippi? Was he, in fact, still his father's son? Or was he freed by his father's desertion to be nobody's son, to be his own father? Could he disavow his father and live? And if so, live as what? As whom? And for what purpose?"

"Well," said Pam, swinging her hair over her shoulders

and squinting her small eyes, "if his father rejected him I don't see why Wright even bothered to go see him again. From what you've said, Wright earned the freedom to be whoever he wanted to be. To a strong man a father is not essential."

"Maybe not," said Sarah, "but Wright's father was one faulty door in a house of many ancient rooms. Was that one faulty door to shut him off forever from the rest of the house? That was the question. And though he answered this question eloquently in his work, where it really counted, one can only wonder if he was able to answer it satisfactorily — or at all — in his life."

"You're thinking of his father more as a symbol of something, aren't you?" asked Pam.

"I suppose," said Sarah, taking a last look around her room. "I see him as a door that refused to open, a hand that was always closed. A fist."

Pamela walked with her to one of the college limousines, and in a few minutes she was at the station. The train to the city was just arriving.

"Have a nice trip," said the middle-aged driver courteously, as she took her suitcase from him. But for about the thousandth time since she'd seen him, he winked at her.

Once away from her friends she did not miss them. The school was all they had in common. How could they ever know her if they were not allowed to know Wright, she wondered. She was interesting, "beautiful," only because they had no idea what made her, charming only because they had no idea from where she came. And where they came from, though she glimpsed it — in themselves and in F. Scott Fitzgerald — she was never to enter. She hadn't the inclination or the proper ticket.

2

Her father's body was in Sarah's old room. The bed had been taken down to make room for the flowers and chairs and casket. Sarah looked for a long time into the face, as if to find some answer to her questions written there. It was the same face, a dark Shakespearean head framed by gray, woolly hair and split almost in half by a short, gray mustache. It was a completely silent face, a shut face. But her father's face also looked fat, stuffed, and ready to burst. He wore a navy-blue suit, white shirt and black tie. Sarah bent and loosened the tie. Tears started behind her shoulder blades but did not reach her eyes.

"There's a rat here under the casket," she called to her brother, who apparently did not hear her, for he did not come in. She was alone with her father, as she had rarely been when he was alive. When he was alive she had avoided him.

"Where's that girl at?" her father would ask. "Done closed herself up in her room again," he would answer himself.

For Sarah's mother had died in her sleep one night. Just gone to bed tired and never got up. And Sarah had blamed her father.

Stare the rat down, thought Sarah, surely that will help. *Perhaps it doesn't matter whether I misunderstood or never understood.*

"We moved so much looking for crops, a place to *live*," her father had moaned, accompanied by Sarah's stony silence. "The moving killed her. And now we have a real house, with *four* rooms, and a mailbox on the *porch,* and it's too late. She gone. *She* ain't here to see it." On very bad days her father would not eat at all. At night he did not sleep.

Whatever had made her think she knew what love was or was not?

Here she was, Sarah Davis, immersed in Camusian philosophy, versed in many languages, a poppy, of all things, among winter roses. But before she became a poppy she was a native Georgian sunflower, but still had not spoken the language they both knew. Not to him.

Stare the rat down, she thought, and did. The rascal dropped his bold eyes and slunk away. Sarah felt she had, at least, accomplished something.

Why did she have to see the picture of her mother, the one

on the mantel among all the religious doodads, come to life? Her mother had stood stout against the years, clean gray braids shining across the top of her head, her eyes snapping, protective. Talking to her father.

"He called you out your name, we'll leave this place today. Not tomorrow. That be too late. Today!" Her mother was magnificent in her quick decisions.

"But what about your garden, the children, the change of schools?" Her father would be holding, most likely, the wide brim of his hat in nervously twisting fingers.

"He called you out your name, we go!"

And go they would. Who knew exactly where, before they moved? Another soundless place, walls falling down, roofing gone; another face to please without leaving too much of her father's pride at his feet. But to Sarah then, no matter with what alacrity her father moved, foot-dragging alone was visible.

The moving killed her, her father had said, *but the moving was also love.*

Did it matter now that often he had threatened their lives with the rage of his despair? That once he had spanked the crying baby violently, who later died of something else altogether . . . and that the next day they moved?

"No," said Sarah aloud, "I don't think it does."

"Huh?" It was her brother, tall, wiry, black, deceptively calm. As a child he'd had an irrepressible temper. As a grown man he was tensely smooth, like a river that any day will overflow its bed.

He had chosen a dull gray casket. Sarah wished for red. Was it Dylan Thomas who had said something grand about the dead offering "deep, dark defiance"? It didn't matter; there were more ways to offer defiance than with a red casket.

"I was just thinking," said Sarah, "that with us Mama and Daddy were saying NO with capital letters."

"I don't follow you," said her brother. He had always been the activist in the family. He simply directed his calm rage against any obstacle that might exist, and awaited the consequences with the same serenity he awaited his sister's answer. Not for him the philosophical confusions and poetic observations that hung his sister up.

"That's because you're a radical preacher," said Sarah, smiling up at him. "You deliver your messages in person with your own body." It excited her that her brother had at last imbued their childhood Sunday sermons with the reality of fighting for change. And saddened her that no matter how she looked at it this seemed more important than Medieval Art, Course 201.

3

"Yes, Grandma," Sarah replied. "Cresselton is for girls only, and *no,* Grandma, I am not pregnant."

Her grandmother stood clutching the broad wooden handle of her black bag, which she held, with elbows bent, in front of her stomach. Her eyes glinted through round wire-framed glasses. She spat into the grass outside the privy. She had insisted that Sarah accompany her to the toilet while the body was being taken into the church. She had leaned heavily on Sarah's arm, her own arm thin and the flesh like crepe.

"I guess they teach you how to really handle the world," she said. "And who knows, the Lord is everywhere. I would like a whole lot to see a Great-Grand. You don't specially have to be married, you know. That's why I felt free to ask." She reached into her bag and took out a Three Sixes bottle, which she proceeded to drink from, taking deep swift swallows with her head thrown back.

"There are very few black boys near Cresselton," Sarah explained, watching the corn liquor leave the bottle in spurts and bubbles. "Besides, I'm really caught up now in my painting and sculpting. . . ." Should she mention how much she admired Giacometti's work? No, she decided. Even if her grandmother had heard of him, and Sarah was positive she had not, she would surely think his statues much too thin. This made Sarah smile and remember how difficult it had been to convince her grandmother that even if Cresselton had not given her a scholarship she would have managed to go there anyway. Why? Because she wanted somebody to teach her to paint and to sculpt, and Cresselton had the best teachers. Her grandmother's notion of a successful granddaughter was a married one, pregnant the first year.

"Well," said her grandmother, placing the bottle with dignity back into her purse and gazing pleadingly into Sarah's face, "I sure would 'preshate a Great-Grand." Seeing her granddaughter's smile, she heaved a great sigh, and, walking rather haughtily over the stones and grass, made her way to the church steps.

As they walked down the aisle, Sarah's eyes rested on the back of her grandfather's head. He was sitting on the front middle bench in front of the casket, his hair extravagantly long and white and softly kinked. When she sat down beside him, her grandmother sitting next to him on the other side, he turned toward her and gently took her hand in his. Sarah briefly leaned her cheek against his shoulder and felt like a child again.

4

They had come twenty miles from town, on a dirt road, and the hot spring sun had drawn a steady rich scent from the honeysuckle vines along the way. The church was a bare, weather-beaten ghost of a building with hollow windows and a sagging door. Arsonists had once burned it to the ground, lighting the dry wood of the walls with the flames from the crosses they carried. The tall spreading red oak tree under which Sarah had played as a child still dominated the church-yard, stretching its branches widely from the roof of the church to the other side of the road.

After a short and eminently dignified service, during which Sarah and her grandfather alone did not cry, her father's casket was slid into the waiting hearse and taken the short distance to the cemetery, an overgrown wilderness whose stark white stones appeared to be the small ruins of an ancient civilization. There Sarah watched her grandfather from the corner of her eye. He did not seem to bend under the grief of burying a son. His back was straight, his eyes dry and clear. He was simply and solemnly heroic; a man who kept with pride his family's trust and his own grief. *It is strange,* Sarah thought, *that I never thought to paint him like this, simply as he stands; without anonymous meaningless people hovering beyond his profile; his face turned proud and brownly against the light.* The defeat that had frightened her in the faces of black men was the defeat of black forever defined by white. But that defeat was nowhere on her grandfather's face. He stood like a rock, outwardly calm, the comfort and support of the Davis family. The family alone defined him, and he was not about to let them down.

"One day I will paint you, Grandpa," she said, as they turned to go. "Just as you stand here now, with just" — she moved closer and touched his face with her hand — "just the right stubborn tenseness of your cheek. Just that look of Yes and No in your eyes."

"You wouldn't want to paint an old man like me," he said, looking deep into her eyes from wherever his mind had been. "If you want to make me, make me up in stone."

The completed grave was plump and red. The wreaths of flowers were arranged all on one side so that from the road there appeared to be only a large mass of flowers. But already the wind was tugging at the rose petals and the rain was making dabs of faded color all over the green foam frames. In a week the displaced honeysuckle vines, the wild roses, the grapevines, the grass, would be back. Nothing would seem to have changed.

5

"What do you mean, come *home?*" Her brother seemed genuinely amused. "We're all proud of you. How many black girls are at that school? Just *you?* Well, just one more besides you, and she's from the North. That's really something!"

"I'm glad you're pleased," said Sarah.

"Pleased! Why, it's what Mama would have wanted, a good education for little Sarah; and what Dad would have wanted too, if he could have wanted anything after Mama died. You were always smart. When you were two and I was five you showed me how to eat ice cream without getting it all over me. First, you said, nip off the bottom of the cone with your teeth, and suck the ice cream down. I never knew *how* you were supposed to eat the stuff once it began to melt."

"I don't know," she said, "sometimes you can want something a whole lot, only to find out later that it wasn't what you *needed* at all."

Sarah shook her head, a frown coming between her eyes. "I sometimes spend *weeks,*" she said, "trying to sketch or paint a face that is unlike every other face around me, except, vaguely, for one. Can I help but wonder if I'm in the right place?"

Her brother smiled. "You mean to tell me you spend *weeks* trying to draw one face, and you still wonder whether you're in the right place? You must be kidding!" He chucked her under the chin and laughed out loud. "You learn how to draw the face," he said, "then you learn how to paint me and how to make Grandpa up in stone. Then you can come home or go live in Paris, France. It'll be the same thing."

It was the unpreacherlike gaiety of his affection that made her cry. She leaned peacefully into her brother's arms. She wondered if Richard Wright had had a brother.

"You are my door to all the rooms," she said. "Don't ever close."

And he said, "I won't," as if he understood what she meant.

6

"When will we see you again, young woman?" he asked later, as he drove her to the bus stop.

"I'll sneak up one day and surprise you," she said.

At the bus stop, in front of a tiny service station, Sarah hugged her brother with all her strength. The white station attendant stopped his work to leer at them, his eyes bold and careless.

"Did you ever think," said Sarah, "that we are a very old people in a very young place?"

She watched her brother from a window of the bus; her eyes did not leave his face until the little station was out of sight and the big Greyhound lurched on its way toward Atlanta. She would fly from there to New York.

7

She took the train to the campus.

"My," said one of her friends, "you look wonderful! Home sure must agree with you!"

"Sarah was home?" Someone who didn't know asked. "Oh, *great,* how was it?"

"Well, how was it?" went an echo in Sarah's head. The noise of the echo almost made her dizzy.

"How was it?" she asked aloud, searching for, and regaining, her balance.

"How was it?" She watched her reflection in a pair of smiling hazel eyes.

"It was fine," she said slowly, returning the smile, thinking of her grandfather. "Just fine."

The girl's smile deepened. Sarah watched her swinging along toward the back tennis courts, hair blowing in the wind.

Stare the rat down, thought Sarah; *and whether it disappears or not, I am a woman in the world. I have buried my father, and shall soon know how to make my grandpa up in stone.*

Automatic Timer

LYNDA BARRY

My father. For a long time I thought about him and then I didn't think about him and then yesterday I started thinking about him again. I was in the basement, and for no reason I went around under the steps and suddenly saw his camera case on this high shelf, and it was like that thing of where you're drowning and your whole life flashes in front of your eyes. Except it wasn't my whole life. It was just one day from a million years ago when he lived with us still and this room was glowing red from the darkroom light. I was standing on a chair, watching his hand pull a piece of paper back and forth under the water, him saying, "Watch honey, now watch." And then I saw the reverse disappearing ghost of my face showing itself slow onto that paper, and him saying what he always said when he did something like that. "Okay, honey. Who's the best dad?"

Some nights he would tilt out the lamp shade in the front room and set his stacks of pictures on a TV tray under it. I'd

94

watch him smoking and coloring me and my sister and my mom with Q-tips and oils and special midget paint tubes and then, for his last finishing touch, he would draw on our eyelashes with a tiny red pencil with Life Magazine printed on the side. He would ask me to hold it up for him to look at and I'd watch him lean back and say "Ahhhhhhh. Another Perfect Masterpiece by Ramond Robert Arkins!" And then my mother would see it and yell at him for making us look like a bunch of Mexican whores.

Mom found a picture of another lady colored the same way. It was in the street in front of our house. I guess it fell out of his car. It was Pat, the checker at his store. Pat with the small teeth who did a wink to my mom and rang our meat up really cheap. Pat colored in and smiling under a tire mark, with her hands up behind her head and no top on. My mom put it on our front door with so many rows of Scotch tape that it looked like Pat was sinking in a deep aquarium.

I can remember the sound of my dad's feet coming up the steps and then stopping. Then him coming in and saying it didn't mean anything.

A long time later, when my dad left, my mother took everything that ever belonged to him and put it out on the front porch for Goodwill. Afterwards, I remember coming into the kitchen and seeing her holding her curved fingernail scissors, flipping through all our photo books and cutting his head out of every picture there was of him. I remember the pile of my dad's heads in the ashtray, her cigarette burning on top, and her singing along with the radio. I remember hearing the bathroom door close, me sneaking into the kitchen and taking three pictures to save. One of him and her holding me, one of him squatting on a beach in an Air Force uniform, and one of him laughing with his eyes shut, holding a dog I didn't know and a glass of beer. That last picture he had colored. He colored the dog in blue.

I reached my hand up and pulled down the camera. It was

the kind with the flip-open top viewer and I remembered once how I watched him and Pat drunk through it, them singing upside down at the company picnic. My mom was at work and Dad took me and my sister. He kept singing "Welcome to my world" and she kept laughing. I won the footrace and I ran to show him my silver dollar, then me seeing them kissing, and then her trying to act nice to me, and later in the car him telling me how lucky he was to have a kid like me. A kid who understood his saying Don't Make Waves.

I saw a yellow number eight through the square glass window. There was still film. My hand started to kind of freak out. It was like a backwards version of that Alfred Hitchcock Hour where the camera comes from something like the thirteenth dimension and can take pictures of the future. The moral of it was something like, Don't Mess With Your Regular Life. I put the camera back on the shelf, and then I took it back down. I put it under my shirt and walked up the stairs past my mom in the kitchen.

My friend Vicky Talluso's brother Victor has a darkroom in their rec room bathroom and said for two joints he would develop the film for me. I had one roach. He said okay. Me and Vicky stood in the pitch dark and I could hear Victor dropping things and saying "Fuck." Then he handed me a container and he said keep shaking it and he lit the roach and Vicky lit a Kool and Mrs. Talluso pounded on the door yelling "What in the hell is going on in there?" She made us come out and each blow on her nose and busted Victor and Vicky for smoking and made me go home.

This morning at school Vicky came running across the parking lot saying she had a present for me. She opened her folder and handed me some pictures. "Only three came out," she said. The first one was of Pat in front of a car. Then two kids at a birthday with Pat smiling and talking on the phone. Then my dad and Pat with their arms around each other, kissing.

I remembered the sound of the automatic timer. How my dad would set it and run fast across the room to get into the picture.

"Who's it of?" Vicky says.

Mr. Davidoff's Will

MEREDITH ROSE

Everything he says sounds delicious. Sounds like manna from heaven. He writes letters. From one end of the city to the other they are posted. I open them in my studio apartment. He says to me: microwave oven, VCR, money market fund. From the heavens these things must drop, I think. Like virgin births they come direct from the lord, bypassing Taiwan and the World Bank.

He says to me, "Becky, you can't live like you live. It's not healthy. " This from a man who smokes a pack-and-a-half a day, a smokeless ashtray in every room, tiny burn marks decorating his cardigan. "No arguments," he says, "you will always be my little girl."

If Ma was on the other line she'd say the same thing, but now he has taken on her responsibility.

"Are you eating enough?" he wants to know. "Did you get my letter?"

These days I'm afraid to read his letters. He wants me to

want so much. For my own good I should want these things, but instead I grow anxious. My father does not lie, but he cannot bear to hear the truth. When I tell him I'm not interested in owning a computer he asks what he has done wrong. On the phone his voice trembles. When we are together his tanned face becomes flushed. He paces back and forth and brings a cigarette to his lips. He does not light it until after he has calmed down.

He sends letters though we live only ten miles apart. Me in town, and he in the suburbs in his big, now almost empty house. When I come over the television is on. He says he wants to be informed. I believe he is trying to muffle the sounds that aren't there anymore, but that seems too obvious. The house dwarfs my father as he pads quietly from room to room. When I visit I ask him to turn off the set, but we compromise instead. He turns the volume down completely and we sit in the TV room and talk. I can hear the birds calling, the sound of a lawn mower a few houses away. The back yard is filled with hard woods. The evening sun hits the patio and shines through the leaves on the trees. I feel a sadness then. This neighborhood lies sleeping. The world enters by invitation only. We sit, my father and I, and talk. Pictures flash on the screen, video from all over the world. Like a well-behaved child the news is seen but not heard.

"Becky," he says, "I spoke with your mother again. She asks about you. What am I supposed to say?"

"Tell her I keep her picture by my bed and I love her."

"She knows that, Becky. She wants to hear some news."

"Then tell her about the butterfly I had tattooed on my shoulder last Monday. Tell her it's yellow and outlined in green, and has red tinges to its wings."

"She doesn't want to know that, Becky. What should I say?"

"Tell her my name is Rebecca."

My father breathes in deep and his body rises. He breathes out and eases down to his slouched position. His silver hair is combed back behind his ears. It is all one length and he applies hair tonic to keep it from moving around. He offers me a glass of iced tea, something sweet. His overture is part of our ritual. He is hoping that if he is gracious, I in turn will be kind and not let my life story come pouring out of me, as if he really was my mother. I miss her constantly, but this we never talk about. Instead, I tell him about my job and my meetings. Each scrap of biography deepens the wrinkles on his forehead. He wants to know, but is afraid to ask, so he waits, hoping I will say something which will make him smile. Eventually, our talk turns to his business and the small amount of money he wants to loan me, which he can turn into a wise investment on my behalf.

The conversation is unsettling, even though we have had it before. The numbers frighten me. They are so tempting. I picture myself saying yes to everything and leaving the house a wealthy woman. Money could do this to me: make me wear different clothes and want more. He says it would make my life easier. We frighten each other with stories about enough. He says a social worker's salary does not fit in that category. I breach confidence and tell him details about my clients: how devastatingly poor they are; the struggle involved living day-to-day. He looks at me in disbelief and uses these stories to make his point: I must get rich quickly, or get rich slowly, but still I must get rich.

Before I leave we survey my father's holdings, his one-and-a-half acres. We walk the outline of the back yard, then along the low stone wall that marks the property between his yard and the neighbor's.

"This house could be many things," I say, as we walk towards the car. "It doesn't have to be a big, empty house."

"You'll have your chance," he says, kissing me on the cheek. "We must visit your mother soon," he shouts as I pull out of the driveway.

From the suburbs to the city I drive the commuters' four-lane headache. The road doesn't move, but the land on either side is in flux. Now there are shopping centers where there used to be forest, fields of parking lot in place of meadow. The city and the burbs meet somewhere among these asphalt tracts which fill and empty like a mechanized tide. My father likes it in the suburbs. It's easy to buy things and his house has tripled in price.

When I get home there are messages on the answering machine. My father gave me this device because he was afraid I did not love him. He thought I refused to answer the phone because he could be on the other end.

"I don't answer because I'm not home," I had told him — on the phone.

"No one's that busy."

"I am."

"Prove it."

I listed my meetings. When I got to the Democratic Socialists he hung up.

"Something's wrong with the line," he said when I called back. "It sounds all scratchy."

"I'm busy, Dad, but I do love you."

"Why don't you tell me in person?"

Then I hung up.

My father gave me the answering machine, and started sending me letters, last year. Tonight there are calls from my friend, Trace, and from my supervisor at work, and a message from my father, though I left him less than an hour ago. He shouts into the receiver, afraid I won't hear him ten miles away.

"We should make it definite. Next Saturday we visit your mother. You pick me up at eleven. 'Bye."

Trace says I should be patient because he is my father and that gives him a right to harass me. She is pregnant with her first and is getting used to the idea that she will unconsciously ruin her child's life. On the way to our monthly Food Co-op meeting the next night she tells me about the new psychology, how it's possible to be an imperfect parent and still reach nirvana.

"He'd tell me what to wear if I let him," I say.

"That's allowed."

"You don't understand. I could make him proud if he'd give me a chance." Trace doesn't answer. She lets me listen to the sound of my words, but I turn on the radio instead.

Tonight our meeting is about Benny, who manages the Food Co-op. Already he has stolen two thousand dollars. Liora thinks we should kill him. She has offered to do this. She was the last woman to have slept with Benny regularly, so she feels doubly betrayed. The meeting room is small and crowded. Spring water and tortilla chips have been placed on the table. Trace takes notes in the corner. In this room we hold on to our beliefs like winning lottery tickets. Our sense of purpose inspires us to scream when a shout would be sufficient. Fingers are pointed. Fists are pounded. The hours bail out of the room while decisions are debated and finally, near midnight, consensus is reached.

My father does not understand this type of group process. He wants me to join the Jaycees because he is certain they don't yell at each other.

"They accept girls now," he says. "They're a nice group."

"Come over for dinner this Friday. You can meet some of the people in my group. They're nice too."

"You come here. I'll fix a big steak."

"I don't eat meat," I remind him.

"Then I'll fix a chicken. You sleep over. The next day we go visit your mother."

I carry our loss alone when he refers to her this way, always as "your mother," never as "my wife."

Our conversation is a standoff, but in the end I win, a minor victory which Trace glosses over. She has read books on aging; now she is aware. Trace says I should be patient because he put me through school and loaned me money for my first car. She thinks he is lonely because he used to love more people, but now they have moved away or died. She tells me that decency is not so painful a virtue.

Everyone takes my father's side, even me, and the stack of correspondence he sends grows higher. My father writes letters, but he never says anything. Instead, I open envelopes containing the latest gold index, or pamphlets offering advice on stocks and bonds. He enters sweepstakes in my name and in the back of the closet, in a shoe box, I keep my winnings — watches that don't work and fake diamond jewelry. I wouldn't know what to do with all that money even if I won, so he tells me: Buy an electric can opener, some nice clothes, save it for when you're old. He worries that when I am old I will also be poor, and he knows that is not a good combination.

My father arrives early Friday night with his gifts. In the department store and the winery he has spent the interest on his hard-earned money. The wine we will drink during dinner. The Water Pik will be consigned to the top shelf of the bathroom closet. My thank you will fill the space in his bank account where the Water Pik and the bottles of wine used to be. Tacitly, we will call this love.

He sits on the sofa while I finish making dinner, his unlighted cigarette moving from hand to hand. The apartment makes no sense to him, though he's had previous opportunity to figure it out. Shelves of store bought books line a wall with the city library only a few blocks away; collections of rocks and sea shells lay about the room, but no art that merits a frame; and finally, my bed is made high in a loft, instead of on the floor, where I won't have as far to fall. My father finishes his survey and concludes that I need a bigger place.

"I like it here. It's perfect for one."

"That's another problem. I'm not the only one who thinks so."

If Ma was still with him she would agree, but now he is the only one who worries. He worries about my friends. Where are they? What are they? He is afraid they are communists, or feminists, or environmentalists — people who are dissatisfied and unable to keep quiet. When he meets them, though, he is the perfect gentleman.

"My name is Harold," he tells Trace and Liora, "but you can call me Mr. Davidoff."

The four of us sit at the table. We eat spaghetti and talk about things that don't matter. There is the weather, which is ever changing; and baseball, with its endless statistics; and a particular eczema on my father's elbow, that the doctors say is incurable. All this we discuss in exacting detail, enthralled by the gorgeous weather and the lousy Cubs and the noxious eczema. And the bottle goes around again though Trace has had her share.

"You don't care for red wine?" my father asks.

"I love it. I just have one glass because of the baby."

My father stares, so she helps him out.

"I'm only in my third month."

"Oh," he says, still looking, scrutinizing her left hand, looking for the ring which will make it make sense.

"Trace is going to be a single mother," I tell him.

"Oh. I'm sorry."

"By choice," Trace says, her voice and smile a gentle lullaby to soothe the wrinkles on his brow.

He cannot be soothed. Liora wants to know one more time how Trace was impregnated, and Trace wants again to tell her. My father listens, his forehead resembling a harrowed field, while girls gossip about donors and sperm counts and ovulation cycles. I assure him this is normal, that this is a way babies are created these days.

"Like that," he says. "Without love."

"With lots of love," Trace says.

My father does not believe her, but is too polite to say. As he arrives early, so he leaves early. He is tired. There's a show on TV he wants to watch. I walk with him to his car.

"About tomorrow," he says, "you pick me up at eleven, right? That's not so early."

"That'll be fine. I'll bring flowers."

He gets in his car and hands me some magazine clippings. "I forgot to give you these upstairs. Some articles about the commodities market."

"No thanks. Too risky."

"Take them. You never know." He lights his cigarette, the smoke taking over where our good-bye kiss of garlic and wine has left off.

Upstairs my friends are cleaning up from dinner. I sit in the rocker and listen to them talk about my father. They hold the views which I have held in the past, but their tone is off. They speak of Mr. Harold Davidoff as though he were shallow or belligerent or insensitive. I ask them to shut up, but I say it nicely. Trace is apologetic. She is sorry for the lectures she gave on parent-child relations. Now, she understands.

"He's a very generous man," I tell them.

"I'd love to own a Water Pik," Trace laughs, but when I retrieve my father's gift she refuses to accept it.

"I was just kidding," Trace says.

"Me too."

I set up the Water Pik by the bathroom sink. When I come back Trace and Liora are ready to go. I walk with them to the bus stop under the camouflage of our friendship. Still, Liora cannot believe and she says in awe, "The way he talks about your mother, as if she was still alive."

"What's wrong with that?" I ask.

Everything he makes is inedible. He makes lunch. On the counter in the kitchen he assembles the foods I don't eat anymore: bologna on white bread, soda pop, cakes wrapped in cellophane. A child's lunch, pre-fab and easy to swallow. I place the cooler in the trunk of the car, on top of the blanket, and we drive from the suburbs to the cemetery.

Along the way my father remembers, but only in the present tense. He says, "Her favorite color is blue."

"I couldn't find blue flowers."

"Stop here." He points to a shopping center. I wait while he goes in the dime store to buy blue plastic flowers. They sit in the back seat, next to the fresh white daisies, her favorite blossom.

"Now," he says, "I will tell you stories."

He talks about my mother as if she were still alive. He does this for himself. There is no room for my sadness, for my sweet sorrow, only his memories, bright and alive. In one recollection they never argue and in another he does everything she asks. Her past is his present, and his present he ignores. When I bring up last night's dinner he has little to say, no lectures on the importance of knowing the right people.

"They're your friends," he says. "That doesn't mean we have to play bridge together, does it?"

"I want you to know they're good people."

"You're a good person. That's all I need to know."

My father wants this to be a happy day. We are visiting my mother. She will be glad.

At her gravesite it is difficult for me to tell. She lies silently in a vast treeless field. Patches of bright color pepper the grounds. The eternal plastic flowers will never turn to dust and because of this they belittle the dead, who do. We place our bouquets by her tombstone and spread the blanket on the grass. Her marker was dedicated a couple of months ago, which makes her presence more real, but still she does not speak to me. My father does instead. He likes to talk about his will. He says, "Becky, your mother has everything. You can have it too."

"We don't need to discuss this here."

"But it's true. She's a smart lady. I've given her everything she's ever wanted."

Across the field grave diggers are preparing the soil. My father takes out a note pad and pen, though he has no idea how to spell the things I really want. The last time he did this I grabbed the list and went and sat in the car. He didn't ask what was wrong, but he offered to drive home. Now I stretch out and enjoy the warm sunshine, watch yellow jackets dance around the open cans of soda. Everything he writes down will be mine, and especially the things he doesn't. This is our unstated compromise, silent and manifest. My father sits on the blanket, his back propped up against the tombstone. He smokes another cigarette as he transcribes my future possessions. In her own way my mother approves of this. She agrees with Mr. Davidoff and continues to keep quiet, as if she really were alive.

My Sister's Marriage

CYNTHIA RICH

When my mother died she left just Olive and me to take care of Father. Yesterday when I burned the package of Olive's letters that left only me. I know that you'll side with my sister in all of this because you're only outsiders, and strangers can afford to sympathize with young love, and with whatever sounds daring and romantic, without thinking what it does to all the other people involved. I don't want you to hate my sister — I don't hate her — but I do want you to see that we're happier this way, Father and I, and as for Olive, she made her choice.

But if you weren't strangers, all of you, I wouldn't be able to tell you about this. "Keep yourself to yourself," my father has always said. "If you ever have worries, Sarah Ann, you come to me and don't go sharing your problems around town." And that's what I've always done. So if I knew you I certainly wouldn't ever tell you about Olive throwing the hairbrush, or about finding the letters buried in the back of the drawer.

I don't know what made Olive the way she is. We grew up together like twins — there were people who thought we were — and every morning before we went to school she plaited my hair and I plaited hers before the same mirror, in the same little twist of ribbons and braids behind our head. We wore the same dresses and there was never a stain on the hem or a rip in our stockings to say to a stranger that we had lost our mother. And although we have never been well-to-do — my father is a doctor and his patients often can't pay — I know there are people here in Conkling today who think we're rich, just because of little things like candlelight at dinner and my father's cigarette holder and the piano lessons that Olive and I had and the reproduction of T*he Anatomy Lesson* that hangs above the mantelpiece instead of botanical prints. "You don't have to be rich to be a gentleman," my father says, "or to live like one."

My father is a gentleman and he raised Olive and myself as ladies. I can hear you laughing, because people like to make fun of words like "gentleman" and "lady," but they are words with ideals and standards behind them, and I hope that I will always hold to those ideals as my father taught me to. If Olive has renounced them, at least we did all we could.

Perhaps the reason that I can't understand Olive is that I have never been in love. I know that if I had ever fallen in love it would not have been, like Olive, at first sight but only after a long acquaintance. My father knew my mother for seven years before he proposed — it is much the safest way. Nowadays people make fun of that too, and the magazines are full of stories about people meeting in the moonlight and marrying the next morning, but if you read those stories you know that they are not the sort of people you would want to be like.

Even today Olive wouldn't deny that we had a happy childhood. She used to be very proud of being the lady of the house, of sitting across the candlelight from my father at dinner like a little wife. Sometimes my father would hold his carving knife poised above the roast to stand smiling at her and say: "Olive, every day you remind me more of your mother."

109

I think that although she liked the smile, she minded the compliment, because she didn't like to hear about Mother. Once when my father spoke of her she said: "Papa, you're missing Mother again. I can't bear it when you miss Mother. Don't I take care of you all right? Don't I make things happy for you?" It wasn't that she hadn't loved Mother but that she wanted my father to be completely happy.

To tell the truth, it was Olive Father loved best. There was a time when I couldn't have said that, it would have hurt me too much. Taking care of our father was like playing a long game of "let's pretend," and when little girls play family nobody wants to be the children. I thought it wasn't fair, just because Olive was three years older, that she should always be the mother. I wanted to sit opposite my father at dinner and have him smile at me like that.

I was glad when Olive first began walking out with young men in the summer evenings. Then I would make lemonade for my father ("Is it as good as Olive's?") and we would sit out on the screened porch together watching the fireflies. I asked him about the patients he had seen that day, trying to think of questions as intelligent as Olive's. I knew that he was missing her and frowning into the long twilight for the swing of her white skirts. When she came up the steps he said, "I missed my housewife tonight," just as though I hadn't made the lemonade right after all. She knew, too, that it wasn't the same for him in the evenings without her and for a while, instead of going out, she brought the young men to the house. But soon she stopped even that ("I never realized how silly and shallow they were until I saw them with Papa," she said. "I was ashamed to have him talk to them."). I know that he was glad, and when my turn came I didn't want to go out because I hated leaving them alone together. It all seems a very long time ago. I used to hate it when Olive "mothered" me. Now I feel a little like Olive's mother, and she is like my rebellious child.

In spite of everything, I loved Olive. When we were children we used to play together. The other children disliked us because we talked like grown-ups and didn't like to get dirty, but we were happy playing by ourselves on the front lawn where my father, if he were home, could watch us from his study window. So it wasn't surprising that when we grew older we were still best friends. I loved Olive and I see now how she took advantage of that love. Sometimes I think she felt that if she were to betray my father she wanted me to betray him too.

I still believe that it all began, not really with Mr. Dixon, but with the foreign stamps. She didn't see many of them, those years after high school when she was working in the post office, because not very many people in Conkling have friends abroad, but the ones she saw — and even the postmarks from Chicago or California — made her dream. She told her dreams to Father, and of course he understood and said that perhaps some summer we could take a trip to New England as far as Boston. My father hasn't lived in Conkling all of his life. He went to Harvard, and that is one reason he is different from the other men here. He is a scholar and not bound to provincial ideas. People here respect him and come to him for advice.

Olive wasn't satisfied and she began to rebel. Even she admitted that there wasn't anything for her to rebel against. She told me about it, sitting on the window sill in her long white nightgown, braiding and unbraiding the hair that she had never cut.

"It's not, don't you see, that I don't love Father. And it certainly isn't that I'm not happy here. But what I mean is, how can I ever know whether or not I'm really happy here unless I go somewhere else? When you graduate from school you'll feel the same way. You'll want — you'll want to know."

"I like it here," I said from the darkness of the room, but she didn't hear me.

"You know what I'm going to do, Sarah Ann? Do you know what I'm going to do? I'm going to save some money and go on a little trip — it wouldn't have to be expensive, I could go by bus — and I'll just see things, and then maybe I'll know."

"Father promised he'd take us to New England."

"No," said Olive, "you don't understand. Anyhow, I'll save the money."

And still she wasn't satisfied. She began to read. Olive and I always did well in school, and our names were called out for Special Recognition on Class Day. Miss Singleton wanted Olive to go to drama school after she played the part of Miranda in *The Tempest,* but my father talked to her, and when he told her what an actress's life is like she realized it wasn't what she wanted. Aside from books for school, though, we never read very much. We didn't need to because my father has read everything you've heard of, and people in town have said that talking to him about anything is better than reading three books.

Still, Olive decided to read. She would choose a book from my father's library and go into the kitchen, where the air was still heavy and hot from dinner, and sit on the very edge of the tall, hard three-legged stool. She had an idea that if she sat in a comfortable chair in the parlor she would not be attentive or would skip the difficult passages. So she would sit like that for hours, under the hard light of the unshaded bulb that hangs from the ceiling, until her arms ached from holding the book.

"What do you want to find out about?" my father would ask.

"Nothing," Olive said. "I'm just reading."

My father hates evasion.

"Now, Olive, nobody reads without a purpose. If you're interested in something, maybe I can help you. I might even know something about it myself."

When she came into our bedroom she threw the book on the quilt and said: "Why does he have to pry, Sarah Ann? It's so simple — just wanting to read a book. Why does he have to make a fuss about it as though I were trying to hide something from him?"

That was the first time I felt a little like Olive's mother.

"But he's only taking an interest," I said. "He just wants us to share things with him. Lots of fathers wouldn't even care. You don't know how lucky we are."

"You don't understand, Sarah Ann. You're too young to understand."

"Of course I understand," I said shortly. "Only I've outgrown feelings like that."

It was true. When I was a little girl I wrote something on a piece of paper, something that didn't matter much, but it mattered to me because it was a private thought. My father came into my room and saw me shove the paper under the blotter, and he wanted me to show it to him. So I quickly said, "No, it's private. I wrote it to myself, I didn't write it to be seen," but he said he wanted to see it. And I said, "No, no, no, it was silly anyway," and he said, "Sarah Ann, nothing you have to say would seem silly to me, you never give me credit for understanding, I can understand a great deal," but I said it wasn't just him, really it wasn't, because I hadn't written it for anyone at all to see. Then he was all sad and hurt and said this wasn't a family where we keep things hidden and there I was hiding this from him. I heard his voice, and it went on and on, and he said I had no faith in him and that I shouldn't keep things from him — and I said it wasn't anything big or special, it was just some silly nonsense, but if it was nonsense, he said, why wouldn't I let him read it, since it would make him happy? And I cried and cried, because it was only a very little piece of paper and why did he have to see it anyway, but he was very solemn and said if you held back little things soon you would be holding back bigger things and the gap would grow wider and wider. So I gave him the paper. He read it and said nothing except that I was a good girl and he couldn't see what all the fuss had been about.

Of course now I know that he was only taking an interest and I shouldn't have minded that. But I was a little girl then and minded dreadfully, and that is why I understood how Olive felt, although she was grown-up then and should have known better.

She must have understood that she was being childish, because when my father came in a few minutes later and said, "Olive, you're our little mother. We mustn't quarrel. There should be only love between us," she rose and kissed him. She told him about the book she had been reading, and he said: "Well, as it happens, I do know something about that." They sat for a long time discussing the book, and I think he loved Olive better than ever. The next evening, instead of shutting herself in the bright, hot kitchen, Olive sat with us in the cool of the parlor until bedtime, hemming a slip. And it was just as always.

But I suppose that these things really had made a difference in Olive. For we had always been alike, and I cannot imagine allowing a perfect stranger to ask me personal questions before we had even been introduced. She told me about it afterward, how he had bought a book of three-cent stamps and stayed to chat through the half-open grilled window. Suddenly he said, quite seriously: "Why do you wear your hair like that?"

"Pardon me?" said Olive.

"Why do you wear your hair like that? You ought to shake it loose around your shoulders. It must be yards long."

That is when I would have remembered — if I had forgotten — that I was a lady. I would have closed the grill, not rudely but just firmly enough to show my displeasure, and gone back to my desk. Olive told me she thought of doing that but she looked at him and knew, she said, that he didn't mean to be impolite, that he really wanted to know.

And instead she said: "I only wear it down at night."

That afternoon he walked her home from the post office.

Olive told me everything long before my father knew anything. It was the beginning of an unwholesome deceit in her. And it was nearly a week later that she told even me. By that time he was meeting her every afternoon and they took long walks together, as far as Merton's Pond, before she came home to set the dinner table.

"Only don't tell Father," she said.

"Why not?"

"I think I'm afraid of him. I don't know why. I'm afraid of what he might say."

"He won't say anything," I said. "Unless there's something wrong. And if there's something wrong, wouldn't you want to know?"

Of course, I should have told Father myself right away. But that was how she played upon my love for her.

"I'm telling you," she said, "because I want so much to share it with you. I'm so happy, Sarah Ann, and I feel so free, don't you see. We've always been so close — I've been closer to you than to Father, I think — or at least differently." She had to qualify it, you see, because it wasn't true. But it still made me happy and I promised not to tell, and I was even glad for her because, as I've told you, I've always loved Olive.

I saw them together one day when I was coming home from school. They were walking together in the rain, holding hands like school children, and when Olive saw me from a distance she dropped his hand suddenly and then just as suddenly took it again.

"Hullo!" he said when she introduced us. "She does look like you!"

I want to be fair and honest with you — it is Olive's dishonesty that still shocks me — and so I will say that I liked Mr. Dixon that day. But I thought even then how different he was from my father, and that should have warned me. He was a big man with a square face and sun-bleached hair. I could see a glimpse of his bright, speckled tie under his tan raincoat, and his laugh sounded warm and easy in the rain. I liked him, I suppose, for the very things I should have distrusted in him. I liked his ease and the way that he accepted me immediately, spontaneously and freely, without waiting — waiting for whatever people wait for when they hold themselves back (as I should have done) to find out more about you. I could almost understand what had made Olive, after five minutes, tell him how she wore her hair at night.

I am glad, at least, that I begged Olive to tell my father about him. I couldn't understand why at first she refused. I think now that she was afraid of seeing them together, that she was afraid of seeing the difference. I have told you that my father is a gentleman. Even now you must be able to tell what sort of man Mr. Dixon was. My father knew at once, without even meeting him.

The weeks had passed and Olive told me that Mr. Dixon's business was completed but that his vacation was coming and he planned to spend it in Conkling. She said she would tell my father. We were sitting on the porch after dinner. The evening had just begun to thicken and some children had wandered down the road, playing a game of pirates at the very edge of our lawn. One of them had a long paper sword and the others were waving tall sticks, and they were screaming. My father had to raise his voice to be heard.

"So this man whom you have been seeing behind my back is a traveling salesman for Miracle-wear soles."

"Surrender in the name of the King."

"I am more than surprised at you, Olive. That hardly sounds like the kind of man you would want to be associated with."

"Why not?" said Olive. "Why not?"

"It's notorious, my dear. Men like that have no respect for a girl. They'll flatter her with slick words but it doesn't mean anything. Just take my word for it, dear. It may seem hard, but I know the world."

"Fight to the death! Fight to the death!"

"I can't hear you, my dear. Sarah Ann, ask those children to play their games somewhere else."

I went down the steps and across the lawn.

"Dr. Landis is trying to rest after a long day," I explained. They nodded and vanished down the dusky road, brandishing their silent swords.

"I am saying nothing of the extraordinary manner of your meeting, not even of the deceitful way in which he has carried on this — friendship."

It was dark on the porch. I switched on the yellow overhead light, and the three of us blinked for a moment, rediscovering each other as the shadows leaped back.

"The cheapness of it is so apparent it amazes me that even in your innocence of the world—"

My father was fitting a cigarette into its black holder. He turned it slowly to and fro until it was firm before he struck a match and lit it. It is beautiful to watch him do even the most trivial things. He is always in control of himself and he never makes a useless gesture or thinks a useless thought. If you met him you might believe at first that he was totally relaxed, but because I have lived with him so long I know that there is at all times a tension controlling his body; you can feel it when you touch his hand. Tension, I think, is the wrong word. It is rather a self-awareness, as though not a muscle contracted without his conscious knowledge.

"You know it very well yourself, Olive. Could anything but shame have kept you from bringing this man to your home?"

His voice is like the way he moves. It is clear and considered and each word exists by itself. However common it may be, when he speaks it, it has become his, it has dignity because he has chosen it.

"Father, all I ask is that you'll have him here — that you will meet him. Surely that's not too much to ask before you — judge him."

Olive sat on the step at my father's feet. Her hands had been moving across her skirt, smoothing the folds over her knees, but when she spoke she clasped them tightly in her lap.

She was trying to speak as he spoke, in that calm, certain voice, but it was a poor imitation.

"I'm afraid that it is too much to ask, Olive. I have seen too many of his kind to take any interest in seeing another."

"I think you should see him, Father." She spoke very softly. "I think I am in love with him."

"Olive!" I said. I had known it all along, of course, but when she spoke it, in that voice trying so childishly to sound sure, I knew its absurdity. How could she say it after Father had made it so clear? As soon as he had repeated after her, "A salesman for Miracle-wear soles," even the inflections of his voice showed me that it was ludicrous; I realized what I had known all along, the cheapness of it all for Olive — for Olive with her ideals.

I looked across at my father but he had not stirred. The moths brushed their wings against the light bulb. He flicked a long gray ash.

"Don't use that word lightly, Olive," he said. "That is a sacred word. Love is the word for what I felt for your mother — what I hope you feel for me and for your sister. You mustn't confuse it with innocent infatuation."

"But I do love him — how can you know? How can you know anything about it? I do love him." Her voice was shrill and not pleasant.

"Olive," said my father. "I must ask you not to use that word."

She sat looking up at his face and from his chair he looked back at her. Then she rose and went into the house. He did not follow her, even with his eyes. We sat for a long time before I went over to him and took his hand. I think he had forgotten me. He started and said nothing and his hand did not acknowledge mine. I would rather he had slapped me. I left him and went into the house.

In our bedroom Olive was sitting before the dressing table in her nightgown, brushing her hair. You mustn't think I don't love her, that I didn't love her then. As I say, we were like twins, and when I saw her reflection in the tall, gilded mirror I might have been seeing my own eyes filled with tears. I tell you, I wanted to put my arms around her, but you must see that it was for her own sake that I didn't. She had done wrong, she had deceived my father and she had made me deceive him. It would have been wicked to give her sympathy then.

"It's hard, of course, Olive," I said gently. "But you know that Father's right."

She didn't answer. She brushed her hair in long strokes and it rose on the air. She did not turn even when the doorknob rattled and my father stood in the doorway and quietly spoke her name.

"Olive," he repeated. "Of course I must ask you not to see this — this man again."

Olive turned suddenly with her dark hair whirling about her head. She hurled the silver hairbrush at my father, and in that single moment when it leaped from her hand I felt an elation I have never known before. Then I heard it clatter to the floor a few feet from where he stood, and I knew that he was unhurt and that it was I, and not Olive, who had for that single moment meant it to strike him. I longed to throw my arms about him and beg his forgiveness.

He went over and picked up the brush and gave it to Olive. Then he left the room.

"How could you, Olive?" I whispered.

She sat with the brush in her hand. Her hair had fallen all about her face and her eyes were dark and bright. The next morning at breakfast she did not speak to my father and he did not speak to her, although he sat looking at her so intensely that if I had been Olive I would have blushed. I thought, He loves her more now, this morning, than when he used to smile and say she was like Mother. I remember thinking, Why couldn't he love me like that? I would never hurt him.

Just before she left for work he went over to her and brushed her arm lightly with his hand.

"We'll talk it all over tonight, Olive," he said. "I know you will understand that this is best."

She looked down at his hand as though it were a strange animal and shook her head and hurried down the steps.

That night she called from a little town outside Richmond to say that she was married. I stood behind my father in the shadowy little hallway as he spoke to her. I could hear her voice, higher-pitched than usual over the static of the wires, and I heard her say that they would come, that very evening, if he would see them.

I almost thought he hadn't understood her, his voice was so calm

"I suppose you want my blessings. I cannot give them to deceit and cowardice. You will have to find them elsewhere if you can, my dear. If you can."

After he had replaced the receiver he still stood before the mouthpiece, talking into it.

"That she would give up all she has had — that she would stoop to a — for a — physical attraction—"

Then he turned to me. His eyes were dark.

"Why are you crying?" he said suddenly. "What are you crying for? She's made her choice. Am I crying? Do you think I would want to see her — now? If she — when she comes to see what she has done — but it's not a question of forgiveness. Even then it wouldn't be the same. She has made her choice."

He stood looking at me and I thought at first that what he saw was distasteful to him, but his voice was gentle when he spoke.

"Would you have done this to me, Sarah Ann? Would you have done it?"

"No," I said, and I was almost joyful, knowing it was true. "Oh, no."

That was a year ago. We never speak of Olive any more. At first letters used to come from her, long letters from New York and then from Chicago. Always she asked me about

Father and whether he would read a letter if she wrote one. I wrote her long letters back and said that I would talk to him. But he wasn't well — even now he has to stay in bed for days at a time — and I knew that he didn't want to hear her name.

One morning he came into my room while I was writing to her. He saw me thrust the package of letters into a cubbyhole and I knew I had betrayed him again.

"Don't ally yourself with deception, Sarah Ann," he said quietly. "You did that once and you see what came of it."

"But if she writes to me—" I said. "What do you want me to do?"

He stood in the doorway in his long bathrobe. He had been in bed and his hair was slightly awry from the pillows and his face was a little pale. I have taken good care of him and he still looks young — not more than forty — but his cheekbones worry me. They are sharp and white.

"I want you to give me her letters," he said. "To burn."

"Won't you read them, Father? I know that what she did was wrong, but she sounds happy—"

I don't know what made me say that except that, you see, I did love Olive.

He stared at me and came into the room

"And you believe her? Do you think that happiness can come from deception?"

"But she's my sister," I said, and although I knew that he was right I began to cry. "And she's your daughter. And you love her so."

He came and stood beside my chair. This time he didn't ask me why I was crying.

"We'll keep each other company, Sarah Ann, just the two of us. We can be happy that way, can't we? We'll always have each other, don't you know?" He put his hand on my hair.

I knew then that was the way it should be. I leaned my head on his shoulder, and when I had finished crying I smiled at him and gave him Olive's letters.

"You take them," I said. "I can't—"

121

He nodded and took them and then took my hand.

I know that when he took them he meant to burn them. I found them by chance yesterday in the back of his desk drawer, under a pile of old medical reports. They lay there like love letters from someone who had died or moved away. They were tied in a slim green hair ribbon — it was one of mine, but I suppose he had found it and thought it was Olive's.

I didn't wonder what to do. It wasn't fair, don't you see? He hadn't any right to keep those letters after he told me I was the only daughter he had left. He would always be secretly reading them and fingering them, and it wouldn't do him any good. I took them to the incinerator in the back yard and burned them carefully, one by one. His bed is by the window and I know that he was watching me, but of course he couldn't say anything.

Maybe you feel sorry for Father, maybe you think I was cruel. But I did it for his sake and I don't care what you think because you're all of you strangers, anyway, and you can't understand that there couldn't be two of us. As I said before, I don't hate Olive. But sometimes I think this is the way it was meant to be. First Mother died and left just the two of us to take care of Father. And yesterday when I burned Olive's letters I thought, Now there is only me.

Extremes of High and Low Regard

LOU ROBINSON

My father writes for *Rod Action* and *Old Cars*. He has worked on hundreds of cars and cycles in his life; he respects nothing. In his column he curses cars with nostalgic relish. All his stories have a curious mixture of macho and humility. They are all at his own expense. He wants to be the first to say, "the old fool."

He tells me about being arrested for riding his 1945 Harley with a taillight out (a long story that includes going to court with Hell's Angels, being forced to take the riding test over, blasting around the barrels on 'Grandpa' and miraculously not falling flat . . .) he says, "You missed your father in his finest hour." His motorcycle belt says Eddy in rhinestones.

When I visit him, he makes me read his latest column the minute I step inside the door. "You're my best audience." I never show him anything I write because it's so often about him and it might hurt him so he would have a stroke and need to be nursed for the rest of my life.

I sold Eddy's motorcycle jacket in the early '70s. For years I wore it, sleeves dangling half empty to my knees. I was wearing it when I went up to Jill Johnston at a reading and Jill said, "I like your style." On the radio a woman describes why she makes videos: The only time she ever saw her father cry was in front of the television when Kennedy was shot. I have the obverse goal: How can I appropriate the emblems that made him appear invincible?

I also took and lost his marine jacket. He likes to remind me of the time he drove me to the bus and watched me, wearing his jacket, board along with twenty marine recruits. He didn't know if I made it to Cincinnati alive.

Once when I had a broken heart, I called Eddy and asked him to find me a motorcycle. He hauled one all the way from Ohio to New York. I rode it around the driveway for several weeks and then sold it.

I studied the man. Very early I remember being depressed that I couldn't wash my whole head like he did, with a washcloth (or wash rag as he calls it, thinking each time of how his third grade teacher said he talked like trash).

He claims a resemblance to Robert Mitchum, which is actually evident in a certain permanently wounded attitude, a stoic but wronged set of grimaces and sighs. His face relaxes from this into tragedy. And from his side, he will suddenly say, "There's a girl who runs the salvage yard here — your age, looks and talks like you." And later, "In my novel the main character, a female, your age, wears a sweatshirt all the time, too. I scrapped the first two chapters, but you might like to take a look at the third. . . ." I move to protect my stomach. No protection felt. Banished from the head, but something in the gut mourns over the necessity of manifestation.

My natural coating-like bark curls up showing the seam of the supposed results of will and the place it has found. This reserve proves itself in the body. Every tribe has its casualties, its downward spiral. I remember when he told me the story of his mother, Edna, whose mother was a Blackfoot Indian, an herbalist from Kentucky, who died just after Edna was born. Edna's new stepmother despised her husband's Indian kid, and one morning hung the child's dog from the branches of the oak outside her bedroom window. He has too many of these stories. I tune out. They register instead in my stomach. Quick lunges may upset the counter momentum, but no masking can counter the brooding and seething — it has its own reasons.

On the phone he says, "I guess you can't make it down for the Kentucky reunion. I wasn't even going to mention it. It's Grandma Birdie's one-hundred-and-one birthday."

Trace Branch, where he comes from, where she hung the dog, was the phrase I fixed on. I heard that story very early. I focused on the plight of animals, speechless creatures who could vanish without a trace. I spent my childhood in anguish on their behalf. After Gail and Eileen Irish, two Quaker sisters from down the lane, dropped out of the club I formed, I scoured the country lanes alone, looking for hurt creatures. My Band of Mercy, my club of one. I found birds, mostly; they didn't make it. One white chicken lived for a few days in the basement. But I bore witness. When Linda Walters strapped her horse in a standing martingale and whipped it, I called the SPCA — "I want to report a crime" — and hung up with the familiar sinking feeling of futility. The same sinking as when Eddy tried to tell me that in movies the horses don't really get shot or fall over the cliff. There was an organization to protect them. Right. I read his books. I knew what people were capable of.

Eddy was titillated by the Band of Mercy. He caught me with a quick question as I was coming up from feeding the chicken in the basement, and, surprised, I let slip the name of my club. I saw his face twist with the struggle not to grin.

I hate to be laughed at and he loved to laugh. One tease could drive me into a week-long silence. I froze him out from the beginning. From the beginning he pushed, he used his very agile mind to get inside my fortress. It was a constant battle which drove us both to extremes. Once I heard him exclaim to my mother, in disgust, as if I were a criminal or prostitute, "Why does she keep the door shut all the time, Mona? All she wants to do is be in her room with the door shut. Six years old and a misanthrope. What does she do in there anyway?"

In there I made paper horses the size of my thumb. It was not easy. Having started so small, I was forced to make the curry combs, brushes, bridles and halters the size of fingernail trimmings. Each horse had a blanket with its name on it, and a tab like paper doll clothes. My favorites had one version of themselves standing proudly, head raised to the wind, and one leaping in air. Each horse had a little me to go with it, with a tab that fit in the saddle, and a blob of red at the top so there would be no mistaking who owned this fabulous stable. I had a green blanket on my bed. Behind my door, I would pose them on the hills and valleys of blanket over pillows. I spent long hours devising plans to ensure their safety if the house caught on fire. In my plans, I saved everyone. But I wanted to be prepared. I didn't want to have to make choices.

And I read: *The Yearling, Where the Red Fern Grows, Black Beauty, My Friend Flicka, Coaly Bay the Outlaw Horse, Beautiful Joe, The Red Pony.* At night I made peanut butter and banana sandwiches and watched animal movies on TV: *Biscuit Eater, Old Yeller* . . . or failing that, Ida Lupino. When my Aunt Verlan sold the motel, she gave all the old TVs to Eddy, so we had one in every room. I didn't like to watch with people. I liked to watch, maybe even the same show, alone, in my bed, with my horses. This drove Eddy crazy. I wanted to be absorbed, out of the body, into the scene with the dog that sucked eggs, doomed; cradling Beauty's scarred head in my hands — room for emotion. I did not ever want to be watched.

Eddy found projects for the two of us: sanding the Harley pieces, cleaning pistons, shoveling gravel — things horrible in their monotony — but what made me dread them was his huge talking, thinking, prying presence. I had to hear things I did not want to know. I heard them all in the garage.

Garage is not the right word. It was a giant quonset hut Eddy had taken apart at an abandoned army barracks and moved to the back field. He widened the roof with a wooden extension and a row of windows that broke the curve, jutting out like a strange ship, where hundreds of pigeons roosted. More like a barn, but that is a word for animals. This vast place was for cars, motorcycles, tractors, workbenches, tools. House items discarded from our earlier years found their way here and stayed forever, turning black with oil: my old yellow chenille baby spread, an Easter muff now used to buff out polish. There was a clear space only in the middle, to drive in a vehicle for repair. The rest of the floor was covered with greasy black things of all sizes. White enamel pans held lakes of black sump oil twenty years old. Acetylene torches, oxygen tanks. Goggles and a gas mask hung on a nail, covered with cobwebs. Anything hanging on a nail was never used. Frequently used things were on the inner circle of the floor heap. "Go look for a bolt about this big" he'd say, holding out his blackened thumb and finger. Or "Go get the ballpeen hammer. It's over by the basket of Indian parts." I never found a single thing I was sent to look for. I never had the satisfaction. I'd stir it around hopelessly for an interval, then trudge back. He'd say "Oh Jesus Christ" and I'd watch his bent back disappear. I spent a lifetime in there on a stool, learning about how to adjust spark plugs, set timing, take apart a piston. I don't remember how to do a thing. "Hold this as hard as you can while I turn." It would spring back in our faces. I never had the strength. Saturdays Mona would say, "Eddy wants you out in the garage," and she'd pat my back in sympathy as I laid down Isl*and Stallion Races.*

Once I came running into the garage, screaming that my dog was stuck in another dog. I had to hear about animal — and then people — sex. I knew a lot already, from reading My *Secret Life,* and books by Henry Miller and Mike Hammer off of Eddy's shelves, but I didn't believe anyone I knew did these things in real life. He went on from dog and people sex to perversion. Telling me about Mr. Stouffer, my geography teacher who had left in the middle of the school year. Because, Eddy said, he had taken six seventh grade boys on a field trip to St. Louis, where he paid them to tie him to his hotel bed and whip him with their belts. Eddy sounded like he didn't really want to have to tell me this. He was polishing the gas tank of Grandpa, the older Harley, the one that had been his father's. I was staring at a calendar of a very fat naked woman, given him by his friend George Brey. George thought it was funny. Eddy didn't take it down because he didn't want to hurt George's feelings. George lives alone with his pit bull at the Radnor junkyard. He is a damn fine mechanic. Eddy and George ride abreast to Indianapolis once a year for the races. They ride straight through cities at 80 miles per hour. It always rains. They sleep in the park under picnic tables, with a plastic garbage bag over the boards and one on the ground. When they come back I help Eddy fix Grandpa, which has invariably broken down somewhere on Route 71 and been patched up with wire, a stub of a broom handle. . . .

In the garage he tells me about the Hell's Angels. This time they played a game with a hot dog hung from a wire stretched between two trees in the campsite. The men have to roar their hogs down the path between the trees and catch the hot dog in their mouths. After awhile, one of the women, in a dog collar, goes over with a jar of mustard and crams the dangling hot dog in it, to make it more slippery we guess, and they start again. He couldn't believe it, he says.

I know this has to do with sex. Why does he tell me? Am I different from my mother, less innocent somehow? Does he think I am more like him? Everything in me slinks away. In private, aroused, I muzzle my stuffed collie dog and pretend to drown it behind a chair. I peel the skin off hot dogs and hack them to bits. But I want to be more like him. I do not ever want to be the one on the calendar, the one holding the mustard.

We have photos of Eddy and me together, lolling on the floor with Gill, his English bulldog. In one photo he lies on the floor with his knees bent and I use him as a chair, my own legs crossed suavely at the knee, my one foot dangling in his face. I remember when his bulk seemed a necessary part of me. I loved him with fierce pride and fear of separation. He was the one who taught me everything, to read, to ride a bike, to climb a tree, to figure things out. He was the one who fixed things for people. He went out into the world and made speeches to crowds. He once marched in a parade next to Yul Brynner. He met Dinah Shore. He had a purple heart and a silver star. When my foot got caught high in the oak and he had to climb up to release it, I fell on the ground in a rage. I could not stand to be so helpless.

We played a game — knocking our heads together at the forehead until someone's eyes watered. I would never quit. If he quit, I was sure he was letting me win. Mona would say "Jesus Ed, is that a game for a *child?*"

When I was a year old, Eddy put me on a merry-go-round horse, blue-grey, I swear I do remember that color, at the Delaware County Fair. The man was supposed to hold me, but I kicked him away with my hard little white baby shoes. I wanted to do it alone, and I promptly fell on my head. I always had rages — when the bacon fell out of the BLT — whenever he could manage something that I could not.

Then suddenly, I couldn't stand to be alone with him. I don't know what changed between the ages of three and six. I don't know where my mother was while all this was happening. Off in her own dream. Alone together, Mona and I either made cookies, cried over TV shows, shopped for school clothes, in perfect bliss, or else fought furiously over things like washing my hair. She says I drove her crazy. But the way I remember it, it was casual. Nothing sly and shaping about it. I wasn't her. She didn't know who I would be but she assumed I would be different. She wasn't bribing companionship from a child.

But I don't remember why I suddenly dreaded Eddy's company. I had grown up riding on the back of motorcycles as calmly as playing horse with a broom. But I developed a dread of this as well. I didn't like to have to press my chest against his back. I didn't like that he would speed to give me a little terror. I got on each time in silence and pride, without a struggle, but never without the thought, "If I die, I will come back as a quarterhorse. I won't have to go to school with boys. I won't have to sand primer."

That's when he gave me the pony. Papaw Harry actually bought Star for all the cousins. But I was the only one who wanted it, and Eddy hauled it from Indiana to Ohio, its eyes rolling white over the cab of the maroon pick-up. Together, we built a barn for it out of metal shingles. I stood on a ladder in the wind, leaning my weight against a sheet of rippling metal, trying to line up a screw and a hole. Or I crouched beside Eddy as he heaved and sweated over fifty-five postholes. I straightened old nails, as he had done for his father, Harry. I was overwhelmed. I would think, "Is this any kind of work for a child?" I wore out. It was over the pony. Another noble sacrifice backfired on him.

I switched affection to the stubborn creature Harry had bought at an auction. The pony was getting even for a life of abuse. He bit, kicked, squeezed us against the wall. Until we got the fence built, he dragged me an acre on my stomach, morning and night, as I staked him out to graze. Finally I won him over, but he never gave in to anyone else. I took off on his back for hours alone, exploring. Eddy was jealous; he was also bit harder and more often. One day he confessed to having gone out and burnt the pony on the nose with a cigarette, after watching him drag me through the field. I lost all respect. But I had to endure this and the rest now, to keep the pony. I had to become duplicitous. I no longer wanted to be like Eddy. I didn't want to be the son he was to his father.

What was his childhood really like? I don't want to ask. If I could swallow it all quick, once, in private, I might have only compassion — no rage. I know from my mother's few words and angry silences on the topic that she thinks Papaw Harry was a cruel man. It is a very sad story, even the little I know. It is too much to bear. That's why he talked to me endlessly in the garage. Somebody had to hear it. He talked to me about his father. How Harry had made him stand in the dark alley for punishment, then crept up on him from behind and scared him speechless for a week. How they were building houses together when Eddy was six. Endless stories of old bikes bought together, fixed together, wrecked together. How Harry was in the KKK in Kentucky, before they moved to Indiana. Then he worked shoulder to shoulder with a one-armed black man, shoveling coal, and got respect for the colored. I was six, seven? Was this about the time Harry left my grandmother for a younger woman?

I have always believed that to write this story would be to bury Eddy. The same suspicion that stopped me from taking his photograph when he would leave on a motorcycle trip. But I have been saving it to the point where I am stub up, a bag of tears. Something spills and must be caught before it disappears into drier memories, all you have left when someone is gone. Old men's bare backs, bent working in the sun, make me sob. I bury it, but hairline fissures open, threatening to gape. Opening not on a void, but on a presence staring back. Solomon, prescribing death as a test of loyalty. Making me fear his death whenever I see his face. His hazel eyes looking up, humble and coy, masking some raw cry. Named Eddy Ray after Sugar Ray. We're bound by romanticism and infection, like lovers. Same anger at not being known, same determination to remain secret. Same stab of remorse when this denial hits its mark. Giant sparring shadows joined at the forehead. No, this story is between the living.

The Day My Father Kicked Me Out

SANDY BOUCHER

It's Sunday evening. We're sitting at the table in my parents' house in Columbus, Ohio, and I've brought a friend with me. I've invited my friend Nyla to dinner, honestly, as protection. It's been eight years since I've come out from San Francisco to visit my parents, and I'm having difficulty being here.

So anyway, we're sitting at Sunday evening dinner, which is tuna salad, as always, and my father begins his lecture on John Dillinger and Pretty Boy Floyd. This discourse is really about law and order, with these two renowned bank robbers of the thirties as villains. He rambles on about their exploits, and then he asks Nyla, Do you know what they did to Dillinger and Floyd when they caught up with them?

Nyla: What?

My father: They shot them.

My father is a big man, and he leans in on you physically when he talks to you. You can feel him pushing on you. Now

132

he leans in on Nyla and says, And do you know what I would do *these days* with people who break the law?

Nyla has just gotten out of the hospital, where she had surgery: she's a bit weak and not quite in control. I notice when he asks her that question she starts to twitch a little, her face begins to tremble and the corners of her mouth jerk. And I remember that when Nyla and I had lived in a women's liberation collective in San Francisco, I had received a barrage of letters from my father, and the lecture on John Dillinger and Pretty Boy Floyd had been in those letters, word for word as he is giving it right now. So Nyla is having a bit of a hard time here, and my father repeats the question.

Do you know what I would do with people who break the law *these days?*

She: I think I do.

He: What?

She: You'd shoot them.

That's right, he says.

And she goes over the edge in a cascade of giggles.

I'm appalled. This is surrealistic, for as soon as Nyla begins to laugh, I lose control too. We giggle and snort like ninnies, and neither of us can stop.

Caught in these convulsions, I realize how trying these three days with my father have been. When he wasn't criticizing me for the way I live, he has been lecturing me about Richard Nixon's innocence and how the press always persecuted that unfortunate man. He's obsessed with Nixon, and set on convincing me of his views, and he has pushed me out to teeter on the edge of hysteria.

Nyla tilts me right over.

My mother's action at this historic juncture is to get up from the table and go out on the front porch to sit on the swing.

My father tries to go on with his talk, but pretty soon it's obvious that we're laughing at him, even though we pretend we're choking and we hold our napkins over our mouths. As soon as Nyla gets herself in control, I start again, and then when I stop, she starts.

So my father gets mad. He stands up, bangs against the table, knocks his chair over on its back, and calls us some names. (It's a funny thing, I can't remember the words he used. He may have said weirdos, and I wonder if he said queers: at that point in time he wasn't sure about me.) Finally, he goes stomping out to the porch, and he sits down next to my mother and starts to swing back and forth.

We're left in the dining room, Nyla and me, and we cannot yet stop laughing. We're helpless, the tears are running down our faces. It feels so good, it feels wonderful, yet we *know* what we've done.

We can hear the swing out on the front porch. *Scree, scree.* They're not talking, but the swing is squeaking.

At last we are calm, only an occasional giggle buzzing like a crazy hummingbird through our now-earnest talk. How are we to get Nyla out of the house?! I mean, they're on the front porch: she has to get past them somehow. Sneaking out the back door would be too cowardly. We sit here. We don't know what to do. And Nyla has developed hiccups.

Finally I agree to go with her to the front porch. We stand up and check out our faces for telltale signs of mirth; Nyla hiccups, claps her hand over her mouth, and holds her breath, bugging her eyes at me. With a long look at each other, we start for the door.

On the front porch, my parents swing back and forth — *scree, scree* — and my father stares into space as if we do not exist.

Thank you very much, hic, for having me to dinner, Nyla says.

My mother replies, You're quite welcome. We enjoyed having you.

Nyla walks down the porch steps, gets in her car, says goodbye to me with a sneaky little wave, and drives off.

Here I am, left. I go back in the house, clear the table, start washing the dishes, and I think, Well, now, what am *I* going to do about this? The longer I stay in here washing the dishes, the harder it's going to be to go out on the porch. Finally, I decide that I must go out right now to say *something*. Through the dining room and living room I go, and step out on the porch. My father swings back and forth, back and forth, staring straight ahead. *Scree, scree.*

I'm sorry we laughed at you. (This is the truth, I *am* sorry.)

And he starts in, You bring your weird friends here and you laugh at a man in his own house, and etcetera on and on, very loudly, and he makes me mad.

Ever since I *arrived* you been laughing at *me!* I yell. Everything I do you put me down, you don't like what I do, you laugh at me, it's about time somebody laughed at *you!*

And my mother says, Please, we *do* have neighbors.

Well, the argument goes back and forth between me and my father, because I feel outraged, and *he* feels outraged. And finally he says to me, if somebody laughs at me in my own house, I'm gonna kick their ass out the door, and yours too!

I see my chance. Does that mean you'd like me to leave? I ask.

Now that really puts him up against the wall. What can he say?

Yes, it does!

I get up from my chair and I spit out, Well, it's a relief!

I go in and slam the screen door and stamp upstairs to pack my bag.

Now I'm up here putting things in my suitcase and I begin to feel ridiculous. This reminds me of a scene in a C-movie.

But Mom will be down there on the porch talking to him, saying, Now Jack, you know how Sandy is, and the two of you don't get along, but, etc., etc. She'll be busily smoothing the whole thing over. So I listen, but I don't hear a word from downstairs. What's going on? That's her role, to smooth things over: *she's not smoothing things over,* what's going on? So I keep on packing. Pretty soon the suitcase is all packed and I still don't hear any voices downstairs.

Now I have to go down there with my suitcase. My father's still out on the porch, but he's alone; my mother is sitting in the living room. As I come down the stairs, she says to me, Can I drive you to the bus?

Is it true? Have I heard the words properly? Yes, no way to get around them. With those seven words she defines her loyalty, her limits, her self-interest, her temperamental proclivities. That phrase is a masterpiece. The inevitability of it! The many layers of significance. At once simple and pithy, it does the job.

When I recover sufficiently to speak, I manage a belligerent Absolutely not! I'll take a taxi!

Then I lean down to the screened window that separates the living room from the porch where my father's swinging back and forth, and I come close and say, loudly, Do we really have to play this scene? He acts as if he doesn't hear me.

So I let my mother drive me to the bus.

On the way, I'm ranting in the car, saying, How can he really believe that nonsense he's talking about Nixon's innocence! I can't understand why he's saying those outrageous things! And she says, Of course he believes what he's saying. *I* certainly do.

There isn't anything to do but leave. I decide right now to go to New York City on the Greyhound, and I announce (not to be dismissed so summarily), When I get back I'll come to see you before I go on to California.

So I go to New York City where I have business to transact and several old friendships to renew. My time there is tolerably pleasant, and when I come back to Columbus, just an hour before I'm due at the airport to fly back to California, I get Nyla to drive me to my parents' house, where she insists on waiting in the car. I've called beforehand, and the excuse is that I am going to pick up some old pictures. We have to have an excuse: it isn't possible to say we are going to try to make up. So we sit and look at the snapshots, my mother and me, at this very dining room table where the blasphemy occurred, while my father paces like a disgruntled bear behind us.

Here is little Sandy sitting on the back step in her sunsuit, age two. Here are my sister, brother and I lined up stiffly against the living room wall looking like the czar's children staring down the barrels of a firing squad. My mother and I ponder two family dog pictures: this is Ham and this is Freddy, beings immured forever in our hearts. Is that blur in the background my cousin Carolyn? Honeysuckle perfume wafts seductively in through the screened windows, as it has and ever shall in Columbus in the spring.

When it is time to go, I decide to make a gesture of reconciliation. What have I got to lose?

I hug my father. He embraces me with arms of heavy wood, saying, Be a good girl.

Then I go to hug my mother, and I murmur to her, Be a good girl.

I always am, she replies.

And I leave, and have not returned.

The Thorn

MARY GORDON

f I lose this, she thought, I will be
so far away I will never come back.

When the kind doctor came to tell her that her father was
dead, he took her crayons and drew a picture of a heart. It was
not like a valentine, he said. It was solid and made of flesh, and
it was not entirely red. It had veins and arteries and valves and
one of them had broken, and so her daddy was now in heaven,
he had said.

She was very interested in the picture of the heart and she
put it under her pillow to sleep with, since no one she knew
ever came to put her to bed anymore. Her mother came and got
her in the morning, but she wasn't in her own house, she was
in the bed next to her cousin Patty. Patty said to her one night,
"My mommy says your daddy suffered a lot, but now he's re-
leased from suffering. That means he's dead." Lucy said yes,
he was, but she didn't tell anyone that the reason she wasn't
crying was that he'd either come back or take her with him.

Her aunt Iris, who owned a beauty parlor, took her to B. Altman's and bought her a dark blue dress with a white collar. That's nice, Lucy thought. I'll have a new dress for when I go away with my father. She looked in the long mirror and thought it was the nicest dress she'd ever had.

Her uncle Ted took her to the funeral parlor and he told her that her father would be lying in a big box with a lot of flowers. That's what I'll do, she said. I'll get in the box with him. We used to play in a big box; we called it the tent and we got in and read stories. I will get into the big box. There is my father; that is his silver ring.

She began to climb into the box, but her uncle pulled her away. She didn't argue; her father would think of some way to get her. He would wait for her in her room when it was dark. She would not be afraid to turn the lights out anymore. Maybe he would only visit her in her room; all right, then, she would never go on vacation; she would never go away with her mother to the country, no matter how much her mother cried and begged her. It was February and she asked her mother not to make any summer plans. Her aunt Lena, who lived with them, told Lucy's mother that if she had kids she wouldn't let them push her around, not at age seven. No matter how smart they thought they were. But Lucy didn't care; her father would come and talk to her, she and her mother would move back to the apartment where they lived before her father got sick, and she would only have to be polite to Aunt Lena; she would not have to love her, she would not have to feel sorry for her.

On the last day of school she got the best report card in her class. Father Burns said her mother would be proud to have such a smart little girl, but she wondered if he said this to make fun of her. But Sister Trinitas kissed her when all the other children had left and let her mind the statue for the summer: the one with the bottom that screwed off so you could put the big rosaries inside it. Nobody ever got to keep it for more than one night. This was a good thing. Since her father was gone she didn't know if people were being nice or if they seemed nice and really wanted to make her feel bad later. But she was pretty sure this was good. Sister Trinitas kissed her, but she smelled fishy when you got close up; it was the paste she used to make the Holy Childhood poster. This was good.

"You can take it to camp with you this summer, but be very careful of it."

"I'm not going to camp, Sister. I have to stay at home this summer."

"I thought your mother said you were going to camp."

"No, I have to stay home." She could not tell anybody, even Sister Trinitas, whom she loved, that she had to stay in her room because her father was certainly coming. She couldn't tell anyone about the thorn in her heart. She had a heart, just like her father's, brown in places, blue in places, a muscle the size of a fist. But hers had a thorn in it. The thorn was her father's voice. When the thorn pinched, she could hear her father saying something. "I love you more than anyone will ever love you. I love you more than God loves you." *Thint* went the thorn; he was telling her a story "about a mean old lady named Emmy and a nice old man named Charlie who always had candy in his pockets, and their pretty daughter, Ruth, who worked in the city." But it was harder and harder. Sometimes she tried to make the thorn go *thint* and she only felt the thick wall of her heart; she couldn't remember the sound of it or the kind of things he said. Then she was terribly far away; she didn't know how to do things, and if her aunt Lena asked her to do something like dust the ledge, suddenly there were a hundred ledges in the room and she didn't know which one and when she said to her aunt which one did she mean when she said ledge: the one by the floor, the one by the stairs, the one under the television, her aunt Lena said she must have really pulled the wool over their eyes at school because at home she was an idiot. And then Lucy would knock something over and Aunt Lena would tell her to get out, she was so clumsy she wrecked everything. Then she needed to feel the thorn, but all she could feel was her heart getting thicker and heavier, until she went up to her room and waited. Then she could hear it. "You are the prettiest girl in a hundred counties and when I see your face it is like a parade that someone made special for your daddy."

She wanted to tell her mother about the thorn, but her father had said that he loved her more than anything, even God. And she knew he said he loved God very much. So he must love her more than he loved her mother. So if she couldn't hear him her mother couldn't, and if he wasn't waiting for her in her new room then he was nowhere.

When she came home she showed everyone the statue that Sister Trinitas had given her. Her mother said that was a very great honor: that meant that Sister Trinitas must like her very much, and Aunt Lena said she wouldn't lay any bets about it not being broken or lost by the end of the summer, and she better not think of taking it to camp.

Lucy's heart got hot and wide and her mouth opened in tears.

"I'm not going to camp; I have to stay here."

"You're going to camp, so you stop brooding and moping around. You're turning into a regular little bookworm. You're beginning to stink of books. Get out in the sun and play with other children. That's what you need, so you learn not to trip over your own two feet."

"I'm not going to camp. I have to stay here. Tell her, Mommy, you promised we wouldn't go away."

Her mother took out her handkerchief. It smelled of perfume and it had a lipstick print on it in the shape of her mother's mouth. Lucy's mother wiped her wet face with the pink handkerchief that Lucy loved.

"Well, we talked it over and we decided it would be best. It's not a real camp. It's Uncle Ted's camp, and Aunt Bitsie will be there, and all your cousins and that nice dog Tramp that you like."

"I won't go. I have to stay here."

"Don't be ridiculous," Aunt Lena said. "There's nothing

for you to do here but read and make up stories."

"But it's for *boys* up there and I'll have nothing to do there. All they want to do is shoot guns and yell and run around. I hate that. And I have to stay here."

"That's what you need. Some good, healthy boys to toughen you up. You're too goddamn sensitive."

Sensitive. Everyone said that. It meant she cried for nothing. That was bad. Even Sister Trinitas got mad at her once and told her to stop her crocodile tears. They must be right. She would like not to cry when people said things that she didn't understand. That would be good. They had to be right. But the thorn. She went up to her room. She heard her father's voice on the telephone. *Thint,* it went. It was her birthday, and he was away in Washington. He sang "happy birthday" to her. Then he sang the song that made her laugh and laugh: "Hey, Lucy Turner, are there any more at home like you?" because of course there weren't. And she mustn't lose that voice, the thorn. She would think about it all the time, and maybe then she would keep it. Because if she lost it, she would always be clumsy and mistaken; she would always be wrong and falling.

Aunt Lena drove her up to the camp. Sc*enery.* That was another word she didn't understand. "Look at that gorgeous scenery," Aunt Lena said, and Lucy didn't know what she meant. "Look at that bird," Aunt Lena said, and Lucy couldn't see it, so she just said, "It's nice." And Aunt Lena said, "Don't lie. You can't even *see* it, you're looking in the wrong direction. Don't say you can see something when you can't see it. And don't spend the whole summer crying. Uncle Ted and Aunt Bitsie are giving you a wonderful summer for free. So don't spend the whole time crying. Nobody can stand to have a kid around that all she ever does is cry."

Lucy's mother had said that Aunt Lena was very kind and very lonely because she had no little boys and girls of her own and she was doing what she thought was best for Lucy. But when Lucy had told her father that she thought Aunt Lena was not very nice, her father had said, "She's ignorant." *Ignorant.* That was a good word for the woman beside her with the dyed black hair and the big vaccination scar on her fat arm.

"Did you scratch your vaccination when you got it, Aunt Lena?"

"Of course not. What a stupid question. Don't be so goddamn rude. I'm not your mother, ya know. Ya can't push me around."

Thint, went the thorn. "You are ignorant," her father's voice said to Aunt Lena. "You are very, very ignorant."

Lucy looked out the window.

When Aunt Lena's black Chevrolet went down the road, Uncle Ted and Aunt Bitsie showed her her room. She would stay in Aunt Bitsie's room, except when Aunt Bitsie's husband came up on the weekends. Then Lucy would have to sleep on the couch.

The people in the camp were all boys, and they didn't want to talk to her. Aunt Bitsie said she would have to eat with the counselors and the K.P.'s. Aunt Bitsie said there was a nice girl named Betty who was fourteen who did the dishes. Her brothers were campers.

Betty came out and said hello. She was wearing a sailor hat that had a picture of a boy smoking a cigarette. It said "Property of Bobby." She had braces on her teeth. Her two side teeth hung over her lips so that her mouth never quite closed.

"My name's Betty," she said. "But everybody calls me Fang. That's on account of my fangs." She opened and closed her mouth like a dog. "In our crowd, if you're popular, you get a nickname. I guess I'm pretty popular."

Aunt Bitsie walked in and told Betty to set the table. She snapped her gum as she took out the silver. "Yup, Mrs. O'Connor, one thing about me is I have a lot of interests. There's swimming and boys, and tennis, and boys, and reading, and boys, and boys, and boys, and boys, and boys."

Betty and Aunt Bitsie laughed. Lucy didn't get it.

"What do you like to read?" Lucy asked.

"What?" said Betty.

"Well, you said one of your interests was reading. I was wondering what you like to read."

Betty gave her a fishy look. "I like to read romantic comics. About romances," she said. "I hear you're a real bookworm. We'll knock that outa ya."

The food came in: ham with brown gravy that tasted like ink. Margarine. Tomatoes that a fly settled on. But Lucy could not eat. Her throat was full of water. Her heart was glassy and too small. And now they would see her cry.

She was told to go up to her room.

That summer Lucy learned many things. She made a birchbark canoe to take home to her mother. Aunt Bitsie made a birchbark sign for her that said "Keep Smiling." Uncle Ted taught her to swim by letting her hold onto the waist of his bathing trunks. She swam onto the float like the boys. Uncle Ted said that that was so good she would get double dessert just like the boys did the first time they swam out to the float. But then Aunt Bitsie forgot and said it was just as well anyway because certain little girls should learn to watch their figures. One night her cousins Larry and Artie carried the dog Tramp in and pretended it had been shot. But then they put it down and it ran around and licked her and they said they had done it to make her cry.

She didn't cry so much now, but she always felt very far away and people's voices sounded the way they did when she was on the sand at the beach and she could hear the people's voices down by the water. A lot of times she didn't hear people when they talked to her. Her heart was very thick now: it was like one of Uncle Ted's boxing gloves. The thorn never touched the thin, inside walls of it anymore. She had lost it. There was no one whose voice was beautiful now, and little that she remembered.

Home Stretch

AMBER COVERDALE SUMRALL

Matt and I lived in sin together for four years, a time in which my father refused to have anything to do with us. If Matt answered the phone my father hung up. I stopped receiving invitations to the traditional family gatherings and holiday festivities. The substantial Christmas checks were replaced by subscriptions to *The Tidings,* and by Holy Cards announcing a novena of Masses to be offered on my behalf. Matt's name was never mentioned by my father until the day of our wedding. And then the long silence was replaced with non-stop talk, as if he had known and accepted Matt from the very beginning.

"You've matured more in this last year than you have for the past thirty," he told me. "I think all our prayers have finally been answered."

Despite the fact that our union had been sanctioned by Holy Matrimony and blessed by my father we were unable to rise to the occasion. When Matt and I separated, after five long

145

years, my father sent a scathing letter listing my failures as a woman in general, and as his daughter in particular, for choosing such a loser in the first place and then having the temerity to divorce him. He insisted upon addressing his correspondence to *Mrs. Matthew Fitzgerald,* as if to retain for himself some semblance of my identity. And to remind me who I *really* was in the eyes of God: "What God has joined together let no man put asunder," he wrote, urging me to take a giant step backwards. When I asked to borrow a small amount of money with the assurance that I would repay it in less than a year, he immediately wrote back, lambasting Matt for not properly taking care of me, and said he couldn't afford it. He had plans to remodel his house, buy a new Mercedes and take a trip to China.

So I wasn't going to see him this time. Even though I visit southern California perhaps once a year, I had plans only to view the Georgia O'Keeffe retrospective at the Los Angeles County Art Museum, visit a couple of old friends, then return home to Monterey Bay. Los Angeles driving makes me crazy: smog, exhaust fumes from hours of freeway idling and a pace that feels like some bizarre LP tunes played at 78 rpm. Not to mention my instant regression to teenage stupefaction when I get anywhere near the house in which I was raised. I wasn't going to put myself through it all this time.

But in the course of visiting my friend Kathy in Hollywood and commiserating about our respective fathers, I became rather intoxicated. After downing four shots of hundred-proof Russian plum brandy — her antidote to her father's abusive phone calls — I decided to call my parents, let them know I was in town. Of course I hoped they wouldn't be, but my mother answered the phone on the fourth ring, just as the message machine clicked on, and before I knew what I was doing I'd agreed to come for a visit.

On the drive up to their home in the San Gabriel foothills I replayed last year's encounter. We'd planned to have dinner together but when I arrived my father and mother were engaged in heavy verbal warfare.

"Goddamn it, Claire! When *will* you listen to me and get a hearing aid?"

"I was in the bathtub, Paul. If you're so *desperate* to get ahold of me you can install a phone in the bathroom."

"You take baths for *three* hours now! Jesus, no wonder the house is such a mess."

"Don't you *ever* take the Lord's name in vain in my presence."

"Oh I *forgot*. You have a direct line to Him. Why would you even bother with a lowly telephone."

My mother never stands a chance in these exchanges, the most she can hope for is the last word. I jumped in cautiously, the way I used to do with the twirling double jump-ropes on the school playground.

"I have to be back in Santa Monica by ten. Do you still want to have dinner?" They stared at me, startled, as if I had just materialized in their living room. My father reached for his pipe, signaling a time-out.

"We may as well have a bite to eat," he said, puffing smoke rings into the air. "How about La Posada?"

"It's fine with me," my mother said. "I've been craving a tostada compuesta all week."

The tension between my parents didn't dissipate once we arrived at La Posada. My father started reminiscing about World War II: how wonderful it was to be stationed in New Guinea, where the natives wore no clothes and thought the Americans were gods. He had recently retired and seemed to be "slipping" (as my mother put it) into a recurrent nostalgia for the good old days.

"It was the happiest time of my life," he said, glancing at my mother. "No one ever talked back to me."

"Only because they couldn't speak the language," my mother replied.

They have no language for each other either, I remember thinking as I ate my chile rellenos in silence, amazed by their

147

eagerness and capacity for battle, year after year. I could not recall a time when they enjoyed being together. Had they ever laughed, held hands or kissed each other? Told secrets late at night, their arms wrapped tightly around each other? Did they ever make love?

My father had not yet returned from his tour of duty in the South Pacific when I was born. According to my mother, when he finally did come home, he said she seemed like a total stranger to him, preoccupied with feeding schedules, diaper changes and grocery coupons. She knew he was disappointed that the glamorous woman he fantasized about while relaying radio messages on the islands no longer existed. He acted resentful of the time she spent caring not for him, but for a baby daughter neither had anticipated so early in their marriage. Gradually he withdrew from his family and by the time my brother was born three years later, he was spending many late nights working at the radio station.

One of my earliest memories is of lying awake at night watching leaf patterns from a neighbor's backyard tree appear on my bedroom walls whenever car headlights flooded the street. I thought every car was my father's but none of them turned into our driveway. Holding Bear, I would eventually fall asleep, waking hours later from a dream of twin green snakes slithering up the banister, as his footsteps climbed the stairs. A flurry of angry muffled words escaped into the hall as the door to my parent's bedroom closed.

La Posada was the same restaurant he took me to when we had our second "father-daughter" talk, which he initiated in response to my moving in with Matt. It was a secret I had planned on keeping from him as long as possible. Given his propensity for espionage, perfected in the armed forces under General Douglas MacArthur, he found out about my "situation" from Aunt Emily, who takes great pride in being the only liberal in the family. She delights in embracing people and predicaments that the others would find shocking or morally repugnant. Once, when I was in high school my father followed me and discovered that instead of going to the movies on a double-date, my boyfriend and I spent the entire time parked on Lanterman Lane, a scant three blocks from my house (an episode which triggered our first "father-daughter" talk). I was grounded for days. Aunt Emily finally convinced him that I'd end up on a psychiatrist's couch if he continued to treat me like Rapunzel. I suspected it was the fear of what psychiatric bills would do to his wallet that made him relent.

At the time of our "father-daughter" talk at La Posada, I ordered double margaritas as he fired question after question at me like rounds of artillery.

"So what does this guy do anyway?"

"Matt's a carpenter, Dad."

"That's not why I sent you to private schools young lady, so you could end up living with a goddamn carpenter."

"Uncle Kevin's a carpenter."

"And look where it's gotten him! Living all alone in a crummy shack out in the sticks with his wolfdog. Jesus, he's half nuts."

"Jesus was a carpenter, remember?"

"Yeah and he never sinned against the sixth commandment like you and that guy are doing. Don't you know no man wants or respects a woman he can have for free?"

"You mean Matt should buy me like stocks and bonds?"

"That's exactly what I mean. He should be willing to make an investment if he really wants you. But he never will now, you've thrown away your trump card by moving in with him."

"I'm sorry Dad, but I could care less whether Matt and I ever marry. You and mother aren't the greatest role models in the world."

"What do you mean by that remark? How dare you insult your mother?"

The dinner ended abruptly with his dramatic pronouncement that I was no longer a member of his family. It was similar, I remember thinking, to being excommunicated by

149

the Church Fathers for advocating abortion. I retaliated by telling him that I hadn't considered myself part of his patriarchal nuclear family for years, so if the act of disowning me was *his* trump card he could damn well stick it in his ear. And I walked out of La Posada and hitched a ride back to my car, parked in his driveway. We didn't speak until my marriage plans were announced.

I turn off the freeway at the Angeles Crest exit; the smog is terrible, obscuring the foothills. Already it has given me a headache, or is it Kathy's plum brandy? My nerves are on edge. I come away from these visits thoroughly frustrated, with the sense that I will never penetrate my father's armor, the cold steel that encases him. Sometimes I think the only hope lies in terminal illness, perhaps then his stubborn self-righteous exterior might give way to a vulnerable, compassionate core.

When I was five we went to Yosemite for our first vacation. As my mother and father sat outside our cabin in Tuolomne Meadows reading the newspaper I played near the river with Bear, dipping his furry feet into the icy water. He was my best friend; I took him everywhere, could not fall asleep at night without him. Suddenly the current swept him out of my hands. I ran screaming and crying to my father, "Daddy hurry, Bear's gone down the river." In a matter of seconds he'd tossed his newspaper aside and followed me to the place where I last saw Bear. Leaping from boulder to boulder he seemed to be flying down the creek, his red flannel shirt billowing like a flag, finally disappearing from view. When he returned an hour later, drenched and disheveled, he had Bear in his hands. Until that moment I had never been conscious of loving my father. I wonder if he realized then, just how thoroughly Bear had taken his place. And if he knew what a disaster it would be for both of us if he'd returned empty-handed.

Vacations were the time I felt closest to my father. He was

relaxed and easy to be with on our late summer excursions to the Sierra Nevadas. We camped and fished by the high mountain lakes of Mammoth, Silver and Gull. When I was nine I caught the biggest rainbow trout on record that year at Convict Lake. My father was beside himself.

"You landed the granddaddy of 'em all," he proclaimed, as I reeled in my catch. "Now you have to gut and clean him. Your mother will fry him up."

"But I want to cook it. I caught it."

"Let your mother. She needs something to do besides tidy up the campground all day."

"But Dad . . ."

"If you start cooking, pretty soon you'll be wearing frilly dresses instead of jeans. Cutting your ponytail off and hankering after boys."

"I never will."

"'Course if that fish is any indication I'd say those boys won't know what hit them."

The summer I was twelve we went to Baja California and I started to bleed for the first time. My mother bought a box of sanitary napkins from a drugstore clerk who didn't speak English. She pointed to the blue box on the highest shelf, then to me. The male clerk stood on a ladder saying, "Senora, por favor, que quiere usted? Este o ese?" I wanted to die. Later I overheard her telling my father.

"Katie became a young woman this afternoon."

"What are you talking about?"

"She started her period."

"Oh Christ! I'll have to watch her every minute now."

"Paul, she's only twelve years old."

"She may be twelve, Claire, but she's in heat isn't she? Pretty soon the boys will start sniffing around like a goddamn wolfpack."

"You ought to know all about that, Paul."

The next day I met Miguel on the beach. As we sat together, watching the fishermen with their nets, my father

151

came running like a crazy man from the motel courtyard. Gesturing wildly, he came straight for Miguel, yelling "get lost you goddamn Mexican gigolo." That evening, in spite of my mother's tearful protests, he packed up the car and we left Ensenada a week earlier than planned. My father refused to speak to me all the way home. Aside from the wrenching cramps I felt a terrible inner sorrow, as if my changing body and new blood had transformed me into something shameful. Someone to avoid, like a leper in biblical times.

After that we stopped taking vacations together. My father started to play tennis every weekend with a business associate. Charlotte would show up almost every Sunday in her crisp white tennis dress. She and my father would drive off together in her candy-apple red sports car. At dinnertime they'd return and Charlotte would shower, then eat the food my mother spent all afternoon preparing. My mother was nervous when Charlotte was around; she burned her fingers or sliced them open preparing dinner. My father told stupid jokes, inflating himself in front of Charlotte like one of those exotic puffer fish. She looked a little like Ava Gardner, wore a lot of make-up and smelled of perfume. She tried hard to make me like her, buying presents and talking sweet with her southern accent. When I was fifteen I saw Charlotte and my father parked in her Triumph near our house. They were kissing, just like in the movies. It was romantic on the screen but I was disgusted. I wanted to run home and tell my mother but I never did. She'd say I was making it up.

My father became suspicious whenever I had a date, sometimes following us in his car to make sure we went to the movies or out to eat. I had to endure his endless lectures on purity, his placing me on restriction if I came home even ten minutes late. During one session in which he was interrogating me, trying to find out how much kissing I was doing with my boyfriend, I decided to confront him.

"What about you and Charlotte?"

"What do you mean by that remark?"

"I saw you, in her car, kissing."

"WHAT!" He slapped me hard across the face. "You're just like your mother aren't you? Making up lies, seeing things that aren't there. I swear the both of you need to have your heads examined." He grabbed me and shook so hard I felt like I was undergoing shock therapy.

"That's the gratitude I get for allowing you to date. I bet *you* kiss your boyfriend plenty. You must have one hell of a guilty conscience, young lady. If you *ever* insinuate such a thing about Charlotte again, it will be the end of your social life for as long as you're living here. Do you understand me? Do you get it?"

"Yes, I get it." I said, holding back tears. I would not let him see me cry. Breaking from his grasp, I bolted from the room. How did he always manage to turn everything inside out. To make me want to hate him. And myself.

I pull into my parents driveway. My father is standing beside his brand new Mercedes waiting for me.

"C'mere," he says. "I've got something to show you."

"Hello Dad," I say, getting out of my car.

"Get in," he says, holding open the Mercedes door. I slide into the front seat as he gets in on the driver's side. Opening the glovebox, he brings out two miniature bottles of scotch. "Have a drink," he says. He unscrews the bottle tops and grabs two plastic cups from the back seat. He is acting strangely, as if we are accomplices in something forbidden. I tell him I don't want the scotch. That I have a headache.

"Oh, I forgot," he says sarcastically. "You're a vegetarian now. Damn communist propaganda. Did you know Hitler was a vegetarian?"

"Dad, please. I just got here and I can only stay a couple of hours, let's not start. What do you want to show me?"

I am struck by his increasing resemblance to my grandfather. He is now seventy-five, the age my grandfather was when he killed himself. After my grandmother's death, he put a gun to his head one afternoon, in our backyard. My father has aged considerably in this last year; he has lost weight, appears frail and distracted. His hands tremble slightly as he turns the key in the ignition.

"I got this with all the money I saved buying diesel in Tijuana," he says proudly, as the strains of Revelry shatter the Sunday afternoon quiet.

"Every time I go to our condo in Mission Beach I drive across the border and fill up." Nothing excites my father like the possibility of a good deal.

"This horn plays fifty different tunes. What do you want to hear? How 'bout Silent Night?" He punches a button and the Christmas carol rings out over the neighborhood.

"Your mother hates it of course." He takes a sip of his scotch, sinks back against the cushioned seat. "So what do you think. Pretty terrific, huh?"

"It's great, Dad." Between this and his erratic burglar alarm the neighbors must want to strangle him.

The Christmas music triggers a memory of midnight mass many years ago. Our family sat in the third pew so my mother could see and hear the priest well. As the service progressed my father started drifting off to sleep, nodding his head toward my mother's shoulder and snoring lightly. She repeatedly jabbed her elbow into his side but to no avail. Just as Father McCormick finished his sermon my father awakened and began clapping. The congregation burst into laughter, along with the priest, who advised my father, from the pulpit, to go home to bed. My mother, who seemed to have shrunk by several inches, was furious. I was laughing uncontrollably, along with my terribly embarrassed father, and we had to leave the church. We regained some semblance of composure in the vestibule. "Well, we sure got to her this time, didn't we?" he said, as if we were life-long allies.

"Let's go inside," he says abruptly, "I've got something else to show you." He sticks the empty bottle under his seat and quickly downs mine.

154

"By the way, I heard from Steve the other day," he says, looking at me strangely. "He wanted to borrow some money. He has quite a drug problem you know."

"No, I didn't know. I haven't seen him since he left northern California." Steve was my brother's best friend. He lived across the street from us.

"He says he got hooked up in *your* area. As a matter of fact, he says you got him started." My father has a wicked grin on his face like a jack o'lantern.

"Oh well," I say, feigning nonchalance, "you know Steve. Always the victim." I open my door and slide out, amazed at how this game continues year after year. Amazed at the amount of anger, hurt and frustration that surfaces in me.

"One of the best things about the Chinese is that they shoot drug dealers on sight. Now there's a policy I can really get behind," he says, loudly, heading for the backyard.

My mother greets me at the door. She is wearing a quilted pink bathrobe and holding a lukewarm cup of coffee. "I haven't been able to sleep since we returned from China," she tells me, offering her cheek to be kissed. She is still beautiful at seventy-five.

"Well, you look lovely, Mother. How are you feeling?"

"Tired. I'm tired all the time lately. It doesn't help to have your father around either. He wears me out. Oh, what I'd give for him to be back at NBC."

My father fought retirement for years until, finally, the network threatened to replace him. We want "young blood" they told him. He was incredulous, had planned to work all his life. He never thought of himself as anything less than essential, irreplaceable.

"How is Matt," she whispers as if we, also, were accomplices. My mother is still a little in love with Matt. He charmed her: holding doors open, helping her with the dishes, leaning close to her when she talked. She used to giggle and sway like a young girl in his presence.

"He's fine. We had dinner last week."

Her eyes fill with tears. "I just don't see why you two couldn't have resolved your differences."

"Mother, please, it wasn't an easy decision, believe me. I didn't walk away on a whim."

"I bought a few things for your house, for the two of you, before I knew . . . would you like to see them?" Before I can respond she has disappeared into the back bedroom.

My father comes in from the kitchen carrying a black attaché case. He tells me to sit down, make myself comfortable. He wants to show me a video of their recent trip to China. It's five hours long.

"Dad, I can only stay a little while. I'd rather talk. I can see the video some other time."

"You have to at least see the dancing," he says, turning on the set. "And the temple shots."

My mother emerges from the back of the house with several boxes, which she places on the floor next to her feet. Removing the lids she holds the contents of each box up, one by one, as if we were at an auction: a large porcelain statue of the Virgin Mary, a wooden crucifix she tells me is blessed by the pope, a wooden shelf for knick-knacks (to hold the statue no doubt), a set of plastic placemats with a daisy motif and a large framed photograph of her and my father taken to commemorate their fiftieth wedding anniversary.

"I hope you can use these," she says. "Although we did buy them for your home. Yours and Matt's."

"Well, you know I still live in a house," I say, attempting to interject some humor into this exchange.

"The presents were bought for the home that you lived in with your husband," my father says, removing himself from his China re-experience. "Not that communist haven you live in now."

"It's called a cooperative household, Dad."

"Don't give me any of your doubletalk. Do you still have your Marxist mayor? I suppose you're still involved in that so called 'sanctuary' movement? Godless communist dupes!"

He turns back to his video. My mother, father and Charlotte appear in the foreground of a Buddhist temple. Charlotte travels with them now. I can't begin to fathom all the nuances and complexities of their relationship. My father simply never stopped seeing her. Gradually she became an honorary member of our family, participating in holidays and other activities. My mother considers her a friend. I try to avoid her as much as possible.

"Look at these Chinese musicians, will you? Aren't they amazing?" The musicians are playing a smattering of American pop tunes and the tourists are eating it up like hungry puppies.

"I really don't want to watch this, Dad."

"Okay, I'll turn the volume down." He adjusts a knob. "There we go." His eyes stay riveted to the screen. My mother brings in glasses of water and spills the one she hands to me. Her hands are shaking.

"Claire, you having trouble walking? Why not just dump the whole thing in Kathryn's lap." He laughs, looking at me, inviting me to participate in her humiliation.

"Your father was always a bully," Aunt Emily once told me. "Even as a child. His primary objective in life was to make me cry or scream. Don't you remember how he'd tickle you until you could barely breathe? Or slide your favorite food off your plate and into his mouth until you threw such a temper tantrum that we'd all be forced to leave the restaurant? Or tease your cat so relentlessly that she'd never come out from behind the sofa when he was home? And when your mother was horribly ill with migraines he'd insist that she get up and prepare his breakfast. Where he got his mean streak is beyond me, your grandparents were so loving, completely devoted to us kids."

I'm having trouble breathing. All the windows are closed, the drapes drawn tight, as if secret religious rites are being conducted in here. My head is throbbing. Everything is as it was when I was growing up: the anger, the verbal abuse, the coffee table with its silver tray of souvenir matches, the never-used fireplace, the painting of the Sacred Heart of Jesus above the mantel, the photographs of me as a little girl. There is just one in which I am a woman: it is of Matt and me on our wedding day.

"I have to go," I say, jumping up from the sofa.

"Do you want to take any of these presents?" my mother asks. "Maybe you can store them at Matt's for the time being, if you don't have room."

"Matt's living with someone now, Mother."

"Oh no, dear." She pulls a wad of tissue from her pocket and dabs her eyes. My mother has been crying on and off for as long as I can remember.

"Claire, for Christsake, knock it off. The man's a goddamn loser. C'mon, Kathryn, I'll walk you to your car."

I kiss my mother goodbye. Tell her to take care of herself. Tell her to come for a visit, knowing she never will. She never goes anywhere without him.

"Remember, we didn't spend good money on those presents so you could sell them at the flea market," he says as I pile them in the back seat. I resist the temptation to tell him that a statue of the Virgin isn't exactly a hot item in communist Santa Cruz.

"How's the car running?" my father asks.

"Fine."

"You know, I *chose* to retire. They weren't trying to get rid of me." His voice is strained. "I can have my job back tomorrow if I want it."

"I know, Dad." I hug him briefly, awkwardly, before starting the car.

"You know it isn't easy being home all day with your mother. She always finds things for me to do. Well, I guess we'll see you next year. Maybe your ridiculous bumper stickers will have worn off by then."

"Maybe they'll wear off on you," I say lightly, as I back out of the driveway.

He looks weary, leaning against the porch railing, vulnerable in spite of his toughness. Like an old bear, I think. An old bear afraid to come out of hibernation. An image of Bear being carried downstream by the river, with my father in wild pursuit, comes to mind. I hold this memory close, as once I held Bear. Long after my father returns to the darkness of his house I am still holding it.

Meeting My Father Halfway

MARIANNE ROGOFF

It was because my mother didn't love my father that she didn't stay married to him. She told me that. And I decided early on, I guess, that I wouldn't love him either. When she'd ask me if I ever thought about him, I told her no.

The only image I had of him was the wallet-sized, brown-tinted snapshot I saw once. "There's your father," my mother said, surprised she even had a picture of him. A photograph of a young man in a sailor cap, white bells and shiny black shoes, one leg raised, the foot propped against a knee-high cement wall. It had been shot from a distance and the face, besides being wrinkled and faded now, was out of focus. I squinted at it, looking for a resemblance.

I built a legend around him, and the story my mother told of their wedding. A double date, a dare, the drive to the chapel just over the state line, the adventure in their hearts that night. In his absence I created him to my liking. He was mysterious and interesting.

Dear Jewel,

First....I am writing on a xxxxxxxtypewriter so as you can read what I am writing, and do not want you to take it as being impersonal.

I was not only surprised, but also quite pleased that after all this time you should want to get in touch with me, and hope that it does not end here//// To answer your question, if I have thought of you, the answer is yes, quite often. Would have answered sooner, but was out of town.....And that brings up another question of yours about what I am and what I do...What I am is a "Red Neck" and I am sure you have heard the xxxxx expression....I am a construction worker (heavy equip. operator) that travels quite a bit...as I must go where the work is.....was on the Alaska pipeline on and off for two years also....

As for my family (your brothers and sister) they are all in the Marine Corps at this time...and have included there pitcher, and also a pitcher of myself.....

I really can't think of to much to tell you xxxxxxxxa it is hard to talk about myself...and for that part, you more than likely know more about me than I about you....do feel free to tell me what you do and everything about yourself as I am very intrested....also curious if you are the same type person as I am.....meaning if you could belong to a redneck father. somehow I don't think that last part sounds like what I ment.....if you follow me....I think that what I am trying to ask, is are you "High Class" or just kind of like me...It still ///xx don't sound right......whatever I guess ...maybe you can figger out what I am trying to say......

Think I have said enough for now...hopeing to find you in good health...and pleased to hear from your absentee father.....

The Polaroid was so shiny I could see my reflection in it.

A close-up of my face with him standing behind it next to a red pickup truck. He was wearing a sleeveless T-shirt and his gut was hanging over the edge of his pants. His cap was pushed back off his forehead, his eyes were looking right at the camera, his jaw was square and dark from beard growth. Across the bottom of the picture, in quotes, it said, "Your Red Neck Father."

I had never expected him to write back.

The phone rang and when I asked who it was, the voice said, "You don't know who this is? This is your father." Well. We had a little chat and I was thinking, this is pretty strange. All friendly, he called me "Hon." I told him I never knew what to call him when I started to write him, Dear Who? That's why I hadn't written back yet. He told me I should call him Daddy. I called him Dad when I said goodbye.

"Bye Dad."

"He wants to meet me," I told my mother on the phone.

"He already met you once."

When I was six months old, supposedly he came to see me.

"You slept through the whole visit," my mother said. "Face down in the crib, with your ass in the air."

I pointed from behind glass to the man I recognized from the picture. I mouthed, "Are you my father?" He nodded. He looked like the picture but it was different seeing him for real. He was wearing the CAT cap and a denim shirt. I felt self-conscious in my high-heeled boots. We walked the length of the long see-through panel that separated arriving passengers from their waiting parties, and we kept nodding and sort of smiling, like people who don't speak the same language. Mostly we were endlessly walking trying to get beyond the glass wall.

He introduced me to his wife, who shook my hand and we followed the crowd to the carousel. He said to me, while we

waited for my baggage, "This is a weird experience, ain't it?"
I stood next to him not knowing him and said, "Yes."

Outside the terminal, it was dawn in Dallas. We would go
back to the motel and pick up their daughter Jane, who had
flown in the day before from a North Carolina Marine base to
make the drive home with them for Christmas. From Texas,
where he had just finished a job digging for oil, to Michigan,
which was home. I had come from San Francisco to Dallas,
would ride north with them as far as Chicago, then head east
to New Jersey to spend Christmas with my mother and
brothers and sisters.

I never expected to be meeting his wife and daughter too.
They were leery, but we were all polite while the dad hitched
the trailer to the back of his pickup and we stood around the
motel parking lot trying to be helpful. Then Jane and I climbed
in and sat on little stools behind the seat in the cab, with their
dog Rosie. The wife and my dad seated themselves in front.
We rode for a bunch of hours making conversation before we
stopped for breakfast, just over the state line.

December 19, 4pm Oklahoma

Jane and I are sharing a motel room tonight. She's
reading *Glamour* magazine on the bed next to me right
now. We're not doing that bad I guess, considering she's
a Marine and I'm a hippie and we're half sisters who have
never met. I get the impression they don't like hippies, and
San Francisco they call "Faggot Town." I'm trying right
now to just listen and take it all in, no point in rocking the
boat so early on. Since for Daddy and me this will be such
a short visit, we might as well try to be nice.

The dad knocked on the door just as I wrote, "try to be
nice" and handed me money to go buy beer at the liquor store
across the highway. Jane and I went together, but she waited
outside while I went in, because I was old enough and she was-
n't. The dad had said it was OK for her to drink a beer or two

because, "She'll have to learn how to handle it sooner or later."

We hung out drinking in the dad's room and I took some pictures of them. Jane with the Bud can raised to her lips, the dad and his wife not looking at me, and one of him alone in his denim shirt, the Bud on the table in the foreground, him scowling into the camera at me in the back. He didn't like me taking his picture, he thought my camera was "fruity-looking." I set the speeds by hand by focusing on the light in the room: late afternoon winter with the drapes drawn, green motel wall, colonial print bedspreads, shiny fake mahogany dresser, gilded framed mirror. Everything in the room was represented at least in part in that one picture, but it was focused on his unsmiling face.

Back in our room to get ready for dinner at the motel coffee shop, slightly tipsy, Jane and I stood in front of our own framed gilded mirror. She thought there ought to be some resemblance between us. But I was tall and long-jawed in the mirror and she was short standing next to me. Her face was round compared to my angular one. Her hair was striking blonde, mine brown. But pink rosy cheeks and narrow mouths we shared, and very light eyebrows. She wasn't wearing makeup and neither was I. I was wearing wire-rimmed glasses, though, and her eyes were sharp.

"Everyone in my family has good eyes," she said.

"Except for me."

We noticed ourselves standing there then, using the word family, and she sighed and walked to her suitcase, picked out her outfit for dinner and went into the bathroom to change.

The main thing that happened at dinner was I broke my glasses. The dad told me, "Serves you right for wearing such flaky glasses." He fixed them for me with black electrical tape, which of course looked totally stupid.

The other thing was, I ordered liver and bacon, which I had never done before.

•

The second day broke the ice. At first it wasn't anything they said directly, it was just the way the day was going. All morning Jane sat up front in the seat between them, and the dog and I watched out the windshield, past the backs of their heads. The road was straight as an arrow through that midwest section of the country, the sun hanging high over snow-covered prairies, corn fields and wheat. Heavy industry surrounded beltways around big cities, smokestacks making the sky gray and hazy, no view too far. The air was very cold outside the truck window and even the dog curled up with her nose between her paws. Up at dawn again, another day of driving, stopping only when the truck needed gas and to eat and pee. No sightseeing, except from inside the truck.

He's the one brought up my mother.

"How's your mother?"

I'm trying to decide what to tell him, in what order. "It's a long story, Dad." I want to say, but I don't, "Why didn't you stay around?"

But he hadn't really posed a question, he just wanted to give himself an opening for what he had planned to say.

The first had to do with his guilt: "My leaving was your mother's doing. I don't care what she told you." She had told me that they had lived together for two weekends, then she realized she didn't love him. She didn't know she was already pregnant with me.

"I never knew her, never loved her."

I decided that was said for his wife's benefit, because I couldn't imagine he believed that. I had to believe there was love in the story, at least on his side.

He was talking to me in the rearview mirror. "She was a flake from the start. Never the most well-behaved woman."

I didn't answer, just listened, meeting his eyes in the mirror. He was saying, "I only know what I know and I don't stutter." As he put the blinker on to get off the highway, he turned his face from the road toward me. "Your mother was a pig," he said to me.

"You don't even know my mother."

"You shouldn't have come if you didn't want to hear the truth."

Jane said, "You're being too rough, Daddy."

And that's when his wife said, "I knew it was better to let sleeping dogs lie."

I spent the lunch break in the truck-stop bathroom. By the time I returned to the truck, he had decided that dropping me off at the nearby airport in Champaign would be preferable to sticking it out all the way to Chicago. I told him that sounded good, "As long as you can pay the difference for what it costs to change your mind on such short notice."

I told the dad I was glad he had disappeared out of my life. "I hate to think how I would have turned out if you were really my father."

December 20, Champaign, Illinois

I think he has me confused with Mom in his mind. I'm the same age as Mom was the last time he saw her. So he only has me to tell, all the things he's wanted to say to her all these years. I don't know, maybe that's a simplification of an overly complex thing. I guess I can't understand why he doesn't like me, why we can't get along. What happened between him and my mother? How was I born if she never loved him and he never loved her?

Jane waited in the tiny terminal with me while they checked and confirmed my new reservations. When the dad came in wanting to know what it all cost, we followed him out to the truck and his wife wrote me a check for $150. He signed it. I thanked her and apologized. "I'm sorry, too," she said.

"It was nice meeting you," Jane said and hugged me.

My father shook my hand. The look we exchanged I would describe as, hard, but mingled with some kind of sadness.

"It's good we met anyway," he said, "so you have no illusions."

166

My Father's Darling

CAROLE L. GLICKFELD

Before Labor Day, Melva asked my father for some money to buy some clothes for school. I was sitting with the cards on the floor in the living room, playing war with myself, and I saw her follow him into the bedroom to ask. I didn't expect him to reach into his pocket and give her the money right away, but he did. So what did Melva do? She told him ten dollars wasn't enough, in sign language because he's deaf.

"Think me rich?" my father signed.

"You cheapskate," she signed right back, maybe because she couldn't help herself.

In two seconds flat he had her up against the wall and was twisting her arm behind her. I ran to get my mother from the kitchen. She couldn't hear Melva screaming because she's deaf, too. "Afraid break arm," my mother signed before she rushed to the bedroom.

When we got there, Melva was holding her arms crossed

167

in front of her face. My father was smacking the side of her head. He sounded like he had a terrible sore throat, yelling, "Honorfatherhonorfatherhonorfather."

My sister sank down to the floor when my father waved my mother away. "Misermisermiser," Melva said, but not in sign language, hardly moving her lips. Like one of those ventriloquists on Ed Sullivan.

My mother tried to stick her arms between my father and Melva, making noises like she was crying. When he turned around, I looked away because I knew what was coming. He pushed my mother so hard she fell down.

Melva didn't get to keep the ten dollars. "He'll get his," she told me. "Everyone gets what's coming to them." She told me it had to be true because she read it in the Old Testament. And then she cried.

After lunch my father said he was going for a walk. Melva was supposed to do the dishes but she said, "I'm getting out of this hell house." That meant she was going to see her best friend, Toni. So I said I'd do the drying. For some reason, Melva gave me a look like she could kill.

My mother filled up the deep sink with suds and put the dishes in. She rinsed them off in the little sink and handed them to me, one by one, until she stopped to talk to me. "Fine, fine, present necklace," she signed, and then she spelled out "M-r-s. K-l-e-p-p." (It can take a long time to sign and spell out everything, which is why you have to say things as short as possible.) My mother shook her head. She said all the deaf people were gossiping about the necklace. I guess that's how she found out. "Not think first o-w-n daughter," she said.

"Daddy present M-r-s K-l-e-p-p?" I asked. "Why?"

She scrunched up her face like she was going to cry. "Clever, try make like. Understand?" She said my father was probably going to see her on his walk.

I nodded. I didn't really understand why my father was trying to get Mrs. Klepp to like him. She was deaf and lived over on the next block from us.

168

My mother put her hands in the soapy water. When she took them out to sign again, she sprayed me. "Sorry," she said, taking the dish towel to brush off some suds from my hair. "Think high c-l-a-s-s. Real t-r-a-m-p."

A tramp was what Melva called the girls in her high school who smoked in the bathroom. I knew Mrs. Klepp was always smoking, but I don't think that's what my mother meant.

"D-o-n-t tell M-e-l-v-a, S-i-d-n-e-y," she said.

Even though Melva and Sidney were much older than me, my mother talked to me like I knew better than they did.

"Shhh," I told her, hearing the key in the outside door.

My father stuck his head in the kitchen but didn't say anything. I heard him go into the living room where he always took his afternoon nap.

My mother smiled a funny smile. "B-e-t no one home," she said, about Mrs. Klepp.

The next Sunday, when we were all having dinner in the kitchen, my brother asked my father for money to get a catcher's mitt so he could play on the Sluggers. That was the team that was sponsored by O'Hanlon's Tavern on Nagle Avenue.

My father dropped his fork and knife down on his plate on purpose. "N-o play b-u-m-s, Catholic," he signed.

"Not b-u-m-s," my brother signed back. "J-u-s-t play baseball."

"Catholic, no good," my father said, getting a very angry look on his face.

Melva did her ventriloquist act again. Without moving her lips, she said, "Sidney, take it easy."

But by that time my brother was real angry. "I-f Catholic no good, why you friend M-r-s K-l-e-p-p?"

Right away my mother tried to tell my father that Sidney didn't mean what he said. My father told her not to butt in. He told Sidney to go to the bathroom. That meant he was going to get a strapping. For a few seconds we all sat there like stone.

"Go!" my father yelled in his hoarse voice. As he got up he banged his fist down on the table, hard enough to make the plates jump. My mother stood up in front of him but he pushed her down in the chair. He grabbed Sidney by the arm and pushed him toward the door. A few seconds later my mother went running out of the kitchen after them.

"Why did Sidney say that?" I asked Melva.

"He saw them go into a movie together. Downtown. But don't tell Mama. It would hurt her feelings."

"Why does Daddy like Mrs. Klepp?"

"She's a tramp," Melva said.

When we heard Sidney screaming, we went in the living room. We could even hear the belt every time my father hit him. My mother was crying outside the bathroom door.

"I could murder him," Melva said. "He doesn't deserve to live."

I went back into the kitchen and put my hands over my ears.

That night I heard my father come home from the U.L., which is short for Union League of the Deaf, where he went to play cards on Saturdays and some afternoons before going to work at the post office. I would wake up sometimes when he came home and listen to him go through his routine. I could hear him hang up his jacket in the hallway closet and open and close the frigidaire before he sat down in the kitchen to read the *Daily News* with a snack, probably pumpernickel with prune butter, which was his favorite. I saw him once through the hallway mirror, but he didn't see me watching him, and he couldn't hear me, of course.

After he got done in the kitchen, I heard him praying outside the room I shared with Melva, beneath the mezuzah. He made smacking sounds. I knew he was kissing his palm and then the shiny gold case that my sister explained has the parchment with writings from the Bible. I could even hear him mumbling in Hebrew. He made more smacking sounds before he went into the bathroom. Like always, I heard the toilet flush and the sink water running for a long, long time (which I could never figure out), then his footsteps back past our room and into the bedroom where my mother was already sleeping.

"Do you think he was sorry?" I asked my make-believe-friend Mary, who was lying next to me. Mary said if he was really sorry he would stop making everyone so miserable.

"I hate him," I told her.

Mary said that was terrible, especially after how nice he was to me. I was the only one who didn't get into trouble with him. I told her that when she was bigger she would understand, and then she fell asleep. I tried to think of something to do that would make my family happier but I fell asleep before I thought of anything.

On Saturday morning I went roller-skating. Robin Reinstein and Tommy Shanahan came around the corner with me, so we could skate in the street without anyone seeing, but at the last minute Robin got chicken and stayed on the sidewalk, so it was just Tommy and me, out in the middle of Sherman Avenue. The street is a lot smoother than the scratchy sidewalk and doesn't have all those cracks, so it's a lot more fun to skate.

I was coming down real fast toward Arden when I heard my brother's booming voice calling, "Ruthie!" I stopped so fast I fell, and before I could get up I heard a car screeching on its brakes just a few inches from where I was. The next thing I knew, my brother lifted me right up and put me down on the sidewalk where Melva was. They were both dressed up because they had just come from Temple.

"What the hell are you doing in the street?" Sidney yelled, so that everyone could hear, including Tommy Shanahan. When Tommy saw me looking at him, he disappeared around the corner of Arden Street. Robin was gone by then.

"Daddy would kill you if he saw," Sidney said.

"Her? He wouldn't lay a finger on her," Melva said. "She's her father's darling. Aren't you!" she said, smiling real sarcastic like.

"I don't ask for trouble," I said. "That's why I'm around the corner."

"Well if I ever see you skate in the street again . . ." Sidney threatened, but he didn't finish because when I looked down at my knee and saw it was all bloody I started to cry. "Go upstairs and put iodine on," he said.

I skated ahead of them, took off my skates, and ran upstairs. My father woke up from his nap and came in the kitchen while my mother was putting Mercurochrome on, since iodine hurts so much. I told him I fell skating, but not where.

"You not watch right," he said to my mother, practically standing over her.

"Can't know what d-o-i-n-g, every minute," she said to him. She put the Band-Aid on my knee.

"Not f-i-t mother," he told her.

"Why me, me? You never watch," she said. "A-l-l t-i-m-e me."

I got out of there and went to tell Mary what happened. She said it wasn't my fault, and then my father came in.

"Want go U-L with me?" he asked.

"Now?"

He hadn't taken me to his club for a long time. I always liked going, especially because of the subway ride downtown. I said okay.

"First change dress," he said, because he liked me to look nice when I went with him.

He dressed up, too, in his brown suit. I saw him brushing his hair with the brush my Aunt Lois gave him for his birthday. It had a real silver back. He combed his mustache with the matching comb. His hair in both places was strawberry blonde, like in the song my brother liked to sing about this man Casey waltzing.

When we got to the U.L., which is in the basement of a hotel on 72nd Street, my father acted very different. He waved hello to everyone, real friendly, with a big smile. He was very handsome when he smiled, my mother said. The room was smoky on account of the cigarettes and cigars from the men who sat at the folding tables playing cards, waving their arms as they signed and making grunting noises. There were only a few women. They looked up when my father took me a-round. The deaf people always asked the same questions. This time it was Mr. Fiorini who asked, "Can sign?" meaning me.

"A-s-k," my father said, meaning he should ask me, so he did.

"I can sign," I told him.

"Wonderful!" Mr. Fiorini said.

I never knew why they thought it was such a big deal that I could sign, just because I could hear. My father looked aw-fully happy.

We went over to a table where Mr. Weisbaum, Max Cohen, and Mrs. Klepp were sitting right under a fluorescent light, the kind with the long tubes. Mr. Weisbaum was wearing his yarmulke, of course. He and my father made jokes in Hebrew, which I didn't understand. They said the Hebrew out loud (I don't know if you can even sign in Hebrew), reading each other's lips. Both of them were bar mitzvahed, which my Uncle Sol said was really something, because they were deaf.

Max Cohen and my father went to the horse races together sometimes. Max Cohen bet a lot, my mother said, and was always in trouble with his wife, Mrs. Cohen. One year he didn't go to the U.L. because he was in Florida, hiding from the bookies.

Mrs. Klepp was one of the few women who went to the U.L. She got in because her husband was a member, but Mr. Klepp wasn't there. "How g-a-m-e?" she asked my father, meaning baseball.

"Not hear," my father said, meaning no one had told him the score. When Sidney was home, he listened to the game on the radio and told my father what was happening.

As Mrs. Klepp signed, smoke came up from the cigarette hanging out the side of her mouth. When the cigarette was between her fingers, smoke came all around us, because she waved her arms a lot.

"You millionaire," my father teased her, about the money she spent on cigarettes.

"Me win poker, can a-f-f-o-r-d smoke all day," she said, and then they both laughed.

I never saw my father laugh at home. He sat down at the table and I sat on a chair next to him and watched Max Cohen deal the cards. I knew a little about poker but not enough to play. I looked over Mrs. Klepp's clothes. She had on a beige cardigan and a black straight skirt, like a high school girl. My mother wore dresses with flowers on them, unless they were pastels. She said Mrs. Klepp was a show-off, but I couldn't figure out what she meant, unless it was the high heels.

After a while I got up and went to the buffet table to get a slice of American cheese, which I ate real fast. My father didn't like me to eat it without bread, for some reason. Mrs. Jacobs got some paper and pens for me to draw with from the office. I wasn't very good at drawing, so I wrote a story about a boy and his dog. The dog runs away, so his father hits him and says it's the boy's fault, but later the father buys him another dog. I knew my father wouldn't ask me to show it to him.

At four-thirty my father had to leave to go to the post office. He wanted Mrs. Klepp to walk him to the subway but she wanted to play more poker, so she stayed. I had to stay, too, since she was taking me home.

They got a sub for my father in the game, Mr. Fiorini. He teased me about being a great poker player like my father. "A-l-b-e-r-t b-e-s-t," he said. "Me g-l-a-d he leave."

I saw my father take all the coins off the table, so I knew he'd won.

When they were done playing, Mrs. Klepp lit up a cigarette. She asked me, "How brother?" and when I said fine, "How sister?" Then she wanted to know what my mother was doing that afternoon. I shrugged.

I thought we were going to leave when she got up, but she had me walk her over to another table, where Mrs. Gertzner was. She was a friend of my mother's although we didn't see her very often. She lived in Brooklyn, near the Steeplechase, with a blind and deaf husband. He could read the sign language by feeling your hand when you signed. My mother said Mrs. Gertzner went to the U.L. to get away from her worries.

Mrs. Gertzner asked me how my mother was. "Home?"

"Fine," I told her. "Ironing."

Mrs. Klepp said, "R-u-t-h my daughter. See, same dimples. Me her mother."

Mrs. Gertzner said, "You wish."

"You fresh?" Mrs. Klepp asked.

"You hungry A-l-b-e-r-t," Mrs. Gertzner said, meaning my father.

Then Mrs. Klepp said, "I smack your face."

"D-a-r-e," Mrs. Gertzner spelled out slowly. "You d-a-r-e."

And Mrs. Klepp did. Mrs. Gertzner smacked her back. Then they started pulling each other's hair and clothes, until the men stopped them. Then Mrs. Klepp took me home.

On the subway ride to Dyckman Street, Mrs. Klepp told me how fresh Anna Gertzner was. "You see yourself. Fresh. Say me hungry A-l-b-e-r-t."

"Maybe true," I signed, suddenly feeling like I couldn't breathe. My heart was pounding so fast I could hear it over the roar of the train.

"You fresh," she said. "I tell your father."

"I tell my mother," I said, looking right into her eyes, which were like blue marbles.

We went the rest of the way without signing.

When I got home, I wanted to tell Melva, but I decided not to, so I told Mary. She said I should apologize to God for being fresh, and I did. I said that if He didn't let Mrs. Klepp tell my father about it, I'd do good things for people when I grew up, like become a nurse.

The next Saturday my father said he couldn't take me to the U.L. because Mrs. Klepp had a dentist appointment, so there wouldn't be anyone to take me home. I nodded, trying not to show him how happy I was, but I felt like bursting. He looked at me real funny. For a second I wondered if he could read my mind, like he was God.

Behind his back I shouted, "Mrs. Klepp is ugly and stupid!"

My father turned around very suddenly. That really scared me, but he didn't say anything. I started to skip out of the room. "She's ugly and stupid!" I shouted again.

"Ruth!" he roared, real loud. He only yelled that loud when he was very angry. When I turned, I saw him waving at me to come back. I crossed my toes and walked slowly toward him. He reached into his pants pocket and took out a quarter and gave it to me. A nickel was what he usually gave me on Saturdays.

"You love father?" he asked.

I nodded.

"Show me."

I threw my arms around him and hugged him. He gave me a kiss that made a big smacking sound on my cheek. "You good girl," he said.

I took the quarter and put it under my blouses in the dresser drawer, then got my skates. Tommy Shanahan was already on the stoop when I got there. He dared me to skate Nagle.

"You're crazy," I told him. "You can get killed on Nagle from all the trucks."

So we went around the corner and skated Sherman Avenue until eleven-thirty, which is when Sidney and Melva got out of Temple.

On Monday, when I was coming home from school, I saw a police car in front of the stoop. When I got almost to the fourth landing, there was a policeman standing in our doorway. Next to him I saw my father and then another policeman in the foyer, and my mother holding a bloody handkerchief over her nose. The cops seemed very glad I was there to interpret.

"Ask your mother if she wants to press charges," one cop said.

I made the sign for "press" like in "iron" and "charges"

like in "price." I knew that made no sense, but I didn't know what "press charges" meant.

My mother stopped crying. She signed, "Go jail."

"I think my mother wants him to go to jail," I said, not looking at my father and trying not to move my mouth very much, so he couldn't lip-read me.

He looked pretty sick when they made signs like he had to come with them. I grabbed onto his leg. "I'm sorry," the policeman said to me when he took my hands off.

When they left, my mother told me how my father had pushed her down on the kitchen floor and beaten her up. She thought our neighbor, Mrs. Cafferty, must of called the police.

"Who s-u-p-p-o-r-t me and the children?" she kept saying. Then she answered her own question. "S-t-a-r-v-e," she said, meaning we'd all starve with my father in jail. I couldn't help crying. I was afraid I'd never see him anymore.

When my brother came home from working in the cleaners, my mother told him to go to the police station and get my father. "Change mind," she said to tell the police.

"Sonofabitch," Sidney said. "It's one thing when he picks on me, but using his fists on a woman . . ."

While he was gone, Melva came home from baby-sitting. "Oh, God!" she said when she saw my mother's swollen face and the bruises on her arm. "Stay jail," she told my mother. "He should rot there," she said to me. "He deserves to die for every rotten thing he's done."

My brother came back alone. He told my mother that after my father got out of jail he decided to go to the U.L.

"Funny, not work," my mother said.

Then Sidney called the post office to tell them Mr. Zimmer had a toothache and to charge it to sick leave.

We all sat around the kitchen table after that. My mother was knitting a sweater for me. Sidney had the *Daily Mirror* open in front of him on the table but he wasn't really reading it. Melva was saying terrible things about my father and sometimes she'd start to cry, which made me cry.

"Sonofabitch," my brother said again. "I could kill him. Just pick up a knife and let him have it while he's asleep. He'd never hear me coming."

"Sidney!" Melva said. "You better ask God to forgive you."

When my mother asked what we were talking about, all Melva said was "Daddy." Melva told Sidney and me she should be the one to kill him, though, because they weren't so tough on girls. "They might put me in reform school for a while," she said, "but you'd have to go to jail." She meant Sidney.

That's when I got the idea. They would never suspect me if I did it. For one thing, I wasn't a grown-up. For another, I was my father's darling.

That night I woke up when I heard the double locks open on the outside door. Mary and I lay in the dark, listening, while my father went through his whole routine, kissing the mezuzah on the door, leaving the sink water running, and then going to bed. I told Mary not to worry, and then I got up real carefully, so as not to wake Melva, who's a real light sleeper. I didn't have to worry about waking up Sidney. I could hear him snoring as I went past his hide-a-bed in the living room on the way to the kitchen.

My mother came in while I was looking through the kitchen drawer for the big knife. I forgot that the light always wakes her up. It shines into the hallway mirror and into her bedroom.

"What d-o-i-n-g?" she asked me.

"Hungry," I said. "Make sandwich."

"Big girl," she said, but she made the sandwich for me, shmeering some peanut butter on rye bread.

After I ate it, we both went back to bed. I thought a lot about what to do next time. It got light out before I fell asleep.

The next day was Rosh Hashanah. My mother made a big dinner, with chicken soup and matzo balls and potato pancakes. She and my father weren't speaking, though. Her eye was still swollen and there was a little scar under her nose.

After dinner my father didn't go to work because of the holiday. He and my Uncle Sol went to the Orthodox synagogue. Sidney and Melva went to the Reform. My mother and I hung out the window. When she went to the bathroom, I ran and got the knife from the kitchen and put it under my pillow.

As soon as she came back to the window, she asked, "What wrong?"

"Nothing," I told her.

"Devil?" she said.

"No," I said, but she looked like she didn't believe me.

It was hard staying awake after everyone went to bed. I told Mary a lot of stories I remembered from the books I read from the 207th Street Library. When I heard my sister breathing like she was asleep, I took the knife out from under the pillow and went to the other bedroom. I had to stand in the doorway a while, until I could see in the dark, then I went over to the bed.

My heart was pounding so loud that I thought I might have a heart attack and die. I told myself to hurry and get it over with. I jabbed the knife in my father's back, over his pajama top. Nothing happened, except he made some funny sounds before he started his regular snore. I tried harder. This time my father jerked and his arm slapped my mother, who woke up. She saw me right away. I dropped the knife on the floor and kicked it under the bed before she came around to where I was. "Sick?" she asked me.

"Headache," I told her, but she couldn't see what I said, so we went over to the window where there was moonlight. I signed, "Headache," again.

We went to the bathroom and got a Bayer's. In the kitchen she looked in the drawer for the big knife to cut it in half. "Funny, gone," she said. She used another one and gave me half to take. "Go bed," she said. "Me stay read. Can't sleep, think too much A-l-b-e-r-t."

On my way back I remembered that my mother dusted with the mop every morning under her bed, so I couldn't leave the knife there. I went to get it, but I couldn't see where it was in the dark. While I was down on my knees feeling around, my father got up. I rolled all the way under the bed, practically dying. When he went to the bathroom, I grabbed the knife and ran back to the bedroom. I could hardly breathe I was so scared.

After he flushed the toilet, I heard him go through the living room. I put the knife under my pillow and went to the hallway just outside the kitchen and peeked in the mirror.

My father was kissing my mother. Real kissing. On the lips, which I'd never seen him do. He was bending her slightly back over the kitchen table. Their arms were around each other, like in the movies. For a second I thought he might be trying to smother her, but then they stood up straight.

"Bed?" my father asked her.

My mother nodded.

He started walking out of the kitchen. Just before she pulled the light cord, I saw her stick her tongue out at his back.

I ran for dear life through the living room and almost squashed Mary when I jumped into bed. In a little while I heard funny noises coming from the other bedroom. I was scared my father was beating my mother again, but I didn't hear her crying or anything. I put the pillow over my head and Mary's and we fell asleep.

In the morning my mother was in the kitchen, so I couldn't put the knife back. I hid it in the dresser drawer where I kept the quarter my father had given me. When I came home from school, my mother was ironing my father's shirts.

"Make u-p," she said, meaning she made up with my father. She was smiling kind of funny.

I wondered how come. "Daddy pray sorry?" I asked her.

She shrugged. "Brother uncle advise," she said, meaning my Uncle Sol had told my father to do it. "Not believe pray."

"Not believe G-o-d?" I asked her, to make sure.

"Good teach children, that a-l-l."

"S-i-n not believe," I told her, which is what Melva had told me.

"Shh," she said, placing a finger over her lips. "N-o tell Daddy."

I put a finger over my lips.

She gave me a shirt of my father's to hang up. Carefully, I buttoned the top button, like she taught me once. "You very d-a-r-l-i-n-g. A-l-b-e-r-t l-u-c-k-y," she said.

I burst out crying but I wouldn't tell her why.

"You sorry see me hurt," she said, pointing to the large reddish purple mark on her upper arm. "D-o-n-t worry, will better," she said, telling me that she and my father were going to the movies later and my sister would baby-sit me. Then she squeezed me against her soft round belly and big bust.

Later I got the knife back into the kitchen drawer, but I couldn't figure out what to do with the quarter. Mary said I should give it back because I didn't deserve it.

On Yom Kippur, when everyone was in Temple except my mother, who was hanging out the window to see what people were wearing, I did something I'd never done before. I kissed the mezuzah. It wasn't easy, because it was way up high on the doorjamb. I had to jump up a couple of times to reach it and I didn't know the right prayer. I told God I was sorry and that if He could forgive my father, maybe He could forgive my mother, too, because she didn't mean Him any harm. I was going to promise not to skate in the street anymore, but at the last minute I thought of something better. I told God I would bury the quarter in the garden. If it was still there on my next birthday, that would mean I was supposed to have it.

"Hungry o-r f-a-s-t?" my mother asked when I went to the window.

"F-a-s-t," I said. "You?"

She nodded.

"Why? You not believe."

"You devil, t-o-o nosey," she said, but I could tell she wasn't angry or anything.

After I got dressed I went down to the stoop and climbed over the wrought-iron on top of the little brick wall around the garden. I buried the quarter in the ground where we fed the sparrows sometimes, between the middle two bushes, four steps from the building.

As I was climbing out, my father came up the stoop. "Why there?" he asked.

"Play," I said.

"Not play today. Religious holiday," he said.

Behind him, Melva and Sidney were walking up the first level. Sidney was in his good suit and Melva was wearing a coat she got secondhand from our Cousin Rona in New Jersey. But she had on her new shoes, with high heels and straps across, like Mrs. Klepp's.

"What me say?" my father signed to me, real gruff.

"Uh oh, she's gonna get hers," Melva said, loud so I could hear.

"Not play," I said. "Sorry," I told him.

When my father started coming toward me, Sidney rushed up. I guess he thought my father was going to hit me, but all he did was kiss me on the forehead. Melva gave me this look, like she was real disgusted.

My father turned and saw them. His face got all cranky. "Not think sister, bring Temple," he said to them, meaning they should've taken me with them to synagogue. I could see Sidney getting angry back. "Jesus Christ!" he said out loud.

"Be careful," I told them, without moving my lips.

"Shut up!" Melva said to me, without moving hers. "We know what side you're on."

By this time my father was yelling so that everyone on the stoop could hear him. I kept my eyes on the ground, even though I could feel Melva looking daggers at me. Later she would do an imitation of us talking like ventriloquists and Sidney would imitate my father yelling and we'd all get hysterical, but right then I stood there with my face burning, wishing myself dead.

Colors

SYLVIA A. WATANABE

"Last night I dreamed," Little Grandma said, laying half of a purple hula girl next to an orange flying fish. "I dreamed I saw the hungry ghosts coming home across the sea."

Little Grandma was always having dreams. She said the spirits of our kin watched from the shrine on her bedroom dresser and spoke to her while she was sleeping. She said they told her when to go down to the beach to harvest seaweed, and where to hunt when Cousin Makoto misplaced his store teeth, and what chicken to bet on at the chicken fights.

The silver pins glinted in her hands as she laid the patchwork triangles, one by one, into the shapes of stars. The gold cap on her front tooth gleamed. "In my dream, it was dark. There was no sun, no moon, no pinpoint of light in the entire sky."

The scent of Three Flowers Brilliantine and stale urine drifted toward me from where Papa sat dozing in his lawn chair. His head was leaning to one side and there was a large damp spot where he had drooled onto the front of his shirt.

I smoothed the blank surface of my sketchpad and chose an oil crayon from the box on my lap.

"Then, suddenly," Little Grandma continued, "a hole opened somewhere on the other side of the darkness. And it opened, and opened, and opened. . . ."

"We get the picture," Aunt Pearlie said, looking up from her newspaper. She gestured at the article she'd been reading. Increase in Sex Crimes, the headline said. "Nothing's sacred anymore. A woman's not safe in her own bed — not even here in this very village."

Aunt Pearlie was a member of the Jodo Mission Ladies Auxiliary and took an active interest in the moral affairs of the community. There was no better post for carrying out this surveillance work than my grandmother's front yard, which was located halfway between the Buddhist temple and the Paradise Mortuary, at the center of the village social scene. Every morning, after sending her husband Emigdio off to the sugar mill, Aunt Pearlie set out for Little Grandma's where she spent the day "seeing to things."

"Just the other morning," she continued now, "I was talking to Emi McAllister over at the Koyama Store."

Little Grandma got up and threw her shawl lightly across Papa's shoulders. "Koshiro," she whispered. "You're going to catch cold, if you sleep with your mouth open."

He mumbled something in his sleep, but didn't wake.

Aunt Pearlie raised her voice. "And Emi told me that she'd heard that the Laundry Burglar is on the loose again."

Little Grandma settled back in her chair, then turned to me. "Where was I, Hana?"

Pearlie hugged herself and rubbed her upper arms with her hands. "It makes my blood run cold — to think of Someone Like That sneaking around our backyards and doing god knows what to our clean laundry."

Grandma ignored her. "Hana, do you remember?"

"Oh, Mama," Pearlie almost shouted. "Something about a hole in the sky, for Pete's sake. Besides which, if it were as dark as you say, how did you even know where the sky was?"

"Because I was *standing up*." Little Grandma laid down her piecing and looked out across the bay. "Then, as the sky opened, colors came pouring out of it — until there were colors where there'd only been darkness before."

"Then, what?" I asked.

"Then, I woke up."

"What?" Pearlie said.

"That's all."

"What kind of a dream is that?"

Little Grandma serenely resumed her piecing. Each movement fit into the next, like a perfectly-made seam. "It wasn't just a dream. It's how the hungry ghosts come home every year at festival time."

Aunt Pearlie pressed her lips together and frowned at her newspaper.

I watched the cloud shadows moving across the sugar fields. Land curving into sea into sky. Up the road, the gate to the temple stood open, revealing the preparations for O-bon, the annual festival of the dead, going on inside. Workmen hammered at the musician's platform in the center of the yard and strung electric wiring from wooden poles stuck into the ground. Two men drove up in a pickup and began unloading the striped canvas tenting for the concession booths.

Every year, on the first night of the festival season, Little Grandma faithfully put out the ritual servings of ghost food and wine to welcome the spirits of our dead kin. "Here is some wine," she'd say, offering a cup of sake, each, to the photograph of my grandfather, a solemn old gentleman in top hat and formal black kimono, and to that of my mother, who was killed in a car accident when I was three. Then on the last night, when it was time for the spirits to leave, she lighted a paper lantern and walked them down to the sea.

Now, Papa sat up and rubbed his eyes.

185

I rose to go to him, spilling the crayons in my lap onto the grass. Aunt Pearlie waved at me to sit down, then stood and held out her hands to him. "Come, Koshiro. It's time to wash up."

"I'm hungry," he said.

She smoothed his hair with a perfunctory, businesslike gesture, then helped him to his feet. "First, we must wash; then, we will have some cake and juice."

My grandmother smiled as we watched them walk hand in hand toward the house.

The week before, Aunt Pearlie had called me in New York. I hadn't spoken to her or to my grandmother since my husband Ben and I had separated a little over a month before. Grandmother had never approved of him — more on principle than for any personal reason ("Far places never give back what they take away") — and I did not feel equipped to stand up to her knowing, long distance silences.

The phone rang again. It was five in the morning, according to the clock radio next to the bed. Even half-asleep, I missed Ben's warmth beside me, the murmur of his sleepy protests in the dark.

"Hana, where have you been, oh my God," Aunt Pearlie's excited voice came over the line.

I sat up, yawning. "Is something wrong?"

"Did I wake you? I forgot about the time. Actually, I would never have called, but I've just come from Grandma's, and, you know how she is. She won't listen to me. You've got to come home."

I struggled to grasp what she was not saying. It took too much effort. "Well, it's not exactly like crossing the street. Can you give me some idea what all this is about?"

A note of satisfaction crept into her voice. "This evening, the Director of the Aloha Lani Nursing Home called me, just as your Uncle Emigdio and I had settled in front of the T.V. set. We always watch Bonus Bingo on Tuesday nights."

"Go on, go on. Is it Papa? Has something happened to Papa?" My father had been staying at the Home ever since Grandma had fallen and sprained her hip the previous summer.

"According to the Director, your grandmother came by, as she always did, to feed him dinner and take him for a little walk. But at lights out, when they checked his bed, he still hadn't been returned. So that's when the Director called me, and I rushed over to Grandma's. She's stolen your papa out of that place and won't give him back."

I began to be annoyed. "If she wants him with her, I don't see any problem in letting him stay."

"That's not the point." Aunt Pearlie sighed; I was obviously not grasping the Situation. "We're not talking about what people *want*. The point is, your father's condition is getting worse, and he needs to be where they can take proper care of him. Mother listens to *you;* you're the only one who can explain that to her."

I knew there was almost no talking my grandmother out of any course she was determined to follow, but I was worried about my father. The next day, I took a leave of absence from the design studio where I worked, closed my apartment, and caught a red-eye flight from Kennedy.

It had been a couple of years since I was last home, when Ben and I came at Christmas together. He found the tropical heat oppressive, but accompanied me, uncomplaining, on my occasional visits. For five days or a week, he read spy novels set in snowy climates and obligingly baked brown in the sun. Most Christmases, I strapped on snowshoes to keep up with him. We usually vacationed in the cold, pursuing wildlife, with binoculars slung around our necks.

"Look Hana!" he'd cry, in the middle of a frozen field, as I struggled to meet his long strides, and he'd point to the snow spirits twisting off the trees into the wind.

Later, I'd tell Little Grandma about it over the telephone. "Today, I saw the snow spirits dance."

"The dead are everywhere," she'd say. "When are you coming home?"

This time when I returned, I saw that Pearlie had not been exaggerating; Papa's illness was much worse. He was often still lucid, but needed help dressing and feeding himself. He rarely spoke. In the past four years, the "forgetting sickness," as Little Grandma called it, had stolen the names of things from him.

His luminous, unfinished canvasses gathered dust along the walls of his studio. In the sunny corner where he once worked, his easel still looked toward the window; a brush tipped with vermillion lay across the square of plexiglass he had used as a palette. I remembered the sound of his voice, guiding my hands, as I learned to mix colors. "How do you make red redder?" he'd ask. "How many different kinds of black can you see?"

Aunt Pearlie pushed the door open and came into the room; she was carrying her handbag and sweater. For a while, we stood side by side without saying anything, though I felt her looking at me. She tentatively reached out her hand and dropped it again. "Your Uncle Emigdio will have a fit if I'm not home to get his supper," she said, and left.

That night I dreamed again of the snow. The dream never changed. In it, I was crossing a vast snowy field with no trees, or landmarks, or colors for as far as I could see in any direction. With each step, I sank farther into the deep, white drifts — first to my ankles, then to my knees, and finally, up to my hips. As I struggled to get free — quietly, quietly, it began to snow.

I woke, as usual, heart racing. For a moment, I imagined I was back in New York with Ben and almost turned to pull his arms around me. Then, I recognized the mahogany toy cabinet with the china tea set sitting on top, the red wooden child's rocker, my father's paintings of birds and animals upon the walls. Here and there in the moonlight, a tangerine-colored bear or a lavender parrot sprang from the shadows.

The sound of Papa's snoring came from his bedroom down the hall, and I thought of how he was in the days when he made those paintings.

"Come see!" I could hear him calling, as I slipped in and out of wakefulness. "Oh, Hana, come see!" And once again, I was running toward the sound. But as I drew close, and he turned to me, he had Ben's face, Ben's voice. "Look there," he said, pointing to a crown flower hedge alive with monarch butterflies, a mango tree where a mother cardinal was teaching her babies how to fly.

"*Akai tori, ko tori,*" Little Grandma was singing upstairs in the attic. "Red bird, little red bird, why are you so red?" As she paused for breath, I could hear the crisp sound of her sewing shears, snipping patchwork.

"We'll all be in a nursing home before she finishes that thing," Aunt Pearlie said the next afternoon, as we sat at the kitchen table, eating slices of chilled mango and looking out the window at Little Grandma and Papa under the poinsiana tree. "She's been at that same quilt for the past hundred years, I'd swear."

"But we can't *make* her take him back," I said.

"We can't go on like this — that's what we can't do. Besides, what'll Ben think, you being gone so long?"

I reached for another slice of mango and took a bite. "He'll manage, I guess."

"But that's not the point, Hana."

It's not that I don't love you.

"I feel bad, we all feel bad about your Papa."

But a person needs space.

"Life goes on, after all!" Aunt Pearlie cried.

The morning light flickered across the walls. The contours of the room shifted, as the boundaries between shapes melted, and colors slid away into shadow.

"If Mama were by herself, she could sell this place and

come stay with me."

Everything was sliding, sliding. I rubbed my eyes and struggled to focus better.

"You know the Japanese investment company that built the hotel across the bay? Well, one of their representatives dropped by the other day. He said they were interested in buying all the land around this area to make a golf course to go with the resort. . . ."

She sounded as if she were talking about coordinating fashion accessories.

". . . It will cost $1,000,000 a year to be a member. A company like that has got to make a pretty good offer, if you know what I mean."

Outside, the gate squeaked open. Emi McAllister, our next-door neighbor, was coming up the walk. She was carrying what looked like a dish or tray wrapped in a brown grocery bag.

"What's she got there?" Aunt Pearlie reached for the spectacles in her apron pocket and put them on. "Hmmm. Probably some of that brown fudge that sticks to the roof of your mouth." She started for the door. "Or a bunch of those hard little puffed rice cakes."

Emi stopped to talk to Little Grandma, then looked up and waved to Aunty.

"Oh, rice cakes," Aunt Pearlie said, taking the bag as Emi came up the front porch steps into the house.

"Just a little welcome home for Hana." Emi smiled at me. "Your Papa's looking fine."

"You think so? I guess."

"Well, he's not fine." Aunt Pearlie offered the dish of cakes to Emi. "I've been trying to talk some sense into this girl. She's as bad as her grandmother."

"I didn't say he shouldn't go back," I protested. "I said we couldn't force Grandma into taking him."

Emi waved the cakes aside. "Never touch the stuff, too

hard on my old teeth." She patted my hand. "Things going badly, huh?"

Aunt Pearlie frowned. "So, Emi, how're you doing? What's the latest on the Laundry Burglar?"

During the last several summers, the village had been plagued by brief outbreaks of laundry burglaries which never followed any particular pattern and never went on for more than two or three weeks at a time. In the past, missing items had included the scarf from Emi's gardening hat, a pair of Doc McAllister's running shorts, the pink rose from Cousin Missy's scholarship dress. Nothing, however, had ever been found missing from Aunt Pearlie's wash.

"Mrs. Koyama says the dancing school teacher is missing her white satin night cap." Emi reached for a slice of mango. "Everyone knows that woman wears a wig."

"It's disgraceful that this situation has been allowed to go on for so long!" Aunt Pearlie interrupted. "Who knows what a twisted mind like that will do next?"

"You have to admit, he hasn't done much of anything in the last four or five years," Emi pointed out.

"He's probably just testing the waters, that's all. We've been lulled into a false sense of security."

Emi put the last of the mango into her mouth. "It's true, no one can ever really know what anyone else is thinking."

"It's about time the police began doing their jobs."

Emi sighed. "From what I hear, the sheriff doesn't have much to go on. The burglaries always stop before any real clues turn up."

"Meantime, what's a person to do? You don't know how I worry. I can't be here with Mother twenty four hours a day."

Emi clucked sympathetically.

"Look at this place." Aunt Pearlie gestured around her. "It's just too much — especially after she sprained her hip last summer. And with Brother the way he is, you've got to keep your eye on him every minute."

"That's odd." Emi was looking out the window.

"It's more than odd!"

Emi turned to Aunt Pearlie and motioned toward the front yard. "I was just talking to your mother out there a minute ago."

The quilting mat was still spread out under the poinsiana, but the wind had blown the cover off a shoebox full of piecing and was scattering the bright scraps across the grass. Neither Little Grandma nor Papa was anywhere to be seen.

While Aunt Pearlie was checking with the neighbors, Little Grandma came limping up the road to the house. "Hurry," she called. "Call Sheriff Kanoi. Ko-chan has run away."

On a hunch, I slipped away to the beach, while Aunt Pearlie got on the phone to the police. In my childhood, Papa had taken me out to the point almost every weekend in fine weather. At first, he brought along his painting things, but he always forgot the time as he stood working on his canvas, and we ended up staying out too long. Once, he lost an easel when he tried to cross back to shore as the tide was coming in. After that, we took walks to the point "just to look," as Little Grandma put it.

We watched for whales in winter — each of us vying to be first to spot the beautiful white plumes of spray rising above the waves. He taught me how to identify the schools of fish, flashing just beneath the surface of the water. A green flash for *manini*. Silver for *papio*.

"Papa!" I called now, scanning the rocks and tidal pools along the shore. The sky and sea were the color of fire. A wave broke over the lava shelf and came swirling around my ankles. I had to hurry. The tide was rising and the way to the point would soon be under water.

Then, I saw him. A speck of white at the end of the point. I picked my way across the jagged rocks, the waves crashing higher and higher, until I was wading through knee-deep water toward him. "You've scared us all to death," I scolded, as I pulled myself up beside him.

He turned toward me, his face transfixed. "See, Hana," he said. "Oh, see." He gestured toward the glittering path of red and gold, leading from where he stood, across the water, to the sun.

"I just turned my back for one second," Little Grandma was explaining again to Aunt Pearlie downstairs in the kitchen, as I drew the water for Papa's bath.

"That's why I keep telling you. . . ." Aunt Pearlie replied.

Papa sat shivering on the edge of the tub, watching me.

"Just a minute and I'll help you out of those wet things," I said. "I think I know why you run away, huh, Papa?"

He had not spoken since out on the point.

"You feel everyone crowding you."

I unbuttoned his shirt and helped him pull his arms through the sleeves.

"It's like Ben told me once, about needing space."

I pulled Papa's T-shirt over his head.

"Well, maybe it's not the same."

I kneeled before him and began unlacing his shoes. I looked into his face.

"Papa, talk to me. I heard you out there."

"Hard-headed old woman!" Aunt Pearlie shouted. There were heavy footsteps across the living room. The front door slammed.

Papa reached for the gold chain around my neck.

"Talk to me," I whispered.

When I finally got to bed, I lay listening to the sounds of the house — my father snoring, clocks ticking, the back porch door banging in the breeze, and weaving in and out, making a single song of them all, Little Grandma humming upstairs in the attic.

The next morning, I was wakened by the racket of my grandmother's antique washing machine rocking back and forth on the cement floor of the patio, out back. The smell of burning French toast filled the room.

I went downstairs to the kitchen and turned off the stove, then poured myself a cup of the tepid brown liquid from the aluminum coffee pot next to the sink.

"That's for the plants," Aunt Pearlie said as I took my first sip. She'd just come in from hanging the wash. "How about Instant?"

I shook my head and pushed my cup away.

She came over and sat next to me, then began clasping and unclasping her hands as she stared out the window. Finally, she spoke. "That was quite a little adventure yesterday."

"Mmm. Do you know where Grandma is?"

"She and your father have gone to the Prayer Lady's to get a laying-on of hands, or whatever it is that woman does."

I got up and went to fill the kettle. "Maybe I will have some coffee."

"If you ask me, he needs more than a good massage to fix what's wrong with him."

I turned and faced her. "Why do you have to keep going on and on about it?"

"Because someone has to."

"You act as if you want him to be locked up."

She was silent. Her hands lay still upon the table. There was a funny bruised look about her eyes.

"What did he ever do to you?" I persisted. "It's not as if he were some sort of social menace or pathological lunatic."

Her mouth was set once more in an ugly stubborn line. "Oh, no? Look, Hana." She pulled something out of her apron. "Look what I found in your father's pocket." She laid the dancing school teacher's white satin nightcap on the table.

Little Grandma took the news calmly. She agreed with no further protest that Papa should be returned to the Home. Aunt Pearlie said Uncle Emigdio would come by the next day, when he was off at the Mill, to drive him over.

In the afternoon, it was too hot to stay indoors, so we went to sit out under the poinsiana — just as we always did. The sunlight glimmered through the bright red canopy above us, casting a warm glow across the whiteness of Papa's dozing face, the whiteness of the sketchpad lying open on my lap. The sound of drumbeats and the high-pitched notes of a bamboo flute came from the temple, where the musicians were beginning to rehearse for the O-bon festival just a few days away.

Grandma turned a patchwork star in her hands, then pinned it to a square of blue. For the first time since Ben left, I felt the tears begin to come. She put aside her piecing and took my face in her hands. "No tears," she whispered. "We can't have tears." A sly look flickered across her face. After waking Papa, she began heading toward the house. She turned and waved at me. "You come too."

I left Aunt Pearlie snoring in her lawn chair with her newspaper over her face, and followed.

Little Grandma led us up the stairs to her room on the second floor. Inside, it was nearly bare — except for a tiny cot with a hard loaf-shaped pillow, the family shrine on the camphor wood dresser, and a calendar, featuring a different Buddhist saint for every month, from Jimmy's Auto Repair.

"Come, come." She directed us through what looked like a closet door, leading up another narrow flight of stairs, to the attic.

She switched on the light. A quilting frame stood in one corner. In the middle of the floor lay a mat covered with little piles of geometric shapes cut from scraps of fabric. Along each wall were stacks of shoeboxes and grocery bags spilling over with bits of piecing and applique in various stages of completion. I recognized a blue scrap from one of Papa's old painting smocks, a yellow piece from my first going-out dress.

But it was to the far end of the attic that my eyes were drawn. There, hung an immense quilt made of appliqued squares, separated by strips of morning stars. The quilt was not finished, but already it covered the entire back wall, from ceiling to floor. From where I stood, perhaps fifteen feet away, it seemed to contain every color in the entire world.

I moved closer, and the colors began to cohere into shapes. Each square depicted places and people in the life of the village. There were the sugar fields sloping down to the sea. The rows of identical green and white houses with a different-colored dog in each yard. There was the singing tree in the temple square and the old head priest at O-bon, leading the procession of lights down to the bay. There was Emi McAllister in her garden. Every detail was perfect — down to the green and pink scarf on her tiny sun hat.

I looked closer. No, it couldn't be. My heart beat faster. It just couldn't. I glanced quickly over the rest of the quilt — at Doc McAllister out for his morning run, and Cousin Missy standing at the window of her Mama's house, and the Koyama Store Lady in front of her store. It was true. Every image had been made from the scraps of laundry missing in the village over the years.

Little Grandma smiled. "To not forget," she said.

I turned and walked down the stairs and out of the house, into the colors of the afternoon.

People Should Not Die in June in South Texas

GLORIA E. ANZALDÚA

Prietita squeezes through the crowd of mourners and finds a place near the coffin. She stands there for hours watching relatives and friends one after the other approach the coffin, kneel beside it. They make the sign of the cross, bow slowly while backing away. Even a few Anglos come to pay their respects to Urbano, loved by all. But after two-and-a-half days, her father has begun to smell like a cow whose carcass has been gutted by vultures. People should not die in June in south Texas.

Earlier that day Prietita and her mother had gone to the funeral home, where in some hidden room, someone was making a two-inch incision in her father's throat. Someone was inserting a tube in his jugular vein. In some hidden room *una envenenada abuja* filled his *venas* with embalming fluid.

The white undertaker put his palm on the small of her mother's back and propelled her toward the more expensive coffins. Her mother couldn't stop crying. She held a handker-

197

chief to her eyes like a blindfold, knotting and unraveling it, knotting and unraveling it. Prieta, forced to be the more practical of the two, said, "Let's take that one or this one," pointing at the coffins midrange in price. Though they would be in debt for three years, they chose *un cajón de quinientos dólares*. The undertaker had shown them the backless suits whose prices ranged from seventy to several hundred dollars. *Comparron un traje negro y una camisa blanca con encaje color de rosa*. They bought a black suit and a white shirt with pink. "Why are we buying such an expensive suit? It doesn't even have a back. And besides it's going to rot soon," she told her mother, softly. Her mother looked at her and burst out crying again. Her mother was either hysterical or very quiet and withdrawn so Prieta had to swallow her own tears. They had returned in the hearse with the coffin to a house filled with relatives and friends, with tables laden with *comida* and buckets overflowing with ice and *cerveza*.

Prietita stands against the living room wall watching the hundreds of people slowly milling around. *"Te acompaño en el pesar," dice la tía* as she embraces her. The stench of alcohol enters her nostrils when male relatives pay their condolences to her. *Prieta se siente helada y asfixiada al mismo tiempo*. She feels cold, shocked and suffocated. *"Qué guapa. Es la mayor y se parece mucho a su mamá,"* she hears a woman say, bursting into tears and clutching Prietita in a desperate embrace. Faint whiffs of perfume escape from the women's hair behind their thick black mantillas. The smells of roses and carnations, *carne guisada,* sweat and body heat mingle with the sweet smell of death and fill the house in Hargill.

Antes del cajon en medio de la sala aullando a la virgen su mamagrande Locha cae de rodillas persinándose. But Prieta does not cry, she is the only one at the *velorio* who is dry-eyed. Why can't she cry? *Le dan ganas, no de llorar, pero de reír a carcajadas.* Instead of crying she feels like laughing. It isn't natural. She felt the tightness in her throat give way. Her body trembled with fury. How dare he die? How dare he abandon her? How could he leave her mother all alone? Her mother was just twenty-eight. It wasn't fair. *Sale de la casa corriendo,* she runs out of the house, *Atravesó la calle,* she crosses the street, *tropezándose en las piedras,* while stumbling over rocks. *Llegá a la casa de Mamagrande Ramona en donde estaba su hermanito, Carito, el más chiquito.* She reached her grandmother's house where her little brother was hiding out. His bewildered face asks questions she cannot answer.

Later Prietita slips back into the house and returns to her place by the coffin. Standing on her toes, she cocks her head over the casket. What if that sweet-putrid smell is perfume injected into his veins to fool them all into thinking he is dead? What if it's all a conspiracy? A lie? Under the overturned red truck someone else's face had lain broken, smashed beyond recognition. The blood on the highway had not been her father's blood.

For three days her father sleeps in his coffin. Her mother sits at his side every night and never sleeps. *Oliendo a muerte, Prietita duerme en su cama,* Prieta sleeps in her bed with the smell of death. *En sus sueños,* in her dreams, *su padre abre los ojos al mirarla,* her father opens his eyes. *Abre su boca a contestarle,* he opens his mouth to answer her. *Se levanta del cajón,* he rises out of the coffin. On the third day Prieta rises from her bed vacant-eyed, puts on her black blouse and skirt and black scarf and walks to the living room. She stands before the coffin and waits for the hearse. In the car behind the hearse on the way to the church Prietita sits quietly beside her mother, sister, and brothers. Stiff-legged, she gets out of the car and walks to the hearse. She watches the pall bearers, *tío David, Rafael, Goyo, el compadre Juan* and others lift the coffin out of the hearse, carry it inside the church and set it down in the middle of the aisle.

El cuerpo de su padre está tendido en medio de la iglesia. Her father's corpse lies in the middle of the church. She watches one woman after another kneel before *la Virgen de Guadalupe* and light a candle. Soon hundreds of votive candles flicker their small flames and emit the smell of burning tallow.

"*Et misericordia ejus a progenis timentibus eum,*" intones the priest, flanked by altar boys on both sides. His purple gown rustles as he swings his censors over her father's body and face, clouds of frankincense cover the length of the dark shiny coffin.

At last the pall bearers return to the coffin. Sporting mustaches and wearing black ties, *con bigote y corbata negra,* they stand stiffly in their somber suits. She had never seen these ranchers, farmers, and farm workers in suits before. In unison they take a deep breath and with a quick movement they lift the coffin. Her mother holds Carito's hands and follows the coffin while Prieta, her sister and brother walk behind them.

Outside near the cars parked in the street Prieta watches the church slowly emptying, watches the church becoming a hollowed-out thing. In their black cotton and rayon dresses, following the coffin with faces hidden under fine-woven mantillas, the women all look like *urracas prietas,* like black crows. Her own nickname was *Urraca Prieta.*

From her uncle's car en route to the cemetery, Prieta watches the billows of dust rise in the wake of the hearse. Her skin feels prickly with sweat and something else. As the landscape recedes Prietita feels as though she is traveling backwards to yesterday, to the day before yesterday, to the day she last saw her father. Prieta imagines her father as he drives the red truck filled to the brim with cotton bales. One hand suddenly leaves the wheel to clutch his chest. His body arches, then his head and chest slump over the wheel, blood streaming out through his nose and mouth, his foot lies heavy on the gas pedal. The red ten-ton truck keeps going until it gets to the second curve on the east highway going toward Edinburg. "Wake up, Papi, turn the wheel," but the truck keeps on going off the highway. It turns over, the truck turns over and over, the doors flapping open then closing and the truck keeps turning over and over until Prieta makes it stop. Her father is thrown out. The edge of the back of the truck crushes his face. Six pairs of wheels spin in the air. White cotton bales are littered around him. The article in the newspaper said that according to the autopsy report, his aorta had burst. The largest artery to the heart, ruptured.

She had *not* seen the crows, *las urracas prietas,* gather on the *ébano* in the backyard the night before that bright day in June. If they had not announced his death then he couldn't be dead. It was a conspiracy, a lie.

> *Ya se acabó; ¿qué pasa? Contemplad su figura*
> *la muerte le ha cubierto de pálidos azufres*
> *y le ha puesto cabeza de oscuro minotauro.*

Is it over? What's happening?
Reflect on his figure.
Death has covered him with pale sulfurs
and has given him a dark Minotaur head.*

The *padrinas* place the coffin under the ebony tree. People pile flower wreaths at her father's feet. Prietita shuffles over to her father lying in the coffin. Her eyes trace the jagged lines running through his forehead, cheek, and chin, where the undertaker had sewn the skin together. The broken nose, the chalky skin with the tinge of green underneath is not her father's face, *no es la cara de su papi.* No. On that bright day, June 22, someone else had been driving his truck, someone else had been wearing his khaki pants, his gold wire-rimmed glasses — someone else had his gold front tooth.

Mr. Leidner, her history teacher, had said that the Nazis jerked the gold teeth out of the corpses of the Jews and melted them into rings. And made their skin into lampshades. She did not want anyone to take her *papi's* gold tooth. Prieta steps back from the coffin.

The blood in the highway could not be her father's blood.

> *¡Qué no quiere verla!*
> *Dile a la luna que venga,*
> *que no quiero ver la sangre*

> I don't want to see it.
> Tell the moon to come
> that I don't want to see the blood

As she watches her father, a scream forms in her head: "No, no, no." She thinks she almost sees death creep into her father's unconscious body, kick out his soul and make his body stiff and still. She sees *la muerte's* long pale fingers take possession of her father — sees death place its hands over what had been her father's heart. A fly buzzes by, brings her back to the present. She sees a fly crawl over one of her father's hands, then land on his cheek. She wants him to raise his hand and fan the fly away. He lies unmoving. She raises her hand to crush the fly then lets it fall back to the side. Swatting the fly would mean hitting her *Papi*. Death, too, lets the fly crawl over itself. Maybe the fly and death are friends. Maybe death is unaware of so inconsequential a thing as an insect. She is like that fly trying to rouse her father, *es esa mosca*.

She stands looking by the coffin at her own small hands — fleshy, ruddy hands and forces herself to unclench her fists. A beat pulses in her thumb. When her hands are no longer ruddy nor pulsating she will lie like him. She will lie utterly still. Maggots will find her hands, will seek out her heart. Worms will crawl in and out of her vagina and the world will continue as usual. That is what shocks her the most about her father's death — that people still laugh, the wind continues to blow, the sun rises in the east and sets in the west.

Prieta walks away from the coffin and stands at the edge of the gaping hole under the ebony tree. The hole is so deep, *el pozo tan hondo,* the earth so black, *la tierra tan prieta.* She takes great gulps of air but can't get enough into her lungs. Nausea winds its way up from the pit of her stomach, fills her chest and becomes a knot when it reaches her throat. Her body sways slowly back and forth. Someone gently tugs her away. *Los hombres* push a metal apparatus over the hole and *los padrinos* place the coffin over it.

Under the *ébano* around the hole a procession forms. The small country cemetery, with Mexicans buried on one side and a few Anglos on the other, is now bulging with hundreds of cars *y miles de gente y miles de flores.*

Prieta hears the whir of the machine and looks back to see it lowering her father into the hole. Someone tosses in a handful of dirt, then the next person does the same and soon a line of people forms, waiting their turn. Prietita listens to the thuds, the slow shuffle of feet as the line winds and unwinds like a giant serpent. Her turn comes, she bends to pick up a handful of dirt. She loosens her clenched fist over the hole and hears the thud of *terremotes* hit her father's coffin. Drops fall onto the dust-covered coffin. They make little craters on the *cajón's* smooth surface. She feels as though she is standing alone near the mouth of the abyss, near the mouth slowly swallowing her father. An unknown sweetness and a familiar anguish beckon her. As she rocks back and forth near the edge, she listens to Mamagrande's litany: *"Mi hijo, mi hijo, tan bueno. ¿Diosito mio, por qué se lo llevó? Ay mi hijo."*

Next Sunday the whole family has to go to mass but Prieta doesn't want to attend. Heavily veiled women dressed in black kneel on the cement floor of the small church and recite the rosary in sing-song monotones. *Llorosas rezaban el rosario,* hands moving slowly over the beads. *"Santa María, madre de Dios, ruega por nosotros . . .* Holy Mary, mother of God, pray for us now and at the hour of our death." Her mother and Mamagrande Locha dedicate Sunday masses to her father, promising *la Virgen* a mass a week for the coming year. They pay a small fee for each — all for a man who had never entered church except for the funeral mass of a friend or relative.

Her mother wears *luto,* vowing before a statue of *la Virgen de Guadalupe* to wear black for two years and grey for two more. In September when school resumes her mother tells Prieta and her sister that they are to wear black for a year, then grey or brown for another two. At first her classmates stare at her. Prieta sees the curiosity and fascination in their eyes slowly turn to pity and disdain. But soon they get used to seeing her in black and drab-colored clothes and she feels invisible once more, and invincible.

After school and on weekends her mother shushes them when they speak loudly or laugh, forbids them to listen to the radio and covers the TV with a blanket. Prieta remembers when her father bought the TV. The other kids had been envious because hers had been the first Mexican family to have such an extravagant luxury. Her father had bought it for them saying it would help his *hijitos* learn to speak English without an accent. If they knew English they could get good jobs and not have to work themselves to death.

Pasa mucho tiempo. Days and weeks and years pass. *Prieta espera al muerto.* She waits for the dead. Every evening she waits for her father to walk into the house tired after a day of hard work in the fields. She waits for him to rap his knuckles on the top of her head, the one gesture of intimacy he allowed himself with her. She waits for him to gaze at her with his green eyes. She waits for him to take off his shirt and sit bare-chested on the floor, back against the sofa watching TV, the black curly hair on the back of his head showing. Now she thinks she hears his footsteps on the front porch, and turns eagerly toward the door. For years she waits. *Four years* she waits for him to thrust open the sagging door, to return from the land of the dead. For her father is a great and good man and she is sure God will realize he has made a mistake and bring him back to them. *En el día de los muertos,* on the day of the Dead, *el primero de noviembre,* on the first of November, *ella lo espera,* she waits for him. *Aunque no más viniera a visitarios,* even if he only came to visit. *Aunque no se quedara,* even if he didn't stay — she wants to see him — *quiere verlo.* But one day, *four years* after his death, she knows that neither the One-God nor her father will ever walk through her door again.

> *pero nadie querrá mirar tus ojos*
> *porque te has muerto para siempre . . .*
> *como todos los muertos de la Tierra.*

but no one will want to look at your eyes
because you have died forever . . .
like all the dead on Earth.

---

* The lines of Frederico Garcia Lorca are from the poem "Llanto por Ignacio Sánchez Mejías." Translation by Gloria E. Anzaldúa.

Letter to My Father

CAROLYN GAGE

I was surprised and pleased by your offer to have me come and live with you. I have often wished that I might have the opportunity to reciprocate the kind of care I received growing up as a child under your guardianship, and I wonder if this might be my chance to repay you. You have always represented to me the point of view that you were a good parent, and so I can only assume that, in your advanced years, you would want the same behaviors extended to you by your caretaker. If I am correct in that assumption, allow me to outline some of the conditions which would really allow you to reap the benefits of that which you sowed as a father:

First, if I move in with you, you will have to turn over all the money and property to me. You will have nothing that is yours. You will need to ask me for whatever you want to buy, and I will have the right to challenge your requests and turn them down if they don't meet with my approval. This will take the burden of financial responsibilities off you.

I think that you will find that wearing second-hand and bargain basement clothes will give you an appreciation for the deeper things of the soul. Certainly, you will learn not to be vain. Self-conscious, yes — but not vain. You may, of course, learn how to sew — in which case, I would be happy to provide you with fabric. Sewing is a valuable skill to learn, and one which will decrease the burden of your financial dependence on me. Decreasing this burden should become the object of your life. You will need to cut your own hair, because I can't in good conscience support these habits of personal vanity. I understand that no one in your peer group will have these economic strictures imposed on them. You may conclude that they are either spoiled, or that you are exceptionally depraved to require so much supervision.

The only time you will be allowed to use the car is when I don't need it and there is some official function you need to attend which will reflect favorably on me. You will never be able to use it for personal reasons. You may wonder why I never trust you with anything, as you have always been a conscientious and diligent person. I will try to impress upon you that your true nature is inherently selfish, lazy, and wasteful — and could manifest itself at any time if I were to relax my vigilance. I want you to learn not to trust yourself. I will never allow you to make any decisions. This way you will always doubt your judgment and be more likely to let other people decide things for you.

You will learn to feel like a barely tolerated guest in your home. You will never use the telephone when I want it. I will have the right to ask to whom you are talking, and I will have the right to forbid you contact with any person who fails to meet with my approval.

You may watch television, but if there is something I want to see — that's what we will watch. As with any activity of yours, I will have the right to interrupt any time. If you leave any lights on in a room you have vacated, I will discipline you. This kind of wastefulness is what causes seventy percent of the world's children to go to bed hungry.

You may have your own bedroom, but you will not be allowed to have a functioning lock on it. And I do intend to barge into your room anytime I want anything. This accessibility will be useful to me in another aspect of your training, but more on that later.

Because you will have no money, you will of course have to share everything in the house with me. But let me warn you ... even though you will not have the money or transportation to replace toiletries, you are not to use them up! I am sure that as you keep constant watch over the soap, toothpaste, and shampoo, you will grow to enjoy the "zen" of these little things. This discipline will spare you the annoyance of dealing with larger spiritual, political, or artistic issues. Now, as for food. Of course, I will pay for your food. God forbid, I should let you starve! But let's not go overboard. Remember you are not going to be making any money. Everything is mine. I will put up with you, but I do not expect to indulge you. I have calculated that 100 pounds is all you will need to continue functioning. Above that, you are really eating more than you absolutely need. Again, I don't want you to feel guilty eating my food, but just remember, for everything you eat that is over what you need as a bare minimum — you will have to really justify your right to exist on this planet.

And while we are on the subject of food . . . since the money will be mine, you will of course prepare the food. It is important that you observe details carefully. To impress this upon you, I will swear violently and throw the food across the room if I find it doesn't suit me. You will apologize and clean it up. One should never take peace for granted. The world is dangerous for old men, and living with me, you will learn to expect violence at all times. You must never relax.

Now . . . about your social life. Of course, I will need to meet and approve of your friends. I will want to know how much money they have, what their children do for a living, and what their sexual reputations are. If they do not speak good

English, you will not be allowed to see them. You understand, this is for your protection. If there is a friend you seem to be growing too fond of, I will help you to maintain a better sense of balance by discouraging the relationship. I will ridicule and criticize your friend. You will be required to participate in this. If necessary, I will forbid you to contact the person. You will learn that loyalty is a liability.

Also, if you have made plans with your friends, even several weeks in advance, you will need to know that I may decide that morning that I need you to clean the garage — and you will have to cancel your plans. This might seem hard at first. It may even seem inconsiderate to the friends who have been counting on you — but they will soon learn to ask someone else, and you will learn that the way to avoid disappointment is never to get your hopes up about anything. See? Oh, how many people would have been spared heart-aches in this life if they had just learned not to want things! And the way not to want things is to learn that you don't deserve them. This is what you did for me, and I can't tell you how much I want to do it back to you.

Your friends — the ones I approve of — may visit. I will try to make them feel comfortable by making constant refer-ences to their bald heads and their white hair, by making "old geezer" jokes, and by alluding frequently to their inability to "get it up." This may seem rude and offensive at first, but I will actually be doing your friends a favor by preparing them for the real world.

You must never express your opinions unless they agree with mine. This is true in matters of religion, politics, educa-tion, and personal taste. If there is some food substance I don't like, you will not be allowed to eat it. If you wear something I don't like, you will have to take it off. If you express an opinion which is incorrect — that is, which I don't agree with — I will make you stay in your room until you change your mind or learn to lie. You must learn that there is no truth, only approval.

You will never swear in my presence. So that you will know what I mean by swearing, I will use words like "shit," "goddam," "Judas Priest," and "hell" constantly in your presence. I will use them violently, to scare you. This will teach you how I don't want you to talk.

Also, I will ignore, ridicule, and trivialize your good work. If you were a woman, I would be very interested in and proud of your achievements, but because you are male, I will let you know that nothing you do counts very much. Although I will never notice your talent or excellence, I will magnify every one of your mistakes or failures. This will keep things in perspective for you. I want you to learn humility. This is an important attribute for those of your gender. If possible, I would like to have an adult of your gender in the house with us. This person will be yelled at, sexually degraded, insulted, and beaten with regularity. He will be terrified of me and unable to protect you. This will be your role model during the years we are together. The presence of my mother was such a valuable role model for me, that I would wish for you to have a similar experience when you live with me.

And now I am getting to a part which may be very difficult for you to understand. If I ask you a question, and you give me an answer that I don't like, I will have to hit you in the face. And that's not all. I will have to send you away to someone else's house. You will not have any clothes or any of your things with you. When I get around to it, in a week or so, I will come over and apologize. You will then have to come home with me again. You may not want to. You may not believe the apology. You may still be scared of me. But you will have to come home. I may hit you again. Hopefully you will not make this necessary, because hopefully you will have learned to say what I want to hear. How much you get hit depends on how willing you are to learn what's good for you. It's not up to me.

If you have any animals, I will kick them and torment them in front of you. This teaches you to make choices. If you protest the abuse, I will turn on you. If you say nothing, you will stay safe. This kind of decision-making is very important. You will learn that it is a bad thing to intercede for others. They must learn to fend for themselves. You will learn that to care about others will only cause you pain. You will learn not to love.

I hope you will never get sick. I truly hope that, because getting sick is expensive — and every day you know you are getting closer and closer to that bottom line financially. I will do everything I can to see that you never come to me and tell me that you're sick. There are three stages to what I call my "wellness training" program: First, I will call you "The Sickie" if you complain of a problem. I will encourage everyone around you to call you that also. If this is not sufficient to encourage you to be healthy, I will send you to your room. I will make you lie on the bed and face the wall. You will not be allowed to read or watch TV. This will punish you. You will have to decide just how sick you really want to be. If you persist in saying that you are sick, I will — after two or three days — call in one of my friends who owes me a favor, or some relative who hasn't practiced medicine in many years. They will do a sloppy diagnosis and give you sample drugs which may or may not have serious side effects. You will learn to take responsibility for your health.

To sum up, there will be no part of your life — your appearance, your habits, your work, your hobbies, your contacts — that will not be subject to my control. I will make a discipline of ridiculing you and everything you do. I will degrade you, insult you, and make every effort to humiliate you in front of your friends. I will physicaly violate you. I will invade your privacy — constantly. I will deliberately call you names you hate, and amplify any human failings that you have. If you ever do anything you are embarrassed about, I will make sure you never hear the end of it. You will hide your feelings so long and so well, that hopefully you will stop having any. You must never challenge me, never resent me. You must love me. You must understand that I had a hard childhood, and I can't help anything I do to you. You must appreciate your abuse. You must make yourself believe that, in spite of every instinct for self-preservation and every natural feeling of revulsion towards cruelty and domination, that I am really acting in your best interests. You will become humbler and humbler as the abuse escalates and the damage goes deeper. This may seem to be a hard path, but in the end your happiness — your very survival — will depend on your becoming what I want you to be.

This arrangement will come close to replicating the dynamics of my experience as your daughter. Except for one thing. Your sexual abuse of me. It is really impossible to terrorize and sexually abuse a seventy-year-old man. Even if you became confined to a wheelchair, you would still not come close to the vulnerability and helplessness I experienced as a child. Not to mention the destruction of my innocence and trust which made the sexual abuse such a profound violation. It is unfortunate that you will not be able to put yourself in my shoes, because of all the things you did to me, this was the most central experience of my childhood, and has formed a cornerstone of my adult life. If I could find some way to teach you deep terror of all women, shame about your body, and distrust of intimacy — I would. Because I cannot repay you for the trauma of that initiation, I feel that my guardianship of you will fall far short of the influence you have had over me. This causes me a sense of deep frustration.

Should you feel that you are somehow dissatisfied with our arrangement, part of our agreement is that you are not allowed to tell anyone. No one will believe you. If it gets back to me that you have tried to complain, I will, of course, discipline you for betraying my trust.

And as a final condition of my guardianship of you, I will take you to church every week. You will kneel before the Mother, the Daughter, and the Spirit of Women. You will learn that God represents the interests of battered and raped women, of sexually abused children, of helpless animals, of oppressed minorities, of underpaid domestic workers and sexually harassed secretaries. You will learn that God hates your pornography, hates the buying and selling of women, hates incest, hates adultery, hates professional men who take sexual advantage of their female clients, and hates husbands who infect their wives with venereal diseases, as you have done.

You will learn that God hates violent and tyrannical white men who make their living off systems of white male privilege, and who create a deity in their own corrupt white male image and imagine their ill-gotten gain is some sign of divine favor. God hates the greed, hypocrisy, moral idiocy, and self-delusion of men like you. As we worship together in this church, you will realize that the mothers and children of this world are the divine order, and that the compulsive accumulation of property and the systems of violence and extortion which protect this accumulation are abominations. You will learn that the entire system of values propagated by and for white males is evil and pointless. You will learn to be ashamed of things you have been proud of. You will learn that what you thought was important is insignificant. You will learn that actions which you considered so trivial that you have forgotten them, are the very issues of your soul. You will learn that God hears the voice of the silenced woman and of the inarticulate child, and that these voices weigh more heavily in the balance than all the clever and manipulative arguments of men in power. You will learn that in the court of God there is no statute of limitations, because the pain of your victims does not go away after seven years.

As you kneel before the altar of the Mother and the Daughter, you will learn, finally, who you really are and what you are really worth. And in this church, old man, you haven't got a prayer.

Duke

JEWELLE L. GOMEZ

My father had two wives simultaneously when I was growing up (neither my mother) — Henrietta and Tessie. I preferred Henrietta. They lived (still do) in harmony and actual support of each other at opposite ends of our hometown, Boston. Objectively, that's the most remarkable thing about Duke; but the list of things I know from him, about myself and the world, weaves around me like the types of shawls that grandmothers are supposed to make. I feel the nappy wool of his self very close to me; the sensibilities of a charming, black bartender, relatively invisible in an economically depressed city in the 1950s and '60s; in a neighborhood trembling on the edge of something called urban renewal — something called gentrification.

Each weekend I visited him at either one of his two households, trying to slip in between the stepsisters and brothers, step-cousins, step-aunts as if I'd been there all the time and was not a weekend guest. I did chores and went to bed when I was told to. But it was always clear I was there for him. We strode through the South End as a team so clearly cut from the same cloth it hardly mattered if we spoke at all. So many others spoke of us our bond was easily forged. And the charm and style for which he was known was attributed to me almost by default. It was like being the stars of a rhythm and blues song. Duke, Duke, Duke, Duke of Earl.

He was what they used to call "heavy set, but neat." My step-sisters called him Jackie Gleason because he had the same build, wore exquisitely cut clothes and was nimble and witty. It was magical to me that my father was the bronze doppleganger for a famous star. Coupling that with his being well-known and well-liked on the block made him a celebrity to me.

The different strands of thought that come to mind to create the picture of who he was are a wild array. The clothes, of course. Mohair sweaters, Italian knits, sharkskin slacks with knife-sharp creases, perfect cut camel hair coat worn just the way that black men do. My favorite look was crisp Bermuda shorts, black knee socks and loafers or deck shoes. The tempting mocha of his knee showing between the socks and shorts as he glided down West Newton Street turned the heads of most women and many men. Maybe I liked that outfit because it was one I could emulate. Sometimes he'd let me wear his shorts and shirts or sweaters, since oversized clothes were in, and we'd go walking in the neighborhood on errands or for a drive to get his car washed. Duke and Little Duke, as the patrons in the Venice Tavern, the 411 or the Regent called us. He took me on my first trip to an airport. He took me to my first, teenaged music concert — Jackie Wilson — where he got free tickets because he was helping the promoter with security. He always cried when my step-cousins got spankings. When I went to the store to buy his cigarettes I'd repeat the name of his brand, "Herbert Tareyton's," over and over until it became an unrecognizable mantra but Freddie, in Braddock Drugstore, knew me.

I was allowed to stay up until he got in from work. Bos-

215

ton's blue laws brought him in usually by half past midnight. His tip change jangled in his pockets as he loosened the waist on his pants then held them up delicately with one hand, that also held a lit Herbert Tareyton. The other hand usually clutched a mayonnaise jar full of ice water. He moved elegantly across the room to sit at the kitchen table with joy written across his face. If he'd had too much to drink he moved even more elegantly. He was a man happy to have family and having two of them was only one of the indications.

He loved to talk. He'd sit at the kitchen table for hours telling stories about bar patrons, commenting on the news in the *Record American* which he read while eating, watching television and talking. He would tell jokes with no punchlines and we'd all laugh until we cried. He laughed until he cried. Turning the pages of the paper he'd read quietly then look up at the TV and make a trenchant observation about something that'd just appeared on the screen like, "That guy (Ross Martin/"The Wild Wild West") has the worst collection of fake mustaches I've seen since Mona Lisa." And Henrietta, Allen, Bonita, Katherine and any neighbor's kid who might be spending the night and I would fly off on gales of laughter again.

Like all the kids I had tasks but mine were related to my father's room: I refiled his albums—he was always purchasing new contraptions for record storage. I separated his cufflinks, straightened his desk, folded his sweaters and counted and stacked his tip change in neat piles from which he'd pay me.

I'd spend hours in his room just being with his things, reading his stacks of magazines — *Gentlemen's Quarterly, Negro Digest, Ebony, Yachting* (he read this regularly, though to my knowledge he'd never been on a boat in his life). I read *The Well of Loneliness* and my first James Baldwin books from the unceremonious pile of novels that grew and shrunk and grew beside his bed.

I'd play his records as I dusted and returned them to their sleeves. One Saturday afternoon he asked me who my favorite singers were. I said Billie Holiday and Arthur Prysock. He beamed and said, "I knew you'd always have good taste." I was eleven years old and in the thirty years since I've measured all success against the pleasure that his expression of pride gave me. Sometime in my teen years we made a deal: he'd teach me bartending and I'd teach him Spanish from my high school text. He really wanted to learn Portuguese since that's what his father's people had been. But I'd examined the multi-lingual pamphlets that the Christian Scientists left everywhere in our neighborhood and I was never able to make sense of the Portuguese. Our commitment to these lessons didn't last long since his schedule was often erratic and mine became more so as I became more of a teenager. But we really didn't mind since the deal had simply been a plot to make sure we spent time together and that never did change. I'd always wait up until he got home from work or when I started going out he'd wait up for me.

He had beautiful hands which I sometimes manicured. I loved the cool softness of his skin and the way they looked both masculine and feminine. He usually wore one of three rings — a Masonic ring with one diamond, a silver ring with many small diamond chips or an onyx ring with a small diamond in its center. He advised me to never wear diamonds to a job in front of white people. He said that no matter what they said they'd be jealous and not want to pay you properly. He also warned me that gold cars blow up. Not an extreme admonition in light of the fact that three gold Cadillacs had done just that to him. He'd departed from his usually rather conservative beige or blue Cadillac one year to purchase the gold. Its engine exploded. The dealer immediately replaced it with another. Its engine exploded. The dealer immediately replaced that with another. It caught on fire. My father declined a fourth and switched instead to muted pink with assorted customizations thrown in along with a free tour of the big Cadillac showroom for me.

I only saw my father intentionally do something to upset another person once. Every Saturday morning proselytizers would ring neighborhood doorbells to preach the gospel or sell copies of *The Watchtower*. Some people welcomed their visits, usually older folks who received so little attention from the outside world or those who'd been anticipating some sort of conversion for years. But at Henrietta's house it was kind of a joke seeing who'd be stuck answering the bell then have the impossible task of getting rid of them politely. Once I listened (from behind a bedroom door) to my twelve-year-old step-cousin, Walter, stuck for fifteen minutes on the stairwell unable to manuever them back out the door.

One Saturday we all ignored the bell but my father was half asleep and annoyed as hell. He went to the front door naked as a bird, the only thing between him and the gospel was the door's glass window panes. It was some time before they called on us again.

When I think of my father I hear the sound of excited young voices, "Here comes Uncle Duke!" It would spread through the gang of kids and we'd be at the door before he could close the front gate. When any adult got desperate disciplining one of us she'd just say, "I'm gonna have to tell Duke!" and all misbehaving ceased. You could almost sense our actual regret at having ever misbehaved at all. I think none of us wanted to risk losing his respect, or disappointing him or being sent to bed without being able to listen to him tell stories.

He and Henrietta were the only adults to like my hair when I got an Afro in 1968. When I was very young, maybe six or seven, he bought us each a pint of strawberries while we were visiting his mother. She looked horrified when she saw us getting down to the last berry and said, trying not to sound hysterical, "Now, John, you know that girl's allergic!" He looked up at her as if he too were seven and said, "But, Mother, we wanted them." I never broke out in a rash or got sick. It's not a bad thing for a kid to think her parents are magic.

Lumps

HARRIET MALINOWITZ

Every month it comes, always in the same spot just below my armpit. It always startles me at first, like something unfamiliar and entirely unexpected. I usually notice it when I am in the motion of pulling a sweater over my head, the side of my hand gliding up the opposite side of my body, enjoying a brief moment of narcissistic pleasure. But other times I discover it because the tips of my fingers have sought it out; they have instinctively touched that spot at just that time and when they feel it my whole body freezes. I go on to explore it, gently rolling it around under the skin, feeling its size, its shape, its strength. With my other hand I feel the same spot on my other breast, reassuring myself with its smoothness, its perfect roundness which displays no variance. I touch my breasts all over, lying down on the bed with one hand tucked under my head, the other moving in methodic circles over the face of an imaginary clock. One o'clock. In toward the nipple. Out again to the circumference and then

219

two o'clock. In. Out. I am very careful and very honest. I examine any suspicious spot thoroughly, refusing to let it intimidate me. All is well except nine o'clock. There is no getting around the fact that it is there, a tiny marble embedded in layers of secretive membrane. I've never yet caught it in the act of coming. I don't know how it gets there. All I know is that it's not there and then suddenly one day it is.

My father started coughing in February. It irritated me when he would exaggerate his cough for effect, the histrionics of a hypochondriac. In June the doctor said it was cancer. He cut the drama fast enough.

So an insignificant little cough was really lung cancer in disguise. That's how cancers work, invisible insidious little things that thrive on you secretly for months before they pounce.

My vision of life is like a *Reader's Digest* article, entitled, say, "The Unforgettable Ordeal of John Doe." John Doe awakens one morning with a crick in his neck. Must've pulled something lifting those heavy cartons yesterday, he says, and his wife rubs in some Ben Gay and he forgets it. He goes out in a good mood, it's a sunny day and everything is deceptively fine. *Little does he know* that at that very moment he has a brain tumor. His easy, unconscious optimism carries the eerie ring of *famous last words*. The lump is harbored in his brain and he is all oblivious. Ignorance is bliss. But one by one the other symptoms will come and the lump will make its presence known. Pretty soon it will control everything.

The trick is to be in a constant state of suspicion. Early detection is the only cure, we are told, and I am always alert to the possibility of a concealed lump.

Since consciousness, I wished my father would die, and then he did. What was discovered was not a lump, not even a mass, but lungs infested with malignant cells. There was no restricting their activity: there was a coup within my father's body and the cancer cells came into power.

Chemotherapy is like a slow, drawn-out nightmare in which you try to run away from something but can get nowhere. It cannot cure but it can arrest. Chemotherapy confounded me; it seemed a matter of trying to arrest the inevitable. I helped out all I could and became a paragon of devoted daughterness. Usually I forgot my dreams before I was forced to confront them. But the truth of the matter was, I was rooting for the cancer cells.

Once it happened that I was sitting in a class, cramped in a seat whose arm encircled me, becoming at the end of the spiral, a desk. Leaning my head to one side, I cupped my cheek and the loose flesh of my neck in my hand, my fingers spread wide to support them. And then, moving slightly, I felt the lumps. Not one, but two, and as I explored the area I found a third behind my right ear. I tried not to touch them, but the urge was irresistible. There in the receding classroom I fondled the nodules in my neck, sickly thrilling to their rolling motion, and with the tips of my fingers I touched the lump in the back of my ear, small and hard and round like a pearl.

And then the headache came. It started that day and it didn't go away for a waking minute in five months. It was hard to know which came first, the brain tumor or the cancer of the glands, but either way it had spread and was already out of control. For those months I felt my lumps every day, growing more and more acquainted with their habits and patterns of change, becoming tense when they enlarged, briefly at peace when they shrank. They were the first thing to enter my thoughts in the morning, my hands flying to them instantly to make sure that they were still there. It started the month after my father died and I felt fortunate that my suspicions were at that time most keenly refined. Even if it was already incurable, I was nevertheless quite on top of things.

Taking care of my father was like a vaccine. It made me deserve not to have cancer. The thing was, he should never have been a father, but he had me, and he fucked me up, and

221

I hated him, and I wished he would die, and he did. And I think I was justified, too. But I can be objective and of course I followed the truth to its natural conclusion. If ever I, a potentially unfit mother, had a child, I too would probably fuck it up, and it would hate me, and wish I would die, and by all the laws of justice and indirect retribution I would.

But taking care of my father and going through all the motions of regretting his imminent departure earned me brownie points with God. Twenty years of evil thoughts unpunctuated by any Oedipal sentiment were sure to have their repercussions. I only wanted the chance to put in some "good" time so that fate would judge me less harshly, perhaps defer for years the biopsy that was my destiny. I began to work toward an escape from this mortal indictment as if it were a handsome pension to be earned in a very short period of time.

It was the vision of guilt that also incited me. I don't want to spend my life being guilty over my viciousness to him, I used to think. So I went about clearing myself of all incriminating charges. I was an angel; I outdid myself in going against my own grain. I catered to every neurotic whim as I watched him wither away before my eyes. I was leaving no room for self-chastisement, no plausible grounds for future regret. I will never say I could have been better, I used to think. I am as good as gold. I'll never torture myself that I could have done more for him in his dying hours.

Sometimes my father's nonchalance about his impending demise moved me to bizarre fantasies. A relative would come to visit, and upon leaving would say, "I'll be around again on Thursday." My father, lying on the sofa with the mask from the portable oxygen tank over his face, would answer, "Well, I don't know. Hope I'm still around." I used to marvel at the way he said it, so offhand, as though he might be leaving for California if a certain phone call came through. Then my mind would become what I thought of as a "Theatre of the Absurd." I would think at him an equally casual remark, like, "Oh, come on, why don't you wait till next week before you kick the bucket?"

Or I'd be sitting in the room reading as he slept, the loud rasping of his breathing coming in such rigid rhythm that I often found myself compulsively humming to it. I'd lower my book and gaze at him, imagining the breathing suddenly coming to an abrupt end: the moment of death. In the theatre in my head there would be a momentary awed hush — and then, sharply cutting into the silence would come the voice of Porky Pig, pronouncing the ultimate eulogy, "Th-th-that's all, folks."

And then from the region behind my sober inscrutable face would echo the laughter, the screaming laughter which abruptly froze when I said, Thoughts like this must mean I'm going crazy.

I like my period to be absolutely regular. I believe in the sun and the moon and the earth and their interrelation, and rotation and revolution, and days and months and years, but I believe more in the female calendar within me. I know that ideally there are thirteen months in the year, neat little packets of time composed of exactly 28 days each. This system is inherently dependable and singularly reassuring. To be aware of the minute changes that occur and re-occur in one's body — a slight bloating of the stomach one day, a barely perceptible cramp on another, warning signals that are more perfect than any barometer — to be aware and to be able to read and live by these signs is to really have Time well in hand.

But the thing that can really usurp this calendar is a lump. Once, about a month after the doctor pronounced me clear of the brain tumor and prescribed Valium, which I was highly suspicious of and never took, and after the headache and the lumps in the neck went away, something strange started happening in my body. I began to menstruate every two weeks, like clockwork. This grew more and more confusing, especially when I began to lose track of which was my *real* period and which was the *extra* one. I had my period so much that time almost began to seem linear, stretched out in a series of periods and non-periods which occurred incoherently in rapid succession. All my thoughts became swallowed up in the absence of any natural rhythm. But of course I was suspicious from the first; and at least I had the knowledge that my perspicacity in relation to all things cancerous would stand me in good stead.

Yet I found myself once again quivering at the prospect of death. I wasn't sure whether my cancer was of the *uterus* or the *ovary* or the *Fallopian tubes*. I scrupulously avoided reading any literature on the subject, knowing that I was susceptible to suggestion. And of course there was the matter of time bargaining. This was the internal debate I waged, half of me wanting to consult a doctor immediately so that treatment could begin, the other half protesting the futility of it and arguing that confirmation of my prognosis ought to be delayed indefinitely to preserve the illusion of hope. Out of cowardice I waited, the brittle fear always whispering inside me.

My father died during Fred Astaire Week. We were taking shifts staying up with him, my mother, my brother, and I. I had been taking the late shift because the Fred Astaire movie would come on at 11:30 on Channel 9. When we started with "Top Hat" he was already in the wheelchair; the effort of walking took his breath away. I remember he slept straight through "The Gay Divorcee." I was able to totally forget him. But I missed "Silk Stockings" on Wednesday because he was up and talking, talking incessantly about the retirement fund and what a rich widow my mother would be. I had heard it many times before, the financial advantages of his dying, and I was frankly bored with the subject. I listened as he rattled on, feigning attention, knowing I would not have to endure it much longer, knowing that he probably wouldn't live till "Royal Wedding."

He slept almost all the way through "The Story of Vernon and Irene Castle," his labored breathing moving in time with Fred Astaire's taps. But then near the end he woke up and he was in one of those moods I couldn't stand, when he'd get all sentimental about his house, bestowing sad farewell glances on the paneling he'd put up, the furniture, the moonlit tomato patch in the backyard where his own Burpee's Big Boys grew, outliving him. When he'd lapse into this kind of reverence, something inside me would become insane, and the only satisfaction I had was in thinking fast and furiously that these walls which he now regarded as some sort of shrine would soon enough be his tomb.

He lost consciousness two hours before "Damsel in Distress" on Friday night. I was able to watch the movie uninterrupted. Occasionally there would be an erratic gasp in his breathing which would startle me, and my heart would pound until I heard the flow of his breath being exhaled again. I didn't want him to die on my time. I wanted the great passing to occur during someone else's shift. I've always been phobic about being around sick people, especially those who are experiencing overt symptoms like having a heart attack or an epileptic fit, or vomiting. Even seeing someone faint makes me extremely nervous. This is just to explain that although I was more than anxious for my father to die expediently, I was less than anxious to be an eyewitness to the event. Sitting up alone with him on those nights was quite an act of martyrdom on my part, one which I expected God or whoever controlled these things to acknowledge by absolving me of all future incrimination. I figured that whatever I went through then was worth it if it meant a clear mind for the rest of my life.

I was right. An hour before "Royal Wedding" he simply stopped breathing. A minute later there was a sudden flux of air from his throat, but it had nothing to do with living or breathing. It was like the air that escapes from a balloon. I had been sitting there reading, eating a Colonel Sanders wing. I looked up at him when he died, feeling nothing, vaguely shocked by the appearance of this skeletal dead man lying inert with an open mouth and no glasses. I put down my wing. Dying was nothing. It was the easiest thing in the world. Licking my fingers, I thought, Is this what all the shouting's about?

225

•

And to tell the truth, since then I've never really thought about it. The funeral was hard, trying to look glum and having everybody hug me and say the sympathetic things that people say, seeing *them* cry, even some of the people from his office, and knowing they were wondering why I wasn't too. But after the funeral there was food and lots of people for a week, and then I went back to school and that was really the end of it.

I'm glad I served my time then, because he never haunts me now. In a way my worst, best fantasies have come true: I can live out the rest of my life and never have to contend with my father again. It's a special sort of liberation which means everything to me. I never have to torture myself for wishing on him the things I wished on him, because actually they happened and he's not here to screw up my life anymore. Just like that last year when I didn't have to wish he'd die anymore because, no matter what I wished or willed, he was going to die anyway. It's strange how you exert your whole being toward something and in the final analysis it happens through some power having absolutely nothing to do with yourself.

It's the same thing with those damned lumps. Of course it helps to be suspicious and alert about them, but really if you don't get cancer it's just because you weren't supposed to get cancer. And I know it, and it scares me all the more, knowing it's really such an arbitrary thing and you're vulnerable to it no matter how you build your defenses. And it gets confusing when you start to mix up science and superstition, although maybe there is something to mind over matter. Still, I continue to keep my cancer consciousness, always making sure not to forget my suspicions for a moment. The lump still comes in my breast every month and I still haven't relaxed into the fatal mistake of saying, Oh, it's just that same old harmless cyst. I'm still filled with terror when it appears but all in all I'm quite on top of things. It's a means to self-preservation. It's my personal imitation of immortality.

226

The Tangerine Plymouth and the Gilded Cage

RACHEL GUIDO deVRIES

Father Valente died in 1954, the same year my father bought the tangerine Plymouth. One was pomp, the other circumstance. The first event, Father Valente's death, I remember by the scent of incense, and the second by the taste of a creamsicle. For Father, we all stood on the sides of Trenton Avenue in Paterson, New Jersey, and watched the procession on its way to the cathedral. St. Anthony's was the church and school I attended. I was seven. My mother kept a statue of the infant of Prague on the windowsill in our kitchen, and Father Valente looked just like that statue to me; he was clearly a grown man, of course, and not an infant, but he looked like the infant, and was dressed like him, too, with red robes and a golden crown. It seems to me now, thirty some years later, that he was carried in an open casket, framed on all sides with gold, and with clear glass panels, sort of like a gilded cage.

My father needed the tangerine Plymouth because he was

227

a numbers runner and a small-potatoes bookie. He had not yet moved up to the Cadillac or Continental school of thought because he was still peanuts, with just a very few connections where it counted. Years later, Philly Falcone, a police lieutenant and a *compare* of my father's would chuckle about those early years. He'd look at my father and bust his balls about the old days, when, as he said, Pop was ". . . the new kid on the block. Oh yeah, I remember when I first heard aboutcha: Russ Mangicaro, big shot, cuz we all remembered your brother, Patsy, Golden Gloves winner in '47 — had his own trade till he was shot, and there was plenty that pissed off. Then along comes Russell with his bow legs and his busted schnozzole. Skinny and already goin' bald and a tough little bastard you were, Russ."

By then, my father was completely bald and pretty stocky, but he was still bow-legged and still tough as nails, slick as snot. A regular son-of-a-bitch he was. By then, he had also graduated to a pale blue 1981 brand new Cadillac. Philly, always known as a good cop, drove a Ford, not even a Thunderbird, but an Escort. My mother drove a Thunderbird — she'd graduated too — and at sixty she had a license plate that said "over 40 and feeling foxy."

But my father never loved a car the way he loved that tangerine Plymouth. I used to wait for him to come home, sitting on the stoop of the house we lived in then on Alabama Avenue, up on the third floor. We rented from Uncle Tommy Giordano — he was my godfather, though not a blood relation, and his wife Irene, whose brother Mario lived with them. Mario had, as my father said, just come off the boat, a real greenhorn. But Mario was nice. He had slicked down curly black hair and a big cleft in his chin, and eyes so dark they never just looked — they always gleamed. He worked at Uncle Tommy's fruit stand, and sometimes, when I was waiting for my father, Mario'd come home from work first, and he'd give me a peach or an apricot or an orange, depending on the season. Mario always smelled like an orange; not like a creamsicle; more like an orange with cloves stuck in it. Once in a while my father and Mario arrived within minutes of each other. My father would turn into the driveway and slowly pull the tangerine Plymouth right up to the door of the green garage, but never into it, at least not in the summer or fall. He liked to sit out on the stoop and look at it, and when Mario was there, we'd all three sit on the stoop, eating fruit and gazing in the direction of the car.

Every Saturday, I helped my father polish it with Kiwi car wax and a chamois rag. The last step was Windex-ing the mirrors: side view, rear view, and then we were off, just me and him, off to the Italian grocery for prosciutto and salami and provolone; then, if my father was in the mood, we'd stop at Uncle Marty Tango's gas station, which was always good for an orange NeHi, and then to the Buffalo Bar and Grill, where my father talked to Nick the bartender, and I drank birch beer and played shuffleboard.

We'd get back home right around supper time, about six. Mama'd be in the kitchen, breading the veal cutlet we always had on Saturday nights, and my sister Rita, two years younger than me, would be in a corner playing with her dishrags. She had about three of them, and she'd fold and unfold them, sometimes for hours. Nobody thought it was strange, but when I think about it now, it seems very strange.

Father Valente's funeral was my first ceremony, not counting my brother Little Russell's baptism, which, although it was done in Latin, and although Father Vincent was bathed in incense, did not strike me as too mysterious. I was more caught up in a sense of relief, for Russell's soul not having to gamble on Limbo, which I imagined as a bunch of bodiless babies, just a bunch of baby heads floating aimlessly on the clouds. I was six when Little Russell was baptized, but even then the sort of aimlessness that couldn't be changed alarmed me.

The year of Father's death was the beginning of my fascination with ritual and ceremony. He died in April, and in

May I received first communion. Also, in May, Raye Ann Del Guidice saw the Blessed Mother move. The statue moved; the lips moved, and all of the more cheeky girls, myself included, swore we saw it also. *Something* happened: I remember that day very clearly; the early afternoon light filtering through the stained glass, the scent of incense, and the pale pale blue of Our Mother's robes, resplendent to all of us, despite the chipped plaster of the statue, despite the old and rather musty church. And Raye Anne's fervor was something to behold. Of course, Sister Fabia, our teacher, had a fit. She was fond of knuckle rapping and humiliation: I once had to sing Yellow Rose of Texas with Donna Mazziotti, because Sister Fabia caught us reading a *Pop Music* magazine. I hated her anyway, because she was Polish, not Italian, and the last year I had fallen in love with Sister Claire, who was Italian, and whose hand I always held at recess. I fell in love with her because she had the softest hand I have ever held; today, that is what I remember about falling in love. For the life of me, I cannot remember a single feature on Sister Claire's face, though I know she was slender and delicate-boned.

Sister Fabia was fat and burped unashamedly throughout our lessons, and she kept a snot rag shoved up one sleeve of her habit, which always struck me as sacrilegious. She was outraged by Raye Anne's and our behavior with the Blessed Mother, though she had encouraged it by telling us stories endlessly, about miracles that young children like us had a part in. There was one she especially loved, about a boy named Johnny, who was very poor; he had a paper route to help his family, kept a 93 average, and still had time to be an altar boy on Sundays. On top of all of this, he still managed to make a visit to church every day, no matter how busy he was. He made it quick, she granted him that, but every day he'd go into church, genuflect and cross himself, and say, simply, "Hello, Jesus, this is Johnny." The punchline of this story, of course, was Johnny's untimely death, witnessed by several adults. Johnny was struck by a car on his way out of church after his daily visit, and he died on the spot. All those around him unanimously agreed they heard it: the voice from the heavens, saying, simply, "Hello, Johnny, this is Jesus." Well. We were in the second grade, and about to make our first communion, and we knew since we were practicing going to confession that we had reached the age of reason; we were constantly being reminded of the difference between heaven and hell and we knew that you could sometimes get time off in purgatory for things like daily visits, to say nothing of the jump you could be granted for a sign of good grace, such as having the Virgin move her lips in your direction. Donna Mazziotti and I even made a pact about the after-world. We were all caught up in figuring how to get in touch with each other after our bodies, like Johnny's, died. We agreed to meet on the corner near our houses, in front of Verp's Bakery, ten years after we died. We must have thought we'd die at the same time, and it didn't strike us at all odd that we chose to meet at a Jewish bakery rather than church. Verp's had the best hard rolls. We ate them every Sunday, right after nine o'clock mass, when they were still warm and the butter melted right into them, and they tasted great with my mother's meatballs, which we dug into hours before the pasta was served. We were *starved* from the fasting that took place before receiving the body of Christ.

Since my father bought the tangerine Plymouth during the year of my fascination with ceremony, that car has always seemed sacred to me. When I think of it I picture it with an aura: a halo. The day of the funeral, my father dropped me off at the school. He didn't like pomp, didn't much care at all for church, and was particularly suspicious of priests, though he did let Mama get the house blessed. He considered himself Catholic, but not a church goer, certainly not like Donna Mazziotti's father, who worked at Nabisco, and belonged to the Holy Name Society, and who ushered at church once a month. My father would have never done that: he would have been embarrassed to death. I always sort of liked that about him. But when I watched that Plymouth pull out of my sight, halo and all, and I stood in the chilly rain that April and viewed my first dead body, and a dead holy body to boot, and was on the fringes of the procession, the incense wafting up through the rain, all the priests chanting Latin, the altar boys waving the incense decanters, I was suddenly and certainly beseiged by a feeling of righteousness, a kind of breeze of holiness; I felt as though I were lighter than air, borne up on the wind of a young and violent Catholicism. And though my heart and my physical self wanted to be off in the tangerine Plymouth with my father, my soul or my conscience or my newly acquired reason gave me a shove in a holier direction. I knew, even at seven, that my father's business was shady. When I asked him and Mama what they were doing at night — listening to the results, they always said, and I never asked the results of what, I just watched them hunched toward the radio on the center of the table, in the kitchen's dim light, while they wrote some figure down, and shuffled fast through a little stack of tickets with numbers printed on them. "Trestle tickets," Mama said, when I asked what they were. What trestle? And my father would laugh, shake his head, say, "You're a pip, Ma." He always called her that.

All of this was in my mind, and despite the loneliness that watching my father's Plymouth vanish from sight brought me, despite the pleasure I knew would come from that car, I had to breathe in the pomp of Father Valente's funeral and I followed the procession, feeling ancient and pious just the same.

When I was twelve my father bought another car. He traded in the tangerine Plymouth for a brand new 1959 Chevrolet. Black, with black vinyl interior. He was moving up, as his color choice showed. That was also the year I received my confirmation. I picked a middle name — Teresa — for a favorite saint, as my confirmation name, and got to kiss the Bishop's ring.

We still lived in the same neighborhood, but in our own house — half a duplex is what it was, with a kitchen and living room and dining room on the first floor, and two bedrooms and bathroom upstairs. There was a wrought-iron railing around the three steps that led up to our front door. Uncle Tommy Giordano was gone, moved to Jersey City, and Mario had bought the fruit stand. I still saw him once in a while, but hardly ever in the neighborhood. I ran into him with Mama a couple of times downtown when we waited for the bus. He was a wino, Mama said, like poor Winnie Glover's husband, Mike, the one who kicked dogs. Mario was still kind of handsome, even though his eyes had lost their gleam. He still had a full head of black, curly hair, and the cleft in his chin.

By the time my father bought his Chevrolet, I'd become a little snooty towards him. I was still very Catholic, and I knew by now those were no trestle tickets he and Mama'd been using. He didn't use that system any more, of course, but he had a second phone put in, and he hung around with guys with names like Big Sal Polizotto and Twofy Barberio. Twofy was short for Two Fingers, the number he had remaining on his right hand. I asked my father once what had happened to Twofy. Looking over at Mama, and not quite laughing, he said that Twofy had lost his fingers "in college." "Really?" I asked, impressed. It had never occurred to me that men like Twofy went to college. Years later, when my father went to college — the county jail, for bookmaking, along with my Uncle Angelo — I understood, and had to laugh about it. Fortunately, both my father and my uncle left college with ten fingers each, but they learned a lot while they were there.

I've learned some things since 1954, too. Last week I went car shopping. I'm considering a Plymouth. They don't make them in tangerine these days. In fact, I don't remember ever seeing one other than my father's. I've been to a few funerals, but I've never seen one like Father Valente's. Last winter a friend asked me to help her book bets on college basketball games. I couldn't resist, although I felt a little out of my element — I really did go to college, the first and the only one in my family to do so — but I did it, and I loved every second of it. I kept all of my fingers. I do not, though, ever go to church anymore. Gilded or not, a cage is a cage, and I'd much rather live my father's life than Father Valente's. I do cherish the memory of his funeral, and every April, usually sometime around Easter, I rise to the occasion, filling up the house with incense, and trying to remember exactly the way Trenton Avenue looked in 1954. But what I mostly see is the tailpipe of the tangerine Plymouth as it rounded the corner away from me, and I long for the summer, when we'd sit on the stoop, eating fruit and gazing hopefully at that dreamy car.

Dropping Anchor

VALERIE MINER

The sailor leaves his ship, picks up an oar and walks
inland. He cannot stop until someone asks, "What's
that you're carrying?" Then he can rest.

– The Odyssey

Grey. Brown. Beige. The color
of this high desert eludes her. The mountains are rocky ladders
to a flat, pale sky. Macro arrowheads. Otherwise, scrub
stretches for miles to the horizon. This reminds Patricia of
travelling in the South. Perhaps because of the bus. She hasn't
taken a long bus journey for fifteen years.

A Black woman across the aisle places a yellow-flowered
pillow next to herself so she doesn't have to share the seat
when they make the next stop at Murdoch. Patricia had heard
the woman tell the young Chicano soldier behind them that
she is travelling from New Orleans to visit her sister in Los
Angeles. She needs the space to stretch. Who could argue?

A day-and-a-half in this bus, muses Patricia, who has less
than four hours to ride from the El Paso airport to Murdoch,
New Mexico. She glances at the blond sailor sleeping next to
her, head jiggling against the window frame, snoring beer
breath in and out. Now she watches his fog on the cold

window, almost clearing when he inhales, then returning the net of moisture over the glass. Outside the window it is white: snow on the cactus, on the telephone poles, on the road ahead.

Patricia closes her eyes and tries to imagine what her father will look like. Instead, Mother's face appears, objecting to this visit. Patricia argues back, that he is more her father than Mother's ex-husband. Her father. Patricia reflects that she was sixteen when he left the family and she has hardly seen him in twenty years. Oh, they have had the obligatory dinners and brunches when they happened to be in the same port. Three years ago in New York. Five years ago in London. Once in San Francisco. But these infrequent, indigestible meals were ritualized encounters. *She has always been better at observing rituals than at participating in them. Even as a devout child, she found the Eucharist stuck to the roof of her mouth.* Sometimes she wonders if Dad sent a stand-in to the dinners and brunches. Any number of people could have imitated that Boston Irish accent and affected the racial epithets. She wonders again why her father, a merchant seaman all his life, has retired to the desert to raise chickens.

The sailor shifts, disturbing her reverie and she opens her eyes. Snow falls steadily as they approach a town. She consults her watch — almost two o'clock. Yes, "The Rotary Club Welcomes You To Murdoch, New Mexico. Population: 1,376. Elevation: 4,095 feet." Patricia never thought her father would get this far above sea level before he died. She had spent years praying for his death. Now he is seventy years old. He is a hoary, fat old man waving to her from the door of the small Greyhound station.

Patricia is the only passenger to disembark at Murdoch. Do the others know something she doesn't? She resists the impulse to turn and wave to the woman with the pillow; the friendliest gesture she can make is to hustle off this bus so that they can get on to Los Angeles.

Dad waves again as she emerges. He stays inside the station until the driver disengages her bag from the storage compartment. Then her father waddles towards her, pulling a poodle. A standard grey poodle, she notices, like the one they had when she was little.

"Hi there," he says.

"Hi." She smiles and pecks his cheek. 4711. Even in the frozen desert, he wears 4711 cologne.

"You like him?" His accent is stronger. Until now, he might have been any retired rancher. Now, she knows he is her father, displaced from Newton, Massachusetts, and from Dun Laohaire before.

"Cute," she manages.

"Guards against the spics," he says.

Testing her already, or does he always talk like this? She realizes she can swallow the bait. He would love a fight. But it's only sport to him.

"I call him Fritzie. Got two more at home. They couldn't all come to welcome you. So I brought Fritzie. He's the quietest."

"Nice to meet you, Fritzie." She scratches the dog's neck and he rubs himself against her long, quilted coat.

"Better get you in the car," he says, "before you freeze. Crazy weather for New Year's. I said come for New Year's because it's usually hot."

"Weather doesn't matter," she shrugs. "I'm here to see you." It comes out naturally enough because it is the truth. She *has* come to see him. Now and then. She has come to be kind to him. She has come because he may die soon — how can he survive with all that weight? — and she would feel guilty if she hadn't come. Still, she is taken aback by her statement, so intimate and direct.

He walks up to a small, green Datsun truck. She is mildly surprised that it isn't a big, old Pontiac they could sail down the highway. However he is a chicken rancher now.

"Mind if Fritzie rides with us? It's a little cold for him in the back."

"Not at all." She holds one bag on her lap, pushes her suitcase on the floor in front of her and draws the dog closer. The truck smells of country. She checks herself in the rearview mirror: a tall, redheaded woman looking a little younger than usual.

"Sorry I couldn't pick you up at the El Paso airport," he grunts, getting behind the wheel. She feels the truck lower a foot towards the ground. "But those roads were slick and I don't have chains. I knew you'd make it fine, though. Once, I took a bus down the Jersey turnpike in weather like this and we made it fine. Who would have thought — chains in the desert?"

"It *was* fine. Really. I thought about the years I spent on buses, doing organizing at those mills in the South."

"Unions." He clears his throat of phlegm and pulls onto the highway. Fritzie barks frantically. "I still can't believe you threw away your college education to become a union organizer."

She stares ahead into the thick fog and prays they will make it safely to the ranchero. Suddenly, she is overwhelmed with memories of Dad, lit up like a tree and swerving all over the road to Somerville on the way to spend Christmas at Grandma's. But the strongest thing she has smelled today is *4711*.

"Didn't hear from Art at Christmas."

"Oh." She reminds herself that she has promised not to get involved in the feud between Dad and her older brother. "How about Henry? Did Henry call?"

"Your little brother always calls." His voice loses its edge. "Henry's doing great. Made assistant manager of the dealership last month."

"Yes." She smiles at the thought of her gregarious baby brother.

"Say, seriously now, how's your work? Your job OK?"

He's trying, she thinks. The last time they met he didn't ask a thing about her.

"Fine." She nods. "We're working on a new contract.

Management seems flexible. We'll see." She wished she could be forthcoming; wishes she could trust him more.

"The dentist liked your book." He clears his throat again. "He's a reader, that guy. He was impressed that I had a daughter who wrote a book. So was I." He looks at her.

Patricia is glad the weather is so cold; perhaps her blush will disappear quickly. It's a modest publication; more a handbook, really. She remembers a wonderful trip they once took together, just the two of them up the coast. "Tell me about the chickens," she says.

"Well, I got bantams and Rhode Island Reds ... you'll see. Best this year are the pheasants. And I've got one terrific peacock."

"Peacock?"

"Yeah, a gorgeous male, wait till I show you."

She knows his place before he turns up the driveway. The flagpole is an exclamation point in front of the house of Walt Lester, American citizen, who hated all the ports he visited and couldn't wait to retire at home. The front yard is filled with pastel gravel. She sees her father's wife, Dagmar, standing in the living room window.

"Home, Fritzie, whadya say, boy? Glad to be home?"

The dog presses his nose on the windshield, yapping wildly.

A chorus of higher and lower-pitched barks greet him. As soon as her father cuts the motor, Dagmar releases the other poodles from the front door.

"OK, OK, now," he shouts. "Down, boy. Down, girl. That's it, that's a good dog."

Patricia sits in the car, amused and touched by the chaos. Why is she taking it so good naturedly? He used to drive her nuts.

"It's all right." Her father looks over, "They won't bite."

"Oh, I'm not worried about that," she begins defensively and hops out of the car.

"Welcome, Patricia," the tall, blonde woman says. She

begins to hug her and then remembers the cup of cocoa in her hand. "To warm you up, after the trip."

"Yes, thanks." Patricia nods, accepting the cocoa. Should she stand here and drink it? Won't Dagmar freeze if she stays outside in her slippers?

"That's it; that's it." Her father is still talking to the dogs.

Patricia sips the cocoa. "Delicious. Perhaps we should get in the house?" She shifts her shoulder bag and reaches for the suitcase.

Dagmar claims it. "This way, yes, what was I thinking about, serving you on the ice-cold driveway?"

They leave him outside with the dogs. She shivers at the familiar sensation of being abandoned. She remembers, as a little girl, waving goodbye at the side of a big, white roaring ship. Why the panic? He's just gone to quell the dogs.

"Sit," Dagmar instructs, "I'll show you the guest room in a minute. But relax here on the couch. You can see two mountain ranges when it's clear. He's been talking about your visit for months. And he gave your book to the dentist two weeks ago so as to talk with you about it. We're not much on reading."

Patricia looks out the big picture window at the heavy mist sweeping down the street. The barking has grown fainter and she guesses her father has gone to check on the chickens.

"I've taken to watercolors myself." She bobs the marshmallow up and down in her cocoa. "I did oils for a while, but the texture wasn't right for the desert. Too rough. You have to look close to see things here. Sometimes in the middle of nothingness, miles of nothingness, there will be a small gem — literally a gem, or a flower — you know and oils are just not delicate enough for that. I don't suppose you paint. You must be too busy."

Patricia wishes she could excuse herself to lie down for a few moments. "I don't have the talent for painting, for creative things like that."

"Don't be modest, an educated girl like yourself," Dagmar turns. "Oh, now, dear, brace yourself for an invasion."

He walks in, followed by three huge poodles. "Behave," he warns them. "Come meet Patricia and behave, you hear me?"

He introduces Schooner, Taffy and Fritzie again.

"Sometimes he gets mixed up," Dagmar laughs, "calls them your names, 'Art, Patricia and Henry.' Can you believe it?"

Patricia smiles thinly and gulps the cocoa.

"Oh, here, let me get a refill. And some cookies. Your father has been baking all week."

He always did this before he went to sea, Patricia remembers. The house would rise with delicious aromas as he canned peaches and tomatoes and made sauces for Mother to serve when he was away. Then he would disappear. For three months. Six months. "It's his job," Mother would explain. "He doesn't like it any better than we do." Patricia knew she should trust her parents; she knew she was exaggerating her fears. But even when he got a shore job, he would be gone for weeks loading cargo. Then one day, what she had always suspected happened: he left for good.

The dogs continue to bark. Dagmar continues to talk. Patricia and her father exchange stale items of family news. The sky outside grows dark and, finally, Dagmar beckons Patricia to her room at the back of the house.

"It's my room, actually, I can't sleep with your father's snoring. Sounds like a bull elephant, you know."

Patricia thinks how Mother would be happy to hear the old buzz saw at night. Surprised by the reflex to defend Mother after all these years, she declares, "Very cosy. I like the colors." She glances surreptitiously at the silver crucifix knotted with palm leaves and hanging over the bed. She has forgotten that Dad persuaded Dagmar to convert to Catholicism. He had talked his way into an annulment and remarriage, protecting his immortal soul. Our father. It's all coming back.

"I'm glad you like it. I sent to Santa Fe for the curtain fabric. . . ."

That night, as Patricia brushes her teeth, she reads a prayer

241

tacked to the mirror. "Please God, help me remember that silence is golden. When I open my mouth to speak, let me breathe in the glory of your universe...." She has been judging Dagmar too harshly. So she stole Dad from Mother twenty years ago; surely she's had second thoughts. Besides, Mother is probably better off alone. She's more independent, more outgoing than she ever was when Dad was around.

Patricia climbs into the warm bed and considers the first day. She is confused by the great affection she feels for him. Of course he is still bombastic and single-minded. But she keeps having glimpses of him in the past — driving her to a basketball game; winning double pinochle with her against Mother and Henry. They had some good times when he was in port and sober. She reads for a while, then slips down beneath the rustling comforter and fresh yellow-flowered sheets. Yellow flowers. She thinks of the woman on the bus and wonders how many hours she has to go before Los Angeles.

The noises start before light. Roosters. High, shrieking whistles. Dogs barking. Patricia puts the pillow over her head and falls back to sleep. Sun creeps into the room and the back door bangs. Dad going out to feed the chickens. Six o'clock. He always hit the deck early. She draws down the shade and crawls under the pillow again. She dreams she is at Olduvai Gorge.

The barking wakens her. Eight o'clock, well, she doesn't want to be a slouch. Tentatively she sticks one foot out of the warm covers and pulls it back. She reaches over and raises the shade to find the street still socked in with fog. Yawning, she gets up; rushes into her clothes.

"You didn't have to get all dressed," Dagmar greets her in the kitchen. "I'm not usually decent until nine or ten. Your father, sometimes, he wakes the rooster."

He walks in, brushing his hands. Patricia is filled with fondness. His gesture reminds her of a past moment she cannot quite place.

"Ready for a real breakfast?" he asks.

"Starving." Then she remembers how much he piled on her plate the previous night. "Medium starving."

"Your father is such a cook," Dagmar sighs. "Especially this season. When we had Father Bailey over for spaghetti and meatballs, he spent the whole day preparing. I tell him, 'Walt, relax, you don't have to sustain people for the next ten years; it's only one meal.' But he loves it. Loves it. I just wish he would love to wash the dishes."

"Thought we could go visit Admiral Dirk, the breeder, while Dagmar's at the picture framer's today. I mean, we could all drive to town and you and me could check out the new birds."

"Now, Walt, remember, you yourself said we didn't have room. . . ."

"All right. All right. Doesn't do an old man harm to browse."

Patricia remembers her mother's warning that his backyard tomato patch would take over Massachusetts.

"Well, Patricia will be with you. I'm sure that will keep you sensible."

Mother had said this when he went up to Portland to load cargo. Patricia read while he was at work. Then he took her out to dinner and introduced her to that nice woman, Dagmar, who was staying at the same hotel.

In the truck, Dagmar makes Patricia promise that she will drag him away from the birds by ten o'clock, complaining about how he had to extend the pens twice that autumn after shopping sprees. Patricia tenses, resentful of Dagmar's intimacy with him. What does she expect; they have been married for eighteen years. Still, Patricia can't relax until Dagmar disembarks at the picture framer's.

Silently they proceed to Admiral Dirk's. Patricia watches the flat landscape, considering how like the ocean it feels — empty and endless and bare. Dad is captain of his ship as he has never been at sea; Dagmar is his trusty first mate. He hasn't retired so much as gone to heaven.

Admiral Dirk is a few years older than her father, a tall New Englander, cut from a richer crust than the Lesters, but rank disappears as the men inspect the new birds. The cages are smelly, crowded and dusty. The two friends consult about incubating times and pen temperatures. Patricia is drawn away to the high-pitched squawk of a peacock in the far pen. As she approaches, he turns his back, raising his feathers; a fire of iridescent greens and blues. Patricia aches to see him in the sunlight.

"I call that one 'King Walter,' in honor of your Dad." Admiral Dirk comes up behind her. "Likes to show off before the ladies. Best feathers in town."

"Don't listen to this old coot." Her father slaps his friend on the back. "We really call that one Emperor Dirk."

She watches the two men laughing and wonders how anyone can be so easy with her father.

"Promised Dagmar I wouldn't bring anything home," he chuckles. "She sent this one as watchdog."

"OK, Walt, see you soon. Happy New Year. To you, too, miss."

Dagmar is waiting outside the frame shop, slapping her hands together against the cold.

She hops in and blows fog on the windshield.

"Whadya waiting in the cold like a dummy for? You'll get pneumonia."

"I was just trying to make it easier on you." Dagmar shakes her head and turns to Patricia. "He's something, isn't he? You do him a favor and he complains. Hey, Walt, where are you going?"

"Home."

"You forgot that I have to pick up the pattern for Mrs. MacLeod. And the basket of fruit for Hunter."

"God damned church people. You're always running

around doing things for them. And here we have our own family visiting."

"He's such a gentle soul." Dagmar winks at Patricia. "I've got an idea. You two take a ride around town while I run errands. It will only be twenty-five minutes. You'll hardly notice. Here, pull over just here, will you, Walt?"

He checks his watch. "Ten-thirty, sharp. But wait inside Nedley's Grocery, don't stand out in the cold. You'll catch your death."

He rips away from the curb and Patricia thinks how her brother Art was grounded a whole month for making the family car screech like that.

"Well, I guess I can show you the new residential park. Can't for the life of me figure why people come to the edge of nowhere and live in a housing tract."

As they drive, she tries not to be frightened. He's with her now. They're together for a while. And this time she'll be the one to leave — to return to her own apartment in Boston.

"Dagmar has these friends who like to eat out. Now I enjoy a good meal, but there's only one decent restaurant here — a Wop place over on the south highway. Anyway, her friends like to eat at 'Sitting Pretty,' ridiculous name for a restaurant. And the food is like frozen dinners, not always thawed. Or they like the Chink place down the street. Not bad for a Chink place, but they put in so much MSG you can't see straight for three days."

"You all compromised on the Italian restaurant?" Patricia asks.

"Naw, we don't go out with that couple at all no more. Dagmar said I let off my big mouth once too often. We used to go out with the Wops, themselves. They're bigshots in the church. Dagmar met the wife at some knitting thing. But him and me got into a fight about the mob and we don't see them no more. Here, I'll show you where they live in the housing estate — see that pink palace up there, lording it over all the other ticky tackys. That's them, the Antonellis. If that don't

245

sound like a mob name, I don't know what does."

"Remember Father Antonelli at St. John's?"

"Yeah, well, a big family."

The following day he drives them to the taxidermy studio in Silverton. Patricia sits in the back seat, next to a carefully wrapped pheasant. The bird has keeled over suddenly, a perfect specimen. Well, she has wanted to know her father's life. Still, she hasn't bargained for Dagmar's constant chatter. Poor woman, Patricia tells herself, she's lonely. She is doing her best to adapt with the painting and the church activities and the social life Dad keeps ruining. Still, Patricia is beginning to feel like a kidnapped ear.

". . . So what do you think about that, Patricia?" Dagmar asks.

"About what, sorry, I was looking at the scenery." She regrets speaking brusquely, then feels mad at Dagmar for making her mad with herself. As always, Dad seems out of anger's range.

"Leave her alone, Motor Mouth. Let her enjoy the country. She has to get back to that damn city soon enough."

"I didn't mean . . ." Patricia rubs her right shoulder, for she can feel the migraine ticking. "Sorry, what did you ask?"

"It's OK." Dagmar sits straighter and peers across the flat scrub as if scouting for the Strategic Air Command. "Let's just enjoy the world around us for a while."

Patricia tries to stretch away the tension, her hand falling on the dead bird's head. She shivers and stares out the window, counting cactus.

Murphy's Taxidermy Ltd is an inconspicuous enterprise in a green Quonset hut on the edge of town. One could easily miss it. Her father is clearly a frequent patron.

Dad grows enthusiastic as they make their way through the dimly lit, vacant waiting-room. "Come on back. They all work here."

Dave Murphy, a big man wearing casual clothes and a baseball cap, raises one hand in salute. He continues to stitch with the other hand. Nell Murphy turns and rushes to Dagmar. A skinny young man, probably their son, is eating a MacDonald's hamburger at a sawhorse in the middle of the room.

"Like you to meet my daughter," her father calls to Dave. Dave nods, "Welcome."

Patricia reads "Dodgers" on his cap and wonders if the bus has made it to Los Angeles.

"Brought up that pheasant," her father says nervously.

"Get right to it, after this squirrel. One of Leonard's pets — you know the two he fed in the front yard? Just expired."

"Could have been the cold," her father says.

"Yep." Dave concentrates on the small, neat stitches. "Speaking of which, help yourselves to coffee over there. And Skip, hey Skip, offer the visitors some of them fries. Wouldn't mind a couple myself."

"Sure, Pop." The boy unfolds himself and stands about seven feet tall. Even if Patricia had been hungry in the midst of all the carnage, she wouldn't consider taking potatoes from this rake of a lad. Her father grabs a handful and pours her and himself coffee.

She accepts the cup and walks around the cold room. She has never visited a taxidermist or a mortician before. The chill reminds her of church. She stops at one trophy, then the next and the next, hanging at evenly spaced intervals from the wall, like stations of the cross. An elk shot in its prime. A raccoon growing threadbare. Two pheasants. A quail. A blue jay. Suddenly she is exhausted, almost faint. How long are they going to stay here anyway? She notices Dagmar and Nell Murphy sitting at a table of feathers, laughing. Dave and her father are arguing football as Dave sews. Skip is munching his Big Mac. They can't have been here long, she tells herself, if he is still eating the hamburger. Yet she has had enough of the gallery and wanders into the waiting-room.

How had she thought the room was vacant? A grizzly bear feigns menace from the corner. You have to look close in the desert, Dagmar said. A defeated moose hangs his head from the wall over the clock. A coyote prances on top of the wide screen television. *Dad brought her dolls from Japan and fabric from Brazil. She always wanted to say, forget the presents and stay a while. But she had to avoid his answer, which would have been a lie.* Patricia sinks down into the naugahide couch and picks up a copy of *Taxidermy Today*.

An hour later — she has consulted the clock every five minutes — Dagmar and her father come looking for her.

"Always reading," he turns to his wife. "Always that way as a kid. She didn't get it from me."

"How about lunch?" Dagmar enquires.

"Sure," he says. "There's a great steak house on Main Street. You feel like steak, Patricia?"

"To tell you the truth," she says, "I feel like a little air. Why don't I just walk around town while you and Dagmar have lunch."

"What's wrong with you anyway? You used to like to eat. You trying to turn yourself into one of them Twiggys?"

"No, I'm just not hungry. And I wouldn't mind some exercise."

"Let her do as she likes, Walt."

He begins to protest, then his attention is caught by the grizzly. "Ralph Foster got that one, on his last trip to Alaska."

"Why didn't he take it home?"

"Well, it was a tie. I mean Ralph didn't last much longer than it took to fly back to El Paso. Heart attack. His wife knew he'd want the bear stuffed, but then she couldn't bring herself to put it in the house."

"So what's it doing here?" Patricia is appalled by her morbid curiosity.

"For the grandchildren," explains Dagmar. "The Murphys are saving it for Ralph's grandchildren."

•

They drive through Silverton in silence, stopping at the Carousel Steak House.

"Sure you're not hungry?" he asks. "They have a salad bar with garbanzo and kidney beans."

She smiles, touched that he remembers her favorite beans. "No, no thanks. I'll just wander around the shops. Maybe I'll join you for coffee."

An hour later Patricia enters the loud, smoky restaurant, feeling revived by her solitude. "Hi!" She waves, glad to see them. "Hey, I got a surprise for dessert. A lottery ticket for each of us."

"Oh, let me see," Dagmar says. "We need coins to rub off the markings. No, no, I didn't win a thing. How about you, Walt?"

"No, two of a kind, but not three."

"No," Patricia shakes her head, "I didn't win either."

She rises early the next morning in the hope that she will get some time alone with him. Maybe they can feed the birds together. She pours coffee from the thermos and pulls on her coat. Walking along the pens, she is amazed how quickly the chickens skitter, seemingly oblivious to the cold. Her father has explained the elaborate heating system and now she understands how complicated it must be. Sweet that he would go to such lengths for the birds. It is begging the question to ask why he couldn't nurture his own children.

Turning a corner by the pheasants' pens, she sees him, bent over, digging seeds from his bag; his white hair swirling around red earmuffs; his cheeks ruddy; his eyes almost bulging from the strain of stooping so low. Suddenly she notices his hands — small and thick — the fingers more like the dried, cracked legs of a turtle than digits of a man. She has always wondered where she got her tiny hands, for Mother's are large and competent. She is at once repelled and relieved. She had thought there was a mutant gene.

"Shhhh." He turns, as if he had seen her all along. "Come

this way, the Prince of Hearts is displaying this morning."

She tiptoes over the sawdust and straw, inhaling the pungent birdshit and taking a step back upon seeing the peacock, even more glorious than the one two days before. The sun is bright now, a crisp, unfiltered morning sun that ignites the peacock's colors, his feathers like rainbows rippling across a lake. He moves the radiant tail slowly, bestowing his gift.

"Beautiful," she says, regretting she doesn't sound more intelligent, "beautiful."

Her father winks.

Her breath catches at his boyishness, at the clarity of the morning, at the power of forgiveness.

"Here," he hands her the bag with a plastic scoop. "You feed him. I'll take care of the bantams."

The Prince scrutinizes her. He waits until she finishes pouring his food. Carefully he tucks away his glory and walks, as if in stiletto heels, to the dish. He stares at her. She steps back. He begins to eat.

"Good," her father calls. "He never lets anyone watch him eat. You made a friend."

She looks up and smiles.

"How about a ride to Mexico? Just the two of us. Dagmar said we should spend some time alone. I've got a couple of errands. Things are ten times cheaper there, you know."

"Sure," she says, but she is reluctant to leave the bird.

Over breakfast he checks his shopping list. The dogs are barking to join them. "No," he shouts back, "can't take you to Mexico."

Dagmar counts the cash from a canister. "Be careful," she says.

Patricia excuses herself to the living room while they complete their transactions. Fog still shrouds the mountains. It does seem strange weather for the desert. Maybe it will clear tomorrow before she leaves.

"Be careful," Dagmar hugs her. "They pretend they don't speak English and cheat you every opportunity."

"She speaks Spanish," her father explains, with pride or irritation, Patricia can't tell.

"Then take care of him." Dagmar remains anxious.

"We'll be fine," he calls gruffly. "Back about three o'clock."

The ride is flat and white and peaceful. They are silent. He never said much when she was a child. She wonders how he can stand Dagmar's chatter, but she doesn't know him well enough to ask. Maybe next time. Yes, perhaps she will come back. It hasn't been a bad trip. They have been close, on and off. He has made a great effort baking cakes and cookies, loaning her handbook to the dentist, driving up to Silverton and now down to Mexico. So he is still loud and cranky and destroying himself with too much food. She is no longer a child; how can this affect her so? His grammar and lack of sophistication — which used to embarrass her — now seem almost the hallmark of his success in the world. After all, he immigrated with nothing at the age of seventeen. And here he is, owner of a ranch house, friend of Admiral Dirk, caretaker of the Prince of Hearts and father of someone who has been published. Yes, she is gratified that he would count her book among his trophies.

The car is slowing down. Ahead the sign reads, "Mexico. *Bienvenido!*"

"Just wait in the car. With the doors locked. I'm going to change some money." He points to a row of wooden huts. "Be right back."

"Be . . ." she begins, almost repeating Dagmar's warning.

"I'll be fine; don't worry."

He returns promptly. The tires squeal as he speeds towards the border gate. The air in the car is moist and she tries to ignore his heavy dose of cologne which is making her stomach turn.

"Buenos Dias," the guard greets them.

"No speak Spanish," her father says as if he were refusing

251

an exchange of pornographic jokes.

The guard straightens slightly. "Good day. Do you have anything to declare . . .?"

She wants to speak up, to temper her father's rudeness, but she knows that neither man would appreciate the intrusion.

Mother cried for a month after he filed for divorce. Patricia had tried to hold them together, had tried to explain one to the other. She couldn't comfort Mother because for years Mother had comforted her, promising that he would return, that one day he would return for good. And she was wrong.

They are admitted to Mexico.

Los Altos is a small, poor town of tarpaper shacks and muddy roads, made almost impassable by the weather.

"Snow in Mexico; this is ridiculous," her father sniffs as he tries to pull the truck out of a rut.

"We've only driven twenty miles," she snaps in spite of herself. "Did you expect the equator?"

"If they maintained the damn roads, it would be all right. How do they plan to do trade when you can't get in and out of their damn . . ." The engine goes whizz-whizz and suddenly they are out of the rut, almost running over a little boy playing nearby.

"Madre Mia!" the boy's father shouts, shaking his fist.

Her father shakes his fist back, then proceeds gingerly over the corrugated road.

"Damn Mexicans, letting their kids play in the street."

She closes her eyes, knowing not to provoke him for they will wind up in jail if he gets any angrier. *She remembers him sitting in his undershirt and boxer shorts drinking beer in front of the TV and yelling at the umpire, at Edward R. Murrow, at Sergeant Bilko. After a while her girlfriends stopped visiting when he was on leave. She didn't know if it was the yelling or the boxer shorts which kept them away.*

"Here we are," he said abruptly. "Señora Garcia. The only honest woman in town."

They walk into a shop lined with bottles of liquor; boxes of detergent; cans of car oil: an extraordinary assortment of American goods. As Patricia's eyes adjust to the light she finds a white-haired woman knitting behind the counter. An orange cat sits on the empty shelf behind.

"Buenos Dias," he has suddenly become a linguist.

The old woman nods, without recognition.

"Nearsighted," he whispers to Patricia.

"Señora Garcia," he says more loudly, moving closer.

"Si," she says, still apparently without recognition.

"She'll remember me. Dagmar sent a box of clothes for her daughter last month. And once I gave them a fan."

The old woman stands up and asks if she can help.

"No Espanol," he says gently, with a touch of pique. He turns to his daughter. "She speaks perfect English."

"Mr. Lester," he explains. "From America."

The woman nods. "Welcome," she says finally.

He smiles triumphantly at Patricia. "See. Now what do you drink? We'll send you back to Boston with something to see you through winter."

"Oh, I don't know." She is suddenly embarrassed. "I don't drink much."

"Don't give me that bull." He is offended. "You've had a drink with me and Dagmar every night since you been here. Whiskey, I know." He turns to the counter. "What's your best Irish?"

She frowns.

"Ah, never mind. I see some Bushmills. No, Jameson. We'll send you back with a big Jameson."

"Dad, really."

Señora Garcia is climbing a step-ladder, reaching for the bottle.

"See, I told you they speak English when they want to."

Patricia can feel the headache rising up the side of her neck.

"And we'll take two Beefeaters. Two Bacardis. One big

Johnny Walker Red."

Silently the woman places bottles in a box. She writes down the price on a scrap of brown paper bag.

"No way," he explodes. "No way; that's eight hundred pesos too much!"

The woman shrugs, remaining steadfast about the amount.

"You're not gonna rip me off just 'cause you gone mute," he shouts.

Señora Garcia returns to her stool and watches him.

"Eight hundred pesos too much!" he declares.

Patricia hears a giggle and turns to find five children grinning in the doorway.

"Dad," she whispers. "Eight hundred pesos is less than a dollar."

He glowers at her. She remembers years of vengeful silence at home and can't stand this any more. "Perhaps if I translated."

"Translation isn't the problem."

"Well, somebody doesn't understand something," she tries.

"It's a question of principle. It's not the dollar. These people will rob you blind in a flash. She knows the price. I buy here all the time."

Her father puts both hands on the counter and stares at the old woman, like a belligerent teenager. The woman has retreated behind heavy eyelids. The cat purrs.

Patricia looks from one person to the other in dismay. They could stand here all day. For the rest of their lives. Maybe they should call in Skip Murphy to stuff them and create a diorama for twenty-first century tourists.

Patricia has an inspiration. Turning to the children, she asks, *"Tu Abuela?"*

A little girl steps forward, saying yes, she is the old woman's granddaughter. Patricia walks to the doorsill and hands the child two dollars. *"Por Tu. Por Tu Abuela. Por Navidad."* The child's face lights up.

"Hey, hey," her father calls. "Don't play with those kids, they'll ring every last penny from you. They always want pennies. Pennies add up."

Patricia knows he knows what she has done.

Señora Garcia, who has followed the exchange from behind closed eyelids, glances at Patricia neutrally.

Patricia stares at her feet.

The woman stands up to the counter.

"So you've decided to be honest," her father barks, his voice betraying his relief.

She ignores him and crosses out the first sum, noting down the amount he has demanded.

He pays her, picks up the box and leaves, tugging on Patricia's sweater.

Patricia looks back with a mixture of shame and resignation. As a child she knew everything would work out perfectly. It had taken years to develop her dubious talent for compromise.

They cross the American border at the far gate, manned by a friend of her father's. They ride back to Murdoch in strained, not companionable, silence.

Dinner is his famous meatballs and spaghetti. With lots of red wine. And Jameson afterwards. He is sweating as they take their drinks to the living room. She knows he is worn out, creating the perfect farewell.

The snow is heavy as they drive to the Greyhound depot. Dagmar has stayed home so Patricia can have a last private moment with her father. And Fritzie.

"I would of drove you to El Paso," he begins.

"No chains," she says.

"Yeah." He is nervous. "But you'll be fine. Those buses are equipped."

"Yes." She stares at the fog.

"I seen worse snow. Once in Jersey, when I was taking a ship out. Why the bus just crawled along the turnpike. I thought I'd never make it. Hell, forget the ship. I thought I'd never make it to the dock. But it was fine. The bus was fine."

"Yes," she says, patting the dog. "Don't worry."

As they pull up, the Greyhound driver is loading bags.

"Well, this is it, honey. Thanks for coming." He stands stiffly, holding the dog by a leash.

"Thanks for having me." She reaches up and hugs him, resisting the mad impulse to pull him on the bus with her. She used to imagine him carrying her onto his ship just before the gangplank was lifted.

"For the trip." He pulls a brown sack from his pocket. "Meatball sandwich and some cookies."

"Thanks," she says, unable to speak more for fear of crying. She can't hold herself this tightly for long and she is grateful when the driver opens the door.

"Hey, don't forget the booze." Her father hands her a shopping bag. The passengers surge forward. She wishes he would let go of it, so she can get on the bus. She is having a hard time breathing.

"OK." She pulls on the bag and just at that moment someone knocks into her from behind. She teeters to keep her balance. Turning, she sees a large Black woman and for a second wonders if this is the lady returning from Los Angeles.

"Shit," her father shouts.

She hears a crash.

"Damn hippopotamus, can't watch her step." He is shouting at the woman, who has the good sense to ignore him and claim her seat on the bus.

"No, Dad, it's good luck, really."

Patricia rushes to save the situation. "Sort of like christening a ship as it's launched."

He stares at her for a second, his jaw clenched, his brows knit and then he shakes his head. "Yeah." He is almost smiling. "Good luck."

They walk to the bus door and he waves her a kiss as she hands the driver her ticket.

"You'll be fine." He is talking to the bus driver. "Once I took a bus down the Jersey turnpike, snow so thick you couldn't see a foot in front. You'll make it fine."

My Room at Night

JUDY FREESPIRIT

I am lying very still in my bed which has a maple headboard. My bedroom has pink wallpaper with little blue and white flowers on it. The white chenille bedspread is covering me all the way up to my neck.

If I look straight ahead, I can see my blue dressing table with the white skirt around it. There's a matching wooden stool in front of it and a mirror is on the wall behind. Someone is in the mirror: I can't really see him, but I know he's there. He's watching me all the time. I turn my back to the mirror when I get dressed and undressed, so he can't see my face. I'm not really scared of him, it's just that he's always watching and he never says anything and it makes me kind of nervous.

In my room there are three windows with sheer white ruffled curtains. One of the windows is in the door on the wall next to my bed. It goes out to the back porch. If I move my eyes to the right without turning my head I can see the maple chest of drawers with brass handles.

When both my parents are home, I like my room a lot. Some nights my daddy goes out to play cards and my mommy and I stay home. I like those nights. Every week my mommy washes and sets my hair. She whistles when she's putting in the pin curls and the cold air tickles my ear and the back of my neck. I don't like the cold feeling. When I tell her, she laughs because she didn't realize she was whistling, and then she stops for a while. After my hair is set, we listen to the radio. My favorite shows are *Baby Snooks* and *Lux Presents Hollywood*. Sometimes my mommy goes out to play cards or visit with friends, and that's when my daddy calls me into his bedroom and we play games kissing and touching each other. I feel funny: excited and scared at the same time. I'm afraid Mommy will catch us. My daddy said it would be the end of our family if she found out. I wish my mommy wouldn't go out and leave me alone with him, but I can't tell her that. I don't want to hurt my daddy so I do everything he wants me to do. I feel bad that we do nasty things, but I like the way they make me feel.

We live in Detroit in a second floor duplex. We moved here when I was eight. There's an attic in this house. The door to the attic is in my parent's room, which is across the hall from mine. At night I'm afraid of the attic. There are noises up there, creaks and groans, and I'm sure ghosts and Nazis are hiding in the dark. I'm 'specially afraid when I'm alone like tonight with only the man in the mirror to watch me.

My parents think I'm too old for a babysitter, and I'm scared when they're gone. I lay very still so nobody'll know I'm here. I won't sleep until my parents come home, no matter how late it is.

I'm afraid the person who's been chopping up the bodies of little kids and leaving them in garbage cans will climb up to the back porch and come into my room through the back door while I'm sleeping. I watch the shadows on the wall; they dance like ghosts; but I'm not as scared of them or the things in the attic as I am of that man who hacks up little kids. I wonder if it was the man in the mirror who killed all those kids.

Maybe he's a man like my daddy.

If I do everything I'm supposed to: keep my body still, only move my eyes, and say all the right words, then maybe nothing will hurt me. You have to know the right words to keep away evil. So I'm just gonna lay here in bed and say *The Night Before Christmas* real slow.

I wonder if Santa Claus does things to his daughter when Mrs. Claus goes out at night. There really isn't any Santa Claus, you know, but I learned that poem by heart, and if I get all the words right, then maybe he won't hurt me.

It's hard to keep from falling asleep. My eyes keep wanting to shut and I have to pinch myself to stay awake. If I fall asleep, maybe something terrible will happen to me. But I'll stay awake and I'll show them all that I'm stronger and smarter than any of them. I'll trick them. They'll think I'm sleeping, and then when they come to get me, I'll punch them right in the eyes so they can't see. Then I'll be as strong as Wonder Woman, and I'll pick them up and throw them off the back porch. I'm the strongest girl in Detroit.

I hear my mommy and daddy opening the front door now; at least I think it's them. What if it's a burglar, or the hacker? I'll stay so still he won't even guess I'm here. If I close my eyes really tight then nobody will be able to see me.

It's OK now. I hear my mommy and daddy talking. They're even laughing. It's a good thing my mommy is home tonight. Maybe I would've hurt my daddy if he tried to come into my bed, because Wonder Woman never would've let him touch her like that. Lucky thing for him my mommy was there.

But I still have to be careful, even when my parents are both home. You can never be too careful. I know that for sure.

Strike
It Rich

MAUREEN BRADY

Me and my brother and sister sit about three feet from the brand new twenty-one inch T.V. Our baby brother, Dewey, toddles up and down the room on the thatched rug which is the only protection from the cool, hard tile of the floor should he stumble and fall and bump his head. We have just moved to Florida and this is the first T.V. we have ever had. When we lived up north on the chicken farm only our rich neighbors had one, and seeing it required conniving a reason to get into their house, then sidling into the living room where it occupied center stage. I would feel like a burglar stealing into that room, but Mary would push me ahead, saying, "Lee Ann, we're just going to look 'n see what's on T.V." Mostly it was snow until they got hooked up to the antenna on the hill, but we would watch until we got good and bored. Often it was snowing outside, too, and when we'd saturate with boredom, we'd go back out to the real stuff.

It is eleven-thirty on a summer morning. The jalousie

261

windows are open but there isn't much of a breeze. When it does blow, it stirs up the smell of freshly poured cement. The memory is beginning to fade, but only a short time ago we lived in the Royal Palms Motel and drove to this Citrus Estates subdivision every couple of days to survey the progress on the house. We'd stare at the concrete block walls which had been erected abruptly in our absence and realize — wow, this is my room, or — hey, this room is the biggest — is it the living room or the master bedroom? We'd tear about with our confusion. The fact that the floor plans said *master* bedroom; the fact that the neighborhood was called Citrus *Estates;* the fact that our parents tried never to talk about money in front of us children: these facts sat on top of question marks in our nimble, pre-television brains. We knew we weren't rich; we knew this couldn't be an *estate*. We knew we had moved because of money, because our father was going back to sea, where he had come from before the farm, and where he had gone when he was fifteen and his father died and he'd stepped into the role of provider.

We knew without being told that this was mother's house. She'd said, "If *you're* going back to sea, *I'm* going where it's warm," and then she got the map out and showed us all where Florida was, and that turned into wouldn't you like to go there? No, no, no, no, no, I'd hollered inside. All my friends, my room, my house, my barns, my hills, my berry patch, my apple orchard, all settled around me, all woven through me, part of me. I saw myself hiding in the attic of the house across the street, looking out the dormer window onto our house, adoring it — the huge maples that stood so tall in the front yard, the wide sweep of the side porch, which was where we set up rainy day games of Monopoly. From there, I imagined myself watching the family drive away without me, the little two-tone green Nash Rambler station wagon that didn't have room for all of us anyway, loaded down heavy in the back, climbing the hill and taking the last curve out of town. In this way I avoided thinking about actually having to move right up to the very last moment, when I was assigned the middle of the back seat, as befit my role as second child, and was packed in along with everything else we had chosen to keep out of the auction.

The fact of the Florida house going up surely meant we weren't tourists. We weren't rich either, but I'd thought only rich people built new houses. There was a sign out front we always had to pass — NO TRESPASSING — DO NOT ENTER — and the whole time we wandered around those hollow walls, I feared being caught trespassing, never called out to the others but whispered, and often they answered in whispers.

We'd look up to the sky and see the stars and giggle at the idea you could see stars from *inside* a house. For me, I wouldn't have minded leaving it that way. It was warm like Mommy wanted. Imagine standing out at night in shorts and the breeze cooled you by its motion, not by bringing in the north wind. It was consoling to think she must be happy with this. No, I did not want or need a roof on this house. Boring as it was at the Royal Palms Motel, change was coming too fast.

"Next time we come the roof'll be on," Daddy said.

No, I didn't believe it. There were only four carpenters and the construction of a roof seemed an enormous task. We couldn't go and watch them build during the daytime because Daddy went to Unemployment or else was off following up leads, thinking he might find a stay-home job, though we all knew he was going back to sea as soon as he got us situated in the new house. The next day, everywhere I looked I saw ants building ant hills. I wanted them to stop, to rest, but they went on relentlessly, pushing one grain of sand to the top, returning for another. I had to sit on my feet to hold back from flattening the hills with one simple swipe of my big toe.

Sure enough when we returned, the roof was on, settling like doom between us and the stars, but at least the breeze still blew through the holes that were meant for windows. Mom couldn't wait for the house to be finished. She walked around with hungry, decorator eyes, thinking out loud about colors, arrangement of the furniture we didn't have, starting fresh.

"Isn't it nice to start fresh," she'd say, her voice light and airy with bright ideas. Mary, twelve and adventuresome, would agree. I'd say *sort of* even though it had wrecked the first ten years of my life, and terrible Timothy, the grouch, nine, would give her a mean look. Dewey would be toddling around, testing echoes with his screeches in the various rooms, or spilling out huge boxes of sevenpenny nails on the floor. Mommy, surviving inside her frilly fantasies, decided to paint the outside of the house pink. Coral, she called it, and that word built in the imagination, but when it came off the paint brushes onto the concrete blocks, it was just plain pink.

Mary and Timmy and me are sitting all hunched up close, both to each other and to the new T.V. in the new house, on the "grass" rug, which leaves markings all over your bare legs if you so much as watch one whole program without moving around. The NO TRESPASSING sign is down and we are now actual residents of Citrus Estates, though it is still hard to believe this is home the way our farmhouse was. Our farmhouse had a woolly rug in the room we played in and drapes heavy enough to hide behind on all the windows. This place seems more like a cross between our real home and the Royal Palms Motel.

Mary and I have a room together like we did before, and Timmy and Dewey have a room with bunkbeds. Mommy and Daddy have the master bedroom but Daddy has gone back to sea so Mommy has it all to herself (really more space than she needs). Daddy has not yet found a job to take him far out on the ocean, but he works on tug boats in New York Harbor for two weeks at a time, then has one week off. We can't afford for him to come home since we live so far away, (in this place that may one day blow away in a hurricane), so on his week off he goes around trying to get on quiz shows and we stay home, watching for him.

We are watching "Strike It Rich" and we know this is one he has tried for and then Warren Hull is saying, "Our next contestant, Mr. Franklin Sperry," and Daddy is there, flat figure on our screen in the Coral house and we are all calling, "Mommy, come quick, Daddy is on T.V." Dewey comes with his greasy fingers and touches Daddy on the picture tube and Mary lunges on him and pulls him into her lap to watch. Mom stops sweeping the sand, which she claims enters this house as if each of us shoveled the beach into our shoes. She comes and stands behind our backs, propped against the broom. I think she is even more amazed than we are to see Daddy like this. I can't hear anyone breathing. It is like he is watching us, watching our existence in the Coral house, instead of us watching him. His face is broad, as it is in real life, and his look is direct. He smiles for a second, which we take as a message for us, then Warren Hull asks him would he please tell the viewers his story.

I am suddenly, rigidly aware that this is not all a game, that for weeks now we have been listening to the sad stories of the contestants on this program. I have often been quietly moved to tears by them. I have known that telling why you are poor or unfortunate is a requirement for getting on the program, but I have never thought to put this together with a picture of my dad, standing there like he is now, shifting his body slightly inside the suit which I've only ever seen him wear to church. He's saying — my wife, she was a city girl . . . I met her on a cruise on a ship I was sailing then . . . we went up country together . . . hard adjustment for her but she was willing . . . worked hard, both worked hard trying to make it with a small chicken farm . . . no big equipment . . . just the family . . . children worked too, as soon as they were old enough . . . (How fast I'd forgotten the chores — gather eggs, grade eggs, pack eggs, feed my own little bantam hens I was raising for a 4-H project. Life so simple in the pink house, squeezing grapefruit and watching T.V.) . . . bankruptcy . . . give up on the farm . . . go back to sea. Family's in Florida now . . . trying to get back on our feet.

I am crying now the way I do when I am moved by other people's stories on Strike It Rich; the tears rise to my eyes and stay on the edges of them until they evaporate. The word bankruptcy has stuck inside me, making me feel as if a boat has overturned in my stomach. I don't know what the word means but I am riveted to it as a key to my confusion. Does it mean the bank has something to do with our lives? One reason it is hard to figure this is that we didn't even have a bank in our town. Despite the fact that I feel sick, I maintain an appearance of calm but avid interest in this T.V. program, and I suspect I'm not the only one. I don't dare look to see how anyone else is reacting because I can feel that shock has made us all into statues, still and silent to anyone but ourselves. Mom is propped on the broom, her bare arms sticking out of her sleeveless blouse, her bare legs sticking out of her bermuda shorts. We are all very exposed. We have come here to start over, but Daddy is on T.V. in living rooms all over the country and, perhaps more to the point, all over Citrus Estates.

I can see that he would like to loosen his tie. He always does that as soon as he exits from the church, pulls his tie first one way, then the next, then releases the top button of his shirt and sighs, as if he had only been getting a limited supply of air through the bottleneck of his throat surrounded by the stiff collar, the noose of the tie.

His story is finished. Dewey is clapping for Daddy, the audience is clapping, Mommy shifts her relationship to the broom and begins to clap and then we all do. The sounds of our claps ring on the concrete walls, the stark floor. We do not have *enough* in this house yet to be clapping, singing, laughing, shouting. We have a cheap sofa with bolsters, a grass rug, a picture of a lone seagull on the wall. We have a father who comes to us on T.V., working for his honor, telling us about a family we barely recognize.

They have cut to a Fab commercial but we do not cut our attention from the screen except to release Dewey for thirty seconds of toddling. We all stare silently at the woman examining her wash for whiteness and Mommy hums the jingle without seeming to know she is doing so.

266

Now back to Daddy and we are ready to play Strike It Rich except while the camera comes in on Daddy, Warren Hull summarizes his story for anyone who tuned in during the commercial. I hope that he will explain bankruptcy, but of course he doesn't. As the words come out of his mouth, our story becomes a public story. It belongs to the show now, which is fine with me — they can have it. "Come on, come on, let's play the game," Timmy mutters to Warren. The camera is on both of them now, and I like the way Warren looks, so friendly to Daddy and yet so comfortable in his suit.

There are categories such as history, music, sports, famous figures, and sometimes Daddy gets to choose the category, sometimes not. After the category is chosen, he decides how much to put on the question, and the more money he goes for, the harder the question he draws. He starts out slow and easy and he's doing fine. He gets all the answers. He lets go of a little grin after each one, then I can see how his concentration is moving forward to be ready for the next. This is how he was also when he was home with us, after we got the T.V. He would sit on the sofa, trunk bent forward, elbows on his knees, and volunteer the answers to the contestants before they responded. Chuckling lightly when they missed. A big $400 is lit up on the screen. This is what he is winning so far, we are winning so far. We are already spending it, at least I am, and I suspect I am not alone. It feels as if we are all one person at this moment, though I know we will argue later about how we would each spend it if it were our own. I would try to begin to fill up the pink house more.

Warren Hull is saying, "Do you understand?" and Daddy bobs his head. What is to be understood is that he has just put double or nothing on the last question and he does not get to choose the category. If he answers correctly, we will win $800. If he does not, we will lose the $400. We hold our breath. It is unbelievable that our life might change so fast.

I grab Mary's hand and we both squeeze hard. I just know he is going to lose and wish he had gotten on The Price Is Right instead. That is his favorite quiz show and I know he could win on it. He knows exactly how much everything costs. He knows the difference between the price of a Sears refrigerator and a Montgomery Ward. He knows stoves, he knows cars, toasters, irons, washing machines. His hobby is pricing things. While other people go shopping to buy, he goes around memorizing price tags. He comes home and reports to us and tells us his ideas about why Ward's is charging more. He knows motors, too, so he knows they have identical motors, these refrigerators. He wants to understand the psychology of pricing, but he doesn't. He believes no one should charge more than is absolutely necessary. Mom says there are hundreds of reasons why prices might come out different, but he doesn't believe her. He doesn't even ask her what they are and she doesn't tell, so I don't know what to think. Just like with the eggs I didn't know what to think. All the time they used to talk about the egg prices up, the egg prices down — way down sometimes — Daddy frowning, his bushy eyebrows nearly coming to meet. It didn't seem fair that if the hens had a good laying season the egg prices should drop. We'd be working harder and so would the hens. Why then should everyone else be going around rejoicing about cheap eggs? Daddy tried to explain the balance, the system of supply and demand, but I wasn't ever convinced that he bought it. An egg was an egg where we were concerned.

They flash $800 in a light bulb design off and on the screen. This isn't because he has won it already, but to tell how excited we are that he might. Warren Hull's low voice has risen to a higher pitch as if he wants us to win it, and I hope this means he has a way of pulling an easy question for the last one. Mary slips her legs under her, comes up to kneeling, and whispers, "Come on, Daddy, you can do it."

Now the category comes jumping out — MUSIC — and Mom sighs, *oh, no,* and we all droop. Still rapt but we can no longer think of spending the eight hundred. Daddy is tone deaf. He can't sing. He doesn't listen when we do or even when music is played. He reads a paper or watches out the window or goes off in his own mind playing with the prices. This is awful. We try to sink slowly but Mary sinks the fastest because of kneeling. I have just filled up the house with eight hundred dollars worth of stuff and they are playing a song, something familiar but I wouldn't know what to name it myself. I say, *come on, come on, please, Daddy,* over and over inside. *You've probably heard the name of it somewhere. Just relax and let the answer come to you.* His eyes are looking around as if time is taking too long to pass, and I can see he has nowhere more to search for the answer. They only played the first few bars. Now those bars are fading in my memory and in the silence I could make them into almost any song, then venture a guess, but he doesn't even do that. "I don't know," he says, shrugging the weight of his shoulders which are abnormally squared off from the shoulder pads in his suit.

"What is it?" I whisper to Mommy.

"The Blue Danube Waltz," she says, mouthing the title to Daddy, but she knows, we all know, that he will never get it. Timmy is beating his legs with his fists. "I'll give you one more chance," Warren says, and replays the same bars of music. But this is only making it worse. Making us wait and wait, making Daddy shift uncomfortably foot to foot, his eyes losing their sparkle. I am chanting to myself — blue danube waltz blue danube waltz. We know it is lost but we are still trying. Now would be a good time for the hurricane to come and blow us away. Daddy is beginning to look stupid, which finally, is worse than bankruptcy. They ring a bell that means time is up and they erase the light board that was holding our money. At least we can breathe.

"Too bad," Warren says. "Bad luck for our contestant." But now the heartline lights up. This is a telephone with lights all around it and as the phone rings, the lights flash, pumping my adrenalin back up so my heart is a knot. Warren's voice is calm enough to make me think the world will go on, no matter what, as he says, "Well, let's see who's calling." He listens and

269

then conveys the message. The caller is an ex-actor from New York City who moved upstate to try his hand at chicken farming and has been quite successful, so he's donating seventy-five dollars to help Franklin Sperry and his family get back on their feet. "How nice of him," Mommy says. I don't think it's nice at all. How come he was able to succeed? And what will a mere seventy-five dollars be able to buy? I don't want to have to be grateful to this stranger. I don't want to have people all over the country, sitting in their living rooms, saying, "How nice, aren't they lucky this man decided to give them some money." If Daddy had won, that would have been something else. Or if the man was willing to donate eight hundred dollars, I'd be willing to say thanks.

Daddy is gone now. He is off the air and a new contestant is telling her story, but we don't follow her. It seems very pale to watch a stranger on T.V.

Timmy curses and Mommy scolds him for it, but he goes on anyway, a grin loping across his face. "Quite a sob story he told, wasn't it?" Dewey is first to giggle at this, then at me. I say, "Yeah, he really laid it on." I wait for Mommy to say, "No, that was real, that was us he was talking about," but she doesn't. She starts to hum "The Blue Danube Waltz," goes on beyond those first few bars they played, letting the hum swell louder as she goes. We are all a mass of giggles now. Mary rolls off her knees over onto her side, her pretty face away from me, but I hear her join in, saying, "He laid it on pretty thick." I tickle Dewey, then Mary tickles me, then she turns on Timmy. He tries to hold a straight face, to resist feeling. His brown hair waves at the same place on his forehead as Daddy's hair does. He looks like Daddy did when he was waiting out the time. Then tiny little spits fly out of his mouth as he breaks into laughter. This seems very, very funny.

"You're spitting at me, can't you control your spit?" Mary says, as she keeps on tickling him. "Can't control your spit, can you?" She turns back to me. "How about you?" I get serious, hold my breath. Think numb and try not to feel her fingers digging along my ribs except as nuisances, but I hear Mommy still humming the tune. She's gone back in the kitchen with the broom and is sweeping and humming and my throat is filling and I burst, rocking on the grass rug with my laughter that's hurting my stomach and my face.

Still somewhere in the far back reach of my mind, I am doing fractions, which we've been studying at school, and trying to figure out what fraction of $12,000 is $800. Because I think it is $12,000 we are paying for this pink house over the next twenty years. It might be $12,500 because we got a corner lot. We are all rolling and rocking and spitting out our laughter and Dewey keeps running, leaping and then falling onto our mass of bodies, and I don't know how we'll ever be able to stop.

"Stop," I gasp. "We've got to stop."

"Can't," Mary spits out.

We've got to ask *what's bankruptcy,* I'm thinking, feeling the indentations on the backs of my legs from the grass rug as if they were symptoms of some big disease. I can't ask it. Instead, I say, "Maybe tomorrow he'll get on The Price Is Right."

"Yeah," Timmy says, his laughter dying to contempt. "They don't have any *music* on that one."

I wonder when will Mommy be able to have a piano again. It's the one thing I don't think Daddy has priced. But I've never seen them give one away on The Price Is Right anyway. I'm thinking how it's hard to imagine where we would put it in this hollow sounding room so that its notes wouldn't just echo off the walls. Then I realize the house is different now. It does not seem so empty or so new as it bounces our laughter back at us.

It Must
Have Been
December First

JANE LAZARRE

I   *Wednesday*
n front of him on the supermarket
line a woman was unloading two shopping carts filled with
food. The express line was closed down for the evening, the
other cashiers were even more crowded, and here he was, for
Pete's sake, for what could easily be a half hour's wait. So he
was pleased when she turned to him, noticed his small purchase, and offered to let him go in front of her.

"Why thank you," he said — gallantly debonaire — and
did not fail to notice her eyes change ever so slightly. She was
seeing *him* suddenly, not a lonely old man but an attractive
man, older perhaps, but definitely attractive. He had always
been a careful judge of the effect he had on women. He slid
gracefully in front of her and deposited a package of one lamb
chop, a hard roll in a plastic bag, a small container of sour
cream, one banana. The sight of the measly purchases recalled
his depression and obliterated the pleasure of flirtation with
the young woman. He winced. He would never have used the

272

word — depression — if not for his daughter and her maddening involvement with psychoanalysis. He would have said he was sad. Then he mocked himself for the word flirtation. Once he would have made it a flirtation. Maybe only five years ago he might have engaged her in conversation, found out if she was married, asked her to a movie. She wasn't so young — not less than forty-five, just the age he liked in a woman. This was no flirtation, he muttered, mocking his arrogance.

He walked out into the chill of Sixth Avenue and pulled his collar up around his white hair, digging his chin into his old navy-blue pea jacket. Tenth Street was only two blocks away. It would take him no more than ten minutes to walk home even if he dawdled in front of the shops or bought another paper, just the chance to talk to Johnny, an old comrade from Spain who owned the newsstand down the street. He would be home by seven. And then what? Nothing to do but eat and read until the eleven o'clock news.

The lobby was increasingly shabby. The dark purple tiles set in geometric pattern with black cement lines were edged with a film of white. They hadn't painted the walls in years. With the front lock broken, anyone from the street could walk in. He climbed up the two flights, too impatient to wait for the elevator. What was his daughter Anne always saying? Her search for autonomy? Well, he had his fill of autonomy. He would be delighted to make his daughter a present of all the autonomy she could handle.

He shifted his grocery bag to his left arm and unlocked the door, peered into the mirrored wall left over from Jean's endless redecorations, locked the three locks including the chain, hung his coat in the hall closet. To save electricity, he turned on only one light. He broiled his lamb chop, sliced the banana into a bowl of sour cream and ate.

Once, Anne had gone an entire month without seeing him. She lacked autonomy, she had informed him. She was too tied to him, she said. She had to break away or lose herself. She was nineteen and already worried. "You got to be grown up enough to have a self to lose, no?" he said aloud, placing dishes in the sink, wiping crumbs off the brown and white plastic tablecloth with a raggedy, orange sponge. "I'll give you autonomy," he said to her now. "You mean independence? I have independence to spare."

And then, inexplicably, he was back on the crowded front deck of the boat, standing close to his mother. With no warning his irritation at Anne, held grudgingly in place for more than ten years, had become this older anger. His mother was sick, looking old before her time, but radiantly happy to be in America, about to see her three eldest children for the first time in seven years. He, the eldest left back home, had been expected to bring his parents and two younger siblings to America. No matter that he was involved with important — no crucial — work in the old country, he had to bring them here. Obligation, they called it. Autonomy was not the issue. The sky was dark, rainy, grey with early morning fog. His mother and father were wrapped in their warmest coats, scarves, hats pulled down over their foreheads. Olive skin shining rose on chiseled cheekbones. His own fair skin (from his grand-mother, they said) red and raw from the wind.

But he had seen so many pictures and movies, read so many descriptions of immigrants in the last fifty years he hardly knew any longer whether he was actually remembering or if he was projecting all those more recent images layered on top of his experience, driving his personal memory behind the black and white photographic stills of history. Anyway, he never wanted to live in the past.

"The past is barren," he said to his friend Mack who was always reliving the old wars, the strikes, the picket lines and marches for social security — like the time some young cops had dragged them away from a perfectly legal demonstration and beat the shit out of them. "You can't live in the past, Man. History marches on, old boy, in spite of you and me," he told Mack, smiling ruefully and slapping his friend's shoulder. "We're a couple of old-timers, let's face it." Still, a light wave

of pleasure moved through him when he used that phrase —
"old-boy" — like when he said "Cheerio," (as he always did);
the pleasure from the memory of Patrick Flaherty, from the
Irish Brigade in Spain, who always spoke that way and whose
intonations Dave had made his own through use over forty-
odd years.

"We can still ᵇᵉ useful, Dave," Mack had responded. He
was trying to get Dave to speak at a meeting of the Veterans
of the Spanish Civil War. "There are things we can do. We can
teach the young."

Dave shook his head mockingly and said, "Oh sure. The
young." He lit a cigarette and remained silent for a few
moments, paralyzed by the absoluteness of his disagreement.

What was left of the past? The words signaling that feeling
he tried so hard to fight but could never fully manage to resist,
that tangible despair that could blanket him with a strange,
dangerous comfort: a reality, at least; relinquishing the endless fight. Sadness was what he called it, he thought, turning
out the kitchen light and going into his bedroom where he
chose a book and lay down on the bed. Anne called it
depression.

At 9:30 she called, her voice cheerful, purposefully so, he
suspected.

"Hi Dad, how's it going? I finally got my phone."

"Well, hello there," he said, as if she hadn't called in
months, as if she were a negligent daughter, which she really
wasn't. What could she do?

She allowed the meaning of his tone, which he suspected
she did not miss, to pass without comment. "So how are you?"
she repeated.

"How should I be?" he said.

"No really, how are you? What do you mean how should
I be, Dad, for Pete's sake, how are you? How's your cold?"

"Fine," he said, "I'm fine Baby. How's the baby?"

So she told him about Carla, stories about his granddaughter that aroused his true interest for several minutes. "Why

don't you come to see us more often Dad?" she said. "Carla loves to see you. And I got the bed now. You don't have to sleep on the couch. And you know how much Mike likes to talk politics with you. He really misses it when you stay away."

An old man with nothing to do. "I'm busy Sweetie," he said. "I work hard all day in the shop, then sometimes I have meetings. When I don't have meetings I'm tired." *A tired old man.*

"You act like you're eighty, for Pete's sake," she said irritably. "You're only sixty-nine."

"Oh sure," he said, groaning slightly as he shifted position, pausing to light up a cigarette. "Only."

"Well other people do things, you only work part-time. You could take a course — something you always wanted to study. You could spend more time with us. You seeing a woman these days?"

"What woman? Are you crazy Anne? There aren't going to be any more women. I'm an old man, for god's sake. I'll come up soon to see you. I promise."

"Well what about tomorrow?" she pushed.

"I don't know tomorrow. Tomorrow's too soon. Maybe Friday."

"Okay Friday." She grabbed his agreement. He could almost see her writing it down in pen on her wall calendar so it couldn't be erased.

"All right Sweetheart," he said, for some unnameable reason wanting to get off the phone. Why? What did he have to do? "I have something to do now. I'll see you Friday." He cradled the old black receiver. He drew the drapes. Green and blue checks. Very attractive. He'd chosen the fabric himself from some extra rolls at the shop, left over from someone's interior decoration job. Anne had been surprised at his taste. As if he had none. They were pretty drapes. He'd had them made to order. He glanced at the bookshelves, irritated as always by their odd shape. He liked even lines of shelves going up and down the walls. These had been designed by Jean. And then she'd walked out. Leaving him with his apartment redecorated to her *meshuggeneh* taste. Among other things, these oddly shaped bookshelves, not wide enough for his old volumes of Marx, Lenin and Gorky. Not long enough for the endless stream of paperbacks Anne gave him, always hoping to stimulate some brand new interest. At his age. He lay down and read while he listened with his one good ear to a soft concerto on QXR. At least he had books. They took the burden of time away for a while. What did lonely people do who didn't read? He read until eleven o'clock, as he always did. No one else called. At eleven he turned on the news and, while he endured six commercials which preceded the superficial headline treatment of the day's events told by a couple of Hollywood beauties, he changed into his old, soft, grey pajamas, took his nitroglycerine tablet and brushed his teeth.

It was November 30, a Wednesday night.

She remembered because it was the day they had finally put in her phone. A strike of the installation workers had delayed it by two weeks, which didn't bother her much. With the baby, her work, and the house, it was a pleasure not to be bothered by the constant ringing every evening. The only thing that troubled her was her father. That she couldn't call him and he couldn't get in touch with her if he needed help.

She and her family had just moved into the nieghborhood and she was testing out various supermarkets. Impatient on the long line, she pushed one full cart of food in front of her and pulled another, filled with several boxes of Pampers and dozens of jars of baby food, behind. Carla sat in the front seat of the first basket, and she was starting to whine.

"Come on Carla, don't cry," Anne pleaded. "We have a phone now, did you know that? A red one. A real red phone."

Carla's eyes widened.

"Want to talk to Grandpa tonight? If you're a good girl

now, we'll call Grandpa when we go home."

Carla nodded her head vigorously and reached behind her to grab for the pretzel box. Anne took it from her, opened the lid and gave her daughter the whole box of pretzels to finger through, to stuff in her mouth, to lick the flickers of salt from. At least she would be quiet and Anne, never patient, tolerant of neither children's whines nor long lines, would be free, for a while, to stare.

She recalled vividly the narrow bed of her childhood room where she used to lay for hours and just stare. It was the same room she and Carla slept in whenever Mike was out of town and they stayed with Dave. But now the room was bare, the windows still uncovered except for old venetian blinds, the only furniture the large crib bought from the Salvation Army and the old double bed that had once been her parents.'

"For Pete's sake Anne," Dave would explode, standing in the doorway to her room, blowing smoke out fast and impatient, "you've been lying on the bed just staring for more than an hour." When she turned her face from him he would gesture at her furniture with a disapproving wave of his hand. "And what the devil's the reason for all this black?"

The black tweed spread was freshly washed. One orange pillow relieved the darkness at the head. On the floor a scatter rug — black and white circular patterns. Käthe Kollwitz lithographs on the white walls.

"What do you want for Christ's sake," she answered him roughly. "There's an orange pillow." She pointed defiantly at the bright color.

"But black,"' he pleaded. "Black spread. Black chair. Black rug, for Pete's sake, Anne, it's depressing."

"I think it's peaceful. I'm eighteen, Dad, can I please decorate my own room?"

"Your mother had such pretty pink curtains," he said, pointing to the worn, uncovered blinds, assuming a dreamy expression.

"Well she's only been dead eleven years, Dad," Anne

responded sarcastically. "Let's get her aesthetic opinion."

"Oh. Aesthetic. Excuse me. I wasn't aware we were discussing aesthetics. I thought I was having a simple conversation with my daughter, expressing my concern about her depression, which incidentally will not be resolved just by staring into space, commenting on the need for maybe a little activity, a little color in the room. But now I understand." He turned to leave, gesturing again to some invisible personage, a disinterested judge this time who was enjoined to determine the winner of their endlessly reenacted battle. "Now I understand," he repeated, "aesthetics." And clicking his tongue with sincere amazement he whispered, "Hot stuff, Baby," as he left the room.

She caressed the soft black spread, stared at the walls until they disappeared, until everything disappeared except what she saw inside her head. Later, she could never remember what she had seen. If anyone asked her, what are you thinking? she would really not know, but her inside rhythm moved from fast to slow, thoughts pouring like honey, images overlapping each other, images of his face, his misinterpretations, the paper she was writing for school and couldn't finish, the terribly embarrassing mistake she had made that afternoon in English class — all her mistakes and failings would funnel into pure shape and color that soothed her like a song in the dark. Out of the colors some grand victory would take shape in her mind — some absolute recognition — either she would be admired for her beauty — she would be graceful, thin, her hair perfectly cut — or she would be receiving a prize for some important gift to humanity. Depending on her mood, Dave would be proud or he would be shocked, lighting up a cigarette as he whispered, "Well, I'll be damned."

A loud crash and Carla's energetic scream sent Anne rushing to retrieve the dropped box of pretzels from the floor. It was her turn to load the groceries onto the counter belt. She lifted several gallons of milk onto the counter and allowed Carla to hand her half a dozen boxes of cereal. She packed meats neatly on one side, the juices down the middle, on the other side fresh vegetables. Four packs of toilet paper, two boxes of cookies, several cans of tomato sauce, noodles — none of this would last more than a week, she thought in disgust. Then she noticed the old woman behind her. She was hunched under her large, black coat. Her head was covered with a dark velvet beret fastened to her thin white hair with a long pearly pin, the kind Anne's grandmother used to wear. She leaned over her cane and clutched three packages to her bosom.

"Why don't you go ahead of me?" Anne said, moving back for the old woman to pass. With a smile the woman nodded her thanks and placed her packages on the counter in the small space left by Anne's gargantuan order. One chicken breast. One quart of milk. A small box of cookies, vanilla creams.

Suddenly Anne wanted to hurry home so she could call Dave. Maybe he'd come for dinner the next night, maybe even sleep over now that she had a comfortable bed for him. Whether it was guilt or love she never knew, but she worried about him living alone, stubbornly refusing to accept half the invitations he received — and something had happened recently, she was sure of it, because there was some woman he used to talk about, a real interest for the first time since Jean left, and then suddenly he dropped all reference to this new woman. Every time Anne dared to ask he would only way, "What woman? There's no woman." Lately, all he ever did was read and watch the eleven o'clock news. Every night the same thing, like an old cat.

When the order was finally rung up, she bundled Carla into her folding carriage and left before the groceries were boxed for delivery. It was cold on the wide avenue. She felt better, calmer, as the cold washed over her cheeks, relieved as the wind slashed across her forehead. She pulled Carla's scarf up over her nose and walked slowly down the street toward their new apartment building. She was glad she was no longer on Greenwich Avenue. It was more picturesque down there than this neighborhood with its ever multiplying high-risers, its dull, functional architecture all slabbed up in the last ten years. But here it was all wide avenues; the lobbies were spacious and uncluttered. It was not complicated like her old home. Like him.

Recently, knowing it was crazy, she had finally said it to him. "Look Dad, you're not well. I have the room. Move in with us." They were words she had once sworn she would never say. But then she had been twenty, caring about nothing more than her independence, drawing her boundaries as tight as possible, shutting out that bossy, intruding old man. Now she was thirty-one. She had her own child. And she knew her father was genuinely sick. Two heart attacks in two years. The last time the doctor had asked her if he'd had a recent emotional upset, he said that Dave didn't seem to have much will to live. Anne communicated the conversation to her father.

"You've got to want to get better, Dad," she had said to him softly as she stroked the old, pale forehead, brushing back his still lush, wavy white hair. His face had seemed completely vulnerable in that moment, with the hair pulled back, vulnerable and young, like Carla's.

"Oh yeah, sure." Dave had responded. "What for?"

"For us," she had said, and the stinging tears that gathered in blinding pools in the crevices of her lower lids had broken over the side and rushed down her face. Dave reached up with old, yellowed fingers and brushed his daughter's tears away while his own eyes filled with resignation.

"I know Baby, for you. It's true. I do have you. And your old man's gonna get better. You can bet on it."

She lay her head down on his bone-thin chest and for a moment felt it weighted there, her ear suctioned around the small percussion of his heart beat. She felt as though she might never lift it again.

But he had refused her invitation to move in. And when she said in that case he would have to change, fight the sorrow and dullness of his life, he only sighed in just the way she hated most. She nearly hung up on him that time, relieved and mysteriously lightened by an anger that she nursed for weeks.

She entered the new, clean space of her home, instantly taking in the pattern of delicate wallpaper against the white molding, the recently vacuumed rug, the well-organized books stacked against the wall, ready to be placed in the freshly painted white shelves. She switched on the TV — *Sesame Street* — so that Carla would be silent while Anne took off her snowsuit, made her a fresh bottle, and got dinner ready in the hour she still had before Mike came home from work. These activities, when free of Carla's gurgles and whines, were almost as good as the old blank stare. She poured herself a tall glass of chilled wine. Her phone hung securely on the kitchen wall. They'd call him after dinner.

Thursday

He moves slowly tonight. No rush. An odd sense of relief suffuses his insides that are usually knots of anxiety. "The creeps," Anne used to call that feeling, and he had picked it up for his own use. "No creeps tonight," he thinks, surprised and grateful as he eats a light meal of strawberries and sour cream, a piece of salami on rye. With a certain unfamiliar or long-forgotten grace he carefully cleans his plate, washes his dish, places it to drip dry in the worn red, plastic dish drain. Tonight he does more than shoot a fast stream of water into the sink to rid it of crumbs and bubbles. He sprinkles Ajax around the porcelain sides, sparks of shining blue, and carefully rubs until the old white gleams new. A grace born of belief — tonight it seems to matter that he cares for himself this way. He does not feel his usual impatience to be prone on the bed. He rarely uses the living room any more, except when Anne and her family visit, but tonight he goes in there, even turns a light on, and pushing the old but still pretty white chiffon curtains aside, he gazes out on the street. And in a flashing moment remembers all the other gazing out of this window, and the scenes he saw.

His first wife, Anne's mother, coming back from a trip abroad. He recalled vividly her navy-blue suit with the artificial red rose in the lapel, the way she looked up at the window, saw him, smiled — a beautiful woman. The day she died he had stood there and watched the long black hearse park. He had watched Jean leave too, the last time. And every time Anne came with her family he had watched them trudging down the block, his son-in-law laden with all the baby's paraphernalia, looking tired and irritated, having no idea how lucky he was; watching them he savored the last few moments of waiting for the bell to ring. Sometimes he watched nothing in particular — the sliver of sky visible behind the buildings, the passers-by — or the small residential houses replaced over the years by gaudy store windows filled with plastic of every imaginable size, function and shape. The world of his child's childhood, of his youth, completely gone. Like his mother, gone. Even the world of the shtetle in the old country. Everything gone.

Back in his own room, again uncharacteristically, he remains dressed when he lies down on the bed. And still the odd, welcomed sense of relief suffuses him, allows him to rest before he reads or switches on the radio. An unmasked moment of knowledge comes — *that's how he feels* — he needn't resist it any more, and his face glows red with a deep, sad smile.

It was cruel, there is no other word for it. A cruel promise, destined to be broken. That life could have a little bit of meaning one more time. As cruel as the central fact of life itself — the horror of death. He recalls feeling this low only once before, long ago when Anne's mother was dying. He would sit in the semi-dark by her bed and trace a gentle finger down her face. Her cheekbones were horribly prominent by then, her cheeks sunken craters beneath them, her naturally wide and sensuous mouth looking wider now than ever before, too wide for that tiny, cadaverous face. Her legs too thin to stand on. Her fingers, narrow as a child's. He blocks out the awful thoughts as he rises from his bed.

And now Ruth was dead too. Cancer, just like before. And young. Too young for him, he told himself when he felt that remarkable feeling he had never expected to feel again. She, not even fifty. He, almost seventy years old. It was crazy. But Ruth hadn't thought so. "Why?" she had said in her wonderfully innocent voice. "What does age have to do with it? We both feel it. We've both been terribly lonely. Why should there be any question at all? Don't be ridiculous, Dave." And she had kissed him. With her simple belief in the power of desire she reminded him of Anne.

When she got the final diagnosis she had told him she was moving to California. She had only several months to live and wanted to be with her sister and her sister's children. He had been hurt. He had wept. So she had confessed that she was doing it for him as well. "You can't go through it again, Dave," she had told him. "I won't put you through it." In one month less than the predicted four, he had received the letter from her sister. Ruth's death had been quick and for these cases, relatively painless. She had spoken so warmly of her last year with Dave. The sister hoped they would meet some day. Actually, it had been quite a bit less than a year. Only a few months of that weird, unexpected, suddenly remembered happiness. A cruelty.

He had tried to write about his feelings to lighten the weight. Anne would have approved. He had put the scratchy notes in his desk, in the envelope with all the important papers, his bankbook, his will. And he had forgotten about it.

"You've got to fight the resignation Dad," Anne was always telling him. And then she would come up with her absurd suggestions. Take a course. Screw some barely known woman. Even live with *her*. But he smiles when he thinks of Anne. She was only thirty. She still thought all pain was transcendable, all joy a matter of will. Maybe the only thing he would concede to her was a firm belief in the impact of childhood. His had been poor, brutal and deprived. His hopes had been nourished on one belief — that a new world he would help to build—perhaps even see—was on the horizon. With the end of that dream, he had no strength to redirect his life. He didn't even blame Jean for leaving. "I want to share your life," she shouted once, "not your death. If you want to die slowly do it without me. I intend to be happy."

Intend. He had never thought of it that way.

He stops pacing and turns on the eleven o'clock news. He turns the sound down so the commercials won't blast him out of this rare serenity. He walks to the closet and sways suddenly from a heavy blow to his chest, his arms crackling whips of stinging pain. He reaches for the bottle of white nitroglycerine pills but misses the closet shelf and falls to his knees. Momentarily, he thinks of the phone. He may be able to crawl over and call Anne, or 911. But the old green rug which looked shabby the night before now looks soft to him. For a moment, he thinks, I will rest. He brings his knees up slightly to his chest, places one hand under his cheek to protect it from the scratchy pile of the old rug, rests the other hand on his slender hip. Perhaps he will sleep a minute before he calls Anne.

He imagines her shaking him the next day. "Dad? Daddy! Are you all right? . . . It's all right Duvidal, darling," she says, calling him by his old-country name because now it's his mother's voice. Then Anne again—"Dad!" Anne and Anne's mother and Jean there too. And Ruth, all the women he had loved cradled the head and brushed the wavy hair—white, blond—back from the confused, weary face, smoothed the lines of vague, lifelong anxiety from the forehead and touched the heavily folded eyelids closed.

Contributors'
Notes

Gloria E. Anzaldúa is a Chicana tejana lesbian-feminist poet, fiction writer and cultural theorist. She is co-editor of *This Bridge Called My Back* and author of *Borderlands/La Frontera: The New Mestiza*. Her forthcoming books include *Making Face, Making Soul/Haciendo caras: Creative and Critical Perspectives by Feminists-of-Color* (Spinsters/Aunt Lute, 1990) and *Prietita Tiene Un Amigo/Prietita Has a Friend* (The Children's Book Press, 1991).

Lynda Barry is a cartoonist and writer whose published works include *The Good Times Are Killing Me*, (which was also adapted for the stage), *Down the Street, The Fun House, Big Ideas* and *Girls and Boys*. She has been a guest commentator on National Public Radio's *All Things Considered* and her illustrations frequently appear in national publications such as *Savy, Harpers* and *Esquire*.

Sandy Boucher is the author of four books, both fiction and nonfiction, including *Turning the Wheel: American Women Creating the New Buddhism*. For a number of years her major interest has

286

been women's spirituality; she recently earned a Master of Arts degree from the Graduate Theological Union, Berkeley. She is now at work on an autobiographical novel.

Maureen Brady is the author of a collection of short stories, *The Question She Put to Herself,* and two novels, *Give Me Your Good Ear* and *Folly.* Her third novel, *Rocking Bone Hollow,* was recently completed. She has been awarded grants from CAPS, New York State Council on the Arts writer-in-residence program, Money for Women/Barbara Deming Memorial Fund and The Ludwig Vogelstein Foundation.

Laura Davis is the co-author of *The Courage to Heal* and author of *The Courage to Heal Workbook.* "Waiting for the Beep" is a semi-fictional, mostly true account of her wacky relationship with her father, whom she loves very much.

Rachel Guido DeVries, a poet and novelist, is the author of the novel *Tender Warriors.* She directs The Community Writer's Project, Inc., in Syracuse, New York, and is a resident faculty member at The Feminist Women's Writing Workshops at Wells College. She is the fiction editor of the magazine *IKON.*

Judy Freespirit lives in Berkeley, California where she works as an Administrative Assistant at the University. Her writing has appeared in the following anthologies: *Shadow on a Tightrope; Love, Politics and Therapy; Lesbian Love Stories; Finding Courage; Word of Mouth* and *Speaking for Ourselves.* Her short stories, essays and poems have appeared in a number of feminist and lesbian journals, including *Sinister Wisdom, Common Lives/Lesbian Lives* and *Lesbian Ethics.* "My Room at Night" is part of an as yet unpublished manuscript, *Keeping it in the Family.*

Carolyn Gage is a lesbian playwright and performer who lives in Ashland, Oregon. She is currently touring with her award-winning one-woman show, *The Second Coming of Joan of Arc.* She continues to showcase women artists through her theatre company, No To Men Productions.

Carole L. Glickfeld's collection of short stories, *Useful Gifts*, won the Flannery O'Connor Award for Short Fiction and was recognized by the New York Public Library as an "outstanding" book of 1989. A Fellow of MacDowell Colony and Bread Loaf Writers' Conference, Glickfeld was recently writer in residence at Interlochen Arts Academy. She is currently at work on a novel, *The Salt of Riches*.

Jewelle L. Gomez is the author of a collection of poetry, *Flamingoes and Bears* and a vampire novel, *The Gilda Stories* (forthcoming from Firebrand Books in 1991).

Mary Gordon was born in Far Rockaway, New York. She is the author of three novels, *Final Payments, The Company of Women* and *Men and Angels,* as well as the short story collection *Temporary Shelter*.

Jane Lazarre's most recent novel is *Worlds Beyond My Control: Notes of a Woman Writer*. She is the author of *The Mother Knot, On Loving Men, Some Kind of Innocence* and *The Powers of Charlotte*. She is the director of the writing program at the Eugene Lang College at the New School for Social Research in New York City.

Audre Lorde is a black lesbian feminist poet, prose writer and essayist. Her books include *Our Dead Behind Us, The Cancer Journals, Sister/Outsider* and *A Burst of Light*. "Zami: A New Spelling of My Name" is excerpted from a full-length work of that title, which Audre Lorde identifies as biomythography.

Harriet Malinowitz's short fiction has appeared in a number of journals and anthologies of women's writing. She received the Harvey Swados Fiction Prize in 1978 for her short story "Lumps." Her first play, *Minus One,* was produced in June 1989 in New York City. She is presently working on her doctorate in composition and rhetorical theory at New York University.

Valerie Miner is the author of *Blood Sisters, All Good Women, Winter's Edge, Movement, Murder in the English Department* and

Trespassing and Other Stories. She earns her living by teaching and by travelling around the country giving readings and lectures.

Joyce Carol Oates is a prolific author, well-known for her many novels and short story collections, among them *American Appetites, Solstice, Bellefleur, Marya: A Life,* and *The Assignation.*

Edna O'Brien was born in Tuamgraney, Ireland in 1936. She has an international reputation as a novelist and short story writer. Her books include *The Country Girls, The High Road* and *A Fanatic Heart.*

Cynthia Rich is the author, with Barbara Macdonald, of *Look Me in the Eye: Old Women, Aging, and Ageism.* Her most recent book, *Desert Years: Undreaming the American Dream,* is based on her life in a trailer on the Anza-Borrego Desert, where she and Barbara Macdonald have spent the past six years.

Lou Robinson lives in Ithaca, New York and works at Cornell University Press. Her writing has appeared in the anthologies *Through Other Eyes: Animal Stories by Women* and *Word of Mouth,* as well as in the following journals: *Trivia, Quarterly #7, Conditions, Paragraph, Phoebe, Frontiers* and *f(Lip).* Top Stories published a chapbook of her fiction (#27). She is co-editing, with Camille Norton, an anthology of innovative writing by women, *Resurgent.*

Marianne Rogoff has published short stories in *CrazyQuilt, The MacGuffin, Marin Review* and *Earth's Daughters.* She has taught creative writing at San Francisco State University and California College of Arts and Crafts. Her story, "Meeting My Father Halfway," is from her novel *Cradle Songs.*

Meredith Rose lives in Western Massachusetts. Her short stories have appeared in the anthology *Through Other Eyes: Animal Stories by Women* and in the journals *Sinister Wisdom* and *Common Lives.* She is currently at work on a novella entitled *The Way She Looks.*

Ellen Shea has been a reporter, editor and English teacher. She currently works in public radio in New York City. Her fiction has been published in numerous journals, including *Denver Quarterly, Black Ice* and *Cutting Edge Quarterly.*

Irini Spanidou was born and raised in Greece and came to the United States in 1964. Her first novel, *God's Snake,* was published in 1986. Her latest novel, *Fear,* will be published in 1991 by Knopf.

Amber Coverdale Sumrall is co-editor of *Touching Fire: Erotic Writings by Women.* She is also co-editor of *Women of the Fourteenth Moon: Writings On Menopause* (forthcoming from The Crossing Press in 1991). Her poetry and prose have appeared in *The Women's Review of Books, New Voices from the Longhouse, Conditions,* and *Sonoma Mandala Review.* She is presently working on an anthology, *Catholic Girls.* She lives in Santa Cruz, California.

Alice Walker won an American Book Award and the Pulitzer Prize for her novel *The Color Purple.* Her other novels are *The Third Life of Grange Copeland, Meridian* and *The Temple of My Familiar.* She is the author of two short story collections, four volumes of poetry and two volumes of essays.

Rosalind Warren has edited an anthology of feminist humor, *Women's Glib,* which will be published by The Crossing Press in 1991. She received a 1990 Commonwealth of Pennsylvania Council on the Arts Fellowship, to be used towards the completion of a short story collection. She has published short stories in numerous magazines including *Seventeen* and *Iowa Woman.*

Sylvia Watanabe is the co-editor, along with Carol Bruchac, of *Home to Stay,* an anthology of Asian American women's fiction. She is a recipient of the Japanese American Citizen's League National Literary Award and an NEA Creative Writing Fellowship in fiction.

Irene Zahava (editor) has owned and operated a feminist bookstore in upstate New York since 1981. She edits feminist titles and the WomanSleuth Mystery Series for The Crossing Press. She has compiled several short story anthologies of women's writings, including *Through Other Eyes: Animal Stories by Women, Finding Courage, Lesbian Love Stories, Speaking for Ourselves, Word of Mouth* and three volumes of contemporary mystery stories by women, published as the *WomanSleuth* anthologies.